The
OUTRAGED
TIMES OF FERMENT

Aditya Sudarshan is a novelist. Author of *A Nice Quiet Holiday*, *Show Me A Hero* and *The Persecution of Madhav Tripathi*, he won the Hindu Metroplus Playwright Award in 2011 for his play *The Green Room*. He has been a scriptwriter for NDTV's political satire show, 'The Great Indian Tamasha' and a columnist in *The Hindu*'s Literary Review. His literary criticism and book reviews have been published in various newspapers. He lives in Goa at present and is working on a true crime book.

The
OUTRAGED
TIMES OF FERMENT

ADITYA SUDARSHAN

RUPA

Published by
Rupa Publications India Pvt. Ltd 2018
7/16, Ansari Road, Daryaganj
New Delhi 110002

Sales centres:
Allahabad Bengaluru Chennai
Hyderabad Jaipur Kathmandu
Kolkata Mumbai

Copyright © Aditya Sudarshan 2018

This is a work of fiction. Names, characters, places and incidents are either the product of the author's imagination or are used fictitiously and any resemblance to any actual person, living or dead, events or locales is entirely coincidental.

All rights reserved.

No part of this publication may be reproduced, transmitted,
or stored in a retrieval system, in any form or by any means,
electronic, mechanical, photocopying, recording or otherwise,
without the prior permission of the publisher.

ISBN: 978-81-291-5180-3

First impression 2018

10 9 8 7 6 5 4 3 2 1

The moral right of the author has been asserted.

Printed by Thomson Press India Ltd, Faridabad

This book is sold subject to the condition that it shall not, by way
of trade or otherwise, be lent, resold, hired out, or otherwise circulated,
without the publisher's prior consent, in any form of binding
or cover other than that in which it is published.

Contents

Prologue, or A Prayer vii

PART ONE
I The Artist and the Idler 3
II The Man of War 10
III The Black Sheep 18
IV A Significant Extra 34
V At Ahishor's 44
VI The Knight and the Hunchback 57
VII At Ahishor's (Contd.) 69
VIII Confessions and Revelations 79
IX Two Prophets of Doom 94
X An Eventful Night 109
XI The Bald Girl 121
XII Delhi–Mumbai 134

PART TWO
I Mother and Daughter 147
II Indignation 154
III A Walk Down J.P. Road 166

IV Mahayogi Navy Baba 178
V A Shadow on the Heart 197
VI Guilt 210
VII On the Festival Circuit—Part One 225
VIII On the Festival Circuit—Part Two 238
IX 'A Condemnable Incident' 252
X Friends of Freedom 263
XI Tara Krishna 274
XII Sasha's Red Letter Day 284
XIII A Family Gathering 301
XIV Desires and Delusions 314
XV First Blood 329
XVI Maithili's Messenger 343

Prologue, or A Prayer

God save me. God preserve me. I am fighting my own embarrassment at such antiquated phrases. Two years ago, I would have sneered at an account that employed them in any but the broadest mockery. Now I shall face the irony. It is not the only one.

I came to the city neither naive nor wary, but primed and eager for battle. I knew of the hardships, the famous 'struggle', and I was raring for it. I wanted no favours; I was glad to pay the price of belonging to our great and vibrant artistic community. In the company of my comrades, I was ready to work wonders. I was going to ferret out the stories—all the wonderful, moving, poignant, tragic, hilarious stories of our time. With the pride and joy of an actor, I was going to bring to life every shade of 'character' in this matchlessly interesting metropolis.

It was not that I was proved wrong. In a sense, my twenty-one-year-old self was perfectly correct. The dreaded 'struggle' for work and money never overwhelmed me. The stories, the characters, they were all there, all more or less easily at hand. It was the other struggle, the one that nobody ever talked about; the other story, the one I never saw coming, that turned my pride and joy to this fear and trembling, with which my fingers still tap the keyboard. This telling is no triumph to me, perhaps it is my penance. All that I neither witnessed nor discovered, I have wracked my mind in imagining. Once again then, God save me, God preserve me, and so to begin.

One

I

The Artist and the Idler

Two years ago, one warm March afternoon, the Delhi–Mumbai Rajdhani was speeding towards its destination. It was after lunch, the plates had been cleared, and many of the passengers in the second-AC compartment were in the midst of last little naps. As often happens at such times, two young men who, quieted by the weight of the long journey, had previously only made a nodding acquaintance, now found themselves in a position to talk. While the others in their carriage stretched out in slumber, they sat opposite each other by the side window of the train.

Physically, they presented a complex set of contrasts. The one who stared out at the fields was baby-faced and well-groomed. His hair rose in combed waves. His clothes, a kurta-shirt, slim-fitted trousers and laceless leather shoes—one dangling above the other— looked new. There was about him the aura of the dandy—or would have been one, had he made a certain minimum effort. But he seemed to lack the inclination, and perhaps the bodily strength, to put on any personality at all. Therefore, one noticed also that he was frail, awkwardly built with high shoulders, thin legs, and a slight but noticeable hunchback.

His dark eyes brooded endlessly on the vistas beyond.

Facing him, scruffy and comfortable in a grey T-shirt and frayed blue jeans, sat Ahishor Frances. Flecked with audacious grey, his hair grew unkempt down to the back of his neck and framed his thickly stubbled cheeks, like a halo. It was true he had slept a great deal on the journey, but this perhaps only accentuated his natural impression of an unmade bed. God knows it was a deceptive impression. Health and energy danced in his eyes that were trained on the figure opposite. His build—compact, well-proportioned, muscular—was healthy too. And when he grinned, as he did now, he radiated attentiveness.

'I was wondering,' said Ahishor.

His companion turned gravely towards him.

'I noticed you were reading *Anna Karenina*. There's a short story by Tolstoy, called 'The Coffee Shop at Surat'. I was wondering if you've read it.'

'No, I haven't read much by him.'

'I was thinking about it when our train passed Surat. This story is literally about a coffee shop in Surat—our Surat. Some place in the nineteenth century where people from all over the world came to smoke opium and drink wine, and coffee, and talk philosophy. That's my personal idea of heaven.'

The young man smiled.

'Surat is a port town, isn't it?'

'Yes. And in fact, I'm told there used to be a place like that in Mumbai too. Just a few decades ago. A restaurant in Dadar, but not like any ordinary restaurant. It had no proper floor or furniture, it was like a big sandy playground, and sailors and travellers from all over the world came to sit there and drink and chat. What a pity I never saw it! I always feel like I was born in the wrong era.'

'You are before your time?' A little gleam, not unattractive, had appeared in the other's eyes.

'After it! By the way, I'm Ahishor Frances.'

'My name is Sasha,' said the young man, and they shook hands.

'Just a fancy of my father's,' he continued quietly. 'He travelled a lot to Russia, on work. Moscow was his favourite city.'

He seemed to suddenly fall silent. Ahishor did not notice.

'Moscow's a beautiful city! I would love to shoot there some day.'

Then he too said nothing. For a few moments they were both looking out of the window. The outskirts of the city were upon them now. In amongst the tropical green, dense little hutments were popping up over boundary walls that were painted over neatly with advertisements. They tore past the slums at a shocking nearness.

'Wait,' said Sasha. Ahishor turned at once. 'Ahishor Frances. I've heard of you. You're a film-maker.'

'I guess I am,' Ahishor mused. 'It's funny, for a long time I never knew how to describe myself. I was interested in too many things besides film. I still am. Everything from science and philosophy to magic and shamanism...to farming! But you're smiling—you knew that already, of course—you've seen my film!'

'No, no, I just read about it.'

'Oh. Well, yes, there has been a lot of hype. I don't consider it anything special you know. Globally, my film is nothing special, nothing very very special that is. But relative to the nonsense we make in this city, I suppose it does stand out.'

'I'm very glad to have met you,' said Sasha. The words emerged oddly heartfelt, as though they were not, and had never been, a cliché.

'And I am very lucky,' said Ahishor gaily. 'It's not every day you meet a Tolstoy fan on the Delhi–Mumbai Rajdhani. You've vindicated my faith in the nutritive value of train journeys! So, what do you do, Sasha?'

'At present... Well, not anything in particular. I am just moving to Bombay for now.'

'Hmm. I see there's a story here that you're not telling me.'

The young man looked chastened. A wave of emotions passed over his face, in expressions both bitter and bashful.

'Never mind!' cried Ahishor, laughing. 'I won't probe! You're going to enjoy Bombay. It's a fantastic city.'

'Yes?'

'Oh yes it is, it is. Maybe things today aren't what they used to be once upon a time—but things are changing too, yes they are. There was always energy in this city, and there's still hope. Whereabouts in Bombay will you be staying?... Versova? Oh really? That's where my office is. I'm there every other day.'

'Oh!' Sasha arched back in his seat, with a look of open enchantment. 'What a coincidence!'

'You'll enjoy it there,' said Ahishor, 'it's charming. There's the beach. And the energy.'

I hope, he thought to himself, I have not gotten myself entangled with some out-of-work actor.

Exhaling loudly, he rose deliberately to his feet and glanced down the carriage.

'You don't smoke?'

'No, thanks,' said Sasha. He had sat up and uncrossed his legs to make room for the other. His hands were clasped together in his lap.

By the time Ahishor returned, the carriage at large was awake, and readying itself for the end of the journey. Bags and suitcases were being pulled out of corners; the train staff was collecting the bed sheets. A man was talking loudly on his phone; another had suffered a coughing fit.

Sasha's own two suitcases, sleek and new, were standing in the corridor. He had a hand over them, as though to claim them, or keep them stable. Though this perhaps was unnecessary. Waiting for the signals to change, the train had been halted for a full minute already.

Ahishor, as usual, was travelling light. Pulling down his lone rucksack from the upper berth, he flopped himself down, ready to go at a moment's notice. It was then that he followed Sasha's gaze.

The view outside was much the same; buildings, trees, slums near the tracks. In the anticipation of arrival, it was of course more generally riveting. But the young man was looking at something specific.

A woman in a sari was standing beside the tracks. She was a plain woman from the slums. She stood, steeped in thought. Her face was thin and composed. Her arms hung heedless by her side and her head was inclined, as though listening for something. A basket full of stones rested by her feet. She stood like a living statue.

'Incredible,' breathed Ahishor. 'She sure is beautiful,' he was about to say, and then he saw how deeply Sasha had blushed already. He grinned excitedly.

'We never think of them this way, do we? When we think of slum-dwellers, they're always cooking, or carrying things, or scolding their children, they're always *working* in some way. They're always *active*. And the women most of all. We never think of them as thinking human beings with a sense of mystery, with dreams and fancies. That's what makes her so astonishingly beautiful, that she's absolutely *idle.*'

'You are right,' Sasha nodded, 'I never thought of that.'

The train shuddered into motion. Sasha was still wreathed in smiles.

'When I was pitching my script, I can't tell you how many people told me: philosophy doesn't sell. The masses aren't interested. I tried to explain to them, philosophy is the massiest thing in the world. Everybody has a philosophy. Everybody lives and dies by their philosophy!'

'She reminded me of my mother,' said Sasha.

Ahishor felt himself forcing a smile, and then, suddenly irritated, he reached for his cell phone and conversation ceased.

He was good-humoured again when they were out on the platform, with the station's familiar commotion encircling, and the warm air of the city rushing him so gladly. He breathed in its well-known medley of smells, that came always packed, and cooked, as from an oven. Sasha's face, in the meantime, was tense with concentration; Ahishor noticed, and all the more was flooded with confidence.

Coolies approached, businesslike. 'You will need a coolie.' He engaged a man in Marathi.

'Pay him sixty rupees when you're in the taxi.'

'Aren't you coming too? Can I drop you somewhere?'

'Carry on,' Ahishor grinned, 'I have some things to do.'

He had nothing to do, but that was just it. He wanted a moment by himself, to exult in his personal and magical gifts, in the plans and prospects that awaited him, and differentiated him from the crowd of passengers, all moving monotonously in the same direction. She must have been on his mind too, of course, swimming up to the very surface of it now, in anticipation of their meeting. But of that in due course.

'Well, goodbye,' said Sasha.

'Ciao ciao. Take my number,' added Ahishor suddenly.

Later, he wondered why he had said that. It ran clean counter to the decision he had reached, as he smoked and mused in the space between the carriages, not to encourage Sasha's friendship. Then again, why had he made that decision in the first place? It was not really because he anticipated, in this stranger, a professional hanger-on. There was something else in the young man's personality, an elusiveness even in the face of innocence, that made Ahishor intuitively uneasy. And now his impulse had contradicted his intuition.

But Ahishor prided himself on both his impulses and his intuitions, and therefore concluded that whatever had happened, had happened for the best.

II

The Man of War

The following is printed as I found it in Sasha's diaries.

10th March 20__

On the whole, my apartment pleases me. It ought to be twice as large for the price, and it is not in the best repair, but I don't need a lot of space or polish either. The landlady told me its first owner was an actor. That would explain the preponderance of mirrors, and perhaps the angles of its 'cut'—if that's the word I'm looking for. It is a neat, private and tasteful apartment, with a reasonable-sized kitchen and bathroom, and the latter, I have quickly realized, is a real luxury in these parts. What is more, the broker was right. I hardly needed the fan today, the place was so cool with the sea breeze. Yes, its windows open to the Arabian Sea!

So I am living next to the sea. I, who ache for the cold, crystal air of the mountains, for the heightened awareness of my blood and my breath when I walk through alpine forests, for the solitude of cliff-edges with not a soul in sight. What made me change my mind? I could have been in Arunachal by myself with my books and my thoughts. Far, far from the stench of selfishness and pettiness.

Instead, I am confronted with this amazing pulsing mass that I have never known what to make of, and chased by the clamour that I hate and detest—for, of course, the other window looks to the street! Have you trapped yourself, Sasha, all too literally, between the devil and the deep blue sea?

And yet—if I could put that down in so many words, I must be in good spirits after all.

* * *

22nd March 20__

This is the first evening in the last two weeks I have felt strength enough to write. I have been sapped by chores and my own ennui.

There were carpenters in the house to fix the sliding doors, and the plumber and the electrician to fix the rest. I have bought furniture, kitchenware, gas, buckets, brooms, the Internet. I have hired a maid. All this was necessary, but I have not been able to see any of it as work. I know this, because work gives me strength. Why is it that settling my flat has only distracted and dispirited me?

Partly it is my guilt about money. I've already spent a lot and I know I will continue to. I tell myself it is rightfully my money, not his, it is only the money that he owes me, as a father.

He hasn't replied to my email. In a way, I am glad. It is better he stay quiet than spin more self-serving lies. For my part, I am glad I wrote. He should know where I am, and that I've not run away. But if he was to come here—I don't think I could stand to see him.

Meanwhile, I feel I must live well, not to please myself, but to give me strength for my work. It seems so horribly easy in this city to immerse oneself in squalor. To make merry in it! I must avoid this trap—it is a sort of death wish—or I will swiftly be capable of nothing.

Of course, 'nothing' is just what I am doing at present! That's the real cause of my tiredness. I told the society people I was a 'writer'. (Versova must be one of the few places in India where writers are a dime a dozen.) Perhaps that was true—once upon a time.

Something read and remembered to lift my spirits before I close: 'A ferryboat knows its whole route before it departs; a man-of-war only gets its orders at sea.'

* * *

3rd April 20__

General Thoughts. Mumbai and Versova.

Walking down Yari road, I feel a carnivalesque atmosphere. Shops and stalls on every inch of the pavement, chaat and sweets, toys and trinkets, barbers and butchers, people everywhere. I am reminded of Premchand's 'Eidgah'. Yet here in the city, the festive fare is laid out day after day, on street after street. If it impresses me, how much more must it impress the young men of small towns?

But these impressions soon alter. A festival, by its very nature, is a special event. If it happens every day, it is not a festival. It is business, trade, work—survival. The energy is still heady but the energy is not the same.

At night, the pavements are strewn with bodies. They lie in their shabby clothes in the yellow sodium glow. They remind me of soldiers, sprawled after a battle.

They call it the city that does not sleep. It is true, there are people on the streets at all hours. The shops run till late. But to work through the night—does that create a 'nightlife'? Surely there is a difference between the vitality that wakes after dark, and the exhaustion that cannot even sleep.

On Friday, once again, I took the train to Churchgate. The famous local trains! They are indeed an experience. When you watch these machines tearing in and gliding out with supreme unconcern, while masses of human beings chase after them, hurl their bodies at them, cling on to them in thick clots of limbs—well! I have felt this once before—during the bus journey to Pushkar—and I feel it again now, clearer than ever: we subjugate ourselves to our machines, like no other people in the world. There is not even a pretence among us that the machine is the slave. Another thing—perhaps nowhere else do people so closely resemble insects. Ten people die every day on these trains, made as meaningless as cockroaches—a mind-boggling statistic.

I am setting things down as I find them. I also love the train journeys. There is a sense of speed and freedom, the wind whips in, there is camaraderie, for in these trains people do not resent the presence of other people. In the trains one is literally close to one's fellow man and that does matter. Without literal closeness any other kind can so easily become a fraud.

It's interesting when a 'big' station approaches—Andheri or Santa Cruz or the most fearsome of them all, Dadar! People line up near the doors, well in advance of the station. They do this to steal a march on the crush of inward traffic, which at rush hour is truly tremendous. They do it by habit though, at all hours. On Friday, I realized what this 'formation' reminds me of. It reminds me of the soldiers in war movies, readying in their boats for an assault on a beach—then charging.

This is the second time I have used a military metaphor for something seen in the city. Have I stumbled onto a truth? An atmosphere of war is indeed compatible with the strain, the exhaustion, even the camaraderie and the jauntiness, even the carnival fatalism, the young man's exhilaration, hanging off a packed train, flirting with death.

And the glamour? (The glamour which, according to my broker, I am actually paying extra for!)

No, here things are blurred. For glamour is a function of how one presents oneself. In spite of everything, Mumbai does not present itself as only, in essence, a battle for money and survival. It calls itself the city of dreams.

Walking through the Seven Bungalows area I often catch sight of a beautiful face slipping into an autorickshaw and speeding away—into the chaos. I suppose what happens in five-stars and nightclubs adds nothing to the world outside. But these 'rick-girls' of Versova are real.

What does their beauty represent? Is it all only deceit, just a cover for grasping, another means to wealth and fame?

Or are they beautiful, in answer to something beautiful?

This section of Bombay's film-world is interesting to me. Perhaps it isn't coincidental that I find myself living next to it. Or that I met Ahishor Frances in the train.

* * *

7th April 20__

Today evening, I walked the length of Versova beach. The sea still baffles and amazes me. It is quite the opposite of the mountains, which one can be in the midst of and be elevated by. No—the sea stands distinct, overweening. One can frolic at its edges of course. That only emphasizes one's sheer distance from it.

The weakness, I know, is in me. I am too fond of feeling secure—not in any material sense—but in my soul. This great sea mocks my eager mind that strives to understand all things, and my heart that yearns to anticipate and prepare for every pain. I think perhaps that is why I have come here, in order to be mocked.

Other people don't seem to suffer so. Without any fuss they simply adore the beach. Well, I looked to learn from them. There is cricket and football played along the sands, there are young boys, sure of a safe landing, practising acrobatics. Small and obedient horses are trotted out for rides by the breakers. They are popular with the children. Stray dogs sit right in the surf, getting wet and cool.

I love them all, but I cannot learn from them, for they seem not to share my trouble. They simply are. Oh, I love them so much I cannot even look at them long! I fear my own malaise may infect them.

Along the rocks, as far as they extend, sit the lovers. They have made of this fearsome sea, a backdrop. Perhaps they are too young to realize what they are doing, or perhaps they are self-centred, impudently exalting their private pleasures— or perhaps they have achieved exactly what I desire, only so consummately, that I cannot even begin to follow them.

Meanwhile, on the sand, on the rocks, on the steps to the street, there are men and women of all ages, alone and in groups, staring towards the horizon. I recognized them. I looked to them for comfort and inspiration. Like me, they had brought their dreams to lay by the sea—by the infinite.

But what then? It makes me anxious, for there is danger here. I sense in their faces a resignation, and a comfort in resigning, though their attitude is the stock attitude of resolve and hope. I distrust it just because it is so aesthetic. 'Hope', when it becomes languid, becomes hopelessness. And it is extremely seductive for that very reason. Don't I know this myself? I too am drawn to casting my wishes onto the sea, to laying back in infinite detachment. But if I truly had hope, I would expect the sea not only to take my wishes but also to bring them back.

I walked further along the beach. I walked in the direction of the slums. Suddenly, I could hardly forgive the slums. Here too, in the face of the infinite ocean, they must set up their clatter of pots and pans, spreading filth and garbage, living hand to mouth, as though nothing else mattered—but that they should keep on living!—but the functions of the body! No—poverty does not excuse degradation. A human being's needs are never only carnal—let nobody forget that!

In anger, I turned away and returned the way I had come. Always, after such anger, I chastise myself. Perhaps, in their circumstances, I would have lived like this too. I only pray that if I did, I would take upon myself, in addition to all my other worries, the guilt of using the seaside so basely. It is as though, for lack of a table, one should eat off a woman's back!

The sun was setting by the time I left the slums.

I wandered for a while among the figures on the beach. I found myself sighing, almost laughing. Where can you walk in this city without your nerves being shaken and jangled, without myriad and contradictory stimuli playing havoc with your self-absorption? Perhaps the only way is to accept every influence with humility, let oneself be shaken.

It is late at night. I am now reaching the reason that prompted me to write this.

Beyond the football games and the gymnasts, I noticed a little lingering among the beach-walkers. They were not gawking, but they were diverted. A girl was being photographed. She was standing in the surf.

I don't think she was a professional model. That wasn't how it appeared. She was being photographed by another girl. As I walked towards them, the photographer was chatting informally, with a high, shrill cadence. I think she was cajoling her friend to pose. She had to cajole a great deal.

I passed them and walked on. I found the way to the street. I only looked back once.

The sky was red behind her. The tide was rising; the waves surged over her body. Suddenly, I seemed to see the whole ocean, ranged against the pettiness of the shore. The dogs, the lovers, the families, the cricketers. The city lights at one end of the beach, Madh Island at the other, and she, on the sands. In her eyes was patience wearing thin; weariness turning to contempt. She was one with the sea in scorning the earth, and everything on it.

The same mystery that I fear and dread was lashing about that girl.

III

The Black Sheep

As for myself—I saw those photos on Facebook the very same week. In April, when Sasha encountered her on Versova beach, I had known Maithili Krishna for some months already. She was by no means a friend, although, as is not uncommon among Mumbai's theatrical folk, she had once told me things I wouldn't have told my best friend. But I find myself unable to lump her with the rest.

On the evening that I first met her, I was at Ahishor's rented flat in Pali Village. I had heard he was looking for an editor for a short film that one of his friends had shot, which he was helping complete. I need hardly say I grabbed at the chance. In the first place, I was hungry for any kind of work. Moreover, like everybody else I knew, I was in awe of Ahishor.

His flat was a charismatic mess of books (more than books on film, I saw Hegel, Schopenhauer, George Bernard Shaw and Nietzsche), DVDs, which included a great deal of classical music, and paper-strewn tabletops. It was always full of people, chatting animatedly, moving busily in and out of rooms, smoking on the roofless terrace.

At the time I only registered that she, like many others,

was young and attractive. Later, I grew more aware of the more disturbing elements of her beauty. Maithili had mixed blood. Her mother was from the hills of Kumaon and her father was Tamilian. But she was very fair, almost white. Her cheeks were like porcelain, her lips thin and pale, her teeth spotless and, as one noticed when she laughed, rather sharp. She did not laugh a lot though. On the whole, her face was still and expressionless—a mask-like face. (A liability, I remember thinking, for an actor.) Yet she never looked merely blank either, because her eyes, which were long and narrow beneath high, curved eyebrows, were always darting with something. I don't know what. Irony, perhaps.

I saw her a few times, on and off, while I was working from the Pali Village flat. I gathered she was making a documentary of some kind—on psychedelic drugs—which Ahishor was producing. Of her more intimate relations with him I knew nothing, though I had noticed some raillery in this connection, among certain sections of his coterie. I wasn't curious. As far as I was concerned, Ahishor could have anybody—and probably did. Soon we had finished the editing, I stopped going to Bandra, and I saw no more of Maithili, outside, of course, of Facebook.

Nevertheless, it was not long after that one startling conversation, during which she had informed me she was 'the black sheep' of her family (though that was not the startling part of it), that I learned in detail, from an independent source, of the Holi party at her house that year. In retrospect it seems to me that many hints of what was to come were let fall that day, and many things set in motion.

She lived in Malabar Hills, in South Bombay, in a vast apartment looming over the sea. It was owned by her parents, but they had been for some years in Washington (where her father had a job in the World Bank), and it was her grandfather who actually occupied it. This gentleman had fought in the freedom struggle, spent multiple terms in Parliament, and later been a highly respected state governor. A widower, he lived alone, save for a little retinue of faithful servants, and while he never complained of loneliness he had welcomed with gladness Maithili's decision to return to India after college. Others in the family had been more doubtful. This included Maithili's brother, Vishnu, a Ph.D. student in Philadelphia.

That Holi afternoon, they were all together in Mumbai, and with the additional family excitement that Vishnu was newly engaged. The young woman herself (her name was Sukanya) was in California with her parents, but her uncle and aunt, who lived in Delhi, happened to be in the city.

And there was one other guest who rang the doorbell that day, who was neither family nor going to be.

'Some *gulaal*,' mumbled this visitor, pushing forward small packets full of coloured powder as soon as the door was opened.

'How prim and proper,' teased Maithili's mother, 'I expected you to come in drenched!'

'In that case, your guard wouldn't have let me in. But you know I've always preferred a dry Holi, Tara.'

'Nonsense, you're just being boring. So are we all. At least the young people are out playing. Suraj! Jatin's here!'

'If there is one place,' he told me later, 'one place, in the whole of this wretched city, where I enter and actually feel— aaaah! I have space!—it's that apartment.'

Jatin Khanna, my ex-boss, was an old school friend of Maithili's mother. She had been (so I gathered from some stray sentiments he had let drop) the one great love of his youth. She remained an affectionate, sisterly presence in his life, which had passed stormily from advertising to fiction writing (a single unknown novel) to movie-making (a single feature film that flopped), and thence to a perfect tumult of ideas and activity whose general tendency nobody could quite divine. He was a big, booming man, possessed of incredible energy, that flared up frequently in angry outbursts, and shrunk in doglike guilt.

They went to the drawing room which was flanked on one side by a dining table set out with sweets, snacks and plates of *gulaal*, looking like fairy dust, and open on the other to a balcony bringing in the warm sea winds. Sporadic shrieks were floating up from below. Holi was in full swing on the streets.

The uncle and aunt of the fiancée aforementioned were seated already on a sofa, their cheeks smeared with colour, feeding on gujiyas and thandai. They were both rather fat; he quite bald, she with her imposing white hair up in a bun, plumly dressed in a kurta and sari respectively.

Maithili's father was making his way down the staircase, clutching a thick book in his hand and looking pleased with himself. This goodwill evidently transferred to Jatin during the fresh round of greetings, but once the new guest was settled beside the others, it seemed to revert to its true origin.

'Here,' he said enthusiastically, 'this is the one I was talking about. Paranjpe's new big book!'

Smiling from the sofa, the uncle extended a hand, but quickly had to use his other hand so as to avoid dropping the tome. His wife too, glanced at it with interest. But their attention soon wandered.

'I love Holis in Bombay.' Tara Krishna was striding towards the balcony, taking a deep breath of the breeze. 'Diwali in Delhi, but Holi in Bombay.'

'Yes, it's the festival of madness,' Jatin grinned, 'just like this city.'

'Oh they all are,' the uncle looked up. 'All our festivals are absolutely barbaric.'

'They can be pretty too. Isn't all this pretty?' questioned Tara.

'All this,' said the uncle, with a cryptic smile, 'is not all that.'

His vague gesture seemed to take in the whole city, the whole country.

'They were just simple festivals,' his wife added slowly. 'Holi is about natural colours, the changing season—now you have these awful chemical paints and hooliganism. Diwali is a festival of lights, not firecrackers and pollution. But yes, in today's time, if we talk about the culture in the cities, which is of course influencing everybody else, it is quite disturbing.'

'I couldn't agree more,' said Jatin. 'By the way, I'm a big fan of your work.' He had only just recognized the lady.

She smiled and nodded, though no doubt she was a little taken aback by this open appreciation from a contemporary. Ira Joshi was a writer and translator, in Hindi and English, a columnist for several newspapers, and a regular invitee at the various literary festivals that had cropped up throughout the country. To these her husband often accompanied her. His own long-planned novel had not yet achieved fruition, but as a well-connected civil servant his presence at such gatherings was always welcome. Together, they were personal friends with important people from all walks of life, and so well-entrenched in the world that it was difficult to believe (yet true) that they had met each other as young Naxalites.

'Someone is yelling,' said Jatin suddenly.

They turned around on their sofas to listen. Indeed, a girl's voice was faintly audible from the direction of the balcony, which overhung the boundary of the apartment complex—she was probably shouting from the lane outside. Jatin rose at once to look. Called back from the kitchen by her husband, Tara came up behind him.

'There were three of them, standing in the sun,' Jatin told me later. 'Maithili, her brother and one other girl—the Joshi's daughter. They looked like popsicles. Maithili was the one shouting. Her brother was trying to shush her—at least I think he was. Some random people on the street had stopped to watch. Basically, she wanted a T-shirt thrown down to her. The one she was wearing had gotten a tear in it.'

At that stage, he had flushed strangely and said no more on this particular point. But I gathered she was rather dishevelled.

From the height of the balcony it was not possible to argue. The cries of 'What happened!', 'Come up!', and even the conciliatory 'Come for lunch!', went as though unheard. Harried into compliance, Maithili's mother quickly fetched something from her daughter's bedroom, and threw it down to the street. The moment she had caught hold of the shirt Maithili marched out of sight. Her brother shot up a strange, contemptuous look. Then, he disappeared after her.

Meanwhile, catching wind of controversy, the Joshis had remained diplomatically on the sofa. Mr Krishna was frowning hard and exchanging odd glances with his wife. The servants went on laying the table for lunch, but there was a strange atmosphere in the room. Nobody was quite sure what had taken place below.

Presently, the conversation continued. Mr Joshi gave his balanced opinion of the new State government in Delhi. It had failed to fix the water problem, but had done something for the roadside hawkers. Jatin exploded into a sudden eulogy of Delhi street food, and since they were now on the subject of food, Tara unveiled her plan for a chain of 'real' artists' cafes, where writers and painters would be encouraged to linger for hours, in green and peaceful surroundings. Everyone thought it was an excellent plan, but Ira Joshi suggested that contrary to what one might imagine, it was an idea better suited to India's small towns than its cities. 'There are truly passionate artists there, who only lack for encouragement.' Listening to the others talk, Mr Krishna gradually regained his good humour. He had started on an anecdote about his English teacher in high school—an amazing man who had never travelled beyond his district in Tamil Nadu yet knew and loved the literature of the whole world—when the doorbell rang, several times.

At the very first ring there fell a silence. One of the figures from the kitchen went to the door, while an array of tense half-smiles appeared on the faces in the drawing room.

The young people poured in unreservedly. In clothes and skin that were coloured from head to toe, they resembled an alien species.

'What's for food?' cried Maithili, 'I'm famished!'

Her smile, shy and brilliant, took in everybody. It was noticed discreetly that she was wearing the new shirt (played-in, but intact) and that there was no sign of the old.

'Aren't you going to change first?' Tara laughed.

Drawing closer to her daughter, she added cautiously, 'Are you okay?'

'I'm not going to change now,' Maithili shook her head. 'We're all dry anyway.'

With a sardonic smile, Vishnu moved away from her. Soon his expression transformed to a big grin as he greeted the Joshis. He was a tall, plump, bespectacled young man. His features lacked the perfect symmetry of his sister's, but perhaps by the same token they were warmer and friendlier.

Anamika, the Joshis' daughter, began to say something in a low voice to Tara, until Maithili, returning from a quick inspection of the food in the kitchen, took her by the arm and led her into the house. She turned back once on the way.

'Where's Dada?'

'He's still in his room, but he'll be out soon. You have time to get ready.'

As it happened, they all did wash and change. It was some time, therefore, before the three generations of the Krishna family, along with the guests from Delhi, and Jatin Khanna, were all together at lunch.

I cannot now picture that gathering in Malabar Hills, without my thoughts travelling further and wider afield. Perhaps this is because any whole example of the family unit (a rarity, by the way, in these scattered times) excites one to imagine the yet larger units of society and nation—just as the sight of an animal in the wild recalls the category: 'habitat'. For I am not merely foreshadowing what they talked about. Such talk could be heard anywhere, as a running noise, a more or less ineffectual chatter. In those days, the discomfiture within our elite and English-speaking circles had grown such, that we were all more or less squirming where we sat. Some spoke blackly about the rise of the Hindu right; some evinced a desperate confidence in the country's surge towards richness, and they were often the same people, at different times of the day. It was difficult to say where anybody stood exactly. It was a time of many a dark foreboding, many a blithe surrender.

Individually, therefore, they might well have discussed what they did, as everyone else was doing, and to as little consequence. But the political heft of their being one family charged that afternoon, and lent its discourse its secret significance. Here is a call for the reader's patience: for beneath these tediously twinkling waters, great waves are forming.

In the room's oldest armchair sat eighty-three-year-old Purushottam Krishna—Suraj Krishna's father, Maithili's grandfather. He was a short man, with a well-groomed grey beard, and sad, stern eyes behind elegant spectacles. Vertical lines furrowed his forehead deeply as he sipped from a mug of soup.

'It must be so nice for you,' said Ira Joshi, 'having your granddaughter around,'

The old man's voice boomed surprisingly. 'It would certainly be nice, if she ever were around.' He smiled and suddenly looked like a chortling baby.

'She was out of Bombay a lot last year, shooting,' Tara explained. 'There was one in Haryana and one in...Calcutta, wasn't it Maithili?'

'You know where it was.'

'When are all these films going to release?' said Mr Krishna idly. He was working away at his plate of puri and sabzi. 'They seem to keep shooting but nothing ever gets released.'

'It takes time. These directors don't have money for big releases either. It's independent cinema.'

'Not independent of audiences, one hopes!' Mr Krishna laughed.

'I guess the good thing about doing these movies,' said Vishnu, 'is that as opposed to mainstream Bollywood, at least you're working in good stories and stuff.'

Here Jatin was seen to restrain himself from expressing some powerful opinion. He would likely have failed had Dipankar Joshi not spoken first.

'Ira and I saw a wonderful film recently. It's called *Schrödinger's Cat*, by a young director, Ahishor Frances. If you haven't already, you all must see it.'

'I know,' Maithili smiled. 'I know Ahishor.'

'An amazing talent! The movie is quite brilliant.'

'True,' said Jatin, seeming to check himself. 'In this particular case, it is true.'

'What's it about?' Tara was curious. 'Maithili never told us.'

She smiled with mock-censure at her daughter, but Maithili did not catch her eye. She was looking calmly into space.

'Haven't you heard about it?' Mr Joshi began, 'I believe it's the talk of the town. It's about—well, it's actually three separate stories. But they're all based on Schrödinger's Cat—the famous philosophical thought experiment.'

A ruminative silence followed. Maithili got up to put away her plate; she had eaten very little.

'There's a new biography of Schrödinger,' said Mr Krishna. 'A fascinating character—he was an avowed atheist, but deeply interested in Vedic philosophy. Tremendous womanizer too.'

As she returned demurely to her chair, Maithili's face was suddenly wreathed in smiles. Diagonally across the room from her, Anamika Joshi was darting regular glances her way. Anamika was a stocky girl with thick, long hair. She made little impression that afternoon, so Jatin informed me. He had put her down as dull and perhaps not very intelligent.

'Can someone explain the story of the film?' asked the elder Krishna suddenly.

'Oh!' laughed Ira Joshi, 'Well, it's a bit complicated—you really have to see it—but I can try.'

When she had finished, the old man frowned.

'And what does she do then?'

'Who?'

'The woman who's lost her family in the accident.'

'I don't want to spoil it for anybody,' Ira smiled. 'It's hinted that she is able to fall in love again. Because when she was much younger, she had resisted her parents who wanted her to get married at once. Which itself—it's very interesting—which itself was because of all the Hollywood teen movies she happened to be seeing at the time. So she went out and had boyfriends instead. And having that life experience in storage, it gives her extra choices when her husband dies.'

Dipankar Joshi nodded. 'One of the characters in the movie says, that whether Schrödinger's cat is going to be alive or dead when that button is pushed, when that radioactive gas is released—'

'Poison,' said Ira.

'Or poison, or whatever it is, that perhaps it all depends on the whole life story of the particular cat in the box!'

'Something like karma, I suppose,' said Ira.

The grandfather lapsed into silence. Once he opened his mouth as if to speak but then closed it again, with visible discomfiture. Then, smiling fondly, he turned to Maithili.

'Your film,' he said, 'on the subject of female foeticide—now, that is a vital subject.'

Maithili nodded briefly but said nothing, even when the Joshis looked at her with interest.

'Yes, an important subject,' said Vishnu, 'but who's going to watch it?'

'Why won't they?' demanded his mother. 'Don't be negative Vishnu.'

'I'm not being negative. Even a very talked-about film like *Schrödinger's Cat* is, relatively speaking, a box office failure. Anyway, obviously Maithili's film isn't really aimed at the box office. But firstly, it's in English. So you're basically preaching to the converted.'

'That's not true, that assumption's not true.'

'Let's not quibble. The core offenders here are not typically English-speaking. But even if the film was in Hindi or Kannada, people aren't going to flock to it anyway. People want to be entertained. Look at it this way: if the public was so enlightened as to want enlightening films then they wouldn't be aborting girl children to begin with.'

'That's...too cynical,' said Tara. Her husband, however, was chuckling, while Ira Joshi smiled thinly and Dipankar Joshi looked impressed.

'So I'm curious,' said Jatin, fastening an eager gaze on Maithili. 'You've been acting in Bollywood for about a year now, right? What are your own impressions? I'm just asking generally.'

She was so expressionless that for a moment he wondered if he had even spoken. Then she answered:

'It's been fine.'

'I'm asking because I personally find it very frustrating. At many levels.'

'It doesn't bother me,' said Maithili. 'For me the problem is our whole modern civilization. It's gotten corrupt. We have to destroy it, and start again at the beginning.'

She had spoken with soft sincerity, but in the aftermath she blushed a little. Around her had fallen a discreet silence, as though everyone was trying to put behind them the gaucherie of such a pronouncement.

'I must say,' Dipankar Joshi said eventually, 'I share Vishnu's scepticism. To change such things in this country...it's going to need some very major intervention. And when you talk of the girl child or women's rights, I mean, it's still the seventeenth century here in India.'

'Even more so now,' Ira murmured, 'with the right-wingers getting stronger every day. We're basically at the mercy of misogynist thugs.'

'Why is nobody having dessert?' Tara cried. 'Vishnu and Maithili, please serve everybody. Vishnu!'

He rose, smirking, and she, impassively. Jatin looked anxiously at his old friend; she was plainly put out. The Joshis had introduced into the pleasant Holi afternoon a discordantly grim note—while all the while gorging themselves. No doubt she was worried too about Maithili playing Holi in the street, and how her shirt had gotten torn.

'Let me help,' Jatin leaped to his feet. 'No, no please!'

'Why are you troubling yourself?' spoke Purushottam Krishna. 'Where are Mohan and Laxman?

'In the kitchen, Appa,' said Tara. 'If I ask them to serve, then the children protest and if I don't, then you protest!'

'I am not protesting,' said the old man gently, and handed his soup-mug to Jatin. 'Now, what were we talking about?'

'What were we talking about?' Mr Krishna smiled. 'I'm not sure.' Suddenly there were smiles all round.

'Anyway,' said Mr Krishna, 'we all have high hopes from the younger generation.'

'Oh absolutely,' Ira Joshi nodded portentously. 'It's honestly all up to them now. If they can move beyond the old stigmas...'

'Just focus on their careers,' muttered Dipankar. 'That's what they should do.'

'I believe *you* just finished studying?' said Mr Krishna.

'Anamika,' said her mother sharply.

The girl seemed to start from a daydream. 'Almost finished. I have my last semester. It's art school, in Greece.'

'Near Athens,' said Dipankar Joshi. He looked for some reason uncomfortable. '*Khair* (anyway), now we are all looking forward to when Vishnu and Sukanya finish! You must come visit us a great deal, Vishnu. By the way, with all due respect to this fine city, I trust you will do the smart thing and live in Delhi?'

'If I can get Suki to leave California first,' said the young man. 'I do expect to work in Delhi.'

'This is also an interesting thing,' said Mr Krishna, tucking into his ras malai. 'In spite of everything, I find that young people today want to come back to India. It's a heartening trend. It shows that... What happened? What're you doing?'

'Heartening?' said Maithili, holding away the bowl she had just grabbed from his hands. 'Heartening?' The word sounded absurd as she deliberately rolled the 'r'. 'But it's bad for your heart! Oh take it!' She returned the dessert with a sudden, bored laugh and then flashed a glance at Anamika, who was staring at her intently. Then she moved quietly and gracefully to her chair.

As Jatin recalled later: 'It was just a weird moment. There was nothing for anyone to say about it. It was over very quickly and when she was sitting again she looked perfectly polite. Almost docile.'

In any case, he had been too taken himself by the turn in the conversation, to dwell on a distraction.

'Suraj, do you really reckon that's true?' said Jatin, 'I was talking to a musician friend of mine the other day. He's gay, and his thing was that boss, I'd get out of this country if I had the slightest chance. I only stay because I have no choice.'

'Of course,' said Mr Krishna, 'Of course, everyone knows India is a difficult place, for all sorts of reasons. However, let's not be blind to our achievements. We do have a growing economy.

That's more than you can say for a lot of the world. With all its faults, we do have a democracy. There is a certain vibrancy here, a certain stimulation. Ram Guha called India "the most interesting country in the world"—and I agree. Paranjpe makes many of these points himself.'

He lifted with fondness the book he had brought down, that the Joshis had set aside. Cradling it in his palms, his voice seemed to gain conviction, and to more and more resemble a speech.

'Liberal intelligentsia optimistic banalities,' was how Jatin described it later. 'Our five thousand-year-old civilization, our history of tolerance—bah! I couldn't decide if he had his head in the sand, or up his arse! Nobody could get a word in edgeways.'

But someone had been trying, and with such effort, that suddenly everyone turned to look.

The retired governor was leaning forward in his chair. His hand, half-raised, was visibly trembling. Indeed, everything about his age was suddenly exaggerated. He sat unsteadily. His brow was mapped with lines, his eyes were sunken, and his lips quivered with the force of the thought that seemed ripe to burst from them.

Suddenly, he cried out. Something fell with a wet splash onto the carpet in front of him. It took the whole company a moment to register what it was.

What happened next was, if possible, even more unexpected. Maithili was on her feet. She dashed the heavy book from her father's lap and marched into the sunshine of the balcony, from whence the balloon, full of water and chemical paint, had entered.

She went straight to the parapet. Screaming, 'Go away! Go away!' she hurled down Paranjpe's masterwork, before the incredulous eyes of every person in the drawing room. (Thus did those lofty words at last come in contact with the street.) There were gasps indoors, a stifled cry of anguish from Suraj Krishna, and the sounds of mingled astonishment and laughter from the street, that died hurriedly as a watchman now hollered at the miscreants.

Returning inside, she began to run up the stairs. Midway up, she paused, and looked over the bannister.

'Dada, don't worry,' said Maithili, gazing at the old man. Then she seemed to sigh, as though all her heightened energy was ebbing away all at once. 'They were just a bunch of idiots.'

After that, the guests did not linger long. But when the Joshis were readying to leave, so Jatin recorded, Anamika went upstairs in person to say goodbye to Maithili.

'She looked extremely concerned,' he told me. 'She looked as worried about Maithili as her own mother did.'

IV

A Significant Extra

I pass now to the following month, to a certain hot, muggy night, when I found myself walking as fast as I could towards the Nana-Nani Park in Seven Bungalows.

As on every night, the roads were choked with vehicles. Buses were making their last return to the depot off Yari Road. Sleek-looking cars swerved unpredictably. I waited at a bend, perspiring impatiently, grimacing at the bright queue of traffic and trying to concentrate. It was not just the honking I was fending off, but the abounding distractions of bustling roadside stalls and perpetual streams of people. Now that I recollect it, I was well and truly in the city's grip, overstimulated, looking for a break. But when I heard my name being called out, I turned almost at once.

From the coffee shop down the road, Ahishor was waving. I hurried towards him. As I drew closer, my excitement momentarily vanished. Also at his table, practically laughing in my face, was Bharat Mishra.

It is possible my dislike of Bharat was snobbish. Unlike me, he had not grown up in a big city. Nor had he been to film school (although for that matter, neither had Ahishor). Perhaps

I was also jealous of how much Ahishor seemed to value him, though he was only an odd-job man, with no particular skills in any aspect of cinema.

These, at any rate, were his own explanations, and he found ways to let me know that they were. He had a long jaw and a toothy grin. I found him cloying, deceitful and malicious.

'Have an iced tea,' said Ahishor, manoeuvring me to a seat. 'Although you look like you need something stronger.'

'Just on my way to one shoot,' I explained. 'Just running a bit late.'

'Why are you late?' he asked, unexpectedly.

I was on the verge of lying, but there was a sparkle in his eye, as though somehow he already knew.

'Where are you coming from?'

'Just, I had gone to see one woman in Lokhandwala. She's a...supposedly she's a clairvoyant. My mother knows her. She's the one who wanted me to go, she believes in all this stuff.'

Bharat's constant grin was bobbing beside me.

'Did she predict your future in the industry?' he said. I ignored him. Ahishor was looking thoughtful.

'That's an interesting coincidence... I'll tell you why I say that. But why are you embarrassed, Dhruv? There are more things in heaven and earth, are there not?'

'I guess, but I don't believe in all this.'

'Don't worry about belief. Take an interest in such phenomena, an objective, detached interest. Occult phenomena are objectively interesting. You can believe *that*, can't you?'

'I guess,' I nodded.

He pushed the menu towards me. I shook my head quickly.

'I really have to go.'

'Where are you going? Malik's shoot?'

'Yeah. I have a small part.'

'He's roped everybody in,' Ahishor laughed. 'Why are you doing this film? Just for the experience? Or because you think it's any good?'

'Probably a bit of both.'

'I am fond of Malik,' he said, after a moment, 'and I know he really loves movies. He's mad about them. But his mind is so terribly confused. What is the point of showcasing all this violence if you don't even begin to make an inquiry into the psychology of it? Then you are simply exclaiming, not even communicating, leave alone instructing. It's a general problem among us folk. We have nothing to say. We just want to say something.'

I kept quiet, though I flashed a scowl at Mishra, who was smirking unaccountably.

'As for experience,' Ahishor smiled into his beard, 'experience isn't just about doing things, is it? It's also about rejecting things. In a general sense, everyone experiences twenty-four hours every day, don't they? So meaningful experience must be a product of selection and discrimination. If you don't discriminate, you are not gaining experience, you are just being buffeted about... Do you understand?'

'I know... I just figured it's better than sitting at home.'

I didn't catch his eye. But I was aware of a certain flushed pleasure, due solely to the interest he was taking in me. He was silent now, smiling slightly, exuding a calm authority.

'*Khair*, at least you aren't doing more extra-*giri*,' said Bharat, 'Or are you an extra only?'

'No I'm not,' I said, 'but Malik did ask me to find extras if I could. Why don't you come?'

Bharat laughed and slapped my back.

'No seriously,' I said.

Our table was beside the pavement, where the passers-by walked to and fro. I remember it was about then that a rather overdressed young man, carrying a bag of groceries, stopped and glanced over the railings. I looked up into a thin face that seemed to be burning with happiness. That was my first sight of Sasha.

They greeted each other with surprise and evident pleasure, but Ahishor did not at first introduce us, nor did he invite Sasha to join us. It was in the wake of a polite query (I noticed that an unusual formality had entered Ahishor's manner)—to which the stranger replied that he wasn't doing anything in particular, 'just settling in'—that a thought seemed to occur to Ahishor.

'Would you like to see a short film being shot?'

'I would like that.'

'Dhruv, meet Sasha. Sasha, Dhruv. He'll tell you about it.'

'Do you know Gemini's?' I said. 'You know it, right? We're shooting there tonight. We'll just need you to sit in the background. It may take a bit of your time though. Like a couple of hours.'

'All right,' he nodded.

'Great, thanks. I'm actually going there right now. If you can get there as soon as you're free, maybe in half an hour, that would be great. Take my number.'

Afterwards, he went on his way, his shoulders high above his back, and his feet as though on springs. There was something doll-like about Sasha's figure, with the fine clothes as though placed upon him and worn dutifully thereafter. Bharat stared curiously.

'Who is he?'

'One of the thousands of melancholy souls,' said Ahishor,

'who come to this city for answers.'

'He didn't look that melancholy,' I ventured, with a smile. 'Thanks, by the way.'

But Ahishor seemed not to have heard. He was suddenly deep in thought. I got up to go.

'Listen,' he said, 'come over after the shoot. I'm staying at my mother's place tonight, I'll text you the address. Bring Sasha too. We'll have a drink.'

I nodded, with an excitement building slowly. I had talked to Ahishor often enough, but an invitation to his mother's suggested a new degree of closeness.

Looking back, I don't know what I was thinking. Perhaps it was my soaring presumptions of close friendship that prompted me to say what I did. Yet even that does not explain what I meant by it.

'Maithili's also there,' I said, offhand. 'She's also at the shoot, I mean.'

The moment I spoke I stood steeped in my blunder. Ahishor's face leaped with a vivid offense. His mouth parted wordlessly. It was clear he hadn't known at all. I was suddenly aware of his vulnerability, of how, for all his spirit and wisdom, he never could conceal his feelings. In the same instant I saw Bharat Mishra staring, his mind working shamelessly. I spoke on quickly.

'Anyway, bye, thanks! Thanks! I'll come as soon as the shoot is over.'

'Bring Sasha too.' Ahishor lifted a generous hand. I hurried away in strange torment.

* * *

Gemini's was unrecognizable. Its open-air environs had always, in my knowledge, exuded the jaunty vibrations of money and pleasure; throbbing with music and laughter, packed close with lovely bodies, with slick-haired young waiters slipping smugly in between them. Now there lay bare the peeling paint on the walls, the chips in the wooden furniture, the surprising paltriness of the space itself. It was cinema, of course, that had so humbled it, that it might afterwards exalt it. But for the time being, the place seemed in shock. I felt rather sorry for it.

Malik came up to me with a distracted look.

'You got your lines, *na*? Cool cool. We have to finish fast, permission *nahi hai*. How is it looking?'

'Nice,' I said.

'Fuck, short film *ne bhi ma chod di*! Not slept for two nights!'

He moved away to discuss some point of lighting with the man behind the LEDs. But I felt a spurt of irritation. I was thinking suddenly of how fat and sweaty Malik was, how wild-eyed and unhealthy his whole appearance. It was an unexpectedly mean feeling. I stood for a moment, trying to compose myself, when someone came up beside me. It was Sasha, smiling shyly.

As I introduced him to the faces I knew, the strange animosity persisted. It was taking them all in its sweep. None of them, I felt, kindled in me any real recognition. There was Tanvi, a breezy, busy line producer, who worked at an ad agency, and was considered extremely efficient at everything she did. She was an automaton to me. There was Mehboob, the lead actor in the film, silent and standoffish. He had arrived with his wife, who was wearing a hijab and sitting amongst everybody, while not saying a word to anyone. Then there were the aspiring film-makers themselves, come to assist one of their own—Varun, fashionably bespectacled with crew-cut hair and a muscular frame; Arshdeep, overweight, cringing and forever cajoling people to 'not mind' his requests; Sushant, a slender and lascivious pot addict [of whom, I have much more to say later].

I knew this latter bunch was full of passionate opinions and secret ambitions; they swore in multiple languages; they smoked and drank at the hole-in-the-wall Woodcon pub in Seven Bungalows with the table fans whirring and forgotten bodies slouched alongside; they downloaded movies all day and watched them all night; they were 'characters'. But that night, as I showed Sasha around, giving and receiving ebullient greetings, trading hand-clasps and nods, I thought they were as flat as they were colourful, exaggerated and unreal people, neither individuals nor a collective, but something half-done. And I was a middle-class boy from West Delhi, with parents who worried if I was eating well, who liked to know where he stood.

The clairvoyant had talked in discomfiting riddles. But among them had been one warning I thought I understood. It had to do with the quality of my company.

'Sorry,' I said to Sasha, 'this may be a pain for you.'

Sasha shook his head. He was looking around with great pleasure, when Maithili walked out of a corner and strolled into the light.

I noticed her specially myself. She sat by herself at a table, waiting for the camera to roll. Her thoughtfulness and composure contrasted mightily with my impression of everybody else. She looked very young in her shorts and sandals, her hair falling freely over her white shoulders. I was reminded of a child in a sandbox, building something after its own designs, gravely oblivious to the world.

Malik was explaining to Sasha what was required of him. 'All you have to do is sit with her like you're having coffee with her. Talk about anything, we aren't recording your voices. *Beech beech mein* (in between), she will keep looking at that other table, where Dhruv will be talking to Mehboob. Whom she will later kill after he tries to rape her. Eheheh! But fuck that *abhi keliye* (for now). Okay? You got it, right? Dhruv, you're ready *na*? We'll start soon, *thoda lighting ka locha hai* (there's a bit of trouble with lighting).'

When I saw the footage later, I had eyes of course for my own performance. Yet I did wonder what they said to each other. They were both smiling intermittently. He was doing most of the talking, his gaze was often concentrated in delight, while hers regarded him with a constant, friendly amusement. I noticed, however, that when, as per the script, Maithili glanced away, Sasha looked up at her, and at those moments, in his troubled eyes, was not the ghost of a smile.

Much more than an hour passed before the scene was done. I went up to Sasha who was standing beside Malik.

'You go,' said Malik. 'Leave Sasha. We'll use him in the next scene too. Shirt *badal ke* (Once you have changed your shirt) you can sit at another table, okay?'

'Ahishor asked him to come too,' I said.

'His Highness has commanded?' Malik grinned. 'A royal *hukum*?'

I found myself at a loss for words. 'He's Ahishor's friend.'

'*Chal ja ja*. We'll manage. Thanks for coming, Sasha, really appreciate it.'

'It was my pleasure,' he said simply.

I marched towards the exit, but Sasha was slower to follow. When I turned, he was glancing around, plainly in search of something. The others were scattered about the restaurant, talking in pockets, or simply preoccupied. Pursing his lips suddenly, he marched out after me.

Malik's crack was still rankling. As we stepped onto the

pavement, I began to speak bitterly.

'Quite a waste of time! I'm just doing this shoot for the experience. You must have gotten damn bored.'

'It's all new for me,' he said. 'Maybe that's why I didn't get bored. They are really nice people though.'

'They're professionally nice people,' I said. 'They're nice to everybody as a matter of policy, because in this town you never know who's who or who'll be what tomorrow. It doesn't mean anything.'

'Well, I hadn't looked at it that way,' said Sasha, 'Still, I wasn't expecting them to be so...down-to-earth. I liked Malik a lot.'

'The problem with all these guys is they're extremely negative,' I said. 'I find them extremely negative and...frustrated. That's the difference between Ahishor and them. That's why they're small-time and he's not. How do you know Ahishor, by the way?'

'I don't really,' he said. 'We met on the train coming to Bombay. I had heard about him though.'

'One doesn't feel frustrated around Ahishor,' I said keenly. 'He has idealism, positive energy.'

'Yes.'

'Frankly he's the only person I've met in this town who I really want to work with. What about you? Where are you working?'

I was walking very fast. The traffic of the early night had dwindled, and I could manoeuvre more or less freely between the sleeping stray dogs and the dug up portions of the pavement. I was anxious to get to Ahishor as quickly as possible, but Sasha was struggling to keep up. I looked back to see him drawing level with his urgent, bouncy gait.

'Where does he live?' he said.

'He lives in Bandra, but he's at his mother's place right now,' I explained. 'It's in one of those nice, semi-posh lanes behind Yari Road. Close by.'

'I'm not working anywhere,' he said suddenly. 'I just moved here. I have some money saved up. From my father.'

He looked very grave as he spoke. An inquisitive mood passed over me; then I fell quiet myself. We hurried on in silence.

V

At Ahishor's

Ahishor Frances's mother was an extraordinary person. I had seen her only once before, but it was not a sight I would soon forget. She had entered suddenly during one of our more boisterous sessions in Pali Village. With a smile on her face, she had walked up to Ahishor, spoken to him in a soft, musical tone, and the rest of us had been silenced, not from discomfiture, but awe and envy. She was slim, muscular and oval-faced, in a dress that showed her bare arms and shoulders. Everything about her suggested elegance. I don't know how old she was, but she looked no more than thirty-five.

I learned later that she had brought up Ahishor almost entirely by herself. In her twenties, Nalini Malvekar (as she then was) had acted in a number of Marathi plays, but she had given up a potentially very successful career on stage to be a wife and mother. Three years later, her husband, a scientist at the Tata Institute, was killed in a car accident. There had followed a period of quite serious financial difficulty, during which she was obliged to borrow money from friends and relatives. She had managed, however, to secure a position teaching English to college students, and had performed so successfully that some years down the line, despite having only an MA degree, she was designated a professor.

It was to his mother that Ahishor owed his extensive and precocious reading, his diverse creative flair (she had encouraged her son to paint, write, act and shoot videos as part of a rigorous homeschooling that ran parallel to his formal education), and I suppose, most significantly, the continual nourishment of his self-belief.

In the meantime, while Nalini had never remarried, there had ensued a relationship. It was apparently common knowledge in theatre and film circles, but I was amazed when I first heard of it. Karim Azad was a legendary figure, both for his prolific lyric-writing in the film industry, and his ferocious intellect that spared none of his contemporaries. He was Bollywood's most ruthless critic, and in my college, he had been revered more than anybody else in Bollywood.

But while his presence at the flat should not, therefore, have surprised me, my heart still stopped when he opened the door. It was only several minutes after I was seated that I felt confident enough to speak without stammering. I seemed to have entered a room full of royalty: Ahishor, his mother, Karim Azad! Imagine my surprise, then, to discover that they were all listening rapt to a complete stranger.

A short young man wearing a denim jacket and a yellow sports T-shirt, whom I had never seen nor heard of, was holding court in the living room as Sasha and I arrived. When I think back, I cannot recall him even breaking stride to greet us. It was just as though we were slipping in late to hear him speak.

'...was called more names in that one week than the rest of my life put together. But they don't realize I enjoy it. I will provoke them all day long, it's my greatest pleasure. One very funny thing happened on Facebook, by the way. I posted an article by PBL. I don't know if you read that one, it was a very academic, closely researched piece on the history of fascism. So I posted this piece, and I tagged two of these Hindu trolls, saying "So-and-so and so-and-so. Would greatly appreciate your inputs to better understand this analysis".'

The young man began to laugh, in the most unusual way. It was a controlled and continual cackle, with the head held straight and the eyes staying fast on his audience, the better to gauge their reaction. During the course of this laugh he turned to me too. There was bonhomie simply dancing in his eyes. I realized I was smiling myself.

'And they took the bait too,' he went on. He had turned his gaze briefly to Sasha, but now was looking at me again. He was rather ugly, yet endearingly so, with a high forehead, close-cropped hair, bushy eyebrows, plump cheeks, and a thin moustache. His voice was high and nasal. 'The sweetest thing about the online mafia is their complete lack of irony. By the way, Ahishor, when were you planning to introduce me to your friends?'

'When you were done with your joke,' Ahishor smiled. 'Mihir Malhotra, journalist, general purpose pundit, and a freshly minted Columbia graduate. Dhruv, a very talented young actor [I blushed], and this—this is Sasha who's just moved to Mumbai. Dhruv, you've met my mother, haven't you? You have, of course you have. Sasha—meet my mom and Karim.'

'How do you do?' said Nalini Frances. She looked as fit and youthful as I remembered, in a checked shirt and jeans. 'Dhruv I know about, but Ahishor has never mentioned you to me. Are you also an actor?'

'We only met recently,' said Sasha. 'I'm actually not doing anything at the moment.'

She smiled as though with perfect understanding. My eyes strayed towards Karim Azad and I nodded respectfully, but it went unnoticed. The great man, kurta-clad as was his wont, was looking into the middle distance, with a sardonic smile resting upon his lips. His cheeks were sullen and his face was thin, with a mop of curly white hair and a white goatee. The rest of him, however, was a lot larger than it looked on television.

When Ahishor offered us drinks, my polite protests were overlaid with a real uneasiness. I don't know what I had expected from his invitation—if it really had been an invitation. (But he had made a point of asking me.)

'Oh!' cried Sasha suddenly. 'Your table is a bath tub!'

I thought for a moment he had lost his mind. But he was right. The table in the living room was an inverted bath tub, with a door placed on top of it. It must have been remarked upon many times before, but pleased nonetheless, Nalini told us how she preferred curtains to doors and considered bath tubs a waste of water because of the amount of water that is used when using a tub. Sasha gazed, openly charmed, at her handiwork, while I grinned too and for the first time, considered the room with freedom. It was an exceptionally pretty flat. There were plants growing thickly in the tiny balcony. The lights were soft and shapely, and the furniture, when it wasn't bespoke, was cane and wood. Paintings hung on the wall, which was itself covered with patterned wallpaper. Later I learned that the paintings had all been done by Nalini herself. They were all uniformly picturesque, with one striking exception. Between a landscape of waves striking a rocky beach, and a man leaning on a railing, contemplating a grassy field, was a picture of Christ on the cross. It was clear that the image was intended for its aesthetic and not its religious value, but I thought the success of this piece of creativity (unlike the others in the room) was doubtful. Among all those embodiments of health and beauty, that emaciated body simply didn't fit.

It was Mihir, not Ahishor, who came around to give us our drinks. I had not noticed him getting to his feet, but he was now rushing about the room, attending to all manner of things. He went to adjust the air conditioner (it was nice and cool in the room already), then fetched an ashtray for Karim Azad who was getting ready to smoke, drew the curtains at the balcony, and came bounding back with a laptop which he placed and opened out on the table in the middle of the room. Then, rather noisily, he drew up his chair. I was a little shocked at these proprietary presumptions, but Nalini and Ahishor were both looking on with indulgence and it seemed that all his behaviour was somehow kosher.

'I'm so excited,' said Mihir, 'I hope you don't mind that I'm so excited. New ideas always get me like this. I don't drink, you know. I just get high on ideas!'

'You get high on people,' said Ahishor.

'People, ideas, people with ideas. I don't need the chair! I'll stand.'

Suddenly the young man looked straight at Sasha. I couldn't understand why. He was more or less laughing, but there was a strange light in his eyes. 'May I begin?' he said. 'With your permission?'

Not waiting for an answer, he turned the laptop around so that it could face us all.

On the screen was a photograph of a wildly bearded man in saffron robes. He was sitting on a bench, with his arms folded loosely in his lap. Behind him was a lake overhung by the thick green canopies of trees and surrounded by shrubbery.

The man was laughing, showing slightly discoloured teeth and many crows' feet around his eyes.

'This,' said Mihir, 'is the so-called Swami Anandavardhana. He is what we in this country call a "God-man". And in my opinion he is one of the most influential persons in our country. More than the prime minister. More than many big corporates. Why do I say that? You name the business tycoon and there's a good chance I can show you a photo with Ananda. As for the PM, in the real sense Ananda has been his closest adviser ever since the PM was six years old. Now, apart from having amassed a huge personal fortune—despite preaching the virtues of poverty—this Anandavardhana has also written whole books on the merits of child marriage and the greatness of the caste system. Isn't it amazing that he isn't more talked about? Do you remember, back when Barrack Obama was campaigning in the primaries, what a big furore erupted over Obama's relationship with his old pastor, Jeremiah Wright, because of the things that Wright had said about American arrogance and racism? All very true things, by the way. But the point is, it was understood that Obama had to account to the public for what his guru had said. Here in India, we are so enamoured of authority figures all around that we would have said, "Oh we mustn't inquire, it's his private life!" But it's not his private life. It's the ideology he is steeped in. It's the root of all the evil.'

'But forget Ananda,' said Mihir, snapping the laptop shut. He began to move back and forth on the wooden floor, with his head bent towards his chest and his chin bobbing there as he spoke.

'He is just one of hundreds. That's the irony. No country in the world is as dominated by God-men, and nowhere are they as little scrutinized. There was the biggest of them all, Sai Baba. All the allegations of fraud and sexual abuse couldn't stop the guy from getting a State funeral with every politician in attendance. There are people like Chandraswami, who had Narasimha Rao in his pocket... Baba Ramdev, who wasn't even behind the scenes, he was openly political. The list goes on. There was that so-called seer Shobhan Sarkar, who had a dream—except not like Martin Luther! I mean, we have to be the only country in the world whose Archaeological Survey spent taxpayers' money digging for gold because a sadhu said he had a dream! You're all smiling, it's so ridiculous, but it happened! Then there's all the countless babas and fakirs who prey on ordinary people. The "hugging Amma" from Kerala—you know that one? There's Meher Baba's cult in Aurangabad, Nirmal Baba, the train babas—I call them train babas—you've seen the ads they stick on the locals? This list is endless.'

'Gandhi himself...,' Karim Azad paused languorously to exhale his cigarette smoke. I felt a little thrill at hearing in person that cadence and baritone. 'Gandhi himself was part of this...phenomenon, if one can call it that. In the matter of rationalism, among many others, it was certainly Ambedkar who set the superior example.'

'Oh Gandhi was an incredibly smart politician,' said Mihir. 'Like all saints he was a better politician. He knew very well that this mindset is all over the country. We are born and bred to mysticism.'

'It's been good for our tourism,' said Nalini.

'That's about the only good it has been,' Mihir scowled. 'And that's bad for the rest of the world. *Khair*, the Western world sends a few of its deluded here. But we have a *billion* deluded on our hands. Okay now, somebody might say, what's the problem, it's been like this forever. To which I say, yes and we've been in the dumps forever too. I certainly don't believe in any Golden Age theories of Vedic times or what not.'

Karim Azad had begun to nod continuously.

'That's why,' Mihir had stopped pacing, and was now standing quite still, stroking his chin unselfconsciously, 'I never say this is our worst moment in history, as far as irrationalism and stupidity are concerned. Obviously in the past we've had religions sanctioned by rulers, enforced by the sword. But I do say it's a deadly dangerous moment today, and something similar is happening today, just in a less overt way. There's a cocktail of superstition and money and power out there—a violent cocktail. Look at the recent past. That Swami Aseemanand was convicted in the Samjhauta Express bombing. Even worse, he was later acquitted! Right here in Mumbai, poor Sanal Edamaruku—the famous rationalist—he had a case filed against him by a church for debunking some silly miracle. He was forced to go into hiding in Finland. In Pune, the activist Narendra Dabholkar was murdered in cold blood. Then our new government was formed. Meanwhile, there's the Hindutva trolls on Twitter, getting more and more fanatical. Look, we all know what's been happening. But what are we doing about it?'

He looked at us all with great anxiety. For some reason, even though everything he had said was perfectly serious, his expression made me smile. Then I heard a little sound by my side. Sasha was leaning forward from the *takhat* where we sat, breathing strangely hard. I think he had started to speak, but his speech had halted.

'It was awful about Dabholkar,' said Nalini, contemplatively, 'I knew him a little. Ahishor won't remember but he met you as a child too, Ahi. But you know, it's interesting what you're saying. One of the things I've always wondered about is, how does one distinguish between superstitions and religions? Because we often complain about God-men, but they don't exist in isolation, do they? Even Dabholkar's movement was only against superstitions; he always said he kept God and belief out of it, in public anyway that was what he said. But, I wonder, on what basis can one do that?'

'On no basis whatsoever,' declaimed Karim Azad, coughing gracefully. 'Religion is simply superstition on cocaine. Whether I believe that a black cat crossing my path is responsible for my catching a fever or that an invisible being in the sky is responsible, in both cases I am equally irrational.'

Suddenly, I found myself speaking.

'It takes a lot to make that argument though,' I said, feeling a hot flush spreading over my cheeks. 'In this country, it takes a lot of courage.'

The great man smiled. I spoke on rapidly. 'Actually, scientists have done studies on the capacities—on the capacities that human beings have for delusions, for deluding themselves. So belief in God can be explained as a kind of motivational tactic that we use, to make our lives easier by imagining it has this larger meaning and purpose.'

'Dawkins has written about it,' Nalini nodded.

Karim took another thoughtful drag.

'But does it make our life easier? I don't see how. It seems to bring on a whole bunch of extraneous concerns. With or without God, the sunset is as beautiful, women are as beautiful, murder is as ugly, life is as melancholy. And whisky tastes just as good. But with God, I can't enjoy it the same way. The fellow cramps my style.'

I am not sure but I fancy I heard Sasha clicking his tongue and even speaking.

'The whole point—'

'On the other hand,' Karim went on, 'how many wars, how much violence, how much ugliness is perpetrated in the name of God? It is false! It is false to say that the idea of God gives life meaning. Rather, it avoids the necessity to look for meaning, to find one's own true meaning. It gives an easy escape route to the weak and those lacking in confidence and it gives cunning people a means to dominate them. If I am intelligent and you are a fool [he was looking at me as he spoke, but I didn't mind, I understood the role-playing], then all I have to say is "God has commanded it", and I—not God—I become your master. Brilliant!'

'Still,' said Nalini, 'life is full of mysteries.'

She was pouting thoughtfully, looking at Karim. I was suddenly extraordinarily envious of her whole being, the company she kept, the world she inhabited, the conversations they had.

'Of course it is,' said Karim. 'And science has unravelled a good many of them. What it hasn't, it might tomorrow. And if it doesn't, well, we must admit our ignorance. But the moment I bring in this God fellow, I get an excuse to stop looking for answers and at the same time to stop feeling ignorant. God is a kind of...fake alchemical process by which ignorance is simply converted into certainty.'

'But one can't disprove God either.'

'Of course one can't, but the onus is on the believer! For that matter I cannot disprove that there are invisible spiders flying about this room as we speak!'

'That's true,' I laughed.

He reached out a casual hand, and it met Nalini's hand, that was already dangling in the space between their chairs.

Their fingers coiled and intertwined.

Mihir, who had been standing and listening all this while, sat down with a loud sigh, as though he had just put down a heavy load. His eyebrows were knotted; he was still full of purpose. Then suddenly, he glanced up.

'Were you saying something?' he said. 'Sorry, I forgot your name.'

'Sasha,' said my companion. We all looked at him. He half-rose from his chair to put his glass on the table (he had hardly touched his drink). In the same motion he began to speak.

'I did want to say—that this whole discussion about God—I think the whole discussion is misconceived. Pardon my saying so. But it's a mistake to ask for proofs of the existence of God. Anything that can be proved becomes trite in the same instant. Do you see? And conversely, nothing that is sublime can be simply proved. What proof is there for love?'

A slow smile spread across Karim Azad's face, in which there showed both tremendous interest and boredom.

'If she leaves you in misery with no answers, leaves you to commit suicide, destroys you slowly by herself, or hires somebody else to destroy you quickly, I assure you she doesn't love you... *Mujhe yaad aata hai*, H.G. Wells *ka ek lafz* (A verse by H.G. Wells comes to mind)...in a letter to his wife. He wrote, "My dear Rebecca, I cannot bank on religion. God has no thighs and no life. When one calls to him in the middle of the night he doesn't turn over and say, 'What is the trouble, dear?'"'

We all grinned or laughed wisely. Karim continued: 'Arre bhai, *jab hum Manmohan Singh ko itna koste hain, ki bhai tune desh ko theek nahi chalaya...toh iss paramatma ka kya kahna, jo ki* omnipotent *hai, sarv-shaktishaali hai! Aur uss omnipotent bhagvaan ne duniya ko iss haalaat main rakha hai?* Either God is not God, but the Devil, or there is no God. No third option is reasonably possible. Mind you, I say "reasonably".' (When we curse Manmohan Singh so much, that you didn't run the country well…then what can we say about this God of ours, who is omnipotent, is all-powerful. And *that* omnipotent God has left the world in *this* state?)

But Sasha's eyes were flashing.

'Don't you see,' he cried, 'your own comparison proves your error! How could the works of God possibly be understood in the same way as a prime minister's? And all that you said about being in misery and dying—it is all compatible with being loved, all of it. Can't the miserable and dead be loved? Yet one may not realize one is loved! Because love is not a trite thing that assures us warmth and shelter and…[he suddenly broke off]. It is a matter of the heart and it cannot be understood reasonably; it must be grasped, passionately!'

He was sitting on the very edge of his chair now. Karim was regarding him with raised eyebrows, and I saw many questioning glances going Ahishor's way too.

Ahishor threw his head back and laughed. 'Sasha, my good man! And here I thought you were as shy as a mouse.'

'I hope you don't mind,' said Sasha at once, 'I'm surprised myself. Something strange has happened tonight, I don't know why I'm so excitable. I never expected to speak like this—and I'm seeing you all for the first time! And you know, I've never even had any answer to your reasoning, Sir, to that kind of reasoning against God. But at the same time I've never been convinced by it either. It's not because of any counterarguments in my head. Only there is something I experienced, when I was much younger. I could tell you. Would you like to hear the story? But what's wrong with me, I'm going on about myself and making a fool of myself! Ahishor, do forgive me...'

'On the contrary,' said Ahishor, 'I love it when people come out of their shells.'

'Do tell us the story,' added Nalini warmly, 'I'm sure we would all like to hear it.'

'You are all very kind,' said Sasha, with a sudden break in his voice. I was watching him in amazement. 'I am afraid I will be digressing from what you were telling us.'

Mihir, who had been addressed, took a moment to speak. Then he smiled.

'But you don't know what I was telling you. Don't worry on my account.'

'Then I will tell the story.'

'Freely, speak freely. Speak like—what was her name? Scheherazade.'

Sasha gave his story no title that night, but I have remembered it ever since under a name of my own making.

VI

The Knight and the Hunchback

When I was nine years old, [so began Sasha's story] my father left the United Nations, for a job training young judges at an institute in Dehradun. My mother and I followed him there. It was the first stint in India for both of us, after five years in Indonesia and four in Norway, which is where I was born. People can't usually make out by looking at me, but I am half-Afghan by blood. My mother was an Afghan woman, an immigrant in Oslo.

She met my father there one winter evening, when he was out shopping in a mall. He was a policy adviser to Norway's Ministry of Justice at the time and she was a saleswoman at a department store. Why and how he wooed her is a story I would rather not tell. Of course I only know it in bits and pieces myself. In brief, he overwhelmed her with adulation, gifts, an intimidating knowledge of her own country, Afghanistan, and bundles of money. I suppose she had never encountered such persistence, at least never from a man so much richer, so much better placed and more experienced in the world. She was only nineteen. In any case, he had his way with her in the end. He then promised to marry her, but my father did not marry my mother. Then, by the time I was born, she had nowhere else to go. Her ties with her own family had snapped unequivocally; shamed and cast out, she entered his household.

Wherever my father was posted, as far as I can remember, he found himself a bungalow to live in. He always managed to have servants, even in Oslo, though it was in Jakarta that he lived on the grandest scale. There was a tall white house there, with servants' quarters and a big garden, where we children ran races and climbed trees and played with my father's Alsatian dog and the two stray cats who had made it their home too; I remember them well. My playmates were the children of the cook, the driver, the maid and the odd-job man. It was with them that my mother lived, in the part of the establishment that is called 'below stairs', while in the main mansion my father entertained his friends, both male and female, from all over the world.

I wonder at the fact now, and it is likely that apart from being carefully sheltered, I was also a selfish child, but my own memories of this time are uniformly happy. I seemed to have no inkling of the daily hurt my mother must have suffered. In my own world, I felt nothing amiss. I did not know how other parents normally lived or behaved with their children. I realized that as compared with the cook and the driver, my own father was exalted and aloof, but this I simply accepted as the way things were. As for the household staff, they were so fond of my mother, they made sure I never sensed her indignity, and in consequence my own.

Everything changed in India. I had cried copious tears when I was parted from my friends in Indonesia, and there must have been some premonition in my self-pity. I may express it by saying that there seemed no place for us to hide here, no nest or hole or burrow to be alone in. It was not in the foreign lands of Norway and Indonesia, but in India, my father's home, that for the first time I felt an outsider.

My mother and I came under scrutiny from every passing eye. I was examined because I did not speak Hindi or Pahadi, because of my unusual name, and because I was her son. But it was far worse for her. I think, at first, she tried to conceal her relationship with my father, to pass off simply as a maid. But his own behaviour made that impossible. He was brash and jovial when my mother strained for delicacy, and withering when she attempted terms of equality. He was drinking more than ever. (I think his new assignment was overwhelming him, it was no sinecure.) I remember him as laughing a great deal in those days, walking through the house with a glass in his hand, shaking with laughter, dropping off stray lines that brought angry tears to my mother's eyes, and rapt interest and gathering judgement from the rest of the staff.

In such an atmosphere, it was not surprising that she soon fell ill. By our second month in Dehradun, she had grown too weak to walk up and down the stairs from our house to the street. Soon she could do no chores even around the home, and a continual fever forced her to bed rest. Then at the start of the third month—it was the beginning of June—my mother passed away, in her sleep. The doctors were astonished; they had throughout predicted her imminent recovery. But in retrospect, I am not surprised. So long as she was working in the household, I think she felt her dignity was shielded, but when she could no longer work, she would not abide being simply kept by my father. My mother was an intensely proud woman.

During the last fortnight of her life, when she was consigned to bed, my father's behaviour towards her had suddenly changed.

He ordered the staff to keep a constant watch on her, and spoke for long hours to the visiting doctors. He had her shifted to one of the guest bedrooms, and every morning and evening, he would himself tend to her. Often, I watched from the doorway while he stooped by her side, whispering soft and urgent endearments. As far as I remember, my mother was always silent. One evening in particular, I recall him pressing her arm tenderly, waiting for a reply to something he had said. He was growing insistent, the question was clamouring in the air, and then she lifted her arm wordlessly and turned over on her side. I am sure she never returned his blandishments.

After she died, my father locked himself in his room for two days, stopped eating, and refused to answer any calls. Then, on the evening of the second day, wan and bloodshot, he emerged suddenly onto the porch of the house and began to holler my name. I was nowhere to be found. Within minutes the servants were galvanized and a search party dispatched in every direction.

I had gotten deliberately lost. It had become a habit with me. I would step off the gravel paths and run into the mountainside, to be by myself in the stillness and the shrubbery. At other times I would climb up to the main street and hurry along it till I found a certain secluded turn in the road, out of sight of the town's buildings. There was a bench at that turn, overlooking a beautiful drop full of pine and deodar trees. There I would sit, crying softly to myself, letting my tears flow freely. Only the occasional car or truck roared by and when they were gone I felt only closer to the panorama that had stayed with me. In my time of sorrow, the changelessness of the hills seemed to me, not proof of indifference, but of a profound wisdom. I felt the mountains were always watching over me, straining to soothe me with their patience and their mysterious calm.

That night I was discovered by the gardener, an old man whom I disliked because his clothes were always smelly and I had never seen him smile even once. In language unintelligible to me, I was upbraided gruffly all the way back to the house.

It was the twilight hour when we entered the gates. My father was gently pacing the grounds. The sky was darkening behind him and the trees turning to silhouettes. When he saw me, he stopped, threw out his arms, and called my name once, plaintively. I approached rapidly without hesitation. He clasped me tightly to his chest. I buried my nose in his sweater and felt the homely woollen fragrance enveloping me. I was starting to cry again. Then he drew me back, and I saw that there were tears standing in his own eyes. My mouth twisted uncontrollably. I burst into sobs.

'She has left us,' said my father heavily. 'Now who will look after us?'

He was holding my arms by my side, the better to look at me. As I cried and cried, his hold seemed to tighten, and though I strained forward to embrace him once again, I found that I could only twist and turn. I grew confused. My tears faltered. He was looking at me very steadily. I felt suddenly that I was required to answer. Slowly, I whispered that I didn't know, and in the same instant I saw my father's eyes widening, his brow growing smooth, and the corners of his mouth twitching upwards. Then, with a long sigh, he let go of me. Shaking his head strangely, he strode back into the house.

The next day, he left for Delhi, not saying when he would return, with no instructions whatsoever as to what was to be done with me. So began one of the most significant periods of my childhood, if the clarity with which I remember it is any indication.

I had been enrolled in a local school that year. It was a small, painted building with flowerpots in the corridors, and a great valley unfurling by its entrance. There was a smell of varnish in the stairwell that made my heart sink every morning. Even now, I can remember vividly how it filled me with anxieties! As I said, I could only speak English, and the constant curiosity about my antecedents from teachers and classmates alike was alienating. But now it took a nastier avatar. As far as I remember, there was no warning. The bullying began all of a sudden, one day during recess, while I was walking down the corridor from the bathroom to the classroom. I heard a shouted word: 'Kubda!'

A group of children was laughing at me. The label caught on. Kubda! I did not understand what it meant until one of the boys performed a helpful mimicry of how I walked, with my back hunched over. You can see my hunchback even now, but it was worse when I was young. I believe it is the kind of condition that can exacerbate under stress.

After that day, the jeering became continual. Every morning, as I walked up to the school courtyard, I would hear the name shouted in the distance. Kubda! It was whispered all around me during class. During recess, unleashing their energies, the children would put on exaggerated renditions of my defect. Soon it was not just my own classmates but children much younger than me too, little toddlers who could hardly speak, who would stare openly and grin. The teachers too grew aware of what was happening. I remember some of my classmates being scolded for passing on chits of paper with caricatures of my hunchback. But the teasing persisted unchecked. Instead, it was I who was exhorted to stand upright, to petition my parents for medical help, and I who felt ashamed that I had neither the ability nor the recourse to 'correct' myself.

One afternoon, after school, I was making my way up one of the narrow paths in the hillside, with my satchel on my shoulders. It was a lovely day, cool and clear, with all the trees waving in a little wind. I was walking slowly, stretching out my moments of solitude, for at home there waited only the resentful looks and grumbling of the staff. I had grown to love my own company, and the mountains'. I looked at all the doors of the houses that I passed, peeped around pillars and over the parapets of terraces. I watched the flight of birds and dreamed of running along with them, over and above the undulating terrain, to the horizon where the hills were blue.

At a certain point in the route, on the far side of a low gorge, I came across a group of my classmates, who began at once to chant my tormenting nickname. As I passed by, trying to ignore them, I felt something strike my bag. One of the boys had lobbed a stone at me. As I swivelled, the next, thrown harder, grazed my cheek.

A frenzy overtook me. I flung my bag to the ground and scrabbled in the gravel. Filling my fists with stones big and small, I hurled all I could at them, one after the other, shrieking insults, one after the other, while hot tears started in my eyes. They were astonished at first, but soon they began to hit back, and they were six against one.

I was lucky not to be more badly hurt. I am sure I would have been, had a figure not run up suddenly and wordlessly, as though from nowhere, to stand in front of me, with her arms stretched wide and her jet black hair flowing down her shoulders. That is how I will always remember her.

She was twelve years old, in the seventh grade at our school. I learned this later, for none of us knew her, on either side of the gorge.

'Put the stones down!' she cried.

'Tell him too,' returned my assailants, though I noticed them obeying. 'He threw them more than we did.'

'He is alone,' she said, 'you are so many. Aren't you ashamed?'

She swivelled suddenly and stared hard at me.

'Why are they hitting you?'

I shrugged; my mouth twisted desperately in feigned indifference.

'Tell me why,' she asked softly.

Suddenly the enormity of my torment, the sheer injustice of it, was unbearable. I walked away rapidly. My eyes were smarting and if I had spoken one word I would have burst into tears.

She did not try to stop me. Instead, when I glanced back, I saw her standing amongst my attackers, while they gesticulated furiously and seemed to plead with her. With a strange anxiety building in the pit of my stomach, I hurried home.

In those days, the caretaker and the maid were looking after me. I remember them only as sullen and silent figures, who performed certain necessary chores, fed me and woke me, and lit the mosquito coil in my bedroom every night. I am sure they were good people who would have shown me real affection, had my father only directed them. Instead they had found themselves burdened with me. Once the caretaker gave me a slap when I came home well after dark, having lost myself walking in the hills. But mostly, I was left to my own devices. Oddly, I was not really unhappy. As I said, I had begun to enjoy my solitude and my unusual independence. I had started to read a great deal too. The vast collection of books that my father had in the house occupied me even when I could understand them very little. But there were times (like the night I was slapped), when my brave facade would crack. I would miss my mother terribly then, and staring at the walls and the high ceiling, cry myself to sleep.

On the evening of the day of my encounter at the gorge, I was holed up as usual in my room. I had with me a copy of *The Lord of the Rings*, which had been rather overwhelming me. But the book was illustrated, and there was one illustration in particular I was poring over that evening. It was of Eowyn, a princess who in the garb of a knight, goes into war. The drawing captured the very moment when, removing her helmet before her enemy, Eowyn reveals that she is a woman. I don't remember what I was thinking, or if I was thinking anything at all, but I recall my heart beating hard as I beheld the proud figure, sword in hand, with her streaming hair.

The next day was a Sunday. In the morning I was climbing the guava tree in our garden, when I spotted the girl from the day before, walking steadily up to our gate. Suddenly, fearful that someone in the house would be rude to her, I scrambled down to meet her.

I saw her clearly for the first time that morning. She was a good head taller than me, and thin and lithe. She was dressed in a faded salwar kameez with a flower pattern. Her hair was tied in a ponytail, and her face was full of concentration. But she smiled the moment she saw me.

'Hello Sasha,' she said, 'my name is Natasha, which is quite similar, isn't it? How are you? I wanted to talk to you about the boys who were fighting with you yesterday after school.'

'They started it,' I said suddenly. 'I only got angry with them because they bully me all the time. They threw stones and they hit my bag and my face—right here!'

'I know,' she nodded. 'They told me they tease you for your hunchback. But I discovered that wasn't the real reason.

Do you want to know what it is?'

She touched my shoulder lightly. We sat down in the shade of the tree.

'The real reason is because they love you and it makes them afraid. Yes, yes, they love you. They want to know you better. I know it seems surprising, but listen to me. When I asked them yesterday what they knew about you, apart from your hunchback, they said your father has left you all alone here and that he never married your mother. Don't be upset, it's okay, listen to me. I asked them what fault of yours that is. They didn't have any answer. They only repeated that your father has left you—and your back is not straight.'

I will always remember that speech, in the cool shade of the garden, so unexpected and arresting that I hardly dared to stop listening for fear she would vanish like a phantasm. It is strange to think that she must have spoken in halting English, for I remember it as simple and flowing.

'I know what you've been thinking. You're thinking, I have suffered and now on top of that they are bullying me, like monsters. That is the frailty in people, Sasha. They are not monsters. It is not really meanness, it is only that they are not brave enough. Because you have suffered they want to care for you—and that is because they love you. But it takes courage to show sympathy. They are afraid for themselves, because if it could happen to you, it could happen to them too. So they try to believe that you are to blame for your mother and father, that you must be different, and somehow at fault.'

'They have bullied me from the start,' I protested, 'ever since I joined, even when my father was here. Just because I'm from outside! They are mean and stupid!'

'Look,' she raised her head suddenly, 'here they are. Neither late nor early, just as I requested.'

Indeed, a row of solemn faces were bobbing their way up the path to the house. At the front of the queue was a boy with curly hair and long eyelashes, whom I considered a particularly dangerous foe. In the playground at school, when I was trying to slip by unnoticed, he was always the first to spot me, and though he was often silent himself, he had a terribly effective way of rousing the other's jeers. It was his thrown stone that had struck my cheek. But now his usually lazy and superior gaze was full of a strange brooding.

'Children are not cruel,' Natasha said quietly. 'Children are only inexperienced in love. When they try to love the person they see, as everybody should, the inexperience shows. But it only shows because they really try, like everybody should.'

It bears repeating, she was only twelve years old, only a child like the rest of us. But that morning she was the leader of us all, with an authority more remarkable than any adult we had known.

The boys trooped up to where I stood, and started to mumble greetings, taking my name. 'Hello Sasha', 'Sasha, how are you?'; I had never liked my name so much.

We stood in a circle under the tree. Natasha was amongst us, speaking gravely but forcefully.

'If Sasha's parents are not with him, you must look after him all the more. He is all alone. It is your choice whether to blame him or to love him. But God says to love him. And I want to tell you something. Even if Sasha had driven his own parents away—even if it was his fault that they did not marry each other—God still says to love him. And he still says to Sasha to love you, even though you have bullied him. God, who has made us all, some tall, some short, some thin, some fat, some with straight backs like tree trunks and some with hunchbacks like mountains. Oh! Do you think God loves the trees more than the mountains? He loves us all each as He made us—always!'

VII

At Ahishor's (Contd.)

Sasha paused suddenly. It took us a moment to realize he had finished speaking. The room was very cool and quiet, and the atmosphere quite altered in a way I couldn't pinpoint. Then Nalini sighed and said something inaudible. Breaking into a smile, she beamed at Sasha.

'It is a lovely story. As you were speaking, I was quite enchanted. I have my own memories of Dehra... The pines, the cold, fragrant air, the warm cooking smells... Ah! So did you make some friends then, after that day?'

'I was taken to Delhi not long after,' said Sasha. 'In the meantime...yes, but it was like a miracle. Those boys did become my friends. It amazes me even now, I tremble even now to think of that morning under the guava tree. She was just a child, like the rest of us.'

'Did you keep in touch with her?'

Sasha shook his head. 'I hardly saw her after that day. But I remember her every time I hear words spoken against God.'

Karim Azad was smoking rapidly. He was growing irritable; I knew the look well from all his interviews. 'While that is understandable,' he said, 'while that is understandable, it is also very personal to you. *Pahli baat*, you must realize your friend was just a child, as you say yourself, she did not even know what she meant when she talked about God. What? You say she did know? You're sure? Haha! Well, very well, even if she was old enough to know...though I doubt it... The point is, one need not invoke God to oppose bullying, I'm sure you can see that. For her it might have been so, but in general, morality need not and does not depend on God at all.'

'It does, it does,' breathed Sasha softly, but so softly that perhaps nobody but I heard him.

'The same applies,' Karim continued, looking at all of us in turn, 'to all the attractive things about religion. And there are attractive things, I don't deny it. A lot of great art, great architecture, songs, dances, festivals. The things *you* like so much,' he turned suddenly to Nalini. 'But those are all separable from the beliefs of religion, which I am afraid are completely irrational, as we were discussing before.'

'If it were not so,' he went on; he was regaining his humour as he spoke, 'if it were not true that achievements in art or science have nothing whatsoever to do with religious belief, then there would not be so many examples of great artists and great scientists who are total atheists. I need not list them, I'm sure.'

'Why should you?' said Ahishor, with a playful smile. 'You're one yourself!'

Karim laughed, which I thought was wonderful to see.

'I am thinking of Niels Bohr, Stephen Hawking, Chekhov, Truffaut,' he said, '*Khair, aapke moonh main ghee shakkar!*' (Anyway, bless you for saying such sweet things!) And we were all smiling with good humour and grace, when Sasha suddenly began to speak very thoughtfully.

'But perhaps all such art is limited,' he was saying. 'Perhaps everything that doesn't have its roots in a true belief, is in some sense frivolous...unreal...a distraction... I don't know... I certainly don't understand yet... But maybe we shouldn't even try to understand! Maybe to try to understand is also a distraction. When I think back to Natasha, she was not artistic or special in any way. She was not clever or beautiful. She had only the force of obedience—that's what she urged upon us all—to obey God and be good; that's what saved me!'

He had gotten strangely excited. His cheeks were reddening and he looked even more baby-faced than usual.

'This conversation has helped me learn!' said Sasha, 'I am grateful!'

Thus exclaiming, he collapsed back into his seat, blushing all over. I stared at him with disapproval—it had welled up in me naturally, the moment he had started this latest speech—but then I saw that Ahishor's eyes were twinkling with fascination. He nodded now towards Mihir, who was sitting quietly; watchful.

'What do you say then? Didn't I tell you Versova discussions beat Defence Colony discussions any day?'

'I am but a humble journalist,' said Mihir, 'I only understand the things I see happening around me. Such rarefied conversation is difficult for me to follow. No, no, seriously, I'm not kidding... But that's exactly why I'm here. Just like our friend, I am here to learn. What I do see proved, right before me, is that our God-men have defenders even among the educated.'

He looked closely at Sasha, who began to shake his head, but then stopped abruptly.

'That itself is very interesting to me,' Mihir continued. 'Astonishing and interesting. But I don't know how to talk about it. You, on the other hand, Ahishor, you do know. You have the ability to analyse mindsets, ways of thinking, at a deep level, a philosophical level.'

He turned as he spoke, not to Ahishor, but Nalini, who smiled and nodded firmly.

'I simply feel,' said Mihir, 'that in the present day, with India going in the direction it is, somebody needs to open up a public dialogue on these issues. Somebody with not just more reach than us print journalists, but also more depth. Though it hurts my professional pride to say it.'

'Mihir wants me to make a documentary,' said Ahishor, 'as my next project.'

'I know *Schrödinger's Cat* was amazing,' said Mihir. 'For a first film especially, I think it was unlike anything anyone has ever made in this industry. I hate that term by the way, "industry", it sounds so overblown—for Bollywood. Forgive me, I'm speaking as someone who absolutely detests Bollywood. But where was I? Yes *Schrödinger's*, it was lovely, at the same time, it was a little abstract... I would like to see Ahishor make a different movie now. Something which marries his theoretical ability with the practical realities of our time. If I'm expressing myself correctly.'

'I liked that it was abstract,' said Nalini doubtfully. 'I thought he could make another fiction film. Perfect that style before trying anything...'

But Karim was nodding animatedly as he leaned forward to stub out his cigarette.

'No, he's right,' he said, '*Schrödinger's* was a nice, clever film but it wasn't terribly socially relevant, as they say. That's not a bad thing of course. But it's not a bad thing to be socially relevant either.'

'A film about religion—and things like that—would be very controversial.' Nalini shot a worried look at her son. 'Even that

Khan movie got into such trouble.' [This was a recent comedy flick, which had lampooned a God-man, against which certain Hindu extremist groups had promptly launched protests.]

'Of course,' said Mihir, 'that's part of why this issue matters, isn't it? Anyway, that movie was fiction, so they complained about depictions and so on. In a documentary, we depict nothing, everything speaks for itself.'

'But in a documentary you're being direct. You can't even say, this is comedy, this is entertainment. It can be far more dangerous.'

'It all depends on how it's told. If it is told in a scientific way, as an examination into mindsets and the reasons behind those mindsets, I think it will be so fascinating there won't be space for controversy. It will actually initiate a dialogue, you see... Questions like—what prompts the success of our God-men? What prompts fanaticism, or blind faith? Is there something unique about the Indian condition that leads to it? I mean, I do share your concern. I just think Ahishor is the only person who could take a subject like this, in a social milieu like ours, and still pull it off because of the way he communicates... If I understand him properly.'

'I like it,' said Karim. 'The subject is terribly important. If he can make it, it might be the most important Indian film ever made. And that's no exaggeration.'

'It's not saying much either,' Nalini uttered a distressed laugh. 'Well... I don't know. There's absolutely no money in documentaries either. You'll never get it released.'

'Things are changing,' said Ahishor simply.

There was a tingling sensation running through my whole body. As I sat there, I thought to myself—these are the beginnings of what will perhaps one day be Ahishor Frances's next big movie, talked about everywhere, screening (like his first) at Cannes. I felt I was present at a birthing, and simultaneously, I felt again undeserving of that privilege. I was suddenly afraid of making the slightest intervention. I closed my mouth tight, and listened with great attention.

Ahishor had stood up and moved aside; he came back now with a glass of plain water, which he soon placed on the mantelpiece. He was fidgety, as he always was when his mind was working hard. His shirt hung loose over his baggy jeans; he ran a hand roughly through his tousled hair. Then he paced up and down, and talked without fuss, just as though he was thinking aloud.

'There was a Dutch biologist,' said Ahishor, 'a man called Niko Tinbergen. He studied the behaviour of herring gull chicks. Tinbergen observed that when these chicks are born they go straight up to their mother's beak, and start to peck on it for food. But then he discovered that it wasn't even the mother that attracted them, it was just the beak, and it wasn't even the beak, because even a stick with a red dot on it—the beaks had red dots—even just that stick made the newborn chicks wild... I always think of this, when I think about human beings and God... What I mean is, I agree with you Karim, rationally you can't make a case for God. But what if God is an irrational instinct implanted in us by evolution, just as irrational as a chick pecking on a stick and hoping to get food? But the instinct is there for a reason, isn't it? That's where I part ways with you a little. In my opinion, a belief in God is not necessarily harmful. It all depends. Even a delusion can serve a purpose. Think of early man, practically every human society in its early stages. There you have low levels of scientific understanding, but high levels of belief, which help people get through their lives on a day-to-day basis, in what would otherwise be an incredibly frightening and dangerous environment. Of course, once societies advance in understanding, once they learn not to be afraid, then they can stand on their own feet, so to speak. The need for God disappears.'

He took a sip of water. All our gazes stayed on him, with varied pride, pleasure and admiration. Only Sasha's expression stuck out. He was staring with a kind of impatience. It irritated me.

'Coming to India,' Ahishor continued, 'I think it's really fascinating. Here you have a society which is changing so fast, getting richer and richer, globalized, modernized—but the God delusion isn't going anywhere. Yet if you think about it, why would it? Just by becoming better consumers we don't become better thinkers. Money on its own can never topple God. Only enlightenment can. It's interesting though, because in this matrix, there is a conflict lying in wait. It all boils down to choice. People have started to appreciate choice. In terms of their material life, what goods to buy, everyone demands choice. Now, the moment people extend this love of choice to their emotional or intellectual or spiritual lives, God's in trouble. For example, take the young man out there, who today wants a choice between every kind of motorcycle that exists, before he makes a purchase... At some point, he will ask: shouldn't I also have a choice between every kind of person, before I get married? Why not a Muslim girl? Why not a tribal girl? Why should those choices be taken away from me?... See, I believe morality, true and false, right and wrong, these are only initial categories. The final distinctions are between choice-expanding and choice-limiting propositions. God—by which I include God-men, fakirs, Babas, the whole shebang—beyond a point, a point which we've long passed, is a choice-limiting proposition. It just needs a certain intellectual push to make people realize that. But that's not happened in India. I suppose that's the burden of our antiquity. The five thousand years of ancient wisdom. Although it's being completely wrongly interpreted, in my opinion. Our true traditions are of debate and reason, not blind faith.'

'Whatever it is,' said Mihir, 'it's keeping us pecking at the beak.'

'Not even the beak. At the stick with the red dot on it.'

'If I understand what you're saying,' said Mihir, with sudden passion, 'it's now or never for India! With all the new forces at work in our society, either we harness them to topple the old superstitions or the old superstitions are going to co-opt them to become even more entrenched! In fact, that's what's been happening all this while. Even as the economy grows, the God-men have been getting richer and richer and more and more powerful.'

'It's something to think about,' Ahishor nodded. 'As you say... yes—it's definitely something to start a dialogue about. In a quite neutral way.'

He looked hard at his mother as he spoke. Suddenly, an almost shy smile stole across her face, and she nodded meekly.

'Neutral is good,' Karim nodded, his eyes narrowing meaningfully and his lip curling expressively (though it was something private and inaccessible that they expressed). 'It's always wisest to be neutral!'

The remainder of that night, I only hazily recall. We all had (at least) another drink and the conversation seemed to fall through completely, in the pleasantest possible way. At some point, Karim mentioned the name of Ritesh, his son from his first marriage, as the movie's potential producer. But in general, everyone was laughing and talking about nothing in particular. Mihir was dashing about the place again, taking an interest in everyone, dispensing a steady current of complimentary or jocular remarks. I remember he told me I looked just like a good Delhi boy, and Delhi boys were all the rage at the time in Bollywood, and therefore I had nothing to worry about—apart from the fact that I was from Delhi. I wanted to remind him that so was he, but I only smiled and took his ribbing. It occurred to me also to ask him how he came to be interested in cinema and Ahishor, and the particular subject of God-men in India, but it seemed somehow heavy-handed and out of key to ask him anything at all. He was extraordinarily disarming.

It was soon after I had gotten up to leave for the first time, and been told to sit down at once, that Ahishor came up to me, and manoeuvring me by the shoulder, drew me aside from the others. His eyes were shining and his mouth twitching with smiles.

'How was her acting?' he said.

It is odd, but I understood at once who he meant—and simultaneously, understood much more besides.

'Fine. It was fine. I didn't stay long though.'

'I'll make this movie with her. We'll make it together. She's going to love it. We were trying to make something before, you know.'

'Something about drugs, right?' I said.

'Drugs? No, not just drugs. It was about altered states of consciousness. So is this one, in a sense, if you think about it... Anyway, that didn't happen, because she's not focused, she's not focused like she needs to be. But we'll make this one...we'll make this one. Even dear Ritesh won't be able to mess it up, though I'm sure he'll try!... I might marry her too, by the way. Don't tell anyone.'

Before I could respond, he burst out laughing and pulled me back into the living room.

VIII

Confessions and Revelations

On an overcast day in the beginning of June, Sasha hurried out of Churchgate station and stepped hastily aside from the moving tides of people. He spent a few moments collecting himself and studying his watch. Then he threw a glance at the old colonial facade of the railway office that fronted the evening sky, and with a deliberate, even stride, moved to cross the road, to where a line of black and yellow taxis waited.

He was wearing a light green collared shirt, tucked into a pair of the slim trousers that he favoured, over which he wore a silver belt. The waves in his hair had been carefully arranged. By and by a perfect stillness had stolen over his features, and the instructions he now gave the taxi driver were spoken offhand. But his excitement showed in the unmeaning glance he continually darted at the sky, and in the beating of his heart. All that week, he had been in a state of torment, an unnatural and ecstatic state that he did not hesitate to recognize.

At twenty minutes to five—twenty minutes early—he stood opposite the Oberoi Hotel and scanned his surroundings with a strange foreboding. Marine Drive was overhung with dark clouds. The waves tossed stormily by the promenade, and the walkers and idlers, the couples on the benches, seemed somehow fatally self-absorbed. Along the streets and the crossings, traffic purred smoothly; various figures blended into one another. Looming above them, dignified and neglected, the old apartment buildings kept a silent watch on the jaunty confusion of the ever-growing city, far across the waters. It started to drizzle.

She was not there one moment, and then she was. Not from the streets or down the promenade, but as though come out of the sea itself, she walked up to him, in a loose white shirt and dark blue jeans, smiling with her sharp front teeth showing, and the salt spray about her hair. When they had greeted each other, they began to walk.

He was loath to say anything trite to her. Maithili spoke instead.

'Are you hungry?'

'No.'

'Are you sure? I've been eating all day, but if you are hungry, we can go somewhere.'

'It's nice to just walk,' said Sasha. 'I don't come here often enough. It's quite something, isn't it?... You don't think so?'

'If these buildings,' she waved a hand at the skyline on the horizon, 'do it for you...'

'You've seen grander vistas, I know.'

'It's not that. But if I was told I had to live in Bombay all my life, I would commit suicide.'

Sasha laughed, yet on her impassive face not a muscle had twitched. Nor had she spoken with bitterness, but only matter-of-fact.

'You are still lucky you live in this part of the city,' he said, and at once realized he was speaking nervously and without understanding what he said.

'Things are very judgemental here,' she said, 'and old and dead. I like the suburbs better. There's more energy.'

'I guess I know what you mean. I wish the energy was less chaotic though.'

She shrugged. 'At least it's closer to self-destruction.'

'Then you don't like it very much after all,' he smiled.

But her face was calm and inscrutable. Quickly, he continued, to find an elevated thing to say.

'Bombay to me—in general, whatever I've seen of it— I think of it as a war zone. It really is very much like a war zone!'

He expanded on the metaphor; anxious to give her his best thoughts. Meanwhile, Maithili was silent. Her eyes rested occasionally on one or the other person they passed, and then a hard glare or a little smile would suggest some secret verdict. Sasha fell quiet and they spent many moments walking in silence; then she nodded.

'Most people never really experience anything. They don't travel anywhere, except on silly holidays. They don't imagine anything. Their days are spent commuting from the home to the office, and back. And when they get back they switch on the TV and sit in front of it. I could never live like that. I need to be exploring what's out there.'

She inclined her head rather skyward than seaward.

'Acting,' said Sasha, 'takes you to new places a lot.'

'Yes. That's one reason I like it.'

'I think it's extremely courageous work! An actor is so vulnerable. Not just physically, but in the mind. When you are playing a character, it must be like letting your own real self be taken hold of and moulded and transformed—and just trusting that you'll come out fine on the other side. It's such a risk to run. It's almost a life and death risk!'

'You're very dramatic,' said Maithili. 'Anyway, what is life without risk?'

Suddenly, she looked up at him, giving him all her attention. A thrill ran through Sasha. It shocked and moved him in every particle. He had not imagined it would be so audacious, and he, so much its slave. She was smiling slightly; her gaze lingered on him.

'Do you like taking risks? What's the most daring thing you've ever done?

'The most daring?'

He laughed, then frowned and was quiet until he felt it a painful necessity to reply.

'I have been alone a lot. I mean to say...in making all my decisions.'

As he spoke, he saw her smile growing assured, with a mingling of triumph and pity that yet struck him as dazzling. For some moments he could barely look at her.

'I think you're someone,' she said, 'who tends to say "no" to new experiences.'

'In conventional terms, yes, perhaps I do.'

'You're being defensive!' She laughed with pleasure, and suddenly, he wasn't enjoying himself at all.

'It's true. I haven't done drugs, for example,' said Sasha. His voice was strained, as though weighed down by some unexpected disappointment. 'I know you are interested in that...that whole subject.'

'As a spiritual matter,' said Maithili. Her gaze had shifted away from him. 'The way we perceive the world is completely changeable. That realization is very profound. The first time I ever tried LSD, it was as though all my doubts and questions were suddenly answered. Everything suddenly made sense!

All the divisions collapsed; I saw how everything was just light... different forms of light. I understood how even with all the wars and the violence, the world is really one...perfect as it is.'

The drizzle had stopped, but the darkness was gathering prematurely. They walked as though in a hurry, occasionally parting ways to skirt around the trees standing in their decorative slabs.

'You skip,' said Maithili.

'What?'

'Every few steps, you do a little skip. Walk a little and let me see... Just walk... No, you're not doing it now.'

'I suppose I'm self-conscious now. But you walk very straight and even. And very fast!'

'It's the only exercise I get in Bombay. When I'm in Goa, I dance for six hours a day and that's my exercise. But here... But tell me if I'm rushing you. No? Are you sure? I actually used to slouch a lot myself. If you work on your core muscles,' she placed a hand on her stomach, 'it helps you stand straight. Another thing I learned doing theatre.'

'So you started doing theatre during college?'

'No, I quit college and then I joined a repertory, in America. It wasn't that I particularly wanted to do theatre. I just really wanted to get done with college. My parents weren't happy. But I was bored in the classes. Formal education is so lifeless. It destroys people's sense of wonder.'

'I agree,' said Sasha, 'it can do that. Although I think it does help develop a critical faculty. I think any formal education helps you discipline your mind, which helps you to know better what you like and what you don't like. Otherwise...it's dangerous to get carried away by things, just because they seem striking or wonderful. You have to know where you stand.'

'It's necessary to spread your wings,' said Maithili.

Lights were coming on in the gradual gloom. A billboard for a horror movie began to glow, revealing hideous monsters crouching behind a girl in a forest.

'What you said about all the violence,' said Sasha, 'and still the world being perfect... But we need to be able to feel that, outside of doing drugs. Just in ordinary daylight, with our five senses.'

'Oh yes,' she said lightly. 'And for that we need to evolve. Human consciousness needs to evolve until the meaninglessness of war and bigotry becomes clear to everyone as a matter of course. It's a long process. Although at an individual level it can be achieved in this lifetime.'

'You sound confident.' He spoke drily.

'It's just evolution,' she shrugged. 'The ones who evolve towards love and peace will survive, and the ones who don't will kill each other off.'

Saying so, she laughed gaily, and in spite of himself, Sasha found himself smiling too.

'I believe that you get what you give,' Maithili continued. 'If you give out good things, you get them back. The Universe is mathematical like that. I've witnessed this myself.'

'Oh yes. Yes, but it's not straightforward. I mean... if you come up against someone who is, let's say, steeped in evil, then no matter how good you are to them, you cannot make them return good back to you. You can't make them. Only they can choose the good themselves. But they can also choose the evil—forever, if they like.'

When she was quiet, he hurried on, suddenly desperate to stall her disagreement if it was coming.

'I saw the trailer of your film.'

She blushed.

'It's a bad trailer,' she said placidly. 'It's not supposed to be a thriller. But I haven't yet seen the movie myself.'

'Your role looked difficult.'

'Some things were difficult... I had a breakdown one day. We were shooting in a field in Haryana, there's a scene where I get gang-raped and then practically killed... No, it was fine, it was very properly done. Nobody touched me where I was not okay with. They were all gentlemen. But at one point I just wanted everybody to go drown. They had to stop shooting. I didn't let anybody near me for four hours.'

'It's good you did that,' said Sasha. 'It's good.'

'Everybody else had friends or family travelling with them. I was alone on the shoot. All my family was abroad anyway, except for my grandfather.'

She spoke contemplatively, without regret or rancour.

'I'm sure your grandfather worries about you.'

'All the time!' she winced. 'He worries all the time.'

'You should try to make it better for him,' Sasha said gently.

'My granddad and I have a great relationship. I've seen my friends, they're so formal with their grandparents, but I high-five him! He's my favourite person in the whole family actually. I couldn't be living with my mother or father, that's for sure. But he worries too much.'

Her step quickened further. The wind was blustering about them. People laughed and preened in the weather; voices lifted in bravado; yet if the threatened downpour materialized they would be scurrying for cover in no time. But perhaps it would not rain after all. The clouds were breaking and parting. The sky had turned a deep shade of ochre.

'Let's sit,' said Maithili suddenly. 'These shoes hurt my feet.'

They went to the parapet, above the famous tetrapod rocks that disarmed the Arabian Sea, though today the waves climbed dangerously and frolicked. She slipped off one shoe and studied her pale, slender foot with absorption. Then she put it back on and glanced up at him.

'Sorry, you were saying something?'

'I was just saying, it's a dangerous thing about movies. I mean, how mechanical they are in their demands. The way that they convert people into props. It's something I thought about even when I came for the short film that day. In movies the demand of the "shot" becomes all-important. You may need just an arm or a leg in the background of a picture—so then for the sake of their arm or leg a human being is made to hold still for hours on end! That's just an example of course. The whole medium is prone to incredible objectification. It's something to guard against I think.'

'It's full-on,' Maithili nodded. 'When you're shooting, there's a collective madness on set. That's the way it is.'

She seemed more satisfied than otherwise. Suddenly, a little smile twisted her lip and a flash of bitterness moved over her eyes, that seemed nevertheless to enjoy its contemplation.

'I was offered another role recently,' she said. 'It was a genius script. But it was full nudity.'

'That's always wrong,' said Sasha, after a moment. 'I don't agree with it at all.'

'Oh I would have done it,' she said, 'but he's a first-time director, and it's a rape scene. Yes, another one. So because he's a first-time director, I don't know how he would have shot it.'

'It all comes from confusion,' shaking his head, Sasha looked away with his brow crumpled and furrowed. 'Everybody is so confused and there is so much frustration all around.'

'What are you talking about?' said Mathili sharply. 'I am all in favour of nudity in fact. Our films are childish; they don't have enough of it... We all are naked under our clothes in real life, you know.'

'We all possess a sense of privacy too,' replied Sasha. 'Then so should characters—if they are going to become real, that is... There are moral duties that we owe, even to the things we imagine.'

'Clothes are just a convention. They're nothing natural.'

'Well, what is natural for human beings? I think wearing clothes is the sort of unnatural thing that expresses our humanity precisely. Just like telling stories and making movies.'

'There are tribes that don't cover themselves. The women go bare-chested.'

'Yes, there are nudists too, I mean there is nothing people can't get used to. But we can't just claim the tribal point of view, from the outside. We have to honestly examine our own feelings. Clothes are dear to us. Look at anyone, even if they have very little, they will value the shirt on their back.'

'Why?' she laughed bitterly. 'What kind of shirts do they wear anyway?'

Her scornful gaze bestowed itself dispassionately amongst the crowds of people, the washed and the unwashed alike. Then very briefly (or was it only his imagination?) she glanced over Sasha's own, well-tailored clothes. She rose quickly and alighted off the parapet. Setting his face suddenly, he followed her purposefully onto the walkway.

Neither spoke for a little while, until he took a deep breath of the sea wind and sighed.

'I feel I was right to move to this city. I mean, I had no clear reason for coming here. I think I just wanted the crowds. To be alone among crowds, to be able to think... I know you said you couldn't live here forever. But are you happy being here, right now...more or less?'

She shook her head with an annoyance that surprised him, and then smiled oddly.

'Look, I came back on the spur of the moment. I was doing theatre in Palo Alto. Hollywood was right there. I was planning to stay on in America but then I started seeing signs everywhere. All sorts of signs that I should go to India. One day I even saw an auto on the road! So I came back. But I'll move on soon. Maybe I'll act in another movie, then I'll make my own movie, and then I want to travel around the world for one year. One or two years.'

She was looking up as she strode straight; a middle-aged lady walking the opposite way had to swerve hastily to avoid a collision. Their shoulders bumped. The woman glared at Maithili, but Maithili did not notice. She was gazing at the moon, that hung pale and gibbous in the early dark.

'I have a friend here. We've talked about it. We both want to go especially to Africa and South America. Also, a few days ago, my ex-boyfriend called me. He was at the Burning Man festival. You haven't heard of it? Anyway, that's another thing I want to see.'

'Travel, of course, travel is...,' but for some reason Sasha failed to finish the sentence. 'You won't miss home?' he said softly.

'What is home? I don't even understand the concept.'

'It's not a matter of merit,' he continued, in an odd, focused way, as though he were concentrating hard on his own train of thought. 'But a place can simply have you—whether you like it or not. You are simply attached to it. I know India is very difficult that way. It's very hard to feel at home here. Even so... But I guess you've never spent much time in India anyway.'

'No, I grew up here,' she frowned, 'I went to school here. My parents were here then too. I was only in America for college. It's the whole idea of home that I don't subscribe to. My mother does! She keeps asking my dad to relocate back to Bombay. They will soon, I'm sure. My mother's very homely. I used to be, but I'm not any longer. I think people should live like nomads, that's the most interesting possible life. And the only reason they don't do it is, fear. They're afraid they won't be able to make money and survive. They're conditioned to live inside bubbles.'

'There are legal obstacles to nomadism,' Sasha thought of saying, but he stopped himself, because the words, that had begun quietly wise, had turned petty in his mouth.

'You're right,' he said instead. 'People are afraid of such things. But don't you see—there may be something good and true underlying those fears. Real attachments to a particular place or people, which one is loath to lose.'

'You keep talking about attachments,' she said. 'I don't even feel attached to this planet.'

And she looked again, with an odd, private pride, toward the gibbous moon.

'Well,' Sasha smiled, 'it's true we come from stardust.'

'There are lost cities under the sea,' said Maithili, 'there are dimensions beyond the boundaries of our consciousness. Monks and shamans have travelled to these places, in trance states, through meditation. What we understand as the world is only a tiny fraction of what's out there.'

'It is an unknown world,' agreed Sasha. 'All things are possible.'

'Exactly,' she said. 'I can't understand people who are cynical.'

'Yes.'

But his mood was flagging. He had a sense of being assailed

by strange, debilitating currents in the atmosphere and of his feet slipping off solid ground. All of a sudden the thought of Maithili's grandfather came to him. He struggled to find a way to reintroduce him into the conversation.

In the meantime, the glitter of the city lights had sprung up all around them, and there seemed to be a palatial building shimmering in the middle of the ocean, though Haji Ali was not near...

'How come you never laugh?' cried Sasha.

She turned and lowered her gaze. A frown had creased the perfect features, glowing softly beside him. Her skin, he saw afresh, was startlingly white.

'I never laugh,' said Maithili, considering the comment.

'No, of course you do laugh! And I also love the way you laugh! You have a wonderful laugh! But it seems like sometimes you laugh at the things you should be serious about and you're extremely serious about the things you should laugh at.'

'You know me so well in such a short time,' she said. 'I'm being sarcastic,' she added, when it seemed necessary. But then she smiled suddenly with a friendliness that leaped out at him, till his heart was bursting in his chest.

He told me later of the marvellous effect of her smile. He was too full of happiness to want to speak, his anxiety was to preserve the moment, while she was silent from her own mysterious disposition. Only dimly did he notice other people shying from the ever-wilder spray that battered the promenade, though he was walking nearest the sea. The traffic too was swelling about them. They passed Chowpatty, the squealing crowds, the dirty sand, the bhelpuri vendors. They came upon the concrete belly of a flyover, rumbling with activity. Suddenly, she stretched a hand to his arm.

'We can walk from here to my house,' she said, 'if you want to walk with me.'

He followed her into a small street between two large, yellowing buildings, and thence into a network of half-lit back alleys. Her step was swift and confident; absently she directed him up a route that turned gradually uphill. They passed a tube-lit shack selling sundry groceries, then a stray cow and a pack of roaming dogs. All around them loomed the backs of safe and wealthy apartment towers that kept the wind away.

'I told you, I went to Ahishor Frances's house,' said Sasha presently. 'His new documentary, the one he's planning, it's very interesting, don't you think?'

'I know about it,' said Maithili.

'I think belief is a subject that's always current. In other words, timeless.'

He wasn't sure if Maithili had heard him. Then suddenly, she began to talk.

'I need to be inspired. For me, work has to be play. It has to be spontaneous. I'm very interested in the moon right now. Yes yes, the moon. The moon is in everything I'm reading. My demon told me too.'

Besieged by queries, Sasha lapsed into a strange, shame-filled silence.

'I'm going to make a short film,' Maithili continued calmly. 'Just looking to raise the money for it. We'll see.'

He was perspiring slightly as they arrived at a set of stone steps, cut into a hillside. When they climbed, the lights of the city receded behind darkly flourishing trees. He wondered what park they had entered, with sudden greenery looming, with the moonlight laid on rough grass. The steps grew steeper but she climbed only faster and soon he was quite out of breath.

Glancing upwards, he saw her smiling at him, just as she had smiled when he had told her what daring things he had done.

Cresting a plateau, they stood in front of another street, from whence arose another discreetly lit apartment tower. Maithili turned to him, breathing just a fraction harder than usual, her white face glowing with unearthly happiness.

'This is where I live,' she said.

'I have to tell you something,' said Sasha. 'I'm in love with you.'

Her mouth moved with irresistible mirth. But his own eyes were incandescent.

'The first time I ever saw you on Versova beach, it was as though I recognized you. I knew at once you were dear to me. Everything I have learned of you after that makes me even surer. It doesn't mean that I want anything from you. Nothing, I don't want anything that's…provisional. I know I'm not fit for that. All I want is to marry you and spend the whole of my life with you.'

'I'm sorry,' said Maithili, between childlike squeals of laughter that had quite shattered her composure. Her gaze flitted over him, full of thrilled amusement. 'I shouldn't laugh!'

'I told you already, you laugh at the things you should be serious about.' Sasha smiled, but there was a weight of sadness in his voice.

'I don't like grandiose talk,' she said, still smiling.

'I love you. That's the truth.'

'I'm flattered,' said Maithili, suddenly stern, 'I really am flattered. But I have no feelings of that kind for you… You've gone very quiet now. Don't go into your shell now.'

Their conversation persisted until the moment they embraced lightly, and said goodbye, but it would be indelicate now to recreate it to the last. Suffice it to say, that even as crushed flowers give off a fragrance, so was Sasha full of bafflingly pleasant, though defeated thoughts, on the train journey back to Andheri. It seemed to pass without him knowing it.

Meanwhile, entering the cool, scented confines of her bedroom, Maithili blinked dreamily and said to herself: 'What an absurd encounter.'

It was some days later that Sasha wrote in his journal:

12th June 20__

I woke up this morning from the most beautiful dream. Last night the clouds had burst with a frenzy. The streets were flooded and choked. I had closed tight the windows in my room, though they rattled continually in the wind and the rain, while I tried to sleep.

In my dream, I woke in the middle of the night. The rain seemed to have long ceased. There was a wonderful freshness in the still night air all about me. I got to my feet and then I saw that the windows in my room were wide open and that all along the two window sills, lay rows of birds, at rest. Their frazzled plumage was folded down, their beaks were buried in their breasts.

I stood near them only to marvel at them. They were all kinds and colours and they breathed so gently and softly. But there was one more glorious than any other. She was bigger, stronger, most dazzling of all. I reached out a hand to touch that bird, and she trembled mightily. I should have withdrawn. But I tried to hold her with both my hands, and then she pecked at me hard (though I felt no pain at all) and then spreading her wings, she took to the skies...

I have tried to write this down with some poetry, but no words can describe the blessedness of the vision.

IX

Two Prophets of Doom

On errands of my own, I saw Sasha more than once, walking the streets of Versova. It was easy to spot him, with his lilting gait and his unfashionably fine clothes. I didn't give him much thought at the time, beyond feeling jealous of his money. I had put him down as a rich and idle loner, but I was soon to discover that he was making the acquaintance of a surprisingly large number of us struggling artists.

One such (though he was forty-five years old) was Jatin Khanna, my erstwhile boss. When I entered his office late that June, for a long delayed catch-up session, the first thing I saw was Sasha sitting comfortably on the office couch, with a wide grin on his face and a biscuit in his hand.

'Do you know each other?' said Jatin, whirling around with amazement.

I said we did.

'Please tell me how the fuck you tolerate him!'

Sasha threw back his head and laughed freely. Jatin, having answered the door, was still on his feet, which were splayed outwards in a kind of fighters' stance. His mouth was working with all kinds of unspoken and unprintable sentiments, while his manic good humour danced behind his spectacles. The whole room was bursting with his special energy, that matchlessly aggressive bonhomie whose dark side I knew all too well. It was with many private reservations, therefore, that I acquiesced with my own smile.

But it is necessary now that I delve deeper into my relationship with Jatin. He was the first person in Mumbai I had approached for work, and he had given it to me at once. In college, I had watched his one and only fiction film ('you and nine other people in India,' he used to joke darkly), and I had liked it hugely for the sheer buoyant energy which was the hallmark of its maker too. Yet I found myself a peaceful and happier person out of Jatin's employment than I had ever been in it. The one year of our near-daily association had been the most exhausting year of my life. Professionally, save for one short film which I was proud of but he scorned, we had failed to see any of his ideas through to any screen, big or small. Personally, I had had pressed on me all manner of authors to read, movies to watch, directors and playwrights whose work I was to follow; my 'politics' (I hadn't known I had any) had been held up to the light and bashed and battered from every direction—ostensibly into shape; my sense of humour, my taste in food and clothes, my English language pronunciation, had all undergone a similar 'improvement', and details of my personal and family life had been ferreted out with extraordinarily invasive concern. But if someone ever told me—as one of my flatmates once did—that 'Jatin truly loves you', I wouldn't for a moment deny it. It was the way he loved that left me wandering into gloomy afterwork evenings, half-chewed up inside, my mind on mute, and white noise playing within.

Nevertheless, I was too fond of him to act decisively on

the resentment (and indeed hatred) that he often aroused in me. He had turned himself into a parental figure, for better and for worse, and I was prepared to perform my filial duty.

Knowing the way he was, Jatin's apparently sudden and intense friendship with Sasha did not surprise me—as far as he was concerned. What intrigued me was Sasha's part in it.

'Why,' I said, 'what's the matter with him?'

The sun was pouring through the curtains, into the tenth-floor room, and the air conditioner was going full blast. I looked around at the familiar, spartan furniture and the two Macs, humming quietly.

'Tell him what you said!' ordered Jatin. 'Go on, let's see if *anybody* thinks that is *not* a lunatic comment!'

'I can't,' said Sasha hesitantly.

'Can't what?'

'I can't say it again. It'll sound pompous, if I separate it away like that. It wasn't a one-liner.'

'That's exactly what it was! Listen to this. He says, "It's okay that books are being banned because nobody reads anyway". Can you imagine a dumber comment!'

'That's not at all what I said,' said Sasha. 'The point I'm trying to make is, there is more than one kind of violence that can be done to books, and the obvious violence isn't the only kind. You can equally kill a society's thinking by banning nothing and trivializing everything.'

'This is nonsense,' said Jatin, 'and I'll tell you why it's nonsense. It's irrelevant theorizing. We're talking about Hindu right-wingers and nutjobs demanding bans on book after book and everybody else being too scared to fight back. That's the context we're in!'

'That's part of the context. But it helps to keep things

in perspective, otherwise we start to feel that things are extraordinarily bad today and that affects our response.'

'They *are* extraordinarily bad. This *is* the lowest point India has ever hit since Independence. But I'm done with this discussion now, it's really starting to irritate me. Dhruv, sit down man, why are you still standing? And where are *you* going, Sasha? No no, stay a while longer, Dhruv has just come, will you have another cup of tea? Dhruv, you? Tea for you too? And we'll have some more of those fruit biscuits, aren't they good? Sasha! Did you like the biscuits?'

In a fit of solicitousness, he moved about us, pointing, waving and jerking like a massive marionette. Sasha sat down again.

'They are good biscuits,' he agreed.

'Arvind!' cried Jatin. 'Chai and biscuits for everybody—and kindly be polite and join us! It's not like you're doing any work anyway! In this office we check Facebook all day long! Not just him, I'm the same!'

A tall, reedy-figured young man loped into sight from one of the small rooms in the back. I had heard of him before. His name was Arvind, and he was Jatin's new assistant on his latest project, which wasn't a film at all. They were building a website that would review the same movie in many different ways, from deliberately different political perspectives, supposedly to eradicate the presumptiveness of a single 'considered' opinion. But I won't attempt to explain the concept any further—I can already hear Jatin in my head contradicting everything I'm saying.

I watched Arvind quietly and uncomplainingly bring in the tea, a job I had sometimes resented but performed innumerable times during my own tenure. Then he sat in a discreet corner, folding his long legs and nursing a little smile. Jatin, however, was not going to let well enough alone.

'Why are you sitting there? We're not good enough for you to sit nearby?'

'I just like this chair.'

'Look at that smile! He smiles like the Cheshire cat! Complacency written all over it!'

Even as I cringed for Jatin, I noticed that his description was not inaccurate.

'MBAs!' he continued. 'The most complacent bunch of people in the country, with the biggest sense of entitlement in the history of the country!'

'I'm actually not an MBA,' said Arvind, still smiling. He had a handsome, though somewhat skeletal face, and dark circles under his eyes.

'By "MBA" I don't mean only the degree! I mean the whole type! You are a manager, aren't you? Do you know he had an offer from Mckenzie? Turned it down, and now he's here. Yeah Dhruv, *wow*, right? What a buffoon right! I know what *you're* thinking!'

Once again, he was not really wrong. By and by, Jatin calmed down and asked me my news. I told him about various sundry auditions I'd been going for (and the one YouTube ad I'd acted in—for a chocolate brand), and then I mentioned Ahishor's documentary.

'I don't know if I'm going to be a part of it,' I said, 'but I really hope so.'

'That's wonderful,' he said. 'Ahishor Frances is the most talented voice we've had in a long, long time. That's really good stuff, I hope it works out.'

As he spoke, my heart was beating hard with a strange exhilaration. To see Jatin quietly and soberly wishing me well was to realize how liberating my proximity to Ahishor could be. Finally, I was cutting the umbilical cord.

'We need art like this,' Jatin was saying, 'that tells about the things happening around us. My only worry, based on what you're saying, is that it will become too philosophical. Even in Ahishor's first movie, it wasn't the philosophy I cared for, it was the storytelling about people like us, our contemporaries. As opposed to gangsters and small-town exotica!'

'I'm sure he will connect it with what's going on,' I said. 'Things like all the books being banned—or forced to be withdrawn—the Muslim guy who was murdered in Pune, it's all coming from a certain ideology, right? I guess he wants to explore that right up to the roots.'

Jatin nodded, ruminatively.

'Tough to make a change though,' said a voice from the corner.

Arvind smiled again as all eyes turned to him. 'I mean, who's going to watch a documentary? Very few people. But the problem's much bigger than that.'

'So documentaries are just a waste of time, right?' Jatin was crouching forward from the couch.

'No, I mean for one's creative satisfaction it's fine of course. But in terms of making a change, it's not going to. That's all I'm saying.'

'Spare me please!' exploded Jatin, 'I've had a tough enough day without hearing an MBA talking about creative satisfaction! It's because of people like you that these forces have come to power in the first place. Because you only care about the "economy" right? Only money matters, social issues don't matter! Violence and bigotry and regressiveness of all kinds doesn't matter. And if you're so interested in making a change, why don't you finance documentaries like this, make sure they get released, dub them into twenty languages, show them all over the country? Then they might actually make a dent right? But that you won't do! Arre I don't mean *you*, I mean your crowd, your business community.'

'You can't expect people to put in money where there's no market.'

'On the contrary, that is precisely how you *create* a market. Risk-taking is the first principle of real business. But enough, I don't expect you to understand this!'

'Ritesh Azad may give money for Ahishor's film,' I said. 'Elevate may be producing it, or co-producing it.'

'Good!' said Jatin. 'But it will need a whole lot of investment without any guaranteed returns at all. I just hope they back it all the way. Wouldn't be surprised if they get cold feet down the line. If they do back out, I'm afraid Arvind is right—not that he should be proud of it!—the film will simply sink and nothing will change.'

He munched furiously at a biscuit and for a little while the sound of his chewing, along with the AC's steady hush, was the only sound in the room. Then Sasha said thoughtfully, 'How do things change anyway?'

'Here he goes again!' cried Jatin.

'No, listen,' said Sasha, 'I think the way in which real change actually happens, is extremely difficult to describe. There's something mystical about the process—as mystical as us changing from babies and five-year-olds to what we are today. So we shouldn't be trite in thinking and talking about making a change. We shouldn't ask to see how it happens every step of the way. It happens magically.'

'Making a movie that nobody sees is not changing anything,' said Jatin. 'Maybe you have that kind of time, money and energy to waste, but most people don't.'

'Instead of talking about changing the world,' said Sasha (just as though he had never heard this barb), 'which simply becomes an overwhelming idea, what if we talked about making an *infinite* change? Remember the whole world is no closer to infinity than a speck of dust is. They're both infinitely less. If we thought in terms of infinity and not massive numbers, perhaps we wouldn't mind doing very small things, because we wouldn't be thinking in terms of big or small at all.'

I looked trepidatiously at Jatin, but to my surprise he had fallen quiet and was listening attentively. But Sasha only said softly, 'I don't know if Ahishor understands this himself.' Then he too said no more, and a strange, befuddled silence slowly filled the room until Sasha spoke again.

'It's irritating, I agree,' he said. 'The gung-ho talk of our business-people, so celebratory, when in reality there is so little to celebrate. But it's dangerous to get too irritated, because then it consumes us, we start imagining devils that don't really exist, so that we can lash out at them. Then we end up in the same place as the simply scared and paranoid.'

He was looking hard at Jatin with a strange, intent concern.

'The devils in human form—,' said Sasha, 'they don't exist.'

'I haven't understood a word you said,' said Jatin. 'And by the way, you're completely wrong.'

While Sasha hesitated in sudden doubt, Jatin turned to me.

'You've gotten over that thing, I hope?'

I blushed and nodded hastily. From Jatin, this was high tact. When we had last met, I had been in torments over my ex-girlfriend and unable to conceal the fact. I still wasn't over her betrayal, but I was managing not to think about it—not too much.

'MBAs, Dhruv,' he made a face, 'in our times they win

all the prizes... Why are *you* smiling? Do you know what I'm talking about?'

Momentarily, I was horrified that he might indeed know, that Jatin might have gossiped. But Arvind was shaking his head.

'But you're happy about it anyway!' said Jatin. 'Sure, why not, you should be happy! It's your world!'

'But I'm not an MBA!' laughed Arvind.

'There's a vision I have,' said Jatin. 'It's a beautiful vision. It keeps going through my head. Just imagine this... All the head honchos from the corporate world, the Shahs and the Mittals, and all the A-list stars, the Khans, the Kapoors, they're invited to one massive party. Everyone's stuffing their faces and drinking and slobbering over each other in one huge hall. There are singers and dancers and all kinds of live performances happening. Then suddenly all the doors are locked from the outside—and starving Asiatic lions are released into the room... The most beautiful part is that for a little while they'll all think it's just part of the entertainment...What...you think I'm sick, don't you? Well, you're right, I am sick, but so is this industry, and so is this country! It's a ticking time bomb, unless someone does something very soon!'

That was when he stopped short and swept a confidential glance around at us all.

'One thing's for sure. If anyone is actually planning on doing something, I'm going to help. Now is the time for good people to act, otherwise...'

No doubt I should have attached more importance to these words of his. But was not Jatin forever prophesying disaster, and forever cooking up new things to do?

* * *

Two days later, it was only my wounded heart that was troubling me. I had rid my lonely room in Four Bungalows and taken to Bandra, hungry for love. There was a girl I had met on Facebook; in fact, approached quite audaciously, and when, amazingly, we came to exchanging many warm and exciting messages, I was quietly congratulating myself on having manufactured a miracle. The fantasy dissipated only minutes after we met, when her face in the flesh reminded me of my aunt's. I was polite, we both were; just as we were both probably straining to end the meeting and get away.

Afterwards, walking in a daze down dark, cobbled inner streets, somewhere off Turner Road, I saw a woman strut by, her shoulders bare, her breasts firm in her top.

Moments later, I stood at a crossroads. An empty auto slowed down before me, though I hadn't asked it to. I turned away savagely and began to walk again, and as I walked, I found Sushant's number and called him.

The truth was, I had been avoiding Sushant for months. Between the night of our one disastrous show and that night in Bandra, I had only seen him twice—once, for a postmortem that degenerated into slyness and backbiting, and once at Malik's shoot at Gemini's. But again, I should elaborate. Like Jatin, Sushant was one of my earliest professional acquaintances in the city. I had met him at an acting workshop. We had gone out for a smoke, and he had offered me a part in his newly written play—which was going to travel to fifteen cities, make lakhs of money, and put us all indelibly on the country's theatre map. There followed weeks of torturous rehearsals in his small, bare, flat off Hill Road (his family in Bihar were wealthy and politically powerful Thakurs, but for whatever reason he only spent enough money to live thus, shabbily, in an expensive locality). In that flat, the smell of weed and staleness filled the air, I was always hungry for proper food, and quarrels erupted constantly—most often between the play's lead actress and Sushant (who was both directing and acting in the lead himself). She left after our first show, amidst private accusations of sexual misconduct, while he insisted (with a shy grin) that everything had been consensual. More fatally for the production, the producer, a banker whom Sushant had somehow convinced to try her hand at the arts, also accused him, of misusing and embezzling her money. But with aggression on the one hand and grovelling on the other, he managed to wriggle out of both messes.

In the meantime, he had tried to make a great friend of me—'my younger brother,' he used to say. During his desperate period after the play he would call me again and again for a drink. I always made excuses. Being away from Sushant was simply rejuvenating. I would think of his wasted, drug-addled frame and the miasma of deliberate, self-destructive unhealthiness that hung about his smoky flat, and wish never to be near it again.

Yet I could not quite get him out of my head. I cannot explain why. I can only say that that actress was a lively, beautiful, intelligent girl. I had never believed she could willingly have slept with Sushant. But as time passed, and I grew aware myself of his insidious seductiveness, I was not so sure.

I met him that night outside St. Peter's Church on Hill Road. From there we were to walk to somebody else's house, where there would be drinks, dope, and women I didn't know. So I hoped and expected.

'You have lost weight, bhai,' he said as he looked me over, 'you're looking good.'

'Well, thanks. I don't know if it's a good thing though. How is everything with you?'

'Everything is fucked.'

He laughed softly, his eyes gleaming. He was dressed as usual, in a loose shirt with the sleeves rolled up, a black undershirt, and jeans that hung far below his waist. He looked like he hadn't bathed for days.

'Everything is fucked, bhai. This town ain't a good place, bhai.'

'Did you pitch those scripts? The TV shows?'

'Bhai, we have not talked for a long time. I junked those long back. I wrote a film script.'

'A full script? A feature film? Wow, that's great.'

'I was thrown out of the office of a producer this week. I told him to his face, *ki* bro, your films are shit. He was like, aah!'

He mimicked an open-mouthed astonishment, and his eyes bulged, cementing the suggestion of the toad that always hovered about his features—not that he was ill-looking.

'What is the script about?' I said.

'I'll tell you *aaraam se* sometime. It's called *The Last Anarchist.*'

'Nice title.'

'It's like Nietzsche's idea of the Superman. It's set in a slum. Bhai, the kind of shit that goes on here, it's hardcore. It's fucked up. As a writer I too have to fuck things up. Then it works, then it flows. You know what I mean?'

He really had read Nietzsche. Rather, he had pored over Nietzsche and Heidegger because his mother was a graduate in philosophy, at the same time as he studied in Hindi medium schools in Patna and roamed the streets with unread companions, teasing girls and picking fights. Then he had come to Bombay and felt for the first time the acute limitations of his English;

his strange accent had gotten stranger still; and he had done a lot of drugs throughout. When Sushant was directing me in the play, trying to make a point, I always knew he really had something to say, or really thought he did. But his articulation was sheer chaos.

'But these motherfuckers are too scared, *woh nahin banayenge*. (They won't make it.) This is my last chance, bhai. My dad phoned yesterday, he was like, *waapas kyon nahi aate*? (Why don't you come back?) They want to fix me up with a petrol pump.'

'Really?'

'Ohhh yeah! They can't understand, they think I'm wasting my time. *Main bhi* focused *nahin hoon na*... (Even I am not focused...) How I wrote this script only I know. The other day, I was thinking about our play. I feel bad about it bhai.'

'It's done now.'

'*Unko chhorunga nahin* (I won't spare them), those two bitches... But now I've understood this scene. These guys don't care about anything bhai. Story, concept, motherfuckers ain't bothered about nothing... Only two things matter in this town. Money and pussy.'

'Have you tried Elevate? They've made some interesting films.'

'They're the worst! The worst! Ritesh Azad *toh*, he is the biggest *tharki* (pervert) in the city. I had a fight with him, *tujhe toh pata hai*... (You know...) Accha I didn't tell you? Oh! You don't know then. I'll tell you sometime. Yeah yeah yeah! Physical fight. Major fight. I would have beaten him badly that day. I wish I had.'

We were walking in the lanes behind the main road, which the monsoons had turned to slush. Ornate little bungalows curved about us, in well-spaced rows, with porches and balustrades and trees between and overhanging. I had heard that these dated back to the 1920s, to Bandra's jazz age, and they were still the prettiest homes in the suburbs.

'Bhai, I'm in a good mood today. I've had some good news.'

'You said everything was fucked.'

'The corporates, they don't like honesty. They're as twisted as anybody but they've got all these airs, they give me these looks, like *this*, and *this*, like they're too sophisticated for me. Talking fancy and pissing farce! That's what I say. Original? Yes, that's an original line bhai. *Khair,* I'll get to them, if not directly, then via the guys who operate for them. Bhai, the deal is, I've found a producer for my film. *Ussi ke ghar jaa rahe hain.*' (Going to his place.)

'Congratulations!' I said. 'Who is this?'

'He has the cash and he doesn't care what I make, *kahaani main bilkul* interfere *nahi karega.* (He won't interfere in the story at all.) You will meet him. You will like him too. Samyak, his name is Samyak.'

His stride quickened, as though the name, spoken aloud, was summoning him onwards. My feet were starting to hurt. I looked at Sushant as we scurried down those dark streets. His face was boyish and his hair was trimmed short. I knew he was badly brought up, full of self-pity, a brat fattened on small-town privilege and the doting fondness of his mother. But when he paused at a turning, lost momentarily amidst old twisted buildings, I was buffeted with strange concern.

We reached a wrought iron gate at a house much bigger than the others, though in the darkness I could see little of its shape. A rainswept wind was stirring the trees, their leaves brushing the grey walls. There was a light behind a curtained window, but it was very quiet everywhere.

Someone mumbled as Sushant opened the iron latch. I saw a burly figure turn away from us and continue urinating. A yellow smiley face gleamed off the back of his shirt. The sound of him on the stone driveway stayed constant in my ears.

Soon a staircase appeared, flooded in white light. There was a kind of red velvet seemingly growing on the walls. We walked up two flights. Sushant pressed a switch but we heard no sound of a bell. Then, as though correcting himself, he simply pushed at the door and it opened.

It was a large, gloomy room, full of couches sunk with silent figures. Sushant disappeared ahead of me. I looked around at the faces above the drinks. A few were smoking quietly. Most, though not all, were young. Then I did a double take. Squatted on the carpet beside one of the sofas was Maithili. She was dressed very casually in slacks, and a kind of smock, and her head was completely bald. White and naked, her face was flickering with strange mirth, while beside her crouched an elderly man who was holding her chin between fleshy fingers and murmuring close to her mouth.

Just a little distance apart from them sat Sasha, his legs folded awkwardly and his troubled gaze fastened on her.

Moments later, Ahishor emerged from an inner corridor and stood with his hands on his hips. He was breathing hard, his grey locks falling wildly about angry eyes. One of the silent figures began to laugh.

X

An Eventful Night

Just then, something heavy collided into me. I turned to see the boy from the driveway. There was a sad-faced emoticon on the front of his shirt, but he was smiling angelically. He had a wide, good-humoured face with fleshy lips and a loose, flabby body all round.

'How are you?' he grinned, grasping my hand and shaking it. 'I'm Samyak.'

I explained who I was and looked around for Sushant. I spotted him in a corner, laughing and patting on the back a bearded figure who was not smiling at all. But next to them was a tired-looking, round-faced girl, all alone, that I fancied at once.

'I'll get you a drink,' said Samyak. 'You know, you look like someone I know. Very dear friend of mine!'

I had to smile. From all that night he was the only person whose name I remembered afterwards. On the way to the kitchen we skirted past Ahishor, who stared at me dully. I don't think we spoke though.

My memory of that night is discontinuous and unreliable. I know I tried deliberately to throw myself into the gathering and not simply to remain a spectator. I must have chatted up the round-faced girl, and there may have been another too. But I seem to have been unsuccessful in focusing my attentions on anyone, for any duration, apart from the one in whom (I firmly believed) I had no interest. Yet it is Maithili's face that glows in my mind's eye. I am aware for the first time personally, of her fearful radiance. That night she was both a sage and a little child—and a continual bafflement to us all.

Not long after I came in, I heard her saying:

'You have mischievous eyes. I see a very young person in your eyes.'

I glanced at who she was talking to. It was the middle-aged man—in his fifties at least—who had just been pawing her face. His eyes, as far as I could see, were beady chinks encased between folds of fat. He was wearing a glistening black shirt with enough buttons open that his chest-hair should sprout free. Only the gold necklace was missing from the very picture of the thug.

Maithili was gazing at him curiously. 'What gives you meaning in life?' she asked. 'Being a producer, being a financier, is that enough to satisfy you?'

'I don't know how to answer this question.' The man cast around, for Samyak, it emerged, with a taut expression of amusement. Later, he broke into chuckles.

'Then you answer it,' said Maithili, looking over him at the next figure—a dark, muscular smoker reclining on a couch. 'What do you want most from life? Is it money? Fame? I want to ask everybody, I'm looking for somebody who can help me.'

'Intoxication,' said the dark man softly. Maithili smiled faintly.

'Happiness, of course,' said Samyak. 'And for me that means family. I want a big, happy family to live and die in. That's the most important thing in the world.'

'Awww! That's so sweet!' My tired girl had perked up alarmingly.

'Love and sex,' spat someone brutally.

'Fuck love,' said another. 'It doesn't exist. Just money. You can buy anything with money.'

'Too boring,' giggled Sushant. 'I want to travel in life. All I want is the gypsy life.'

I was amazed that when it came to my turn I was almost nervous. I said I was confused and didn't know what I wanted from life, and then I gave way quickly to the person beside me. That was Sasha.

'To live it,' he said. His voice at that moment was unusually high and piping, like a girl's. 'Just to live life.'

There were no reactions from the gathering. We looked at Ahishor for something more interesting. But Ahishor was gazing ruefully at the ceiling. He was standing unnaturally still, like a figure sculpted. Somebody prodded him to speak. A moment later, he was laughing.

'Who asked this question? It was you? Well... Why am I not surprised?... Does one want things from life? Or does one want to do things in life? I don't know what to say... Does one want things, or are there such things as ideals—to serve? Who said he wants happiness? Ahh yes... And somebody said money...Who said money?'

He was laughing in a long-drawn, rather horrible way. I had never seen him in such a mood before. The faces around me were slowly turning resentful. I was conscious of something very badly amiss, and anxious and bewildered myself. Only later did I think it through. Then I realized how much of an outsider Ahishor really was, notwithstanding his roots, and his fame in Versova and all the excitement on social media. All 'film people' were not alike, all young people were not of the same persuasion. Those rich, bored bodies were the sons and daughters of the old school, the glamour-struck businessmen and conniving artists who made the blockbusters that Ahishor so frequently denigrated. It was my fault for assuming he did not feel the things he said, and that ultimately, like everybody else, he would always make nice with everybody else.

'Quit fucking around,' said the bearded boy, in a slow, dangerous drawl. Ahishor stopped smiling.

How had he come to be in that room and why was Sasha there, huddled on the carpet, unable even now to take his eyes off Maithili? But my curiosity was only a distraction from the drama unfolding.

'Oh it's my turn, is it? Well, for me the answer's very easy. What I want most from life is to marry you. I only want to marry you, Maithili.'

Ahishor's eyes were glinting with strange triumph, and his lips were moving, as though tormenting a smile into being.

'Marrying you is what will give meaning to my life.'

I looked at her. For a moment she was startled. Then she smirked, and turned to the beady-eyed financier and asked for a cigarette.

A murmur of derision was going about the room. A lone cheer went up from someone half unconscious. 'Was that an actual proposal?' said one of the girls innocently. But my heart was in turmoil. I remembered Ahishor's face, healthy and glowing, when he had last spoken of Maithili. I tried to catch his eye; I didn't know why, but I wanted desperately for him to reassure me that this was all part of a plan.

'Aren't you going to say anything?' he continued instead, 'I know you're very fetching Maithili, but it can't be everyday a guy dedicates his life to you, in public too... And such a fine public too!?'

'Bro!' Samyak, the host, threw up a pacifying hand, 'Chill! And Baba, you've not told us your own answer.'

Maithili looked up coolly. Then she seemed to wait, until everybody's attention had finally left Ahishor and returned to her.

'I want to understand,' she said then, impassively. 'My mind is full of thoughts all the time. They go on non-stop. I want that to be over, and to be at peace. I want to know what this Universe is all about, what all of this means. That's why I'm looking for someone who can help me.'

The round-faced girl rolled her eyes, and very audibly sighed. I wanted to assume a similar attitude, I even formed in my mind the label 'pretentious'. Yet I could not help recognizing the sincerity of Maithili's speech. About her peculiar terseness and her lofty pain there hung the suggestion of a rare and romantic reality.

'So you've not found the person yet?' Samyak asked courteously.

'It may not be one person. It may be a combination of people. Or different people at different times. I made a friend recently... It's been an interesting journey with her.'

Suddenly, Sasha spoke out.

'You won't find help this way. You mustn't go knocking at every door.'

In that instant (it is an image I can't forget), I saw Maithili glare at Sasha with a leaping, ferocious hatred. I don't think he noticed himself. Afterwards, just as though a switch had been pressed, the implacable mask fell over her face again.

'When I was thirteen, I had my stomach pumped,' she said,

in a general way. 'I wasn't depressed that day, I just wanted to experience death, just understand what it was... You need to start experiencing life first,' she addressed Sasha suddenly, and then turned back to the rest of the room.

He stepped away gingerly and found a chair adjacent to me. That was how we were both sitting (I was beginning to feel light with drink), when Maithili began to talk about her film. It was not very late then, but various people had left already. Samyak was sitting to one side of her, with the lecherous financier still installed at the other. Ahishor was watching from a sofa, at the far end of the room.

'I only need...maybe fifteen thousand rupees,' she was saying.

'Fifteen thousand? We could just have skipped the wine at dinner!' said Samyak. 'But tell me, what's your motivation here? Do you want this to go to festivals? Or...'

'First of all, I want to make it,' she said. 'It will help me learn. And also…'

She left the sentence unfinished, and stubbed out her cigarette.

'Instead of a short film, why don't you make a full feature film? There's so much more that can happen. Bertie knows. Am I right, Bertie?'

'Short films are a waste of time,' said the fat man, stroking Maithili's bare shoulder as he spoke. She swivelled with a smile that bothered me.

'But why are you not acting?' he grinned at her. 'You must be getting many offers.'

'I realized something recently,' she told him earnestly. 'In the past, I have acted to avoid being myself. I've been pretending to be other people. But I need to find my own self now.'

Bertie kept grinning widely. Samyak too was smiling, though

he seemed to restrain himself.

'You're doing Vikas's movie in October,' he reminded her, 'in Amsterdam.'

'That fell through,' she said. 'They had selected me. I'd even signed the contract. But then they decided my look wasn't okay, they wanted a leggy model type instead. Now I do have some other meetings lined up, but I've decided I won't say "yes" to any project that doesn't truly resonate with me.'

I quickly deduced which movie Samyak was referring to. It was a collaboration between one of the new and admired 'independent' directors, and a big corporate producer. It was going to be a major release. I was impressed, and curious how disappointed Maithili must have been to lose such a role. But she revealed nothing.

It was Ahishor who sat up, rubbing his scraggly-haired chin and shaking his head.

'Bollywood,' he grinned. 'Oh Maithili, what did you expect from Bollywood? What do you still expect? When one has self-respect, one doesn't keep returning to things that have proven their lack of worth.' He was no longer smiling.

'You know something…,' but it was not Maithili who had replied. The young man whose own beard was shaped and groomed, was sitting up in a corner. 'This is what I can't stand about guys like you. Your so-called indie films only exist because of the money that Bollywood makes. Yet you keep dissing it like immature kids.'

'Are you talking to me?' said Ahishor. 'Then firstly you should know I never use the indie label myself. [This was not strictly true.] I am for good cinema, that's all. Secondly, Bollywood is regressive and idiotic and I don't care how much money it makes. It has entrapped the public in an abusive relationship.

It's an industry without merit, which exists only to propagate the careers of the children of dynasties.'

'Like the Azad dynasty,' smiled the bearded boy.

Ahishor opened his mouth into thin air. The snipe had broadsided him. To this day I regret I did not speak up myself to point out that there was no comparison, that Ahishor had earned everything he had achieved, that after all everybody knew somebody, and that in any case Karim Azad was not his father. But the sight of Ahishor, discombobulated, only stoked his opponent's malice.

'And who're you trying to kid anyway?' he continued sharply. 'Everyone knows you took Danesh Khan's money for marketing your film. Untouchable, immoral Bollywood money!'

'I made my film exactly the way I wanted to. I didn't let a soul interfere creatively. If afterwards somebody appreciates my work and wants to help me in the release, I am gracious enough not to decline, merely because of my own opinion of their past work.'

'Ha! So now it's just an "opinion", is it? Haha! How convenient! So long as you're taking money in any shape or form, just be grateful and shut up about "Bollywood".'

Ahishor's head turned. I followed the direction of his gaze, just in time to catch Maithili's lingering smile. It was wounding even to me, but Ahishor's cheek had flushed as though physically whipped. I felt a hatred welling up, spurting towards her.

Two others were watching closely. For Sushant, a new star was swimming into his Universe, he was swelling with deep, visceral respect, with consequences no one could have foreseen. He told me later that that he had known nothing of Ahishor before that night, and was only vaguely aware of *Schrödinger's Cat*. (Also, that the bearded boy was a 'prick' who deserved a thrashing.) As to Sasha's impressions, they remain a mystery to me. He was like a mournful ghost in the room that night, gazing anxiously from face to face.

'There's one thing I have never done,' Ahishor resumed quietly. 'You're not listening I suppose. [The bearded boy had fallen back among the cushions, evidently satisfied with his work.] That's very rude but it's your decision. One thing I have never done and will never do is beg for money from people who are the scum of our cinema. Not even fifteen thousand rupees!'

Glaring at Maithili, he got up and would, I am sure, have swept out of the house, if Samyak had not risen almost instantly himself.

'Arre! What did I do baba!? Full collateral damage you are making me!'

Meeting Ahishor midway, he put an arm around him. He grinned so likeably that, amazingly, an answering smile appeared on Ahishor's lips too.

What I remember next, is sitting on a jute mattress, out on a terrace, on a very still, cool night, with the street lights twinkling off the treetops. Everyone had left but the six of us— Maithili, Samyak, Bertie the financier, Ahishor, Sasha and I. I was staring in fascination as Samyak cut lines of cocaine on a cane-and-glass coffee table. Earlier, on Sushant's urging that coke would give me the energy I needed to take the round-faced girl home (though he had put it differently), I had snorted a portion myself, for the first time in my life. But I was disappointingly unenergized, and later the girl was gone.

'It's a silly drug,' Ahishor told me. 'It has no complexity. I never do it.'

The anger that had been boiling in him all night seemed to have cooled though. He was looking on calmly enough while

Maithili bent her bald head to the table and ingested line after line. I was shocked myself, though I was not conscious of it at the time. I recall grinning a lot, till my mouth ached.

'My biggest fear,' she was saying, apropos of what I don't know, 'is that I will only remain a spectator, and real life will pass me by. I won't understand or experience the things that I need to. That's what happened to my mother.'

'Don't say that,' said Sasha suddenly. 'Don't talk like that about your mother. Even if it's true, you shouldn't say it to just anybody!'

It was he who looked the most disturbed now. He was staring with wide, alert eyes at the table full of cocaine, and the leering old Bertie, ensconced again near Maithili. But she simply ignored the strange outburst and it drowned quickly in the great strangeness of the night.

'Well, if you're behind the camera,' said Samyak, 'I'm afraid you *are* a spectator.'

'Precisely,' said Maithili. 'Films are rather tame things, aren't they?'

'So then I'm confused!' he laughed. 'Do you want to make a film or don't you?'

Ahishor too made a snorting sound; a kind of guffaw. It seemed then that we were all laughing at her. She was squatted on the mat, flicking up bits of the white powder with her finger and licking it clean. I caught glimpses of a sports bra beneath her smock. In the unholiness of my impulses she had at that moment turned cheap and degraded, a creature to disrespect.

'Actually, it's interesting,' said Sasha, suddenly loudly, 'I think you have to go very close to some things before you realize they are not for you. You have to actually commit to them, in all honesty. There's a realization that comes only at the eleventh hour. It simply doesn't come sooner!'

He flashed a sudden smile at Maithili. We were distracted. Later, when I looked, her aspect had altered. She was gazing at the sky. The full moon was shining behind the trees, and her face too was pale and glowing. There was sweat on her forehead. It occurred to me in passing that she did not look well. Yet she continued on the cocaine with practiced calm, and so did our host himself.

But Ahishor was frowning again. He threw an angry glare at Sasha, and then suddenly rose to his feet.

'Well, I'm leaving,' he said, looking hard at Maithili. She seemed not to have heard. Softening suddenly with a smile, he walked up to her, around the low table at which Samyak's attention was absorbed. I remember him bending down beside her, cupping his hand by her ear and speaking softly for quite a long time. When he was finished, she looked at him in an amused and friendly way.

'Later,' she said. 'Later.'

For a moment, he only stared. Then he turned rapidly and strode back into the house. In another moment I heard the front door slamming shut.

Nobody seemed to remark on Ahishor's exit. Maithili glanced at Sasha, but said nothing. He too did not speak to her, though he was clearly trying to hold her attention. But she only looked at him briefly, and then at me, and then her gaze, dreamy and smouldering, turned inward into itself.

The next thing I remember being struck by was the sight of Sasha shifting up to the financier, Bertie, and engaging him in close conversation. Soon, the paunchy old man was telling him something that, in the telling, was bringing tears to his eyes. 'Ultimately there is nothing but family,' I heard him say, while Sasha nodded sombrely.

When he was done talking to Bertie, Sasha got up, muttering that he had some things to do early the next morning. He looked unhappy, though he was decisive about leaving. I had been feeling purposeless myself for some time, and said I would accompany him to Versova.

Samyak walked us to the door. At the gates of the house, I remember noticing that it had started drizzling again and wondering how they would manage on the terrace.

XI

The Bald Girl

It was less than a week after that night in Bandra, a cold, windy Sunday following a night of heavy rain. Those days, of my own volition (Ahishor had not asked me, but I wanted to be ready), I was researching so-called 'God-men'; ashrams in America, sex scandals, piling wealth, universal love, the joy of life, the oneness of all things, spontaneous bouts of crying in the 'presence' of the guru, enlightenment, nirvana, and fleets of fancy cars. As I lay on my narrow bed with my laptop on my stomach, and my flatmate's video game coming through the door in regular, rhythmic bursts, like free verse, my eyelids began to droop. It was all boring to me. I could not understand the fascination with things so esoteric and removed from the pressing concerns of life as one actually lived it. Turning, I shoved the computer onto the little available space on my desk, trusting it would keep its balance. Then I rolled over and stared at the wall.

After a while, I realized my heart was pounding. I was growing anxious, to the point of feeling cold panic. What about? I was thinking of my career, my chances in the city. Jatin was right. Things were only getting worse. Everywhere, it was either rosy urban candyfloss or small-town gang wars. Why could we not make true and simple cinema like the Iranians? If I saw nothing from Bombay that I even wanted to be a part of, then what hope had I of getting any parts? The theatre too was pretentious and tiresome. Everybody went around with fake smiles and bonhomie, doing terrible, pointless comedies. Nobody had a clue. I couldn't even make quick money in one of the awful television serials, because they demanded hunks, not actors. How long was I going to continue on my parents' charity, unable to support myself?

It began to settle on me, horribly, that I was in the wrong city, in the wrong line of work altogether, in the wrong country. My apartment building was dirty and cramped; outside, the streets were floating in filth. The previous week a child had fallen into an open manhole. Two people had drowned in the sea. We had no such things as lifeguards. But it didn't matter, the carnival of filth would roll on oblivious, let apocalypse descend.

The noise of the video game was growing impossible to bear. I wanted to tell him to switch it off or at least to turn the volume down, but my mouth was too dry to speak. I lay there quietly, almost fainting with suffering.

Sometime later, I woke with a strange resolve. My head felt unnaturally clear, though my heart was still racing. Gathering up my laptop into my well-worn rucksack, I started for Ahishor's newly rented office, in Aram Nagar.

* * *

It did not bother me that, but for the caretaker, nobody was there; I was glad to be alone in that green and meditative environment. In any case, it was full of life. Creepers criss-crossed the boundaries of a small courtyard outside the office proper, which was home also to three mongrel dogs, two cats and, a phalanx of invisible, chirping birds. There were two sofas set out in this space, a cane swing hanging from a sheltering tree and plug points in the walls. Beyond the walls lay the rest of Aram Nagar, the favourite of the new film companies, a wild, rain-splashed expanse in the heart of Versova, sprouting with cottages in crazy lanes. Aram Nagar was not a real village, but something better, a seeming idyll to please the imagination.

I had not been sitting there long, when the dogs began to bark and then rushed all together to the entrance in a frenzy of excitement. Soon two people appeared, petting and pacifying the leaping creatures. Ahishor was with a girl I had not seen before. She was sturdily built, in shorts, a white scarf, and a colourful, patterned top. Her head was completely shaven.

They had not caught sight of me, when she turned back and shouted:

'They won't do anything you silly laddoo! Hurry up or I'll send them after you!'

There came a frantic cry from beyond, and the rotund figure of Mihir Malhotra staggered, as though pushed, into the gateway, where he stopped, paralysed, while the dogs broke away from the other two and sniffed him over thoroughly. I couldn't say he quite resembled a laddoo, though he was endearing enough in his fright. The girl snapped her fingers and spoke a series of words I didn't catch, and the dogs raced back to her, wild with love. I got up, smiling.

'Hi,' I waved, 'hi. I thought I'd just come here to do some reading about the film and stuff.'

'What a coincidence!' said Ahishor, looking more pleased than surprised. 'We were just talking about you.'

'Randeep Hooda!' cried Mihir delightedly (with reference to some fancied resemblance). His nasal tones already felt familiar to me. He was still standing near the entrance, but his spirits were evidently recovering. 'This is an honour!'

'Do you know Anamika?' asked Ahishor. 'Have you met?'

The bald girl had seated herself at the same place from where I had just risen, the better to manage the fawning dogs. I noticed that even the cats had come out of their aloof resting places to watch her from up close. She gave me a curious glance.

'I don't think so,' I said. 'Hi, I'm Dhruv.'

Shaking my hand briefly, she began to speak simultaneously.

'Dhruv, do excuse us. Ahishor and I have something personal to talk about.'

'Of course,' I said, flushing.

'Wait,' said Ahishor, 'this is Dhruv, the one I was talking about.'

'Oh...it's *you*!' In an instant, her expression altered. She had kajal-lined eyes and a nose ring, that seemed to magnify and make extraordinary the sternness of her stare. 'So you abandoned her too? And what was your excuse?'

'Is she bothering you?' Mihir called out eagerly. I turned briefly to see him fitting himself into the cane swing with great satisfaction. 'Don't be intimidated Dhruv! Just tell her who you are!'

'There was nothing for him to do,' said Ahishor. 'Besides, he was quite gone himself.' He turned to me quickly, by way of explanation. 'So apparently Maithili had some kind of blackout that night in Bandra. But that guy Samyak is a friend of Anamika—Anamika knows everyone, by the way—so he called her and she came and took Maithili home. She's angry that I wasn't there to look after her. Which I understand. But yeah, it's nothing to do with you.'

'She might have been raped,' said Anamika, still staring.

'She told me that asshole producer was hitting on her all night. And Samyak had almost passed out himself. If he had actually passed out, I'm sure she would have been raped.'

I was shaken, and beyond that I didn't know what to think or feel. One of the dogs began to nuzzle my leg and then, perhaps feeling that this happy occasion called for more, jumped up to lick my face. I noticed Anamika's gaze softening. She turned back to Ahishor.

'And why couldn't you at least take her calls the next day? I was with her! She tried at least three times!'

Now it was his face that hardened. 'I'll tell the guy to make us tea. Dhruv, do talk to Mihir. He's going to feel left out.'

I moved over quickly to the other side of the courtyard. Up on the swing, Mihir was flicking dust off his collar. He was dressed formally that afternoon, in a full-sleeved shirt, trousers, belt and shoes.

'She's a dear friend,' he said, 'I've known her since we were kids.'

Suddenly, he abandoned the swing and fell gracefully onto the sofa beside me. Crossing his trousered legs, he sat back and examined me with such a droll expression that I felt a smile pricking at my lips.

'But she's always been a bully. Don't take it to heart or you'll end up like me. All right?'

'All right,' I grinned.

'So listen, how is everything? Are you getting lots of work? Are you making money?' There was no raillery in his anxious voice, but I kept grinning.

'Nope,' I said, 'it's a bad scene here.'

'In what way?'

'It's just tough to get work. And if you get work, it's tough to get paid. People don't pay.'

'That's terrible! Who have you worked for who didn't pay you?'

'I mean, they pay,' I said, feeling a strange, reluctant loyalty towards Jatin, 'but not on time. And obviously not much.'

My report seemed to plunge Mihir into anguish. His eyebrows knotted and he chewed his lip.

'You need to find a way, Dhruv. Somebody with your talents. But I guess you don't want to do the crappy Bollywood stuff?'

'No... They wouldn't want someone like me either.'

'Don't say *that*. Forget them, it's for you to decide. But is acting your basic interest or is it directing or what?'

'Acting—yes, acting is my basic interest. But I'm doing other stuff too, assisting people, so that I can learn generally. Also, like I said, acting jobs are tough to come by.'

'Boss, don't get distracted. You need to focus.'

'I know. It's my birthday in November. So I've decided that after my birthday I'm really going to do auditions properly, come to Aram Nagar every day and all that.'

My strategy seemed not to encourage him. He looked at me with the same great concern.

'So right now, your parents are supporting you?'

'Yup.'

'Anyway, you're young... You're what, twenty what?'

'Twenty-one.'

'Wow! Just look at me. My dad's a C.A. He's nicely rich. And I actually *fought* with him to do journalism. Because my thing was, I don't want to just make money. I want to read, I want to write, be socially aware, you know, culturally significant...you understand? So I made sure I went to DU, hung out with the right people. Now I'm fucked because there is no money in print journalism. What? Yes sure, I went to Columbia, but so what? I came back to India right? So now I'm thinking I should get into the movie business. *Jo bhi hai* (whatever it is), there's got to be more money here than in magazines.'

'I guess,' I said, though I remained unsure how far his serious face was covering a laugh. 'I really liked your concept by the way, for the documentary I mean. I was reading about it myself today. God-men and how they operate.'

After a moment's silence, he said:

'I should have become a lawyer. They get money and prestige both. But listen, you really think people will like this film? I think it's an important subject and this is also a good time for documentaries, isn't it? They're even getting big screen releases, I believe.'

'I'm sure if Ahishor makes this, it will be released in theatres.'

'Hmm...I'm telling you, Dhruv, people like us need to step up our game. India is changing. If we want to stay relevant and make money, it's not enough to be fuddy-duddies sitting around on Gymkhana Club memberships. And I say this as someone who spent the first half of my youth completely enamoured of that type! But I find that a lot of people in Delhi are still like that—journalists, academics, policy types—they're still basically snobs. I guess it's different in Bollywood, *hunh*? Snobs can't even live the illusion of superiority, 'coz they're getting rogered so bad, *hunh*?'

'I think,' I wasn't quite sure what he was getting at, but I did have something to say, 'people here are just tired and confused. The film snobs, yeah they're clearly on the margins. But the sellouts also know that their lives are empty. I think the city itself is just too rushed and chaotic. It drives everybody mad.'

For some reason, my words brought a smile to his face. 'Interesting interesting interesting!' he said. 'Well, now, Dhruv, you don't worry. There are always opportunities for men of talent. You and I are going to find them!'

'I hope so!' I didn't know what had convinced him of my talent, but there was something uniquely flattering about Mihir's open interest in my career. I was feeling more confident than I had in a long time—which was thrilling in itself.

He was looking ruminatively over my shoulder.

'Anamika's parents are lovely people. You must meet them. So warm and erudite. And so grounded.'

'You know her a long time?' I said, 'Anamika?'

'Oh she's like my sister. She's just like my sister. We were neighbours in Delhi when we were kids. To be honest, her parents are closer to me than my own parents.'

His voice had turned deep with emotion, and I liked him for that too. Turning, I glanced at Ahishor and Anamika on the next sofa. Their heads were bent together in close conversation, an amusing contrast, when the one was wild-haired, the other bald. I thought of Maithili, freshly bald herself, and guessed vaguely that the two girls must have gone together to get their shaves. Then, a phrase, like a title, entered and stuck in my mind. 'Two Bald Women'. I looked again at Anamika. Her hand was squeezing and stroking the head of the furriest dog. I don't know why, but I felt a frisson of something unpleasant.

When the caretaker brought in tea, and everyone converged gladly, their talk became less guarded. Reaching for a cup, Anamika spoke so we could all hear.

'She's very ambitious. You know that, even if she pretends she doesn't care. She wants to make her mark.'

'All the more reason for her to work with me, right? There's no comparison between this film and her short film which I don't even think she's serious about. She's never once mentioned it before. And anyway, they're not substitutes. She can always do both. Surely she can see that!'

'Ahishor, it's not about rational decision-making all the time. What you have to do is stop taking her for granted. Ask her nicely! That's the signal she's sending you!'

He sat back cross-legged and took a sip of tea. He looked unnaturally calm, like a monk.

'Should I go to her house?'

'Not right now,' said Anamika. 'Right now, she's obviously mad at you. I'll speak to her first. When she's ready, then I'll tell you, and then you come right away!'

'Fine.'

'Uff! Such proud people I tell you!' Sighing and shaking her head, she turned to Mihir. 'Is this also a Bombay thing, you think? Because in Delhi we all love each other and we're not ashamed of it.'

'Dhruv here is from Delhi too.' Mihir slapped my back suddenly.

'I can tell,' she said, staring at me afresh. 'He has "Delhi boy" written on his forehead.'

'Doesn't he just? That's a compliment, Dhruv, don't look so scared. Her bark is worse than her bite. Ahishor! Did you know Dhruv here is already researching for our movie?'

Without warning, my heart began to pound. Ahishor looked up vaguely.

'He will assist me on this. *Tu karega na?*' (You'll do it, yes?)

'*Haan,*' I nodded, and I may have mumbled further without knowing it, for I was lightheaded at once, soaring with euphoria.

I tried then to listen closely, while Ahishor said he was

meeting Ritesh Azad the following week, for a preliminary chat about funding and other things. Mihir reckoned he could raise enough money from 'folks in Delhi', even if Ritesh wasn't forthcoming, but Ahishor said they would need a distributor anyway, and that it wouldn't be a problem with Ritesh. The only problem would be if he got involved creatively.

But the important talk passed by me in a haze. What I remember clearly is Mihir saying, sometime later:

'Yes yes, that character at your house. Charles Dickens! The Dickens of Dehradun! What about him?'

'He's not a friend,' said Ahishor, frowning. 'He just happened to be there—it was my mistake. He has nothing to do with our work.'

'I only saw him that one time,' said Mihir thoughtfully. 'But he seemed...not truthful. Not someone you can rely on, if you know what I mean.'

'That's right,' said Ahishor. 'He's a bit deceptive.'

'This is the guy who was hitting on Maithili, right?' Anamika asked curiously.

'Yes, same guy. God knows how he knows her, or why she ever called him to Bandra. It was supposed to be just the two of us—like I was telling you.'

'Never mind now.' She put a hand on his arm.

* * *

That same evening, an hour before sunset, Sasha made his way to Malabar Hills. It was not by the back alleys and the hillside trail that he came to her house, but in a taxi, on the main roads. In his hand was a cloth bag with a book inside, but the guard at the foot of the apartment mistook it for home delivery and so led him (pressed kurta and all) directly to the service elevator. Sasha's manner must have been unusually deferential for such a mistake to have happened. But I cannot imagine it happening with anybody else.

He was let into the house from a side entrance, by the servants, and made to wait in a wood-panelled hallway, while they retreated to consult. Around the corner a staircase rose, twisting, like an exotic plant. Beyond it, he could see the living room, beautiful and spacious, and the glass-panelled doors of the terrace and the sky that suggested the sea. Presently, he was beckoned forth to the carpets, where an old man sat on an armchair, swaddled in a shawl.

'I'm a friend of Maithili's,' said Sasha. 'I came to give her a book.'

At length, her grandfather gestured for him to sit. It was not a cold evening, but a woollen sweater was visible beneath his shawl. His face showed lack of sleep, and his shoulders faintly rose and fell with every protracted breath.

'What is your name?'

'Sasha. My name is Sasha.'

'Sasha? That's a nice name. And where do you live?'

'I live in Versova, in Andheri.'

'Versova is far.'

'Yes, it is quite far.'

'Maithili's friends rarely come from that distance. She has some friends nearby, you see. But...'

Wordlessly, then, the old man held out a hand. Understanding somehow, Sasha removed the book from the bag. The man's eyes were curious as he set straight his spectacles and brought the title close. A smile of recognition spread over his face.

'Maithili is upstairs,' he said, handing back the volume. His speech was now loud and exact, as of one used to commanding.

'The first door nearest the top of the stairs.'

Sasha had not begun to climb, when he heard footsteps above his head, fast and firm, coming clattering down towards him. He waited at the bottom of the staircase, his heart aflutter.

A girl he had never seen appeared at the turn of the spiral. She was square-built and bald-headed.

'Who is it?' cried Anamika.

'My name is Sasha. I'm a friend of Maithili's.'

The girl stared from the steps. 'Is she expecting you?'

'No.'

'Then I don't understand. Why didn't you call first?'

'I tried calling her a number of times this week, but I got no answer. I was worried about her. I hope she's all right?'

'I've heard about you,' said Anamika. 'Maithili didn't take your calls. Can't you take a hint?'

His gaze flickered with the sharpness of pain, but returned to hold hers with renewed urgency.

'I hope she's all right.'

'If you were so worried about her, you shouldn't have left her alone in a strange house. Anyway...'

Sasha's face fell. 'I felt that I had no authority,' he said, in pained tones. 'She gave me no authority to look after her. But yes, yes, perhaps you're right, I should have stayed.' He looked up, inflamed with emotion. 'Was she all right?'

The girl cast a glance over the bannister, at the armchair where the old man sat in brooding silence. She took a further half-step towards Sasha.

'How can you just show up like this? Don't you have any manners?'

'I told you, I tried calling first. I was worried, so I came.'

'This is stalkerish behaviour, do you know that? Maithili

barely knows you. *This* is why she's not well! She's not well because of Indian men like you!'

'I want to speak to her personally.'

'You can't.'

Suddenly his eyes flashed.

'You have no authority to tell me that.'

'If you try coming upstairs, I'm going to call the cops. I mean it.'

Sasha noticed, from the corner of his eye, Maithili's grandfather turning his head. The old man's face was pinched and troubled. His mouth was drooping with strange, affecting sadness, though he neither moved nor tried to speak.

As though an invisible force holding it buoyant had suddenly withdrawn, Sasha's body went limp.

'It's all right,' he said faintly. 'Can you give her this book please?'

'You can leave it on that table. Yes, that table.'

Swivelling, Sasha spied the side table by the wall nearest the stairs. He put the book down. Anamika stayed watching from her vantage point. He moved robotically in the wrong direction.

'It's the other way,' she directed him. Sasha did not look at her again, though he threw a last glance towards the living room. Old Purushottam Krishna's eyes were closed. He had fallen into a fitful sleep. His chin dug into his shawl.

XII

Delhi–Mumbai

I was home for a fortnight and a week. I lay about in large rooms under whirring fans. I strolled the lanes of our government colony in Central Delhi, and played games of football on the greens between the bungalows. I ate well, and often, indoors, and just down the road at rich and homely Khan Market. There, I met my boys from college and my girls from school, and sometimes their husbands too, while I felt sliding over me Delhi's tight embrace, the safeness and the warmth, the whisper in my ear that there was no reason to leave. There may be tension on the streets, violence brewing easily in the close air, but none of that would penetrate the shielding walls of home and restaurant and car.

Nor were the lucky ones turning a blind eye. Everything was being worked on, everything talked about, in government, in business, in media. There were new faces in the corridors of power, but they were familiar after all. Things were settling down. Worries were proving unwarranted, demons dissolving like harmless dreams. Slowly and steadily, the country was being set right. Life was going to get better everywhere in India—and here in Delhi, it was already the best of anywhere in India.

When it came time to leave, I was full of mixed emotions. Carrying me through my anxiety was the one assurance, that I had a meeting with Ahishor the day after I arrived. I was glad and grateful also that Mihir would be there; Mihir, a knowing Delhi journalist, had come purposefully to link the two worlds. It excited me suddenly that I had manoeuvered myself to the site of such a synergy. This was no ordinary Bombay project, no grubby moneymaker, no desperate venting of frustrated energies, but something new and elevated and important.

I had a lower berth on the train that evening. As long as there was light outside, I sat by the window and watched the landscape. Intermittently, I turned to the book I was carrying—short stories by Chekhov—a favourite of mine, but for some reason I was missing the inner calm necessary to read.

Even as I peered at the melancholy vistas of hut and meadow and sky, night claimed everything. Now the sight of my face in the window startled and (for some reason) depressed me. I stretched my legs out and closed my eyes. Dinner was an hour away, I had heard someone say.

Suddenly, I felt an audacious weight shoving aside my feet, and someone's satisfied sigh as he sat where I was rightfully sleeping. I jerked my head up and found myself glaring into the laughing face of Bharat Mishra. There was a moment's pause, during which competing confusions paralysed me. Then, rejecting the alternatives, I filled with indignation.

'What man!' I cried. 'What the fuck are you doing?'

'Aren't you going to say "hello"?'

'I was trying to sleep! And you...! What're you doing here anyway?'

'Hahaha! I am travelling to Paris.'

I sat up reluctantly, while he leaned back, pushing away

my blankets, as though they were not quite clean.

'I saw you at the platform,' he said. 'I was waving too, but you didn't notice. *Abhi toilet se aa raha tha*, suddenly *tu dikh gaya*. (I was coming from the washroom just now when I came upon you suddenly.) A nice surprise! What, you were in Delhi for some work?'

'Why were you in Delhi?' I countered.

'Some work,' he smiled. '*Aur bataa* (Tell me more), what's been happening?'

'Nothing. You tell me,' I insisted. It was one of Bharat's irritating traits that he always pumped one for information, while revealing nothing concerning himself. He always did this with a great air of modesty and self-effacement.

Ignoring my query, his darting eyes alighted on the Chekhov. He picked it up at once, under my disapproving stare.

'Hmm, nice... But somehow I never got into Chekhov. I prefer Tolstoy.'

I said nothing, even when he looked up with a challenge in his eyes.

'Chekhov is too incomplete, I feel,' he continued, 'he doesn't say enough.'

'Maybe,' I said.

He was flipping the pages brutally. 'By the way, you should tie your luggage with a chain. It's not safe like this.'

'Why is it not safe?' I demanded. 'This is second-AC in the Rajdhani. I'm not going to tie my luggage up like I'm travelling in sleeper.'

'It's your wish,' said Bharat. 'There have been three robberies in the past one week on this train. They happen between Ratlam and Kota, between 12.30 and 3.30 at night. Don't you read the newspapers?'

'I haven't read anything about it,' I said, irritated and disconcerted.

'It's very easy to rob this train. The doors are always open even though they're not supposed to be. And because of the curtains in the compartment the thief can slip in and out without being noticed. Sleeper class or third-AC is actually safer... Lot of crime in North India,' he finished decisively.

'Well it's not just North India. There's crime everywhere—in East India, in South India.'

'*Haan*, but there is more crime in the north.'

He had put my book down on the far side of his body. I was involuntarily tilting my neck to get a glimpse of it, when he brought his feet up and swivelled, cross-legged, to face me squarely.

'You heard about Ruhi Khanna?'

'No. What about her?'

'Oh, I thought she was your good friend?'

I had met this woman, Ruhi Khanna, one time, through Malik, and then once again at an acting workshop at Prithvi Theatre. She was a 'struggling' actor, who lived by herself in a three-bedroom flat in Sewri, bought for her by her father, and she was too old for me. Beyond that, I knew very little about her. I had heard she had a bad temper.

'She's not,' I said.

'Why? Did something happen?'

'No, what do you mean? I just don't know her well, that's all.'

Bharat sank into a strange silence. I pulled at my blankets. It was cold in the compartment and oddly quiet, despite the preponderance of people all around. They were lying at various angles, self-absorbed, or perhaps they were simply tired, as we went speeding and rocking through the night.

'She had a thing with Pankaj Pande,' said Bharat gravely.
'What kind of thing?'
'You know.'
'Tell me properly,' I said, with the beginnings of a smile.
'Arre *nahi* yaar, *kaafi* serious *maamla hai*. (Oh, it was quite a serious matter.) Apparently, he tried to rape her.'
'What!'

Pankaj Pande was an elderly man, indeed, sage-like, with flowing white hair. He had been making movies for three decades, all (with two ignominious exceptions) outside of the mainstream, which made him an icon for our young independents—in name, at least. Jatin, however, truly worshipped Pankaj, he spoke of him as a kind of father figure, and because of the long hours I had spent listening to Jatin, it was in that light that I had come to see him too.

'They met at an acting workshop in Aram Nagar,' said Bharat, 'I think roles *ke chakkar main woh uske peeche pad gayi*, (I think she fell after him in order to get a few roles) messaging all the time, you know how she is—or you don't? *Khair*, the story is—her story is—he called her to his office late one evening. Then they sat on the sofa in his room—near the table—you know how his room is *na*? Yeah, so they were sitting on the sofa and chatting generally and then suddenly he told her he couldn't cast her in anything—but would she like to sleep with him? *Haan haan*, arre, he is like that, he is extremely blunt. She was shocked obviously and said no. But *woh nahi maana*. (He didn't agree.)'

'What did he do?'

'I mean, I don't know the details. But sexual assault, basically. Not rape, but serious.'

I was amazed; or more precisely, I made an expression of amazement.

'So then...did she go to the police? What's happening now? When did this happen anyway?'

'That's the thing. Apparently, this happened two months back. She was too upset to say anything. Even now she hasn't gone to the police, but she has told people privately, so the word has spread.'

'And what does Pankaj say?'

'He says whatever happened was consensual. He says she is lying, except about the fact that he told her he wouldn't cast her, but if she would sleep with him. He admits he said that—admit *kiya*, he is not ashamed of it. According to him, she was offended by his honesty, and now she is getting back at him because *Mumbai Mirror* did a story about the movie. *Woh padh ke usko yaad aaya ki* (Reading that she remembered that) she isn't a part of it.'

I tried briefly to gather my thoughts on the subject, to recall Pankaj Pande and Ruhi Khanna and assess their likely relations. Then a kind of tiredness overcame me.

'It's all fucked up,' I said, 'shit keeps happening in this town.'

I felt a certain shame as I spoke, that drowned quickly in a rising irritation. It surprised and annoyed me that Bharat Mishra was still looking so grave.

'So who told you?' I asked him.

'Ahishor.'

His face, dark, narrow, clean-shaven, was full of brooding. He was a few years older than me, but he seemed at that moment generations removed. I looked him over, in his checked shirt and trousers. (He was always dressed fastidiously—I had never seen him in a T-shirt). Suddenly, I was afraid he was going to ask me if I was doing any work with Ahishor. I wanted to share nothing.

There was a newspaper on the table ahead of me, which I picked up quickly.

'You spoke to him recently?'

I pretended I hadn't heard.

'I have to meet him about some work,' Bharat continued, 'I guess it will have to wait till he's back... By the way, have you been to his house in Mashobara? It's really nice. Mashobara itself is really beautiful... Mashobara. You don't know Mashobara? It's right next to Shimla.'

'He's gone somewhere?'

'Of course, that's what I'm saying. Didn't you know? Accha you have been in Delhi.'

'Where has he gone? I mean, why? Why has he gone?' I could hear suspicion and disbelief in my voice. My hand reached for my pocket, where my phone still held the enthusiastic (though dated) message from Ahishor that insisted on seeing me 'as soon as you get back from Delhi'.

Bharat grinned and adjusted his posture, resting his back and extending his legs onto the floor between the berths. '*Pata nahin* yaar. (I don't know.) He just wants a break maybe... But basically, it's about Maithili only.'

'What about Maithili?'

'She left *na*.'

'Left where?'

'India.'

When I continued to peer at him as though he was playing a series of tricks on me, he explained the whole story.

'In the middle, for a few days, Ahishor was shooting a short film. Nothing serious, it was actually meant to be a birthday present for Karim Azad. Maithili started coming for that. She came for the first few days, and she was very into it, they were talking a lot, laughing, brainstorming. Then, suddenly, one day she didn't come. Her phone kept ringing. Later we found out that she was going for rehearsals for a play instead. She had got selected for something—first-time director, his name is Navjot, you may not know him. Obviously Ahishor was furious. Anyway, we did our work without her. Then some days later, I happened to meet Navjot. And can you believe it? He said she had stopped coming for his rehearsals also! He was desperately looking to cast someone else!'

The train had halted, as far as I could tell, somewhere in the wilderness. Within the compartment, the cold and quiet continued.

Bharat's face was contorted in scorn. I had not seen him thus before; it was a threatening face.

'I always knew this about her,' he was saying. 'She is not a person you can rely on. Even earlier, when I used to talk to her, I felt her mind was somewhere else. And when she looks at you, even if we are just sitting like this, it's as though she is looking from very, very far away.'

'Yes,' I nodded suddenly, 'you're right about that.'

'This time she had some excuse at least. Her grandfather died.'

'Oh.'

'Heart attack. It came in the papers.'

'Was he someone famous?'

'Long back he was governor of West Bengal. But listen *na*... What did Maithili do after he died? She didn't even stay for the funeral! The rest of her family flew in from the States, and Maithili flew out to Greece.'

'Greece? Why Greece?'

'That I don't know,' said Bharat, with a gesture of irritation.

We were moving again. Presently, one of the train staff came by to hand out the dinner trays (vegetarian first, so I had to wait).

'Not for him, he has come from another seat,' I said without thinking, when the man glanced at my companion. Bharat gave me a peculiar smile but said nothing.

'Personally,' he continued, 'I'm happy she has disappeared. Ahishor was too obsessed with her. Except now he has disappeared himself.'

There was something almost maternal about the worry in his voice. But even as I watched, Bharat's downcast face darkened with ferocity.

'And that fellow has gone with him! What's his deal anyway, *tujhe pata hai* (do you know)?'

'Which fellow?'

'Mihir Malhotra. He's gone to Mashobara too. They are both there together, discussing God knows what. Do you know Mihir? Are they doing some work together?'

So there were some things Bharat didn't know. I felt myself seizing up, my hands moved back to the newspaper on my lap, and I shrugged and shook my head.

'I've only met him once,' I said.

'He claims to be a journalist,' said Bharat. 'But he's a fraud! I know for a fact that he never finished his Columbia degree. He was actually going to be expelled for plagiarism. Then he struck some deal with the college and managed to hush it up. But he never graduated. Still, somehow, he is friendly with all kinds of people. I mean very senior people. Vinod Paranjpe is his Facebook friend, they like each other's posts. He knows

Justice Raghavan of the Supreme Court. He is close to lots of people in NDTV. I don't know how he does it. He is dangerous.'

'I'm sure he's not dangerous,' I smiled.

'He is dangerous!' Bharat's eyes were wide with anger. 'Also he is extremely *matlabi* (calculating). Ahishor is not like that. Ahishor trusts people and doesn't use them!'

I noticed a few glances coming our way, passengers looking up from their dinners. I was getting hungry myself.

'Do you have net on your phone?' asked Bharat suddenly.

'Yes, why?'

'I'll show you something,' he said eagerly, 'I'll show you something on Facebook. About Mihir.'

He reached out a hand. I looked at it, and then at him. His face was lit with ugly enthusiasm. His mouth was hanging open, and I could see a row of yellowing teeth. Suddenly, I was repelled.

'No,' I said, 'I'm not interested in all this.'

At the same moment, my food arrived. I took the tray calmly and began to clear a space for it on the berth. I was aware of Bharat, lingering, swallowing his pride, as was his wont. He seemed to be thinking of what to say next.

'Accha Dhruv, I wanted to inform you, *mera ek dost hai* (I have a friend), he is doing casting for a Cadbury's ad. Audition is tomorrow, will you do it?'

'Let's see,' I said, 'message me the details if you have them.'

'Okay... Also, I was thinking, for myself, I'm thinking of trying out voice acting. Can you give me the number of the teacher you went to? Also if you can speak to her about me, it will be good.'

'I'll give you the number,' I said, without looking up, 'but I think her schedule is full already.'

Bharat swung to his feet viciously, and the dal spilled on my tray.

'Bye bye!' he said gleefully, '*Tere* chicken *mein baal hai*!' (There's hair in your chicken!)

When I glared at him, he guffawed and went his way. I looked down. I saw nothing in the chicken, but with the thought planted in my head, I had to throw it away.

Nor did I sleep well afterwards. My dreams were full of threatening stares and sudden bursts of violence. The one definite image I retained, on waking to the sunny fields outside Mumbai, was of Sasha, clad in black medieval armour, sweat trickling down his face, running towards me and shouting something that I couldn't understand.

Two

I

Mother and Daughter

Dear Ma,

I'm planning to restart my blog! My writing blog, I mean, not the art one. I suddenly have so many thoughts flooding my head, which, you know is amazing, because I haven't felt like that for years. Now I know you're waiting to hear about Mr D'Souza and the farm, but I'm going to make you wait. I'm going to tell you about my WHOLE WEEK first, because every bit of it was OUT OF THIS WORLD!

On Tuesday, the exhibition happened. Ohhhh I wish you could have been here! My Bellini sketch was on display and my self-portrait too. And I wore the red sari! Yes, I tied it myself! Everyone was suitably amazed. You would have been proud:-). And Laura and Sophie were looking so beautiful in their gowns. We were all loving each other all day long and telling each other how talented we are and the wine was flowing freely, I'll have you know;-).

You know what's really delightful? Maithili and the gang get along like houses on fire (or do I mean just ONE house on fire?). Before she came, that's the only thing I was anxious about. I wasn't worried about looking after her, because she's the easiest house guest you can imagine, completely hassle-free. She hardly even needs food—I think she runs on thin air! But I was afraid she would go into her shell and not make friends with my friends. (She can be slightly strange sometimes.) But that's not happened, thank goodness. Everybody's really taken to her, in fact it makes me jealous! And proud at the same time, you know?

After the exhibition, all the girls came over to my apartment for a cook-athon (we made pasta and hummus and jam tarts), and there was this one moment when I was standing by myself at the balcony, with the meadow behind me, watching them all just relaxing and mingling and chatting. I felt so...fulfilled. I've realized I'm a 'host' by disposition Ma, I'm like you. I'm happiest when I can bring lots of people together and create a happy time for all of them.

By the way, Maithili and I have finally settled our 'origin' story—i.e., the story of how we came to be friends. ('Family friends' doesn't cut it, you understand.) The story is I was passing through a desert in Rajasthan and I saw her veiled in the distance, like a mirage, only she turned out to be real. She was a queen in exile, and I was a wanderer, and we were both looking for an oasis.

Wednesday! Was the hike in the Pindus. They happen the first Wednesday of every month now. I've done this particular trail twice before and frankly I've been a little bored and tired on the last few treks. (I think I told you.) But this Wednesday I loved it all again, and even better, because I was showing it off to Maithili. It was a perfect day, sunny, with a nip in the air, a brilliant blue sky, and all of us tramping up and down in our sneakers, eating sandwiches and gazing over lush valleys. I realized it's true what they say, the same old experiences get rejuvenated when you share them with someone new. Later, Maithili, Zachary, Laura and I had dinner at Alikis—fried zucchini, calamari and saganaki.

Thursday (I wasn't kidding about telling you my whole week :-)), we went night-swimming on Thursday. At the little lagoon by the rocks. The whole thing was like a dream. The moon was bright and the light in the water was zigzagging like a bunch of beautiful snakes and the water was cold and fresh. I wanted to go skinny-dipping—but Maithili was shy. I don't know why, nobody could see us!

I felt something strange that night. I don't how to explain it. It was like—I was so happy that I was panicking! Everything was right there, perfect and wonderful—the cliff, the water, Maithili...and I already felt as though it was slipping away from me. I was already feeling nostalgic about it, even as I experienced it. I don't know how to explain it better...

Oh, by the way—there's a new cafe near the studio, called The Cat Cafe. You can pet cats as you sip coffee. It's really very sweet. I was thinking, wouldn't it be nice to start one in Delhi too? Maybe we can call it the Cat and Dog cafe? There are so many poor strays on the roads. Do you think it would work?

I've been getting anxious about the end of the semester... And that makes me guilty, because I feel I should be more excited about meeting everyone again—and plus there's Suki's wedding! Maithili's folks are so sweet too (though I get what you said about them being too 'simple'. Maithili says the same.)

It's just that in India, no matter how wonderful a time I'm having, I always have the sense that there's darkness behind me, and someone lurking in the dark, looking over my shoulder. I can't just run towards the horizon, like I can here, there's always something holding me back... How on earth did you and Papa manage all these years?

Anyway, I didn't mean to go all melancholic on you! Just promise me we'll all shift to the hills in a few years. Sophie and Lauren will come too, and Maithili. We'll set up a colony somewhere! I'm serious:-)

Wow, this email has gotten so long and I haven't even told you about the farmhouse yet! Well, Mr D'Souza was a total sweetheart. He was talking really fondly about you and Papa, and he said he wishes you visit him soon. You should! He's got a swimming pool, a tennis court and an orchard. At night there were fireflies in the trees. And he grows all his fruits and vegetables on his own property. (There are two v. cute boys who help him with that.) And he keeps geese too! M and I ate like pigs all weekend. (He also has a great library, it's 'our' kind—full of detective novels.)

Next week we're planning another trek, but this one's something new. Apparently there is a wildlife photographer-turned-hermit who lives somewhere in the woods near Mr D'Souza's farm. We're going to track him down and find out his story. Exciting, right? It was M's idea. She's very focused like this. She knows how to make one experience lead to another, which is uncanny because that's exactly what I used to struggle with. I was telling her this too. It's like I can gather together all the most beautiful flowers, that I can do, but then I don't really know how to string them together.

More soon! Love you long time!
xxxxxx
A.

* * *

My dearest Anamika,

We got a lovely note from Kenneth D'Souza about your visit. I've promised him we'll all go and visit him together, after your convocation.

In the meantime, my dear, could you rest a little please? I was exhausted just reading your email. I'm glad you're enjoying your last semester, but if you relax a little, you will enjoy it more, and perhaps these worries you mention won't come to you either. Trust one who is experienced in the art of enjoyment.

Mihir came home for lunch yesterday, with a friend. Can you guess who it was? Ahishor Frances, the bright young director. That was such a pleasure for Papa and me. Apparently they had just come down from Mashobara. Mihir was looking very healthy and happy. As for Ahishor, he really is a wonderfully talented young man, and extremely knowledgeable about all sorts of things. But I'm forgetting— Mihir says you got to know him quite well yourself, when you stayed back in Bombay—you never told me dear! I was so glad to meet another one of your generation with so much intelligence and energy.

The two of them are planning a very interesting project about God-men. When we were talking about it, I realized just how many people Papa and I know ourselves, who go to some Baba or the other. It really is rather wretched. Ahishor made the very good point that in India, it's God-men who constitute the real Fourth Estate. They're completely free of scrutiny too, even more than the media. That does need to change.

I am so happy for Mihir that he has found such company,

and also come up with something important and useful to work on. You remember what a state he was in after the Columbia episode? But even at the time, I told Papa, I was sure he was going to bounce back. He has had that irrepressible quality ever since he was a child.

Dearest, do give Maithili some good advice. I hope she is not simply abandoning her movie career. Tara Aunty sent me a link to a piece in The Times of India; it seems the movie that Maithili acted in is releasing in November. I'll send that piece to you too. She should really be in Bombay to make the most of all this—it's not everybody who gets to play the lead in a feature film! And you know, her parents were upset about the way she left. It's only natural, anyone would be. It's all very well to be unhappy about things, and of course she was close to her grandfather, but at a time like that one cannot think only of oneself. I know you will agree.

Now there is something important I want to tell you. About India. What you wrote reminded me of Naipaul and his 'area of darkness'. India is not like that any longer, even if it once was. And if your Papa and I could manage to have a great time in the India of the 80s and 90s, you really can do it now, dear. (Of course it's different if you get a job in Europe.) The secret is to learn contentment, in your own space. It's not a bad word, you know, it doesn't mean compromise. It just means that you don't let the burden of your surroundings drag you down so much. Then you can also work to improve your surroundings, bit by bit (it's a process)—but in the meantime you don't forget to enjoy what you have.

You can do this even with the right wing in power. I was doubtful some months ago, but now I can say, thankfully, that things are not absolutely dire!

The other important thing is to set up a home! That's the best way to organize your happiness-es, and enjoy your friends, and the people we know here and the help we have. You really don't have to go running from point to point. That's not sensible at all. I know you know this, that's why your email surprised me a little... But we'll chat properly in person when I'm there.

Lots and lots of love,
Ma

P.S. Of course we shall have a home in the hills, but it will be a second home, when we want a break from Delhi. What is this talk of 'colonies'? Really dear! Pls. call on Sunday. Your Mamma is a bit worried now.

II

Indignation

Sasha walked slowly towards the apartment tower, though it was too vast to register as such. The array of dark and lighted squares that loomed in all directions, suggested instead some piece of machinery, like a telephone switchboard, or an aircraft's control panel, made gigantic. He was sweating from the walk from the station and the hard ride in the local train. He was recovering his breath, also, from the rows of dingy and harshly lit restaurants that were filled with smoke and the smells of frying, and the heaps of garbage that lined the road right up to the gates of the 'Flora Eternis'. Besides, he was nervous, almost afraid, though he couldn't say why.

He had only a floor to climb, so he used the stairs. The door from the stairwell opened almost directly onto the door to her flat, with her name embossed upon it in golden calligraphy. When he pressed the bell, part of an intercom, he felt, by contrast, the total silence of his surroundings. It was as quiet as the corridors of a hotel.

'One minute,' enunciated a voice.

The very next moment, Ruhi Khanna pulled the door open. 'Did you get lost?'

'No,' said Sasha. He leaned unsteadily against a wall, unstrapping his sandals, 'I walked from the station.'

'You should have taken a taxi,' said Ruhi, turning away from his struggles. 'Well, sit anywhere. I've been waiting for you.'

He moved from the passage to the living room, and found her seated already on a sofa-bed, with huge green cushions piled at her back.

'Sit there,' she pointed.

It was hot in the room. A strange, stale smell hung in the air, and Sasha breathed with difficulty. The ceiling fan was twirling slowly. He glanced at it from the chair she had indicated.

'This is for you,' said Ruhi, sweeping her hand towards a row of small, square, brightly coloured trays on the coffee table, each filled with nuts and namkeens.

'Thanks. It looks very pretty actually.'

'I'll show you the rest of the house sometime, but I'm too tired right now. It's a beautiful house. Everybody who comes here is amazed.'

The walls of the living room were bare and whitewashed, and the floor empty of furniture, save for the one section where sofas and cushions proliferated in tumultuous colours. Through an open door, Sasha spied another bleak and empty room, with a lone wooden cupboard.

'Can we increase the fan speed?' he asked. 'It's a bit hot.'

'Do it if you want. The switch is behind you.'

Presently, he sat again, under a whirring fan. 'So how are you?' said Sasha quietly.

She was silent for several seconds. Her mouth drooped and a terrible expression passed over her face.

Ruhi was thirty-three, dusky and petite, with a high forehead, straight black hair, and dark, sunken eyes. From the few times

I had met her myself, I considered her a well-spoken, clearly intelligent and more or less 'nice' person. Yet I too remembered sudden instances when she gazed with mystifying hatred at the person she beheld. I didn't then have the words to describe what had disturbed me.

'I'll tell you, but I have to tell you the whole thing, or you won't understand. So just listen to the whole thing.'

'Okay,' said Sasha.

'For the last three months I have had nothing to do. I am tired of going for auditions where nobody ever gets back. Then there was a phase in the middle when I was really supporting Imran Khambatta's theatre group. I went to their show twice, and both times I met them all backstage. I tweeted constantly about their play because they asked me to spread the word. And I know for a fact that I got at least three new people to watch it—people who would not have watched it, but for my recommendation. But despite that, when I asked when they were beginning casting for the next play, the Mirza Ghalib one, I didn't even get a response. And then Imran unfollowed me on Twitter... Why are you smiling? Do you think it's funny?'

'No,' said Sasha, 'it's not funny. What they did is wrong. But it's also quite normal, isn't it? People do take help from other people and then avoid them. Because they want to avoid the awkwardness of feeling obligated. You mustn't take it so much to heart.'

'I never do such things myself,' said Ruhi. 'So no, I don't understand it at all. Anyway. That happened last month. Then I was out travelling for a week in Karnataka, just recuperating from everything. When I came back, a friend from Delhi was in town, a photographer friend of mine, who's also gay. He wanted to go to Leopold's, so I took him there, and while we were drinking I was telling him this story—what happened with Imran. Suddenly he began to lecture me! Just when I needed support, you understand!'

Already, there were angry tears welling in her eyes.

'He implied that it was my fault! I was shocked. How is it my fault when I am betrayed? Then when he kept talking I began to understand what he was *actually* talking about. He said that he himself had suggested my name to one of his friends in Bombay who is making a movie. And that friend of his told him—No, nobody can work with her, she is "too intimidating".'

There was a catch entering her voice. Her face was rigid with hurt and incredulity. Sasha took his time gathering together a handful of namkeen.

'You wanted to talk about Pankaj Pande,' he said gently.

'I told you I have to tell you the *whole* story! Don't interrupt me please! It stresses me out!'

'All right, I'm sorry.'

'How can someone call me intimidating? I am polite and friendly and always punctual wherever I go! Just because I have a personality doesn't make me intimidating! And yes, I do have a degree from LSE, I have worked for two years at MIT, I didn't just jump to Bombay after school to start struggling mindlessly. I'm sorry, but most actors here can't even write a grammatically correct email!'

'Yes,' Sasha nodded. 'That must be part of it.'

'They like to work with people who don't have any confidence, intellectually, whom they can easily dominate, people like Malik! Or people whom they went to college with, or whose parents are from the industry.'

'You know Malik?' said Sasha, with interest.

'Yes, yes, but don't interrupt. So after that conversation,

I was sitting at home all day long, wracking my brain. At night I couldn't sleep. Because this friend of my friend—he doesn't know me personally, you understand? That means someone *else* has told him about me, you understand? *Who* could that be? This guy is in Bollywood proper, so it must be someone who moves in those circles. But I've never worked with anyone like that! I just couldn't make sense of it! I still can't. The only person I can think of, whom it might be, is Karim Azad.'

'How come Karim Azad?' asked Sasha.

'Well, in July I did a scriptwriting workshop with the British Council, which was mentored by him. We had a fight. And it was so strange because initially I was Karim's favourite person in class, he was constantly praising me and giving me attention over everybody else. Then suddenly things switched.'

'How?'

'Wait, wait!' said Ruhi impatiently. 'I'm telling you.'

She glowered at Sasha while he finished swallowing another mouthful of peanuts.

'It was a two-stage workshop,' said Ruhi. 'First, we came up with ideas for short films, then we went away and wrote our drafts, and then we came back and got a critique from Karim. He *loved* my idea! But during the feedback portion, he was extremely cutting and rude. In my story there was a maid who murders her employer, and according to Karim "the servant did it"—that was how he described it—is a classist plot point. I thought that was absurd!'

'Yes, it's more classist to imagine that a maid cannot murder her employer,' said Sasha.

'*Hai na*? (Isnt' it?) So we argued about it, but then after that, he was taking every opportunity to put me down in front of the whole class. Then, finally, we were supposed to be divided into two groups, one group's scripts would be taken forward for production and the other group would get the option to redo the workshop. Earlier on, Karim had *already* assured me I would be in the first group! But still he put me in the second group... Do you understand? Are you listening?'

'Yes,' said Sasha.

He had turned his gaze to the window. The roiling mess of Sewri lay shrouded in darkness.

'Karim doesn't like being argued with, I guess. But listen, don't get so bothered. It's just a worksho…'

'Somebody is spreading the word that I'm "intimidating" and preventing me from getting any work in this city! How can I not be bothered!'

'You're almost crying, Ruhi... Is this not too much of a reaction?'

'Stop!' she cried. 'I didn't call you here to be negative! Have you come here just to criticize me?'

'No,' said Sasha, 'but I also hope you didn't call me just to be rude to me.'

For a moment he glanced narrowly at her. Then, confronted with her look of confusion, his frown vanished quickly.

'I called you because you're someone I can talk to about myself,' said Ruhi, 'and I *don't* have to think about your feelings while I talk. I don't know why, but that's how I feel towards you. Maybe it's because I don't respect you.'

'You don't respect me?'

'I don't know! And I don't want to talk about it, all right? Now are you listening to me or not?

After a moment, a grimace passed over Sasha's face, and turned it strangely bashful.

'Yes I'm listening,' he said, 'I'm sorry for interrupting.'

'It's all right,' said Ruhi. 'I told you all this so that you understand the state of mind I was in, when I went to Pankaj's office. But just remind me—what did I say to you on the phone? About him?'

'You said he was the one who'd been messaging you, not constantly, but every now and then. You said he wasn't flirting outright, but would give you compliments sometimes. And also say things like "I'm very stressed, I need someone to help me calm down", things like that.'

'Yes,' she nodded, 'he was being very self-deprecating, you understand? I felt sorry for him, that was all.'

Sasha sat back on the plush cover, making himself still and quiet.

'We were having long chats on WhatsApp. He was telling me about the trouble he was having with his Bandra producer, how hard it was to survive here, making the kind of movies he does. He talked about his ex-wife too, a few times. My point is, *he* was sharing his personal life with *me*. I was not. I was just being a friend and a good listener. You understand?'

'Yes,' said Sasha.

'And also, I didn't want to be rude to him, because he's an important contact, professionally.'

'Of course,' said Sasha, 'you were obliged to be polite. It was wrong of him to put you in that position.'

'I guess so. I mean, I'm happy to be somebody's friend... But listen! Then he called me to his office, so naturally I presumed it was about a role. He knew that I knew he was casting for *Shahjahanabad*. So why else would he call me to his *office*? Yes, I did think about the time, because he only texted me at 9.30, but then I know his office works late, sometimes they work all night. Anyway, when I got there, I realized there was nobody else around, but I was already there by then, you understand? So I went into his room, and then he started talking... What did he start talking about?—oh yes, the TV was on, he was watching TV... So he said to me, come here and see this. That's why we both ended up sitting on the same sofa... It was CNN, they were doing a bulletin on American air strikes on ISIS. Then Pankaj started talking about ISIS and how extremism is getting more and more popular these days, as opposed to moderate voices. I said, yes, I agree with that. And then suddenly, without any indication or warning, he just leaned in and kissed me! I immediately pushed him away and he started to say how I was the only person who understood him. He really began to beg and plead. He said he loved me truly, he wanted to spend his whole life with me—he said that too! I said "no" very clearly. Then he said, "okay, okay", he backed off, and started talking about ISIS again. And then suddenly, he went in for another kiss! Again I said no, and again he became whiny and apologetic. He kept saying "I'm sorry". But then again he would try to kiss me! I was amazed, because there was no connection between what he was saying and what he was doing! I couldn't make sense of it at all! And all this while, the TV was still playing!'

Sasha breathed deeply.

'He did it to confuse you,' he said, in a voice that was thickening.

'I don't know, maybe. And this went on and on!'

'You didn't leave?'

Ruhi hesitated. 'No, I didn't leave, because I kept thinking he was going to stop. I just kept my mouth closed. I remember, when he started to...hold me, I remember thinking, I must be a very strange person to be letting this happen... That's when I told him, I am not going to sleep with you for a role. His answer to that was, "I don't want to give you a role, I just want to sleep with you..." When he said that, I was shocked. I should have got up and left then. But I wasn't in a proper mental state. And that's because of all this stress I've been going through. You understand?'

Her eyes were unusually dry and her voice, quite clear. It was Sasha who was blinking in a tide of emotion.

'So did you sleep with him?' he asked, with an effort.

'There was no intercourse,' said Ruhi carefully, 'but there was a lot of sexual activity. We were there till about one o'clock, I think. Then he dropped me home in his car.'

'He dropped you?'

'Yes, I insisted on that.'

They were both silent, while her eyes bored into him meaningfully. Sasha's own gaze moved slowly from the table to the wall to the window.

'He behaved wretchedly,' he said, 'wretchedly, despicably.'

'*Now* do you understand why I am home on Twitter all day?' she cried with triumph. 'There is nothing *for* me outside, there is no reason for me to go out! I am getting no work here! Men here don't know how to behave! But I want Pankaj to pay for this.'

'He should...,' said Sasha quietly, 'he should pay for it.'

'I've told some people, just privately, like I'm telling you. But someone suggested to me that I should out him in public, on Twitter. He's very active on Twitter himself. I think it's an excellent idea.'

Sasha continued softly, 'I'm thinking of the police. You didn't consent, even if you stopped protesting. What he did is still criminal.'

She shook her head with irritation. She was sitting up straight on the edge of the sofa. The cushions lay scattered about her. 'I'm not going to the police. I'm not putting myself through that. Unless you mean your father can help? Can your father do something?... Why are you looking so surprised? You did say he's a lawyer.'

'Yes,' said Sasha, frowning hard, 'or he was. But—I am not on good terms with my father.'

A drumming had started up from somewhere in the night. A muffled but still rasping beat penetrated through the room's closed windows. Sasha cocked his head, as though to listen, but he was not really listening.

'Don't spread this on Twitter,' he said suddenly.

'Why not?' demanded Ruhi.

'Because you can't truly express what happened there, you can only light a match. Then, people who don't know enough about it will start to take sides. Even the sympathy and support you get, it won't have any real foundation. The whole thing will spiral out of your hands.'

'I want it off my hands,' said Ruhi. 'I want to have him punished.'

'But that won't happen in the right way, even if it happens at all. When you whip up a frenzy, it hurts you, it makes you into a straw figure that gets blown this way and that. It will all be ugly and false, Ruhi.'

She stared at him, locks of hair falling over her temples, her coal-black eyes filling with fresh tears. Her mouth was moving with soundless sobs, that climbed continually up her throat. All the while she was shaking her head—significantly, deliberately.

Sasha felt a hot flush crawling over him. He wanted to continue speaking, with renewed sympathy, but there was a savagery in her gaze that haunted him.

'Have you spoken to Pankaj Pande yourself?' he managed to say. 'Or if speaking is difficult, you could write to him. You must give him a piece of your mind! Why don't you do that? Tell him personally how wretchedly he behaved. If you say it to him, he will feel it! And I promise you, you yourself will feel much, much better. When you confront somebody like this, it's a very powerful thing to do...'

She seemed to have grown still and composed, but Sasha was not comforted, because her gaze remained fastened on him, painting him over manically in dark and terrible hues. After a while, he got up with a jerk.

'I'll get some water from the kitchen,' he said.

When he returned to the room, he found her on her feet, setting straight the cushions. It crossed his mind that the long, frilly dress that Ruhi was wearing was also white like a wedding dress.

'You should go now,' she said, with her back still to him.
'Yes, all right.'

He put the glass of water on the table.

'Listen,' he said softly, 'don't stay at home all the time, okay. If you shut down like this, it's not good, you know that.'

Ruhi turned and stood, palpitating with returning sobs, her cheeks already ravaged with tears. Sasha moved towards her, skirting the coffee table. He touched her arm. He found himself muttering that everything would be fine. She pressed closer to him, and he put his arm around her, stroking her shoulder gently. Then, suddenly awkward, he disengaged. She glared up at him, full of hatred and contempt.

'Just go!'

When he was at the door, she called out again.

'You haven't finished your water!'

'I'm fine,' said Sasha, poking his head around the wall. 'It's all right, I'm fine.'

By the time he was out in the night, the drummers were retreating. He walked to the roadside, and lingered in the hot stench for an empty auto. He had a sense of failure and foolishness for having left his home, and the work he was trying to begin, merely on the calling of someone who was barely even a friend. No doubt that was why she had said she didn't respect him.

But why (there rose up in him now, this odd anxiety) had it gladdened him to hear that?

III

A Walk Down J.P. Road

That time of the year is vivid in my memory. While Sasha hurried about the city on misbegotten-seeming errands, I stepped out of my apartment, one September night, into the gaudy cacophony of a Ganpati procession.

Throughout that week, trucks and tempos carrying idols, fitted with loudspeakers, blaring film songs, had passed through my locality, on their way to Versova beach. 'Passed', however, is an imprecision. They loitered lovingly throughout, whilst crowds of revellers danced and swayed on every side of them, and when they did not entirely block the traffic, they herded it into a tiny bottleneck that suffocated it for kilometres.

It was best, therefore, to be on foot, as I was. I picked my way past the Four Bungalows marketplace, where only notional divisions now existed between shops, pavement, and road, because the motorcyclists were on the pavement, the crowds were moving amongst the cars and buses and a frilly green pandal was operating from near the shops to well into the street. As I went by it, I looked quickly for the idol within. There, away on a throne, sat Ganesha, pink, plaster of Paris, sated and decorated, soon to be drowned, eternally smug.

It was the last of the *visarjan* (immersion) days and the frenzy was spiralling. There were trucks every few metres (so it seemed to me), young men, slick with sweat, jeering (for some reason) from their rooftops, and down below, people—armies—marching in both directions. At the bend in the road, beside the cafe where I had bumped into Ahishor on the day of Malik's film shoot, the usual songs ('Chaar Botal Vodka', 'Lungi Dance', and other such devotional numbers) were interrupted by an outburst of political sloganeering.

The drumming—a raucous, catatonic beat—ran throughout; it was the same thing they played at weddings and pujas and everywhere else, a sound which made my spirits sink with a strange despair.

For it was only so long that I could maintain my humour, or brush aside the continual physical and sensory assaults. Retreating into a roadside dairy, whose thick milky smells came buffeting me at once, I stopped and stared at the figures dancing in front of my eyes. It was astonishing to me how easily they danced, how uniform their smiles and their laughter was, how, from the glitter-spangled child chortling in the back of the tempo, with his feet dangling out, to the men in their untucked shirts and pants and the women in saris—everyone was simply 'enjoying' themselves. Even as I watched, my resentment grew. It was not just that they were enthused by the occasion, and I was not—I was always vicariously happy to see people dancing in nightclubs, though I did not dance, or by other people making fools of themselves on alcohol, supposing that I was sober—it was the way in which they were moved that troubled and alienated me. In all their whooping faces, I caught not a glimpse of irony. And that note was not merely absent, but savagely, defiantly absent.

Further down the road, I came across another stall; this was like a vortex in the crowd, attracting hordes. A long table had been set up on the pavement, right in front of an ice-cream parlour, which was still open for business, though impossible to access. (Behind the stall, beyond the shop-windows and on the other side of the counter within, I saw uniformed employees beholding impassively their total barricading.) At the table there moved about a number of women, handing out *vada pav*s, chana and something else I couldn't spot, for the throngs that queued and milled. It was free food.

Suddenly, I discovered the man who was shouting. He had been bothering me for almost my entire walk. His cry of '*garam garam vada pav aur thanda thanda paani*,' uttered with an inflection so lascivious as to suggest unthinkable pleasures, was growing maddening in my ears.

Now I saw him, mike in hand, standing by a pole hoisted with loudspeakers. He was massive and sweaty, in a bursting white shirt, with eyes made small by burgeoning fat. And again he lifted the mike to his mouth and repeated with oppressive energy the same, infuriating lure.

I stood aside and watched him, struggling to damn him with my scorn. How could a lowly *vada pav* and water be talked up so unashamedly? How could they fetch such crowds? The queue for the food was endless. People continually broke off the road to lengthen it. In my eyes the whole panorama was wretched and petty, debasing to everyone involved (even though I was aware my ill-temper itself was beginning to ring absurd).

Turning with an exclamation, I walked on, fast on my feet, though heavy-hearted. But some minutes later, when I could sight in the near distance the way to the beach, and a large Ganesha covered in golden threads, about to be driven down it, there suddenly stepped aside from the pedestrian-traffic the very person I was hurrying to see.

Ahishor was smiling, his long locks fell peacefully about gently creased cheeks, and he bowed before me, full of humour.

'*Adaab janaab*. On your way to conduct a *visarjan*?'

'Are you kidding?' I cried excitedly. 'I would blow this all to hell if I could!'

At once I remembered that his mother was Marathi, and he might be tremendously offended. My sudden horror must have showed, for he looked at me and chuckled.

'Said millions of frustrated Mumbaikars—under their breath! Come this way, we can't stand like this.'

Just then, I noticed he was not alone. Malik was staggering up behind him, in a faded red T-shirt and cargo shorts, his perspiring face full of animal vigour. Ahishor turned, dodging the other's heaving frame, and began to march purposefully. I followed along with Malik, a pace or two behind, while I wondered briefly why they were meeting. They were not friends, at any rate.

As for me, I was going to Ahishor on urgent business. For many weeks after my trip to Delhi, I had heard nothing from him. My messages went unanswered. I was told he was still in Shimla; later, I heard he was back in Mumbai, but not back in the office. I heard various things from various people. He was reading a great deal, busy with 'research', and meeting very few people. He was making short trips to Matheran and Karjat. He was shifting house from Bandra to Versova, to a new flat close to his mother's.

By and by, I stopped inquiring after him. When he finally did call, at eight o'clock one Saturday morning, I was, firstly, startled out of sleep and then completely unprepared for the enthusiasm and energy radiating down the line. With scarcely a nod to the intervening lull, Ahishor informed me that he was about to start shooting. We met the same afternoon. Soon, I was rushing down J.P. Road to Aram Nagar every evening.

A circle of grinning faces came bobbing into our path. Up ahead, I saw Ahishor darting towards the awning of a grocery store. Malik and I waited for the dancing men to pass.

'Good fun *na*?' said Malik suddenly. I stared at his slack-jawed grin.

'It's chaotic and meaningless,' I said.

'Ehehehe! I don't know.'

His whole body was quivering with nervous energy. By contrast, I felt myself growing very still.

'Are you guys coming from the office?' I asked politely (though our voices were raised above the nearby drumming).

'*Haan*? No no. I just had to talk to him—had to talk to Ahishor... This film festival thing *re*. We guys are trying to raise some money.'

'Okay, but did you meet at the office?' I continued pointlessly, as he plunged forward.

We joined Ahishor among the cartons of potatoes and onions, and stacks of chips, at the front of the shop. He was grinning as we approached, with his eyes travelling up and down Malik in particular.

'This is all very cinematic, right Malik? Malik is the ultimate man of cinema! He judges everything in terms of how dramatic a visual it is. Rat-infested, crumbling courtyard in Zohra Aghadi? Yes, okay! Let's live there! Relatively clean apartment building? N.G. [this was film editor's lingo, meaning "no good"] Only I wish you weren't so biased in favour of grunginess...and disorder. There are other kinds of beauty too.'

'I don't have money *re*!' cried Malik. 'That's why I live in Zohra Aghadi!'

'It's a vicious circle, my friend,' said Ahishor. His face had suddenly turned serious, 'It's a trap. First they force you to live in confusion and then they tell you to love it and celebrate it, so you're never going to leave it... Remember what we talked about today.'

As he spoke, he lifted an empty blue carton, turned it upside down, and sat right down, beneath the awning. Nobody in the shop seemed to notice or mind.

I noticed a change coming over Malik. His natural state, which was a great emanation of energy, like a porcupine shaking out its quills, was altering. He was withdrawing into himself. He fidgeted only for the purpose of extracting a cigarette from his pocket, while his eyes fitted out with a mean, cynical expression, the likes of which I had never seen on him before. I glanced at Ahishor, seated on his crate. He was gazing at Malik, with a slight smile, which broadened as Malik's phone rang and a gruff conversation began, though I couldn't catch the words.

'Anyway,' said Malik, turning to us after it was over, and taking another long drag, before dropping the burnt stub onto the pavement and stepping on it. 'I have to get back to writing now. So I shall take my leave of you fine gentlemen. And I hope this is an adequately *non-grungy*...farewell!'

Ahishor threw his head back and laughed. Malik too grinned in a conciliatory way, but as he passed me, I caught again the troubled note on his face. Then his heavy, rollicking gait mingled into the crowd's and presently he was lost from sight.

'It might have been,' Ahishor was saying thoughtfully, 'but for the business with the cigarette... Ahh Dhruv... But I am fond of Malik.'

'What were you both talking about?' I said.

'Funding the film festival. They want to start a "movement". Why are you standing? Come, sit.'

I joined him on a green carton, which he dragged over beside the blue. Surprisingly, as I squatted low to the ground, I felt just as though I had climbed to a vantage point, distant from the festivities blaring all around us.

'You must have heard,' Ahishor continued, in the same ruminative vein, 'the Mumbai film festival has lost its sponsors. It needs money this year, or it may not happen... So, Malik, Varun, et cetera, et cetera, are starting a crowd-funding campaign. He came to ask me if I'd put my name to it.'

Here, as I waited for him to continue, Ahishor started to frown. When I prompted him, he returned to the subject with a start, as though he had been thinking of something else in the meantime.

'What? Oh yes... I said "No". I told him "No, I wouldn't". He didn't like that at all. I said to him, that our job, as filmmakers, our job is to make the best films in the world; it's not to be the biggest film buffs in the world... If this city was actually a great centre of world cinema, the film festival wouldn't need to scrounge for support. But the truth is we make no world-class cinema at all. And if the people who should be making it, people like Malik, if instead they pour their energies into pretending they're part of some great movement...the festival gives us delusions of grandeur, you see? But when you are in a state of poverty, you cannot be living as though you are rich. Then all the more you remain poor.'

'What was all that about grunginess?'

He smiled. 'I'm afraid I gave Malik a piece of my mind. I told him that watching films from all over the world had actually made a fool of him. Malik and the others, I know they are mad about movies, but that's not a pleasant thing. It means they are completely overwhelmed, completely dominated by this endless stimulation of everything they keep torrenting. And it shows, Dhruv. Their own imaginations stop at gangster flicks, heist movies, small-town exotica, inner city violence...am I right? Their movies are full of these bits-and-pieces characters who are desperately striving to get ahead in the world, which is fine, but the characters themselves are never taken seriously, they are never given any dignity. Everyone's just revelling in lives of parody. Exactly like the makers themselves! It's a terrible condition to be in. I mean, you worked with that guy—Sushant—so you know what I'm talking about... Bharat also... Bharat also has suffered. But Bharat is clever, he knows it...'

His voice trailed off into thought.

'You told Malik all this?' I said.

'Someone has to,' Ahishor shrugged. 'It's not his fault, you see, because this...this disordering of a person's mind, it's a very systematic, continuous process, here in India.'

I felt a surge of inspiration. For some time now 'Sheila ki Jawani' had been ringing out across the road.

'Yeah, like this!' I said, '"Sheila ki Jawani" at a Ganpati procession! If that's not a disorder, then what is!'

He nodded. 'But understand how it comes about... It's actually mandated. In a sense it's quite proper. Ganpati is your superhero of the day. Film music is the super-music of your time. So the two must go together, you see. Who cares that the meanings don't match?... It's a simple matter of marrying within one's caste.'

Unlike mine, Ahishor's voice was unexcited, even exhausted, and though he spoke with conviction, it seemed to me again that he was distracted all the while. There were odd pauses and frowns that interrupted his speech. Then I thought of all our recent meetings; and it struck me that these spells of abstraction had become quite pervasive in conversations with Ahishor.

'So yes...,' he was going on, 'it's the same thinking at work... this obsession with status...it's what coerces young Maliks and Sushants to acquire a proper English education...the right cultural trappings. Doesn't matter that Hindi may have been more natural to them...and that their education only ends up breaking up their personalities...hobbling their imaginations... Think about it. How many writers do you know personally in Bollywood who can't write well in any language?'

I thought for a moment. 'Many,' I agreed.

'So then they are suffering, are they not? In the mind. And the vast majority in the pocket too. It's only a few people who make a killing peddling broken-up wares. Ironically, they are the ones who don't care a hoot for cinema. They aren't even doing cinema, so it doesn't matter that they can't. You see?... But everyone who is sincere here, is suffering in every sense. And then when I see one of those people, who I really am fond of, so eager to persist in suffering... Well, like I said, I gave him a piece of my mind... He drinks tap water, you know? Yes, Malik, in his pokey little flat, he drinks water from the tap! That tells you something about him.'

He got up with a grunt, sighing loudly, and, with an effort, injected his voice with energy. 'Come on, Dhruv, let's have free sherbet!'

I thought at first he was joking. But though he was laughing, he was insistent. We navigated into the road and further down it, past the gates to the beach, where police people in khakhi were watching with interest a mid-sized Ganesha, teetering nonchalantly on the shoulders of a human swarm, and thence into another section of familiar cafes upstaged by makeshift stalls. Here both my amazement and my disgust returned afresh. The street was covered, every other inch, with white plastic cups. Even as I gaped, two young men strode forward, tossing off their drinks before tossing their glasses into the sea of litter. I threw outraged looks at them, which they never noticed. Ahishor caught my eye, with an odd, private smile.

'You see,' he said, 'someone else will clean it up....'

Then his smile faded and he said, thoughtfully. 'Can't really blame Maithili for wanting to escape all this, can you?... Although...,' he lapsed into silence.

I pretended he hadn't spoken. For chiefly selfish reasons, I had been deeply glad that he had not mentioned her name all these days. For who could ever tell in such affairs? I was afraid that some anxiety over Maithili might occasion in him another unexplainable retreat to the hills, and obstruct our (my) work. So now I concentrated on developing my ire at the abounding mess. I spoke aloud more imprecations.

'Yes, but it's different when you get involved,' said Ahishor suddenly. Then wordlessly, he pushed forward to the sherbet stall.

There, in the fast-moving queue, I was handed a cup of surprisingly cold liquid, and (thrust awkwardly into my palm by a wide eyed young girl in a frock, who was being encouraged by her mother) a lukewarm bread pakora. We were ejected, a whole body of people, all of us clutching our goodies.

'Haha!' said Ahishor, 'And that was me, once upon a time.'

He was staring at one of the tempos. A group of children were clapping excitedly in the open back. Their Ganesha was gone, but they seemed not to care.

'My mother was never keen on *visarjan*s, but there was an

uncle of hers—he used to take me. I used to have a blast. All the way through all the traffic. Enjoyed myself thoroughly.'

I had taken a bite of the pakora and a sip or two of the sherbet. As we walked on, a new sensation came stealing over me. It was something thick and warm, like the night itself. My mood was changing. I was strangely calm, suddenly no longer bothered when we passed another knot of dancers, another jaunty film song. In fact, it surprised me that Ahishor was still discussing them.

'But it's one thing for children...I think children love chaos, because they have an implicit belief in order. So for them, the existence of chaos only proves the largess of order, you see? And that's quite sweet... But these [he flung a hand about] these are not children. They're not counting on their parents to have everything under control...Then what kind of...'

All of a sudden, he stopped walking. But I had moved on a few paces before I noticed. Swivelling, I saw him, stock-still, in the midst of currents of people and garish lights and sounds, his thick-set, floppy-clothed figure, his bearded face full of the pain of concentration.

I took a step towards him.

'Tomorrow,' he was saying, 'all these people will go back to their lives, just as if a switch had been pressed. Like automatons. Have you noticed, Dhruv, how they dance like automatons?'

'It's not bad dancing.'

'No no, it's wild. But that's not the point. You can programme that.'

'Well, I guess there is something odd about it. Listen, we haven't talked about the shoot yet.'

'Haven't we?' he said, smiling. 'Who do you think presses the switches?'

His lips and his eyes were twitching, as though his thoughts were actually crawling up and down his face, beneath his skin. I stood about, with my confusion and discomfort plain. 'I'm sorry,' said Ahishor suddenly, and I felt, as he said that, a surprising spurt of relief. 'Enough of this...We'll talk about tomorrow...'

But it was only when we had finished the walk to the office that either of us spoke again.

IV

Mahayogi Navy Baba

I am now at that episode which deserves the title 'fateful'. Yet however much I may now wish that it had never happened, it was, and remains, one of the most memorable afternoons of my life.

We did not have far to travel. For our first interview, we had found living amongst us, only a few kilometres from both our houses, just beyond the bazaar of Yari Road, an individual who proclaimed a connection with higher powers. Ahishor had got the name from our producer, Ritesh Azad, who in turn had heard of this man because his devotees, apparently, included a growing number of figures on the fringes of the film industry. So we were starting close to home, in more ways than one.

At the appointed time, in the midday sun, I retraced the previous day's journey to the threshold of Aram Nagar. Ahishor was there already, drinking masala tea bought from a man with a kettle and a string of plastic cups, who came every morning to that dust bowl. I shook my head quickly when he looked at me. It was too hot for chai.

Presently, from within the village, there approached a hatchback, its tyres marking noisy tracks in the gravel and clouds of dust lifting in its wake. The car halted beside us, and I got in the back, with a nod and a smile at the sullen figure in the driver's seat. That was Bharat Mishra.

My disappointment at Bharat's involvement (which had come about in an unquestioned, matter-of-fact way) had been lessened by his own seeming distaste for the project. He had said very little, but from various dark looks and mutterings, it was plain he thought it a bad idea, the wrong subject for Ahishor's all-important second film. I was sure this had something to do with his dislike of Mihir, who had in the meantime departed for Delhi—though Ahishor assured us that he was 'building us up from there'. I had assumed, also, that Bharat considered Babas and Swamis so generally fraudulent as not to be worth a serious inquiry. In this, however, I was mistaken.

That day, as we slid onto the delightfully empty street, Bharat was frowning continually. By contrast, I was full of enthusiasm. When I had finished taking stock, once again, of the equipment beside me—camera, tripod, memory card, battery—fully charged—I sat back and stared at the sights of Versova. Save for the heat (which vanished in our AC), it was a beautiful day. A cloudless blue sky was soaring above the apartment buildings; between them lay glittering the open sea. There were still portions of the previous day's litter on the road, but I was glad to see so much of it cleared already, the stalls taken down, the revellers returned to the places they had sprung from. Through the windows of the coffee shops, I spied Versova's faithful—bearded young men, elegant women, punching away at their laptops. We passed a shopworn young beauty in a thin cotton dress, waving down an auto, her gaze stripped for the battles of the day. Two men in cargo shorts were shaking hands warmly, as they balanced on the narrow divider between the lanes, and outside an ATM I saw a lone, dreamy figure, staring into space.

Meanwhile, all the way down the path, scattered leaves were stirring in the sea breeze.

Something suddenly caught in my throat. I felt terribly happy. A moment later, I noticed Bharat in the rear-view mirror, trying to catch my eye.

'Wasn't that your friend?'

'What?' I said, 'Which friend?...Where?'

But his gaze had turned away in silence. After a while, he looked to his left.

'So, how exactly will it work, bhai? Do I have to translate what he says, or no?'

'I don't think you'll need to,' said Ahishor. 'The guy I spoke to said he speaks Hindi well and a little bit of English too. Just that he's most fluent in Bhojpuri. So in case he slips into that, and if he's saying something complicated, then... He's from your state, Bharat.'

Bharat grimaced, and the ugly look stayed on his face. It was there still as he turned the wheel at the broad turning towards Yari Road. A new gymnasium had come up at this bend.

'So this will work well at film festivals abroad, *hai na*?'

Ahishor shrugged. 'It's most relevant for a domestic audience.'

'But that must be his thinking, *hai na*?'

'Whose thinking?'

'Arre, who else? Mihir Baba.' Bharat laughed unpleasantly.

To my surprise, Ahishor merely chuckled and then yawned and stretched luxuriously in his seat. The sun was falling full on his contented face.

Then we swerved at the next crossing, leaving behind the supermarket and the tree-lined lane that led, by esoteric twists and turns, back to Ahishor's office. As I beheld the familiar vista of Yari Road, my heart performed a little leap.

For six months I had lived on this street, on the fourth and top floor of an old and derelict apartment block where the ceiling crumbled during the monsoons and rats made nests in neglected window ACs. That had been my first home in the city, and it had imprinted on my mind a kind of awe for this streetscape, more than any other that I had known, or was to know. Like ranged gauntlets, there ran past my gaze the barber's shop, the butcher's shop, the mattress shop, the fruit-sellers, the chemist's shop, the pani puri and vegetable stalls, beside which I had cowered one torrential afternoon, while the vendor beneath his makeshift roof laughed at my wind-wrecked umbrella. Here were ugly buildings, with their varied hoards of beautiful girls, Nigerian immigrants, clerical workers, cantankerous old men. There, cheek by jowl on the cobbled stretch, were the mandir and the masjid, Yari Road's most famous landmark. Yari Road! Where the necessities of material and spiritual life were always on display, easily had, but impossible, by the same token, to rise above.

All this I beheld, as I had many times before, but with a subtle darkening of the usual cocktail of emotions. For there was playing on my mind the presence of the mystic, overhanging my old home. Rather, in spite of myself, I felt a gathering excitement. Was my poor, self-absorbed street unaware of the larger powers that swirled above and beyond? Or was there, in its pitiless vitality, an occult purpose that I had simply never divined?

We dove deeper past mandir–masjid. The road narrowed and deteriorated. Gritty slush appeared (I wondered when last it had rained), and turnings into narrow galis, that went past paan shops and smoky food-shacks (focal points for pedestrians and loiterers) into bleak horizons, where, I knew, a mass of slums awaited. There were high-rises in the vicinity too, overlooking what clung to their foundations. But their lofty mien failed to convince. Up in the distance lay land's end, the Versova jetty, the homes of the fisherfolk, more slums, piles of colourful garbage, more dirt underfoot. But we did not have to travel that far.

By and by, Bharat stopped the car in a lane adjoining a series of non-descript, low and boxy apartments, with ugly iron grills imprisoning every window. A few hundred metres ahead of us was a seeming dead end in the form of a freshly whitewashed wall. Beside us, hanging crookedly off a stout tree trunk, was a signboard for 'Best Chinese Cuisine.' The painted arrow was exhorting the viewing public towards the heavens, more or less. As had been discussed, Ahishor made a phone call at this point. Then we rolled down the windows and waited.

It was peaceful where we were. The hot sun came diminished through the trees, falling dully on parked cars. The building compounds seemed filled with silence. Even the usual jangle of daytime sounds—vehicles running, honking, cawing crows, somewhere, an electric drill—were muted and distant; I had to strain my ears to pick them out. Only a handful of figures walked slowly towards the main road—thickly, through the viscous afternoon.

Therefore, the sight of a tall, thin, grinning figure, bounding towards us with unbridled enthusiasm, had all the incredible suddenness of an apparition. Even as I stared, the man's face was by Bharat's window.

'Welcome!' he shouted. I saw Bharat flinch and jerk his head away. Then, in what appeared almost an act of retaliation, he flung open the car door, causing the newcomer to leap backwards.

The face that greeted us, as we stood about the car, was still joyous. He was an extremely young man, handsome, with thick, tousled hair and eager eyes. The sleeves of his shirt were rolled up informally; he wore it tucked neatly into belted jeans, whereupon an unfortunate embroidery traced glittering curlicues.

'My name is Ali! I have come to take you to Swami-ji's place!' he announced proudly, in good English.

In the back of the car, I shifted the tripod to my lap to make room for our fourth. As we began to move down the lane ('right from the end,' Ali instructed), Ahishor asked him what he did, and how long he had known the Swami-ji. The reply was lengthy and breathless.

'I am originally from a village in Bijnor [said Ali]. I came to Mumbai after my 10th pass to join my elder brother. He has a chai stall in Ghatkopar. Yes, far from here! But I was not enjoying that work. I wanted to try something different. My brother said, no, I cannot. For my brother, the chai work is all right because he is a dropout. But I thought I can do other things. So then we had a fight. Not a big fight. But for a few days, I was living away from home. At first, I was just moving about the city. I didn't know what to do. I wanted to work in a proper restaurant but wherever I asked, there was no vacancy. At night I slept on the pavement. One day, I took the metro and came to Versova. When I came out of the station I saw a row of nice restaurants, all people happy and eating and drinking. I went inside the one which had the brightest colours and asked to meet the manager. You won't believe it, but that day itself one staff had left! He gave me a job! Right, I said right!'

I watched with amusement Bharat's furious expression, but he obeyed in silence. We turned into a short gravel path, where a rusting gate, three quarters of the way open, was set back from the lane. On the inside appeared a sprawling network of apartment blocks, short, ugly and featureless as the ones outside. Ali continued:

'But that man was not okay... He gave me kitchen work only, only cleaning. I told him, let me be a waiter, I speak good English also. Am I not speaking good English? [His speech lapsed frequently into Hindi, but the part that was English was, we assured him, excellent.] It's not that I mind such work. But it was difficult to do always and the payment was very less. And...there was some other problem also. So I left that job and went back to my brother. *Le jao*, there is no watchman. *Seedhe, seedhe...* (Take it in, there is no watchman. Straight, straight...) Still, you know, I was not happy. Then one night, a man came to our tea stall. He was a watchman himself, in a society in Ghatkopar. We started talking. I asked him what his job is like, he said it's very bad, very dull. Oh Sir, he had a very sad story. He is actually a chemistry honours, but on the train to Mumbai somebody stole all his papers, all his money... So he had to take up such a job. But it was he who told me about the Swami-ji. One morning he said, "I am going to see him today, do you want to come?" I was going to refuse, but I don't know why, I just said yes. I left the stall that day and came again to Versova.'

We were gliding down a cement driveway, between a wire fence (with wild scrubland beyond) and blocks of flats with washing in the windows. Soon these sights gave way to a large central courtyard, where a dusty garden with the obligatory broken swing was surrounded by more constructions, several covered in scaffolding. There were cars parked beside the garden. Ali told Bharat to stop alongside. But as we manoeuvred to a halt he began to speak with the greatest urgency and excitement, and we all stayed in our seats, in the fading air conditioning, until he was finished.

'After that you won't believe what happened! Swami-ji gave me *this*!... It looks just like a simple metal ring, but he put magic on it! That same day I understood. I was expecting *ki* my brother will thrash me when I return, because I had run away from the stall, but he just said "Come sit". Then he told me *ki* there is a job as receptionist in an office in Lokhandwala. Lawyer's office. One friend of his had told him. Since I am good with reading and writing, I can speak on the phone in English also, so why don't I take up the job? I couldn't believe my ears! I came running back to Swami-ji and fell at his feet! He was not surprised, of course, he only had done it!'

Looking into Ali's beaming, almost blushing face, I could not restrain a smile. Ahishor too was regarding him tenderly.

'Are you still working at the lawyer's office?'

'Yes!'

'So you're working. You haven't become a full-time devotee of your Swami-ji.'

The blush on Ali's face shifted and deepened.

'Actually, I thought about this...just leaving everything and taking up the spiritual path. But Swami-ji said I am not ready for it. He is right of course. Still there are too many distractions on my mind... Better I pay attention to them only! Also, later, I can serve Swami-ji better, if I work hard and make money now.'

'Did he tell you that?' said Ahishor.

'No he didn't say anything, myself I was thinking about it. Frankly speaking, I am a very normal person. I don't have these spiritual powers. Nothing like Swami-ji. Sir, he is very minded! The kind of powers he has! At the age of just three months he started to speak. He had read the scriptures by the time he was twelve. When he grew up he loved to travel, so he joined the navy, he became a captain in our navy. (That's why today a lot of people call him Navy Baba. But not me; to be frank, I find that name quite funny!) Then one day his ship was attacked by pirates. They were Africans.'

'Somalian pirates?' I wondered.

'Yes, yes. The ship was going to be kidnapped, there was no hope. The pirates were too close and they had too many weapons. Suddenly Swami-ji had a vision of his guru, Morya Baba, who lives in the Himalayas. Morya Baba told him not to worry. When he opened his eyes again, the pirates were gone! There was nothing there but sea! After that, when he came back to the shore, he resigned from the navy. He went to live in the forests for ten, twenty years, he was doing sadhana.'

'Was it ten years or twenty?' asked Ahishor innocently.

'Fifteen at least, Sir,' answered Ali cheerfully. 'From this he got all his siddhis, his spiritual powers. *Jaise*, even this ring he gave me, he simply waved his hand and created it out of thin air! He can do so many things. He can see into past lives, he can predict the future... He doesn't even breathe oxygen, like you and me.'

'Really?'

Ali broke out into a triumphant grin, as of one who has played his ace.

'Yes! That's why he is able to live underwater and underground also. He has done it many times! You don't know?'

We stepped out of the car, into the warm and prosaic afternoon that was filled suddenly with the promise of the improbable and fantastic. While Bharat and I gathered our things together, Ali, eager as a child, was already waiting for us to follow.

It was two flights up a gritty, gloomy stairwell, of a kind

I had climbed countless times in Versova. Down such bleak corridors, behind such heavy doors, emblazoned with religious symbols that varied with the landlords' persuasions, were so many rented homes like my own. Enter to discover piles of clothes, mattresses askew on the floor, gleaming MacBooks on crowded tabletops, wet bathrooms, chipped crockery, the harsh sun on tired eyes, the uneasy odour of genteel poverty, and the air weighed down with the vibrations of inflated dreams, puncturing slowly.

The Swami-ji's flat was spacious, sans almost any furniture, with unobstructed air laying still from end to end. In a wide passageway, with a bare, swept floor, we added our own footwear to a cluster of sandals and slippers. Thence we came to a large hall, thinly carpeted, whereupon were seated, cross-legged, a number of silent figures, before an empty chair. The windows were curtained, and two fans spun fast overhead.

'He is shifting soon to Madh Island,' came a whisper from young Ali. 'Here is too less space.'

'It's a big flat!' I murmured without thinking. But just then, a door flung open with a startling sound, and a large figure strode out to the middle of the room, while the desultory silence became at once focused on Ali's Swami-ji, the Navy Baba.

He seemed to be in his fifties. His torso was bare, a hairy chest, a comfortable paunch, between an open, flesh-coloured robe that fell over a creamy white dhoti. He wore a red tweed cap aslant on the top of his head. In the glow of the tube-light, his face appeared lean, clean-shaven and handsome. His eyes were narrowed, and on his way to the central chair, he threw many sidelong, rather unimpressed glances, at the gathering on the carpet. Upon sitting, however, he fixed his gaze upon us, huddled at the back.

Someone left the Baba's side and padded swiftly over to Ali, who lowered his head, grimaced, and nodded many times during a whispered conversation. Moments later, the squatters were shifting on the carpet, opening up a corridor of space between ourselves and the Swami-ji. As Bharat and I carried forward the tripod, the Baba nodded, smiled approval, and remarked, in tones that resounded about the room:

'You are the director.'

'I am the director,' replied Ahishor.

Then a strange thing happened. As suddenly as storm clouds, an atmosphere full of tension and mystery crept over the room. My movements, I recall, became hushed and halting, all through the erecting of the camera, the adjusting of the frame, the testing for sound. Somebody had fitted our little mike onto the Swami-ji's robes; he had made no objection. I could feel a physical thickening of the air—something akin to those unforgettable classroom moments before an examination result was announced. I wondered briefly if this was what was meant by the 'presence' of an enlightened soul. But it was neither sweetness nor peacefulness, rather a sense of drama, that I felt thrumming through my veins, and it was centred not on one man, but the pair of them.

Ahishor had seated himself a few feet in front of the Swami-ji's chair. He was sitting very comfortably, cross-legged, with his back erect and his head held high, to look the other in the eye. His grey hair stirred beneath the fan.

'How,' he was asking, 'do you solve the troubles of the people who come to you?'

'It all depends on the person.' Navy Baba was looking almost bored, but behind the half-smile and the lazy eyes I sensed a total alertness.

'People who come to you want jobs, want money, want to marry the girl who does not want to marry them. How do you solve such problems?'

'When you are an enlightened person, all these things become easy to solve.'

'But how? By what magic?'

The Baba had closed his eyes. I smelled incense in the air, and looking about, spotted where agarbattis were burning under a garlanded portrait of a bearded man. It was the room's only decoration—not counting the motes of dust that danced ravishingly by the windows.

'Please understand,' said the Swami-ji, in easy Hindi. [It was soon apparent that Bharat's translations would not be required.] 'The goal is samadhi. The union with the infinite.' He was speaking slowly, choosing his words, while his deep, rasping voice still carried everywhere easily. 'But for this one must be psychologically...and spiritually...ready. If the person who approaches me is not yet ready for true understanding, he will ask for worldly things, of the kind you mentioned... In such a case I may refuse, if the person is not humble, if his desire is not sincere... Or I may provide him these things, if he shows sincerity and humility... But even when I do this, it is only to show him how easily I can provide for him, so that he will understand that these worldly things are only playthings... Then he will ask for more. He will ask for the source of my powers. Thus from the worldly he may go beyond the worldly.'

Ahishor was expressionless for a moment, with his eyes fixed on the Baba. Then he asked, 'Swami-ji, is it true that you yourself have attained samadhi?'

'Yes.'

'How did you do it?'

'For the complete answer to that question...you have to understand all the sadhana I have performed from the beginning. Not the beginning of this life. The beginning of all my lives. That will take some time. [Swami-ji smiled.] But if you want to know about the final stage...I have performed both Bhoomigat Samadhi and Jal Samadhi, many times in the past twenty years... I will explain. In Bhoomigat Samadhi, you are buried underground for many days, in a small pit of nine feet by seven feet by five feet. These dimensions are important, because they connect us to Venus, Jupiter and the infinite. In such circumstances, no ordinary human being can survive. You have to stop breathing, travel into yourself, you have to become unified with the whole vast earth energy, from which you have been born... Similar with Jal Samadhi. That is performed under water. And there is a third kind also—'

'How,' Ahishor interrupted, 'do you breathe? If there is no oxygen.'

'One does not breathe. One's blood does not flow, one's brain does not function, as per medical science one is dead. But really you are in a state of supreme consciousness...you simply exist... The third kind of samadhi is in an airtight container. I will be performing that in January next year, in Agartala. You are welcome to attend.'

Another period of silence followed. From behind the camera, I could feel the room's attention focused in line with it. Ali, seated informally with his arms around his knees, was gazing rapt at the Baba. I glanced at Bharat, crouching to one side, and did a little double take. For some reason he was looking terrified.

'Swami-ji,' said Ahishor, 'some people say that these are only stunts and tricks, which neither require nor yield any spiritual powers. [The Baba began to chuckle.] But that's not my question... My question is, accepting that you do possess godly powers...and not only you, that other Swami-jis all over the country also have these powers...my question is, why do you not all get together and cure our country's problems?

I looked to see if he was smiling. On the contrary, the colour was high in his face; his shoulders were rising and falling; he was full of passion though his voice was even and controlled.

'India is one of the poorest places in the world. People don't have food to eat or houses to live in. If there are so many of you, who can create objects out of thin air, why don't you create homes for the poor? And why do you not yourself go out into society and help those in need? Why do you wait for people to come to you? Is it because you want devotees gathered around you, people to serve you, and make your life comfortable?'

Because Ahishor did not look left or right, so I restrained my own timid impulse to take stock of the stirring and murmuring that had sprung up across the carpet. Yet soon, the offended noises died away; I heard snickering instead. On the Swami-ji's face, to my surprise, was spreading a look of vast complacency.

'Mr Ahishor Frances,' he said, and I shuddered, though there was no mystery about his knowing the name. 'You are not paying attention. I said once already...the goal is samadhi. It is a spiritual goal. It is not a worldly goal. Giving food to the people is the job of the government. My job is to take them to a higher consciousness... Now, sometimes a child will not listen to a lesson, until he is given a chocolate. So as I said, sometimes I give chocolates. But the purpose of my sitting here is not to give chocolates.'

With a tilt of his head, Ahishor asked in English, in an altered tone, 'Are you getting everything?' It took me a moment to realize that he was addressing me. His face was grim; in his eyes was none of the playful pleasure that, in my experience, debates and arguments usually evoked in him. I made a silent thumbs up.

'There was,' the Baba's voice boomed on, 'a second part to your query.'

I felt, as he spoke, the smugness of one enjoying the movements of his intellect.

'Why do I wait for people to come to me? Understand Ahishor-ji... It is the first test of a person's readiness, to rise, that he seek out help. If he does not seek out, he cannot be helped. This is why I wait... Until, a person comes.'

The Swami-ji's hands had crept out onto his lap and he was clasping and unclasping them in a deliberate way. Suddenly, he leaned forward from his chair, lowering his capped head, with his eyes narrowed on Ahishor.

'You are not yet ready for spiritual teaching. Yet, you have come for help...and I know very well you are in need of help. So tell me. What is the trouble you are facing? Career is running into difficulty?'

From his slumping position, Bharat sprung alert. He strained forward, as though at a leash, glaring at the two of them; then quickly he turned his indignant gaze towards me, though I too ignored it.

'Yes, yes, it's true.' To my amazement, Ahishor was mumbling words that seemed to be welling up from deep in his heart. It passed my mind that he was acting—and if so, what acting!—but I was far from sure.

'When you try to make cinema, that means something in this city... I don't know who or what is to blame...but it's terrible, horrible. It's like trying to communicate with a wall. There's nobody listening. There's only laughter! There's somebody laughing, at you, at themselves, at everything. Maybe I feel it so much because I'm not like the others...I'm not *mad* about movies, you see... For me, it's just a medium, to put across my ideas...But I've failed to do that. They all praised my first movie, but I know the truth...It was a childish movie...it was full of showing off...begging to be praised...That's the reason they praised it...[suddenly he raised his voice] The thing is, it's all a machine. That's the mistake I've been making.'

'Come near me,' beckoned the Swami-ji. 'Yes...good...kneel before me...put your left hand on your head...good...show me your right hand...Yes, that way... Now listen...'

I could hardly believe my eyes. But everything was in frame, being recorded just as it was happening.

'Your career will transform after this project,' said the Swami-ji. 'This will be a launch pad for you. *I* will be a launch pad for you. You understand? You must take this film far and wide... Spread my name, my message...then, and only then, yours will also spread. Do you understand?...Good... Now look here...'

Over Ahishor's outstretched palm, he waved in dizzying circles his own hand, that was encircled by his flapping sleeves. The next moment, he was holding aloft a small, square, white stone.

'The divine prasad of Mahayogi Navy Baba!' pronounced the Swami-ji. He gazed about the room, lingering on the camera. 'It is not an ordinary stone... Stones, you all know, have very powerful memories. This one has come all the way from the Himalayas. I have summoned it from the exact spot where Baba Morya did tapasya for twenty-five years. It is filled with the memory of his concentration.'

I zoomed the camera in, to behold, in stylized calligraphy, the single letter 'M', painted in red, upon the hard surface.

'Here,' the Baba was smiling good-naturedly, 'take it... Keep it in your office. But not on a mantelpiece, remember. Keep it on a separate table with nothing else nearby, and keep that table near your computer. Then do your work—and have faith. Have... What is the matter?'

His mouth hanging open, Ahishor was staring, goggle-eyed, at the object on his palm. I wondered again what had come over him—the trick had been impressive, but we had seen many such on video before, it did not merit such mystification. If he was still acting, he was now being blatant and obvious. And then suddenly he grinned, and began to guffaw.

'Where did you get this from?' His voice was trembling; he was a cauldron of emotion. 'Can you say it again, Swami-ji?'

'You must pay attention!' scolded the Baba. 'I said already that it has come from the Himalayas. See here—it bears the mark of Baba Morya.'

'I see!' It was a near-yelp. Clutching the stone, Ahishor drew back from the God-man. He was smiling and trying not to smile, shaking his head in spasms; while his eyebrows darted up and down absurdly. Then he seemed to take hold of himself. He frowned hard, rubbed his beard on both cheeks, and exhaled forcefully. He spoke, in soft, but clear tones.

'Swami-ji, there has been a mistake. This stone has not come from the Himalayas. This is not the mark of Baba Morya. I know this, because the stone actually belongs to me, myself... Yes, yes, it's mine. I had it made at a souvenir shop in Istanbul this May. It was going to be a birthday gift for a friend. But I never gave it to her. About one month ago, I left it here on Yari Road, in a brown paper bag...I just left it on the street... I was going to put it in a trash can, but I didn't... So you see, there has been a mistake.'

An infinite kindness had entered his voice. My mind was

racing, to what conclusions I couldn't say. But there was no doubt in it that Ahishor was telling the plain truth. Just as it struck me, '*The stone was for Maithili*', I heard someone else's breath drawn in sharply. It was Bharat, his face contorted in an agony of deduction.

As Ahishor retreated to where I was standing, the young Ali broke from the ranks of bemused onlookers, and hurried over to the Swami-ji's side. He bent to whisper in the Yogi's ear. An intense irritation showed on Navy Baba's face. Suddenly, he thrust out an arm that sent Ali reeling backwards. Pronouncing a curse in Bhojpuri, which needed no translation, he rose to his feet, his robes shimmering as they fell.

'Put that off!' he commanded me.

'Put it off,' said Ahishor quietly.

As I hastened to take down the camera, I was amazed to see the Baba grinning again, with his teeth bared.

'For those who doubt the blessings of God,' his voice resounded hatefully, 'there is nothing but suffering. Great suffering is in store for you, Mr Ahishor Frances! All of you who are watching—remember this day!'

Then he strode out of the hall. I felt the eyes of the gathering turned on us. An old man in a white shirt was clicking his tongue. A bespectacled woman, with a huge handbag, began addressing us in a flurry of Marathi.

Ali, herding the three of us to the exit, was full of despair.

'Sir, what did you do?' he kept saying. 'What did you say?'

But when we reached the foot of the stairwell, he suddenly turned contemplative.

'Even if that stone was yours, you had thrown it away, you said so yourself. Then is it not amazing that Navy Baba gave it to you?'

'It's an amazing coincidence that he found it, and chose me of all people to try it on,' said Ahishor, 'because only I can prove that he was telling lies about it... Your Baba is a fraud. Please think about that, Ali. Take my advice...stop visiting him.'

V

A Shadow on the Heart

Some days after the drama of that first interview (how enthralled we all were to watch and rewatch the footage!), past nine o'clock one night, Ahishor lay stretched out on a mattress on the floor, in his new flat in Versova. A lone yellow light in an orange paper shade was forming shadows across the room.

It was a crowded room, full of furniture, with loaded bookshelves, a wooden cupboard with a golden latch, a round table, a square table, many chairs, papers and mugs, plates and pans (the kitchen adjoined it), a mounted globe, a chessboard, potted plants, thickly curtained windows that were parted to let in the spill of the street lights, colourful rugs on the floor, a cuckoo clock, pictures hanging off the walls (notably, not a single movie poster), and patterns painted on the walls. These had been done by Ahishor himself.

Behind the mass of things he lay as though barricaded, and hidden from sight. The clock ticked; one of his two pet cats jumped up onto a high-backed chair to sharpen its claws. But an overweening silence prevailed, within the room and without, until a shuffling was heard near the open door, then a knock, and a cough.

'Come in,' he called out, not stirring.

As he entered the cool darkness of the room, it seemed to Sasha quite empty. It was only when he approached the table towards the centre, with the thought of putting down the spiral-bound book he was carrying alongside the other books, papers and one unusual, decorative stone with the letter 'M' inscribed upon it, that he saw his host, prone on the floor, his eyes open to the ceiling, and his hands under his head.

'Sit, sit,' said Ahishor, 'I'm going to get up myself. Shall we have a drink?'

'I would like tea, if you have it.'

'You don't drink?'

'I do,' said Sasha, 'but right now I'd prefer drinking tea.'

Ahishor grinned, and lifting himself off the mattress, was on his feet with uncommon agility.

'Tea it is! Boiling hot tea, we shall swill it like a pair of Dostoevsky's Russians! Now while I make the tea, you tell me your news. How have you been, where have you been, what have you been doing...I'm listening.'

The grey cat leaped to the floor, and Sasha sat on the chair it had vacated, with the odd sense that it would be impolite now to choose another.

'Well, it's hard to say,' he said, 'I've been meeting various people. Made some friends, I guess.'

'Really,' sang out Ahishor, setting down a saucepan of water on the burning gas ring. Noisily, he opened a cabinet for tea leaves and sugar. 'What kind of people? Here in Versova?'

'Yes, mostly.'

'Making friends with people in Versova! Now that's impressive.'

'Why do you say that?' asked Sasha curiously, but Ahishor,

stirring the pan, made no reply. When he returned, strolling, to the living room area, he was stroking his beard thoughtfully. He did not sit, but paced the floor rug.

'Don't mind my asking,' he said, 'but how do you make a living?'

'My father is a very rich man,' smiled Sasha. 'I am living off his money and pleasing myself... No joking, that's the truth, more or less.'

'Delightful,' grinned Ahishor, 'delightful—and devilish! You know, you are quite an enigma to me. When I first met you, I thought you were an aspiring actor.'

'Oh no, not at all.'

'Yes, I realized that. So what is it? You love movies, do you?'

Again Sasha shook his head, with apparent surprise. 'I watch very few.'

'I myself watch practically none. Though I make them, so... But we're not talking about me. If you're not interested in movies, why did you decide to spend your father's money in Versova—of all places? You could be living anywhere.'

'I suppose,' said Sasha, 'I am just drawn to the people. Your community of artists...the strugglers... I like their company.'

'You like trauma cases?' said Ahishor with a sudden laugh. 'The Versova Shelter Home!' Then he ceased ambling about, and stuck out a hand.

'So is this your script?... Interesting title...what's the story?'

'It's difficult for me to say,' began Sasha.

'That's exactly what you're going to have to do,' replied Ahishor gently. 'Very few people in this town will read what you've written. They'll want your story narrated. In fact, more than that, they'll want your log line, your elevator pitch. You understand that? Short enough to start and finish on a lucky elevator ride with a producer who isn't even really paying attention.'

He thrust the spiral-bound volume back at Sasha, and trotted back towards the stove, where the tea was just starting to boil.

'Should I switch on more lights?' he said in passing, 'I like it dark myself.'

'There is enough light,' said Sasha. Shadows criss-crossed him where he sat, his fingers tapping the plastic cover of his manuscript.

'It's a collection of four short stories which are all set in the mountains. So the setting unifies them, and then the theme... well, I know there is a common theme because I wrote them all in the same state of mind. It's friendship, maybe. Or maybe it's just—people learning to love each other. One of the stories is the one I told you at your mother's house—the story that happened to me, when I was a child. There's another about a mother and daughter—the daughter resents the mother because the mother isn't educated. There's also one about two friends— one who left the hills to work in the city, the other stayed back—and now they meet again.'

'I see,' said Ahishor, 'I see. How much milk and sugar?'

'A little milk. Two spoons.'

'That's a lot of sugar,' Ahishor chuckled and he was still all smiles moments later, when he came back with two steaming cups. Handing one to Sasha, he put the other on the table, and then threw himself down on the mattress. There he hugged a cushion to his lap, smiling and thinking.

'I will read your script, of course,' he said, eventually. 'You said on the phone this is the first script you've written.'

'I wanted to try,' said Sasha, 'but I don't think I'm a writer really.'

'And you've not shown it to anybody else?...Well, I'll give it a shot. Just don't be disappointed if nothing happens. The things we see on our movie screens tend to be very different from this—if I understood the description you gave me. I'm sure you know that already.'

'In mainstream cinema, I know.'

'Everywhere,' cut in Ahishor. 'The mainstream is violent, sexist, populist, jingoistic. And here in Versova, what are we? Violent, sexist, self-conscious, paranoid. I know, because I see scripts all the time. There's someone cooking up something at every coffee shop in this place... And it's all the same kind of thing. Gangsters, frivolity, stupid people killing each other for petty reasons. No critical inquiry of course, no study of violence—just violence! Now, what you have written—that story you told us the other day, it was a simple story...something meaningful... But it won't fit anywhere.'

'But you work here too,' said Sasha. 'If you think this way, then...'

Ahishor settled back against the wall, where the painted rays and curlicues, shooting and swirling about his head, took on spectacular new meanings. He was wondering how freely he could talk. Sasha's gaze upon him was polite, attentive, deferential. And yet...

'I'll be honest with you, Sasha. This is not material I can make anytime soon. It's not that I don't like it, or that I won't like it when I read it. (And I will read it.) It's just that the industry is too rotten, I don't want to work with it any longer. I've realized this. I can't spend six months grovelling before producers and distributors to let me make real movies that say something... Cinema is incredibly powerful, you see, it's a machine, it's like the machine guns in World War I, they were the game-changers. Whoever had control of the machine gun, that side won the battle. And in this country, well in most countries, but in this country without doubt, for a very, very long time all the wrong people have had control. Bloated, greedy, lecherous, bigoted men—that call themselves artists! They've been spilling their rotten fantasies like barrels of bullets...corrupting the whole cultural atmosphere, spreading this kind of mental regression all over the country. Cementing it! It's such a powerful machine... So somebody who thinks differently has got to take that machine from them. That's got to happen first—then stories like yours can be told all the time. Then we'll be living in peacetime! But now, it's time to fight. And nobody's fighting! There was a time when people talked about it. Yes, a few years ago. You've heard of Passion for Cinema? The website? Well never mind, it's history now. Now everyone's running scared. At best they're taking little potshots here and there, but sooner or later they all sign their deals with the devil... For example, look at Maithili. Why did Maithili leave?'

It crossed Ahishor's mind that he had said more than he intended to; he had intended only the general overview. Sasha was listening with the same respectful expression. At the mention of Maithili's name he frowned slightly.

'I don't know. I know her grandfather passed away.'

Then all of a sudden a new mood seemed to sweep over the visitor. He took a gulp from his teacup, put it down beside Ahishor's, and leaned back in his chair with a little gasp, his gaze wracked and inward, the muscles on his face literally trembling.

'With Maithili,' he started to speak, 'I don't know. Because I was never even able to make friends with her. The thing is... I liked Maithili.'

'Sure,' said Ahishor.

'But I wasn't able to get through to her, at all. She thought I was too pushy and also too naive. I could never have any *stable* conversation with her.'

'Don't worry about it!' drawled Ahishor, 'I know Maithili very well. She isn't the way she seems. For one thing—and this may sound rude—but it's the simple truth. Maithili is not very intelligent. She's quite dumb.'

Sasha, still shivering with emotion, sat sunk in silence.

'And that's the whole key to understanding her, and all her decisions. She seems mysterious and profound. I know, I know... She looks that way, she has that kind of demeanour. But it's a deception. The reality is she's completely confused by most situations. It's like when you have a movie actor who never shows any expression. He can get by in a lot of scenes, the viewer's imagination does all the work for him—but he himself has no idea what's happening.'

'That might be true,' said Sasha, 'what you said about an actor anyway.'

Ahishor sipped his tea.

'It's true for her too,' he said. 'Try to realize that, or you'll be lost, my friend. Something tells me you don't have much experience with women... Well, well, we won't get into that. [Sasha was blushing.] The point is, Maithili came back to India, craving stardom—yes, that's another thing, she craves and expects stardom—because she is used to the best of everything, you would know if you'd seen where she lives.... Oh, you have?'

Surprised for a moment, Ahishor reached out a hand to stroke the back of the cat, which had begun rubbing against him.

'Craving stardom...but not in Bollywood, because she is better than Bollywood, you see. I mean, she is, she really is. Unfortunately she finds that nowhere else can give her any limelight. Versova is a mess. So she's confused. So...she escapes.'

He shrugged and broke off. It seemed to Sasha that the sureness with which he had begun his speech had faded as he went along.

Sasha bent forward, shifting towards the edge of his chair. He continued to thrill all over with tiny shudders. Certain things that she had said and written to him were taking hold of him, like unseen assailants at his back. Meanwhile, the dark and the quiet of the flat shrouded him continually; he felt a painful longing to leave, to run into the streets.

'I don't think...,' he began. 'She was not comfortable in India. She has larger ideas, doesn't she? Of how a society should be, the way people should live. She talked about that.'

At once, Ahishor laughed confidently and drank from his cup.

'Drink the tea, it will get cold,' his voice was energetic again. 'When you really have ideas of how a place should be—do you stay and try to make a difference? Or do you run away? You run away when you are *out* of ideas. You're right, she has this thing about modern civilization and how it's all going to hell. But I even told her once, very clearly—I said, it's not the amenities of modern civilization that you dislike, it's the inability to enjoy them properly! Your problem with modern life isn't that it's too comfortable, your problem is it's not comfortable enough. You want your AC *and* you want your unpolluted air. That doesn't happen. So again, there's a conflict. There's a mess to be fixed. And in India there is just no avoiding it, because here the modern, the premodern, the prehistoric!—everything's all together and in your face... I like it better actually, it's more real. In the West, they shove the trouble under the carpet... By the way, remember Leo Tolstoy?'

'Yes?' frowned Sasha.

'I love Tolstoy, but isn't it so typical of an aristocrat to want to renounce the world? And what for? Death? No! Cleaner air, tastier water, fresher milk and cheese! Maithili's like that. She's living in the countryside now, you know.'

'In Greece.'

'No, that was long ago. In New England. She *was* in Greece, then she was in London, and Sussex...now she's crossed the Atlantic. And she won't stop moving either—she can't!'

'She doesn't write to me any longer,' said Sasha heavily. Then, sipping quickly, he added, 'The tea is very good.'

Ahishor was studying him keenly, smiling behind his beard, while his hand kept stroking the purring cat.

'I am afraid I misjudged you, Sasha,' he said, after a moment. 'There was a time when I thought you were—pardon me—conniving and insincere. But now it seems—pardon me again!—that you are just an idiot! This is not how you deal with someone like Maithili! You're stuck on her; you're chasing her. You'll destroy yourself this way, and she won't care a bit, I assure you of that. Other girls would notice—Maithili won't even notice.'

'She is far too self-obsessed,' he continued thoughtfully. 'She is...I don't know the word, but just imagine...her sense of self! Because she cannot live in any one place, so she dismisses all of modern society. Because she couldn't do what it takes to build a career in movies, so she condemns all of cinema. Too "tame", that's what she said. All right for spectators, not for those who want to *live*. Do you remember her saying that? That night in Bandra? You were there too...'

Ahishor began to frown, not because the memory was painful but because it had triggered, yet again, a complicated train of thought that he had traversed repeatedly in the past. His voice turned inward and abstracted.

'It's not that she didn't have a point, by the way. It's not as though I haven't thought about cinema myself... Where it's going, what it's good for... all these kinds of things... But we come back to the same crossroads. Do you run away? Or do you stay and make a difference? The movie I'm working on right now, for example—and Maithili had the choice to be a part of it—it is not going to be tame. No, no!'

He grinned; momentarily his face flamed with satisfaction, before he fastened friendly eyes on Sasha.

'Ah, now I remember! You went and visited her house. Carrying a book of poems!'

'That was silly of me,' Sasha's cheeks reddened, 'I mean... to leave her a book and think that would be enough. She was so restless, that night in Bandra. Reading Rumi has helped me a lot, in my life. But people never react to books the way one hopes they will. Still—you never know—maybe it did help her, or will some day.'

A look of disinterest was creeping over Ahishor's face. Sasha hesitated, then spoke quickly.

'Did she ever talk to you about...'

Ahishor glanced up at him.

'Yes?'

'...about a demon?'

'A demon?'

Sasha nodded. The word, spoken carefully, felt tinged with the ridiculous. But he held fast to it, until it found its place in the room that was full of shadows.

'Once she mentioned being given advice on what to read, by a demon. I didn't ask her about it, but that was what she had said, very clearly. It seemed to me she had used the word literally.'

Ahishor cocked his head and stared at the ceiling, ruminatively at first, and then with little smiles, possibly of remembrance, though when he lowered his gaze, he was wearing a frown, and looking more or less bemused.

'Yes,' he said, slowly, 'I heard something like that too. Well. [He smiled again, mischievously.] I shouldn't tell you in what context...that demon once popped up.'

Suddenly, he shrugged and raised his eyebrows gracefully.

'Maithili talked about many bizarre things. After a while I stopped listening. She had—she has—such an inflated sense of her self, it put me off, to tell the truth. Maybe she saw ghosts and demons and auras, but I didn't. And I think a conversation should be about something both parties understand. Enough about her! Let's get back to you and your visit to Malabar Hills. So that was when you met Anamika.'

'You know Anamika,' said Sasha dully.

'Well, I have tried to avoid her,' Ahishor sighed. 'But it's difficult, because we have so many mutual friends. Anamika has mutual friends with everybody. She loves collecting people, if you know that type. An extremely needy person. When she's in Bombay she keeps calling me to town for lunch... However, she's harmless.'

Sasha was drinking his tea steadily, with his gaze fixed on the far shadows of the room. From where he lounged on the mattress, Ahishor noticed how erect his visitor sat and suddenly felt (as he had before, in the same company) a rising irritation.

'She was very rude to me,' Sasha was saying, with a firmness and decisiveness of tone that also annoyed Ahishor. 'I don't know what she told you, but she behaved badly. To me, she did not seem harmless at all.'

'That's because you came bumbling in like an old parent, interrupting playtime! Anamika simply *dotes* on Maithili. She is gay, you know. Anamika is gay, I mean.'

'Oh,' said Sasha, but this fact did not appear to interest him.

'Yes.' An unpleasant smile had appeared on Ahishor's face, and the hand with which he was petting the cat had grown rough, which caused the cat to meow softly and bound onto the nearest table. 'Of course, Maithili is just using her—in the nicest possible way. But that's why Anamika disliked *you* so much. Basically, she's made the same mistake you have...though with more success. Success, in inverted commas, I mean.'

But Sasha, it seemed, was not paying attention to his verbal finesses. Suddenly, he turned on Ahishor a grave and almost worried look.

'I'm really not an idiot, honestly. I'm not chasing Maithili because I'm besotted with her. I like her, yes...but if I was mistaken I can accept that. What troubles me is when I can't even be on good terms with somebody! She is not even my friend. And then Anamika...the way she treated me. When that happens, I feel something is badly amiss. Something is dangerous then.'

Frowning, clicking his tongue and muttering, 'Nothing is *dangerous*,' Ahishor reached over to the table, where the cat had just knocked over a plastic bottle. He let the bottle lie and picked up the white stone instead and looked it over.

'What's your cat's name?' said Sasha mildly.

'Terrence... After the director.'

'Ah,' Sasha smiled, though Ahishor felt sure he did not know the reference. He glanced at his visitor's empty cup.

'Some more tea?'

'No, thanks, actually I'll leave now.'
'What's the hurry?'
'Oh, I have to meet someone,' said Sasha awkwardly.

Rising, Ahishor gathered up the cups with efficient grace.

'Well, I will read your script and let you know what I think. Just leave it on the chair.'

'Thanks,' said Sasha.

When he was halfway out of the room, he turned with his mouth parted. Ahishor was leaning against the kitchen top, his arms folded across his chest. Something thin and white gleamed in his right hand.

'You forgot something?' he called out.

Sasha hesitated. In his mind was a little speech about how living stories, however unheralded, themselves could combat mechanical ones and how the age of true cinema need not be postponed to after a power struggle. But now those thoughts seemed to sink under their own weight, and vanish in the claustrophobic gloom.

'It's nothing,' he said. 'Sorry—thanks again!'

'Take care,' said Ahishor.

VI

Guilt

A chill had entered the air, the first real whisper of winter. Sasha walked back the way he had come, on quickening steps. Soon he was out on the thoroughfares, which were well-peopled, as at all times, though for now the night remained young. He had grown accustomed to these ways, and he observed without noticing the homeless figures lying in bundles on the pavement and the two tall blondes, in cocktail dresses, hurrying past him on clicking heels. At a corner of the road, his eye went, out of habit, to a cafe alongside, where, in lassitude and in earnestness, young people were still confabulating. For a moment, he thought he had spotted Sushant, with his arm around a girl, and he felt a jolt of pain, remembering that last night in Bandra (he had not seen Maithili since), but he did not stop to make certain.

A short while later, Sasha did pause. There was a smile tugging at his lips. Outside the boundary wall of the 'Palm View' apartment building, that went towering into the hazy sky, a group of stray dogs were resting in the dust. He recognized these dogs. He was fond especially of one with a white coat and a thick black stripe over its right eye which suggested a raised eyebrow and made for a dire and dramatic expression. They turned their heads with interest, some with their tongues lolling out. Standing near them, without moving to pet them, Sasha looked, and spoke softly.

'How are you today?' he said.

The white dog stared back. It was on its haunches, and the others, that were lying, kept studying him too, their stomachs rising and falling steadily, their brave hearts pumping hard as always.

'Good dog,' said Sasha, feeling suddenly overcome. 'All of you.' Then, fighting his own embarrassment, he thought aloud.

'I am like you, you know,' he murmured. 'That's why I like to see you so much.'

A calm descended over him as he left the dogs behind (the white dog half-followed, then watched him go), but strangely, it came mixed with fresh and overpowering pain. His lips moved to worry the wound, yet it was quite self-consciously and even eagerly that he spoke her name.

'Maithili, Maithili,' breathed Sasha, stumbling faster down the pavement.

With the same odd calm, he reflected on his handful of meetings with her, his utter surrender, and how scarcely his feeling was reciprocated. No self-pity followed; instead, he filled with a turbulent pride. It had gratified him (thought he did not dwell on this feeling) to hear Ahishor's view on Anamika. But when it came to Maithili, he thought, Ahishor was wrong. Maithili was not merely rich and spoilt. She was not merely lying, she really was after grander things. Or was he—he grew troubled again—trying to persuade himself? Had he, from foolishness and stubbornness, failed to see through her? He remembered to the word her last email to him (many weeks ago), and now his step slowed and grew wayward, as he read it over in his mind.

> *There comes a time when intuition takes precedence over intellect. Before this there must be a burning away of all expectations, beliefs, learned ideas. In this space the past has been a story that has led you to this point and the future is also visible—not in terms of actual events, but as a feeling. You realize you are in a story whose protagonist is yourself. You become the pilot of your own aircraft. It's very empowering. Very few people have this. Recently I went through a raja yoga initiation. But that's just the beginning. You are trying to use your intellect. You say you want to help me but I think the truth of it is that you are looking for help yourself. I think that the advice you are giving me is something that you are mostly telling yourself by writing to me. I present nothing but a mirror to you. For some reason you are blocked. You do not radiate. Also, it irritates me because you really don't know me at all. You have known me for a tiny period of my life and have only seen one facet of me. I can be generous, cruel, wise, stupid, high and low. And I love every moment of my neurotic humanity.*

Suddenly, Sasha halted. Somebody had spoken, close to his ear. 'Hi, hi,' he heard again. Turning, he found himself face to face with a woman he had never seen.

She was short, and neither old nor young, though her face was wrinkled. She was swaddled in multiple-worn and dusty sweaters. Her hair was up in a bun; her eyes stared sharply; her lips were pursed. She had planted herself directly in front of him, cutting off the horizon.

'Young man,' she stared. 'Hi. Do you live around here?'

Her voice was rough, but her English and her accent were

polished, bred, to all appearances, from society's upper classes.

'Yes?' said Sasha.

Her eyes stayed on him, gleaming, until he felt compelled to speak further.

'Yes, but why do you ask?'

'You see, what has happened is, I left my home without money. I just need a hundred rupees to get home.'

'Oh...'

'I would be grateful for your help. I need a hundred rupees,' she repeated harshly. She was unsmiling throughout.

Sasha glanced around, and hesitated. Nobody on the street was looking at them.

'You don't have an ATM card?'

'No, no, I don't have my purse at all. Can you give me the money? You might be in my shoes tomorrow.'

'Where do you live?'

'In Bandra,' came the answer.

Making up his mind with an effort, he reached for his wallet.

'I hope you really do need this,' he mumbled, tilting his head to catch her gaze, which had now strayed to his hands. The woman said nothing. Grasping the hundred-rupee note, she grunted briefly, then turned and scurried down the road—in the direction away from Bandra. A short while later, she disappeared into a side lane. Sasha watched her go, feeling chastened by the minute.

A con-woman, he thought to himself. But what else could I have done?

Briefly, he remained astonished at the encounter, for beggars were common on the road, but tricksters rare. Then dragging his feet onward, he felt his spirits sinking. His reveries of Maithili had fled from him; she was far away, she cared nothing for him. Was he really what Ahishor had called him, an idiot? Was that the accurate word? Thus filled with troubling and sapping introspections, he reached the dim enclosure of the pub beside the pavement.

As on every night, the Woodcon pub was crowded with men. They were seated in rows at the long, pew-like tables indoors, and huddled in clusters in the cramped space outside, where plants grew along the walls, in low electric light. Looking around, Sasha spotted Malik, his heavy frame bowed over a corner table, where a glass, half-full, stood already. Two men at an adjoining table had their chairs turned towards him; one of them was talking emphatically, while Malik, looking downwards, nodded at irregular intervals.

'I know, because I was posted there,' heard Sasha, as he approached, 'I have been in that situation. You have to let it happen. People are killed, of course—but it is for the sake of peace in the future. Otherwise, violence, a hundred, or a thousand times worse, is *going* to happen... 300 lives today for 30,000 tomorrow! What choice do you have? So don't tell me what people say...they are pussies, they have no idea about governance... It was the same in '84, and in 2002. Realpolitik. You know that word?'

The speaker was wearing a loose, rumpled shirt, with several buttons open at the top. He was middle-aged. Lines of perspiration were trailing down his cheek, although, even in this close enclosure, it was not warm. He looked annoyed and impatient. When Sasha arrived to join Malik, he stared at him, sizing him up, and then, perhaps not quite comfortable with what he saw, repeated the word 'Realpolitik!' twice in Malik's direction, before shifting his chair back to his own table. There had emerged about him an air of injured pride, while his companion, a thin, clever-looking man in a checked shirt, was suddenly full of chuckles.

'*Tune* script *padha?*' (Did you read the script?) inquired Malik, almost before Sasha had sat down.

'Not yet,' beamed Sasha.

'*Kya re* (What's that?)...I thought we would discuss over drinks.'

'I'll read it tonight, after drinks.'

'Okays,' Malik fell quiet.

He was wearing a tight yellow T-shirt that accentuated his fleshiness, grey cargo shorts and floaters. With his disappointed expression he looked specially boyish, though presently he perked up, ordering a vodka and lime soda for Sasha, and providing specific instructions to a familiar, red-jacketed 'Anna', for a plate of boiled peanuts to be mixed with chopped onion, cucumber and lots of masala.

Meanwhile, the aroma of alcohol hung in the air, the tabletops were sticky, the ashtrays spilling over; wads of napkins littered the floor, but there was no music to interfere, nor any overbearing ruckus at the tables, and amidst the crowd of absorbed drinkers, it was easy to talk.

'Busy, yeah, quite busy,' said Malik, in answer to Sasha's query, '*Ek toh yeh* film festival *ka locha tha*. (First there was this trouble with the film festival.) Now it's mostly resolved, *paise aa gaye*. (...the money has come in.) *Haan*, Bollywood people, they stepped in. Then I had gone for two weeks to Hyderabad, research *pe*. And *uske pahle*, (...before that) I was writing the other script, this one—the Roopnagar script. *Padh na jaldi!*' (Read fast please!)

'Yes, yes.'

'Actually, you know what, don't read it. I'm doing a fresh

draft now. I'll send you that one, read that instead...There's one scene I really enjoyed writing. *Sunega?*' (Will you hear it?)

With the vodka to his lips, Sasha nodded.

'So basically, the situation is, there's this guy, who has been kidnapped by this gang. They take him to an abandoned shed, in a completely deserted place, somewhere in rural Haryana. The film is set there. They make him sit on a chair, inside the shed and start slapping him. They slap him seventeen times! And you know what? I want to do the slapping for real, hehehe! Anyway, once they're finished slapping the guy, they are about to murder him, when suddenly he breaks free and runs out of the shed. Visually this part will be a bit like the *Hazaaron Khwaishein Aisi* scene, with Shiney! So he runs, runs, runs, but there is nowhere to go. The whole gang run after him. But now! While they were beating him inside the shed, there had been a storm developing outside. A storm, yes, a weather storm. So it's raining now, they are all running in the rain and then just as the gang catches the guy, there is a flash of lightning and an explosion. They all turn to see that the lightning has hit that same shed that they were in just a minute ago. It's completely destroyed. And then they look at the guy who ran away, because of whom they ran too. They're mind-fucked. They're like—Boss, *isko jaane do*! (...let him go!) We can't do anything to this guy!'

'It's very nice,' said Sasha. 'Except for the slapping part—I mean, you can't possibly do that for real.'

'Why *re*?'

'It's hardly the way to treat people! But the ending of the scene is great. Very unpredictable.'

'Thanks *re*.'

Malik finished his drink and called for another. Then, as the waiter was setting off, he called him back again with an apologetic request for two cigarettes from the paan shop on the street.

'So it's gangsters again,' mused Sasha. 'Your script is about gangsters again.'

'Ehehehe,' acquiesced Malik, 'I just like that genre, I guess.'

'I was talking to Ahishor Frances,' said Sasha. 'He thinks we make too many gangster films, and they tend to be violent for the sake of it, not meaningful. I don't think he is wrong actually.'

A cloud passed over Malik's face. 'Let Mr Ahishor make his grand meaningful movies with French funding and the blessings of his mom's live-in partner! And let him give his opinions to Scorcese and Tarantino!'

'I don't think he is wrong,' said Sasha peaceably, though he felt suddenly on edge.

'Ehehehe! Whaddever!'

For a while thereafter, Malik spoke very little, gazing instead at the ceiling and ruminating over his glass. Later, he was on his third drink and berating Sasha for not keeping up. Hitching up his shorts, he adjusted his seat and begged the waiter to help light his cigarette. Then he sat back, sucking at the cigarette, until the troubled look had left his large and amiable face. But it was visible again when he began to speak.

'Listen, had to tell you something. A very interesting thing happened when I was in Hyderabad. So basically, I had gone there without any agenda. Producer was funding the trip, so the idea was to spend time in the Old City, just meet people and listen to how they talk. They speak Dakhni Urdu na, it's very different. Oh, lots of things. Like they say "*Hao*" instead of "*Haan*", "*Meku*" instead of "*Mujh ko*". And they add "ich" to words, for example "*Woh kab* mental *hoke fatt jaye bharosa*-ich *nai*". We would say "*bharosa*-hi *nahi*"...So like that. Anyway *woh chhod*... (Let it be...) One day, I was chatting with an auto driver, and I was telling him that I want to meet people, local people. That same afternoon he came to my hotel—with a girl. In a burkha.'

'Ah,' said Sasha, as Malik chuckled, but soon Malik was smoking, grim-faced once more.

'A full burkha. Her name was Afroza. Basically, the auto guy was pimping her. But after he left, I told her, look, I'm a writer, I write films, I've come here for research, I'm not going to do anything with you, so just treat me like a brother and let's talk. Because I actually wanted a character like this! In the script, there is a prostitute, she gets picked up by a Don. So I told her I'm a writer, and slowly, slowly she began to trust me...ended up spending three full days with me. I even tried to book her a room in my hotel, but the hotel people were objecting. So in the day we used to meet and talk, and at night I used to drop her near a masjid. She told me she was living there because she had fought with her parents. But I used to drop her some distance away, because she said I must not be seen with her in that area. Because in that place, if a guy is seen with a girl in a burkha, it's dangerous.'

'What things did you talk about?' said Sasha. 'In the three days.'

'Ahh, lots of things. Basically, all the fuck-ups that happened with her, that made her get into this line...I also introduced her to one NGO there, they help homeless women. Anyway, I recorded most of our meetings, you can listen sometime.'

'Okay,' nodded Sasha. Malik seemed distracted. A few moments passed before he resumed his narrative.

'On that first day, Afroza was very quiet. She wasn't talking.

So I bought a bottle of Pepsi and I mixed whisky in it. After she drank a bit, she relaxed... So that worked well... Only thing was, she loved *daaru* man! She turned out to be a full-on alcohol addict... And then on the third night, we were sitting near a *talaab* (pond). Drinking Old Monk. Talking. I was also drunk. I didn't realize how drunk she was. Next thing I know, she's passed out.'

He was staring into the cobwebs in a dark corner of the ceiling. His tongue passed over his lips.

'*Bilkul hi, matlab,* fully passed out. She was gone. And there was nothing I could do! I tried to wake her up, but she was just not responding. And we were quite far from her home, that masjid area. The place where we were, I didn't know that place very well. It was not, like, too safe a place. The biggest problem was, I couldn't even call an auto or a taxi because, you get it right?'

'They would ask what you were doing with her,' said Sasha.

'If anybody at all had seen us, I would have got into serious, serious shit. Not just from the *sadak ki janta* (the public on the road) but even from the police. So there was no escape. So...first thing I did was, I took her phone and I deleted my number from it. I had to, I had no choice... And then I left.'

'You left her there?'

'I had no choice.'

'Did you call her later?' said Sasha.

'I did *re*! Next morning I came to Bombay. Called her up immediately. It said the number is out of service. Since then, it keeps saying the same thing. I can try even now!'

Placing his phone on the table, Malik pressed the buttons furiously. But as the call failed to go through, his manner grew detached. He took a sip of his drink and remarked, offhand:

'See...no reply... I called the NGO people also, the one I had taken her to. I asked the woman there—Afroza *aayi*? She said, *nai aayi* (she didn't come).'

Shrugging, Malik pocketed the phone and drank off what remained in his glass.

'Hopefully, she is okay,' said Sasha quietly. 'I guess you should not have researched in this way.'

'It just happened *re*.'

Sasha was frowning, with his head inclined, and his dark eyes nearly unblinking. He felt assailed by many discomforts, and uncertain of how and whether to express them. Eventually, he raised his head.

'In order to write a character, do you have to actually meet a person, literally get them to tell you things? Why not imagine a character? Isn't this very crude and forced—and also it is using a person. Isn't it?'

'I told her I was a writer *re*! Every writer does research!' Malik was looking ruffled—a rare occurrence. (He had a vast and melancholy self-possession. I had often seen him worried and troubled on his own account, but rarely did he lose his temper with another.)

But Sasha was speaking swiftly now.

'You still have to be careful. What I'm thinking is, if you can't imagine, or feel a character, if you are compelled to go out and *get* her like this, and then you find that you've bitten off more than you can chew—then maybe you are writing the wrong kind of story. Something that isn't close enough to you... Too voyeuristic... It's something to consider,' he finished with such gentleness in his voice that the angry retort on Malik's lips stalled momentarily.

Then, before Malik could speak, a jarring noise split the

quiet. The perspiring man on the adjacent table had dragged forward his chair. Sasha looked into bloodshot eyes, laden with animosity.

'Are you a mental case?' said the man. 'I think you have some problem.'

'Ehehehe,' Malik guffawed indulgently, but the stranger and eavesdropper continued to stare at Sasha.

'Any normal person would say, this was highly, highly *decent* behaviour! And you are pointing fingers at your friend! You take an ordinary man in his position—I'll tell you what he would have—first of all he would have fucked her. Talking, researching, all this can keep happening. In fact, shall I tell you something? The research would have been better with fucking! You would have learned much more! A whore talks the most at that time, when she is supposed to be doing her job. She was pretty *na*?' A sudden doubt seemed to assail him.

'She was pretty,' Malik chuckled, 'but I was obviously not going to do anything, Sir! I have a girlfriend.'

'So what?' the man demanded angrily. 'How would your girlfriend get to know? Anyway—that's your decision—because you are a gentleman.'

'I don't agree with you at all.'

Sasha was sitting up in his chair, his body tensing. He did not try to think. The words came to him quickly.

'I am an ordinary man too. And I would not have slept with her. And I don't have a girlfriend.'

'Ohh tell me,' said Malik suddenly, not noticing the gaze the middle-aged government officer was now casting over Sasha. 'What happened with you and Maithili? You liked her *na*?'

Sasha looked out at the pub's cloying and squalid darkness. It was bearing down on him, holding him fast to the table where they sat, in a corner of the room, pressing his back to the wall. The stranger's attention, he noticed, was fixed shamelessly upon him.

'Yes,' he nodded, 'but nothing happened. Now she's left the country, yes, she's gone abroad. She's travelling. But—I still have hope.'

Malik leaned forward, shaking his head. 'I think you should move on *re*. Like honestly speaking, I don't know her much. Just worked with her on the short film. Had no complaints—though she was not friendly at all. But generally speaking, *aise* situation main, *kucch hone nahi vaale*. (...in this kind of a situation, nothing is going to happen.) If she was going to respond, she would have responded already.'

Sasha felt the truth of the words, that were spoken with wisdom and experience. They stung mightily, but he waited, and endured.

'Now,' continued Malik, 'you are just harming yourself, and annoying her.'

'I don't ignore her annoyance,' said Sasha, 'I respect it every time. But it can't destroy my own obligations towards her. That's how I feel—I have an obligation to Maithili.'

'She does not want your obligation!' cried Malik.

'Come on, Malik,' said Sasha, with sudden vehemence. An ineffable healing was washing over him, strengthening him. 'Everything you're saying is very sensible. And yes, from the outside, I might look selfish and obsessed. But there are deeper truths! Are our obligations to people contractual? Aren't we obliged out of goodwill? Why else are we supposed to forgive even our enemies?... I am sure—it was not for nothing that I fell for her. I can't believe that it was for nothing. Something will emerge from this. It may be that she'll never like me—though

I still have hope. But whatever happens, I must keep caring for her—at least for the time being.'

He sat back, controlling his breathing. The government officer, who had been listening intently, was now looking confused. He beckoned to Sasha with a crook of his finger.

'Before this girl left,' said the officer, 'did you screw her? At least once?'

'No, no,' laughed Sasha, trying to look away. 'Of course not!'

'What do you mean "of course"?' said the man incredulously. Suddenly, his narrow eyes gleamed. 'Tell me something—have you ever screwed a girl?'

Sasha smiled again, but before he knew it, he was shaking his head. 'No,' he said.

'No wonder!' cried the man, 'I knew it! How old are you?'

'Twenty-eight,' said Sasha.

'Twenty-eight, and you've never screwed! Man, what are *you* doing?' He swivelled towards Malik, 'You should be getting your friend laid! What are you doing?'

As Malik fidgeted in embarrassment, the officer's companion, the figure in the checked shirt, who had been silent throughout, reached out a restraining hand.

'It's their business yaar. Ignore him,' he said to Sasha. 'He used to talk like this to me too, and I fell into the trap. It's your life, it's your choice. If you don't want it—'

'He *wants* it!' cried the first man. His eyes were frenzied, as though filled with visions. 'Just look at him! He is not some angel! He has a sick mind! Am I right? Oh, the things he would like to do to them! Oh, such glorious, dirty things! Am I right? Wait, I'm asking him, he'll tell us, I'm not forcing him! Wait!'

The smile had long ago left Sasha's face. He sat, stiff-faced, like one mesmerized. A hot flush, that had come over his cheeks, was draining quickly.

'You are not wrong,' said Sasha, 'But—'

Malik interrupted him with an urgent suggestion that they find another table. This, however, proved not to be necessary, because the government officer was soon being helped to his feet by his companion.

VII

On the Festival Circuit—Part One

At the film festival the previous year, I had watched twenty-seven films in six days. I had pored over the daily schedule, googled reviews, scanned the blogosphere and the twitter-verse for everything that caught my fancy. I had booked my movies punctually at midnight (the minute the website opened for bookings) and walked from hall to hall in the buzzing Andheri multiplex, stoked up with coffee and muffins, content to stand in the lengthiest queues. At excited intervals I had stopped and chatted with friends and familiar faces, but all in the unreal way of one drugged. I *was* drugged—by the hall's inky coolness, the congregation in the darkness, and that magic light from the screen, that brought people and vistas, marching in, pageant-like, from whole other worlds.

Afterwards, I had found time to be critical too, most of all to bemoan how abject Bollywood was, by comparison. But even that anger had been a propellant, pushing me to find like-minded people in my own milieu. It was at the film festival, the previous year, that I had seen *Schrödinger's Cat*.

But that year, I found myself in a strangely petulant state. When I had learned that the festival was in jeopardy, I had felt nothing (not the disappointment I would have expected). Later, when I read that the money had been raised, my first reaction was one of displeasure and irritation. I could not explain it at all. On Twitter, one night, I came across this exultant and much retweeted comment: 'The film festival is our Dussehra, Diwali and Ganpati combined!' It made me cantankerous in a way that I can only compare to an old person, who is bothered by the play of children.

I forced myself to register for the festival (though it felt like a chore), hoping that once I was there, I would be carried away as usual. Instead, I was profoundly restless, hardly able to sit through a single film. It was not that they were bad. I wouldn't know—I simply couldn't concentrate. Most of all, I stayed away from the local films. That too was a reversal of my behaviour the previous year, when I had specially sought them out, so I might later seek out their makers. But now, the whole exercise seemed burdensome—a distraction. Why, and from what, I couldn't say.

All this was most discomfiting, and throughout the festival that year, I hated my own company. Only once did I manage to forget myself. This happened, ironically, during the one time that I stepped into an Indian film. I had walked out of a screening, just a few minutes into it, and walked at random into another hall. No doubt I would have got up again after another few minutes—had Maithili's face, fourteen feet high, not come up before my eyes.

In the film, Maithili played a young, westernized girl doing an internship with an NGO in rural Haryana. She stumbles upon a girl child-abortion racket, bravely or naively takes it on, is attacked and raped in a dusty maidan by drunk and angry culprits, but not before she has forced an end to their activity.

However, a pointless romantic track and a general absence of nuance made the whole thing rather fatiguing viewing. (Later, I read an observation in a review that perfectly expressed my thoughts: 'The socially relevant theme of this movie is made to serve a gangsters' and good guys' plot that would not be out of place in a B-movie. Tragically, our shock at the truly abhorrent practice of female infanticide is undermined by our boredom with the storytelling.')

What made me watch the entire film, regardless, was Maithili—and not at all because I knew her. There was something riveting about her acting. It was not that it was excellent—or even good. At various points, her dialogues and her expressions seemed to me off, 'floating' and out of key with the scene and the situation. Nevertheless, they were impossible to merely mock. They compelled instead an unusual respect—such was the spirit in which they were essayed. She was never simply struggling and failing, or overwhelmed at the task before her—the mismatch seemed rather the converse. She herself seemed larger than the business of pretending. With her slow, curious gaze, her frowning concentration and the minimalist grace of her movements, she gave the impression of a vast, self-possessed intelligence engaged in study, experimenting, as it were, with the character she was given to play.

When the credits rolled, and the lights came on in the auditorium, I looked about on a kind of hunch. Sure enough, it was not long before I spotted Ahishor. He was sitting by himself in a deserted back-corner. The hood of his sweatshirt was pulled back over his wild-haired face, and though his posture was languid as usual, he was scowling fiercely as he stared into space. My gaze swept over the rest of the crowd, searching out other faces I knew. I noticed Sasha, in the middle of a row of strangers, unable, it seemed, to stop smiling. Then, just as I was considering getting up and going over to Ahishor, a ponytailed man who had been hovering near the screen began speaking into a mike.

Certain members of the cast and crew were introduced in person. We applauded dutifully. Suddenly, I saw a handsome gentleman in a blue jacket getting to his feet, and rising with him, an attractive lady in a red sari, who was all smiles and blushes. Seated next to her, clapping his large hands together and quite goggle-eyed with goodwill, was Jatin Khanna.

'The beautiful lead actress, Maithili Krishna, unfortunately could not be present today,' said the announcer, 'but we are lucky to have her parents with us. Mr Suraj Krishna and Mrs Tara Krishna, please join us for the discussion! Everybody in the audience, do remain seated. As I said, before we started, we'll now have a short discussion on the film...the social issues that it raises. Of course, these are vital issues for us all to introspect about. So can we have Chaitanya [that was the director], and Aditya [the lead actor], and Mr Krishna, could you come up front—we have some chairs here—and Mrs Krishna! Mrs Krishna please!... could you come up front...and then afterwards we can open it up for questions...What? Yes?'

Here he broke off, and there followed a brief huddle near the screen, involving the announcer, the director and two young festival volunteers. The upshot of the confabulation was that, due to a paucity of time, the proposed panel discussion was being called off in favour of a series of short addresses, to be followed (the announcer hastened to assure us) by the audience's chance to talk.

Presently, the director, who must have been in his thirties, began to speak in what sounded to my ears like a series of insincere homilies. I heard him declare that he wanted to make his next movie in Hindi, so as to take his vital message to a mass audience, and I fell to sniggering in my seat. He was looking to sell out as quickly as possible! Soon I ceased listening altogether. I stared instead at the Krishnas, husband and wife, and Jatin, in the third row.

I gave my ear to the older generation too, as I was accustomed to doing. When Mr Krishna ambled out into the aisle, and took the mike with an authoritative, though gracious nod, I was content to merely listen. Whatever mutinous thoughts may have been bubbling in my mind, stayed at the back of it.

'A very good afternoon to all of you!' he began. His voice was polished, rather high-pitched and endearingly shaky. He looked happy and excited to be addressing us. Suraj Krishna was a well-built man, bobbing up and down in his suit, with the great white screen behind, and the great red wave of our chairs rising before him.

'First of all, I must confess to being completely undeserving of your applause. I have played no role whatsoever in fostering my daughter Maithili's artistic talent. I myself have not an artistic bone in my body. However, I am happy today to bask in her glory!'

Warm and appreciative laughter broke out in the hall. Here, it was felt, was a sophisticated speaker, some notches above the usual film event fare.

'On a more serious note,' he continued, 'while I am a relative stranger to the world of cinema—not entirely, mind you, because when I was a young man, I did love the French New Wave. Jean Seberg was my first and last on-screen crush! [There was more laughter and applause from one pocket of the hall, especially fulsome from the ponytailed announcer, but also confusion elsewhere and some murmurings of 'Who?'] But my own preoccupation for most of my adult life, which I have spent working with various organizations in and out of India, and for the last several years, the World Bank—has been economic development and social change—which of course, are intimately and crucially related. So I must congratulate Chaitanya and everybody else who has worked on this fine film. It really gives me a lot of hope to see this... Hope, not only for my daughter's career and a further opportunity to share in her triumphs for me—but for the future of the country, yes, for India. I have always felt that if we are going to be successful, in this endeavour, of social progress, of educating and raising the moral standards of our nation, especially as regards the treatment of women—because we all know that there is simply no other matter as vital to modern India as the status of women and the girl-child—then the new generation has to take the reins. You, who are privileged to have had good education, sound upbringing, the opportunities to express yourself, must use those opportunities for the betterment of all. So how wonderful it is to see that you are doing it! And in cinema, especially—there is no medium of communication quite like cinema, is there? Nothing else has the power to move a mass audience in quite the same way. I want to share with you all, my own experience, with a film project that we did at the Bank a few years ago—'

He carried on to describe what I gathered was a short film contest on the subject of climate change. Soon he was telling us the names and histories of the illustrious judges, a witty anecdote about one of them, who was apparently a great personal friend, and the quality and provenance of the contributions. He was speaking slowly, with many rich pauses. There had grown over his manner a certainty that he was being interesting, wise, and much-liked by us all. He returned to his theme about the duties of the younger generation. I looked at my watch, and at the announcer, who was stealing secret glances at his own. The speeches had been intended to keep the programme brief.

But when I turned with a sigh and a click of my tongue, to the person beside me, I found her (a well-dressed young woman, with a scarf around her throat) staring mutely ahead. It seemed to me that such an uncritical blankness was dominating the crowd at large. Mr Krishna went on enjoying his speech, oblivious to the fact that he was personally extraneous to the film, and stealing the spotlight from the film-makers, and yet being met with surprising docility.

'But I am afraid I am speaking too much,' he said at last, with an indulgent smile. 'You haven't come to hear me, after all.'

No sooner had he uttered these knowing words than a terrific clapping broke out from the back of the hall. The sound was produced by only one person, which made it all the more sharply pointed. I swivelled, but was only in time to see the heavy doors swinging shut. At once I looked over to Ahishor's seat. It was empty.

Mr Krishna finished his peroration with admirable composure. (I wondered if he even realized what had happened.) In the quiet that followed, I saw the announcer leaning over the front row of chairs, to say something urgently to Tara. She waved her hand violently, presumably waving away the man's apologies.

'I'm told we need to clear the hall quickly for the next show, so we'll move straight to a couple of questions from the audience. But please—keep them short!...Yes, the gentleman in the middle...'

I did not stay. I suddenly could not wait to find Ahishor.

* * *

After the screening, the Krishnas, with Jatin in tow, went out to one of the cafes in the area, to wind down the pleasant evening. But try as he might (I suspect he never tried very hard) Jatin could not restrain his inner dissatisfaction.

It was what one might call a chronic condition. I have mentioned already that Tara Krishna had been Jatin's first love. The major emotional jolts of his youth had been on her account. I refer to the usual—her rejection of his ardour, her choice of another, whom, even when he accepted his own unworthiness, he could not accept as anything more than a pragmatic match, the concretization of it all with her marriage and the establishment of her household. In one sense, it appeared that time (the intervening decades) and space (they had often been divided by continents) had been wholly successful peacemakers. Over the years, Jatin had spent countless pleasant hours with the married couple. Indeed, in Tara's presence, this bull-like, painfully energetic man was often unrecognizably docile. But I wonder how often, time and space, are truly put to the test. And just because he had continued to hang around, with his heart still in it, so there did occur those moments when all the seemingly long-settled work of numbing and mollification, came off, like the red nose of a circus clown. Now, for example, Tara and Suraj were back in India for the foreseeable future. (There was work pending on his late father's estate, and preparations to make for their son Vishnu's marriage.) Here they all were, together at the cafe. Jatin felt the years rolling away...

He was irritated because Suraj had gone on for so long in the cinema hall, and Tara had been denied the chance to speak. It was she who been a consultant with UNICEF, researched the plight of girl-children in North India—besides, she was a woman herself. Was it right that her voice should have been stifled by a loudmouth? Was that not really the story of her whole marriage? And she had acquiesced to this smug insult, as she had to them all.

Jatin had neither the courage nor the tact to raise the specific issue. But it was not long after their coffee arrived that he began to break out in talk.

'You know, Suraj, sometimes you really haven't got a clue, do you?'

Mr Krishna, who was sipping greedily from his cup, paused and raised an eyebrow. He was not disconcerted.

'All your praise of the new generation—have you seen these kids? They are not concerned about anything beyond their careers. Trust me on that! I'm not talking about Maithili, she is exceptional without doubt. I've always said that. But the vast majority is nothing like her. For example, the guy I'm working with right now, Arvind, yes... I really don't know how long I can keep him on, he is smug and lazy. Intellectually lazy. Dhruv was much better, of course, I like Dhruv, but even he...[here Jatin shook his head violently]. They're all soft, they drift with the tide. They don't think, they don't read!'

'I was speaking,' said Mr Krishna, 'in the context of the film we saw. In my opinion, it was a very good effort indeed.'

Tara nodded, the sight of which struck Jatin like spurs. 'It was shallow and sensationalist. It was a wasted opportunity to actually say something. Honestly speaking, Maithili was the only good thing in it. And the music—though they overused it.'

Mr Krishna said nothing. Jatin's clumsy aggression was familiar to him, though most often as stories overheard and laughed at. But it was painful to experience, and (he thought to himself) embarrassingly jejune.

'You're being extremely harsh,' said Tara. She was not smiling at all. 'You are the one who is constantly complaining about Bollywood producing meaningless films. Now here is a film about something that really matters.'

'Yes, yes! That's why I called it a wasted opportunity. Come on, even you can see that it was sensationalist. Are you saying it wasn't sensationalist?'

Suraj Krishna began to chuckle, while Tara stared at Jatin, still eagerly dwarfing his end of the table. In her gaze was a strange mingling of disappointment and fury.

'Do you know it has won a National Award?' she said.

'Really? In which category?'

'The best English film.'

'Aah! That's not hotly contested, trust me. As for National Awards—well, that's a story of its own. Believe me.'

'Pessimistic as always,' said Mr Krishna thoughtfully. He picked up his cup and placed it back on the saucer, enjoying the resonant click as it settled into the indentation—just so!

'I'm not pessimistic,' pounced Jatin, 'I really hope for good work by young people. That's why I get irritated at their attitude. Remember I'm not talking about Maithili. I'm talking about the majority of them.'

'Well your irritation is irritating for other people,' said Tara, 'as is your presumption that all we think about is Maithili. No, don't start talking again! I don't think either of us is in the mood to humour this right now.'

Jatin sat back, breathing tensely. His lip had curled like a baby's, as it did at such times; he looked not far from tears.

'I'll shut up,' he brought out huskily, 'only because *you* are asking.'

'Please do.' Tara remained unsmiling.

After a few moments, Mr Krishna began to nod, just as though he had been mulling something over all the while.

'Talking of the younger generation—'

'Can we talk of something else?' said his wife.

'No, no, wait, listen. I was thinking about that young man whom Dipankar put through to us.'

'Oh... Mihir?'

'Yes! He really impressed me, I must say. You too, I think? Yes, I thought so. Outstanding young man!'

It transpired that Mihir was back in Mumbai (which I hadn't then known), and that one of the first people he had been to see was the Krishnas, at their Malabar Hills home. There was no particular purpose to his visit, and it was just this that had most pleased Mr Krishna. 'It was nice,' he explained, 'to meet a young man who understands the old-fashioned concept of a courtesy call. I remember how when I went to Delhi for the first time, I was actually carrying letters of introduction from my father. And I did meet all those people—in fact, I got my first job in the Ford Foundation on a tip from N.K. Rao, who had recently retired from the Sri Ram Centre of Industrial Relations. It gives a young man a tremendous boost to connect with important people in the older generation. This boy did his degree at Columbia. He has been writing on liberalism and constitutionalism. Extremely polite and intelligent. We had a really invigorating chat about the Nehruvian culture of open-mindedness which one sees so little of today. I actually suggested to Mihir that he should do a little book—I have wanted to do it myself, but now I don't see myself making the time. A little book on the *foreign* scholars and consultants whom Nehru worked with. There were so many of them, Nehru had no xenophobia, you see, even though India had just gained Independence. Anyway, it was a great little chat we had, I was really glad to have met Mihir, and I told Dipankar that. It seems the Joshis have known him ever since he was a child. So you see,' he concluded at length, smiling sanguinely at Jatin, while patting down his still-thick head of hair (an attainment he was extremely proud of), 'while these may be dark times in some respects, I do have reasons to be hopeful for the future.'

Jatin shrugged sullenly, before glancing up at Tara. She was holding a muffin in her hands, nibbling daintily. A strange sense of betrayal came upon him as he realized she was not going to voice her own opinion.

'Oh, the designer wrote back,' she said suddenly, looking over the table at her husband. 'Let me forward you what he's sent. I like the second option best.'

Soon, they were talking about their son's wedding cards and the wedding preparations in general. Jatin's thumb began to cramp, as sometimes happened when he had been sitting too long with his fists half-clenched. He stifled a cry of pain. However, he was noticed. Tara exclaimed with sympathy, which gladdened Jatin, until he perceived a smile lurking in her eyes. He knew he looked ridiculous, with his crooked and ungainly thumb quite paralysing the rest of him. But the pain was fierce and her laughter (he felt sure he hadn't imagined it) had wounded as well as annoyed him. He pretended the cramp was easing quickly, so the Krishnas would cease being solicitous and go back to their conversation. It took many minutes of discreet massaging before he was all right again.

* * *

In the meantime, I had caught up with Ahishor in the lobby of the multiplex.

'I saw you in the hall,' I said breathlessly.

He frowned. Suddenly, it struck me that I had nothing further to say. He had been moving quickly to the lift. I had held him up. Then he smiled and winked, and my sense of blundering dissipated in relief.

'Are you coming to the office tomorrow?'

The next day was a Sunday, and our next shoot (with a member of the Indian Rationalist Association) was only scheduled for Tuesday. 'Oh! I was thinking of going to the Lit Fest,' I explained, 'the one in Bandra. There's a friend of mine—'

'Go by all means,' said Ahishor, turning on his heel, raising a patient hand, 'it's fine. Say hi to my mother and Karim if you see them.'

I still wonder if anything would have turned out differently had I been present at the office that Sunday. Not that I was likely to perform any heroics. The awful episode would have taken place regardless. But I would have been saved my guilt and regret at the thought of Ahishor being all alone to face it. Could that in turn have stopped me, from plunging so deeply, into all that I did afterwards?

But these too are idle thoughts.

VIII

On the Festival Circuit—Part Two

I will recount the events of that day chronologically, as I experienced them. At ten o'clock, I was in an auto, on the way to Bandra's Mehboob Studios. I had only a vague idea of the literary treats in store (it seemed to me that at least three different literary festivals had taken place in the city that month—though I am probably wrong). I was chiefly excited for my date.

Her name was Janhavi. I had first spotted her in Aram Nagar, stepping out of an audition—we had looked at each other. After that, her face had popped up quite by chance on a friend's Facebook page. This friend I had grovelled before and pleaded with to arrange a meeting. (I surprised myself; I had never pursued someone so openly.) But even after she facilitated a second encounter, it had taken a lot of trying, texting, and bewildered waiting on my part for the date to finally come about. It crossed my mind, as the auto went by Juhu beach, that things had changed a lot since college. Without boasting, I can truthfully assert that girls fawned over me then. I never needed to try. But there were certain things Janhavi had said to me—and she was not the first, since college—that made me feel bafflingly inadequate in some essential way, like a man in the dock, on charges unexplained.

I was only five minutes late, but she was calling already as I walked through the gates. I had already spotted her. She was standing beside the front lawns of the compound, among colourful streamers and advertising banners, in a cream top and grey jeans, her curly hair falling over slender shoulders, her face tantalizingly averted.

'Hello Dhruv,' she was saying, 'I'm waiting. Are you close to reaching?'

'Heyyy Janhavi,' I said, 'listen, I'm so sorry, I just got a call from Aamir Khan Productions.'

'What?'

I walked slowly towards her as I spoke.

'They are shooting their new film, their lead actor suddenly fell sick, so they called me as a replacement. I couldn't say no ya.'

'They called you?' She was irritated, disbelieving.

'I'm in Film City right now. Aren't you happy for me?'

'Dhruv... Are you not coming for the Lit Fest?'

'How can I come for the Lit Fest baba? I'm sitting with Aamir right now. He's wearing a yellow hat.'

'Dhruv...why didn't you tell me in the morning?' She was frantic with annoyance.

'I wanted to tell you in person.' I bowed into view, grinning widely. "I thought you'd be angry otherwise.'

'Fool!' she exclaimed, which was predictable enough, but there seemed such depths to her disgust that I felt shivers going through me.

She was smiling soon though, after biting into a mutton roll, although she had insisted the previous minute that she wasn't in the least hungry and that I was delaying us for the session she particularly wanted to attend.

Standing in the sunshine, eating good food, with a happy-looking crowd milling about us, and Jahnavi looking so pretty, I was bursting with appreciation. I wanted to find a quiet, shaded corner for us to sit in, and there to talk about Manto and Hitchcock (shared interests we had discovered) and her childhood and mine and the music she liked—and so on. But she was adamant. She led me into a huge, sunny, air-conditioned hall, where a packed audience was staring at an empty stage.

'There are no seats left!' she whispered excitedly. I was astonished myself at the turnout. Luckily, we found a pair of empty chairs in a side row, with a relatively clear view of the proceedings.

My surprise only grew when I cast eyes on Mihir, in a blue blazer and a dark blue tie, striding onto the stage. A woman situated on the sidelines began to introduce him (a short introduction that seemed more full of adjectives than information), while he settled himself on one of the two chairs on stage, poured himself a glass of water, crossed his legs and began to drink. Moments later, the hall was filled with applause. A second man, tall and angular, wearing a well-creased shirt with folded sleeves, was shaking hands with Mihir. Their faces now appeared on a big screen by the stage. The newcomer had curving eyebrows and a hooked nose. He was balding, but young-looking, probably no more than forty (a ripe old age, however, for literary success). He stared out at the audience with a piercing, flitting gaze.

'Who is he?' I asked aloud.

'Don't you know?' Janhavi stared. 'That's Giri Joseph. He was shortlisted for the Booker Prize! If you don't know, at least listen to the introduction.'

'Oh ya ya,' I retorted, 'I read about that, of course. What was the name of his book? Have you read it?'

She did not reply but motioned angrily at me to keep quiet. I was about to tell her that I knew Mihir.

On stage, the conversation had begun. I was immediately struck by Mihir's manner. Everything about him, from the shoes up, was polished. He was sitting very still and calm, speaking in polite, restrained sentences. He exuded such an air of respectful deference and admiring scholarliness, as I had never imagined he possessed, but in the comfort of which his interlocutor was blossoming. The caginess had gone from the writer's eyes; the superior light had settled in. He was growing relaxed, a smile came over his thin lips.

Of the actual plot of the prizewinning novel, I did not understand a great deal that morning, though later I educated myself. It was based, apparently, on actual events that had occurred in a group of villages in Tamil Nadu in the late 1960s. A low-caste peasant uprising against high-caste feudal landlords had, in time, been brutally crushed. But not before one dramatic week when the revolutionaries had burned down a police station (killing everyone inside) and derailed a goods train. The planner-in-chief of these operations had been a young Brahmin man, a school and college topper, from a highly educated family of mostly government servants. 'A family not dissimilar to my own,' the writer told us, in dry, carrying tones.

The ironic smile, having once appeared, never left his face. He proved to be full of wry wit and wisdom. With an attentive Mihir providing the leads, Joseph expanded on various subjects—the Naxal movement, caste and class hierarchies, the 'stultifications of the Indian middle class' (his expression), manual labour and modern life, the 'egregious buzzkill' (I quote again) of ritualistic Hinduism.

Very quickly, I was hooked. Joseph's novel (there were copies on stage) seemed so fat, the subject seemed so serious, and the scale of the research seemed so considerable—and yet he spoke about it all with such light-heartedness—almost indifference! I thought he was perfectly cool. His self-awareness, for example, when he said (I am recollecting):

'The modern novel is itself a highly bourgeois product. It is written from a position of leisure and privilege, it is a commodity in the global markets of capitalism. And here I am writing about a revolution... Ha!... Well, well... You see, I have been to those villages. I have talked to the people. And that's why, you know, it amazes me, when I hear writers, particularly in the English language, taking themselves so seriously. Writers and readers and literary festivals and the whole damn jingbang—pardon me... I think we should all be acutely aware all the time, of how insignificant our activity is, when it comes to effecting any real change in this country, that's darn well crying out for it....I think that's a cross we all should carry—it's nothing, but it's the least one can do... Oh I have a lot of fun, don't get me wrong, I have a great time every time I visit India [he had lived in London since he was twenty-five years old]. But by the same token, I despair of India, because I *shouldn't* be having such a great time. Many, many other people are having a rather rotten time... I suppose writing is a kind of expiation, whereby I look at this society and I force myself not to blink. It's so darn easy to blink, or just to look away...so terribly easy to become complacent... "He said, sipping his latte"... [So he was—there was coffee on stage] You see? *This* is why I have to kill myself, writing those scenes...'

As I smiled in admiration of the great writer's honesty, and listened eagerly for more, another, less pleasant sensation began to overtake me. I was hearing loud laughter from various quarters of the audience, and it was getting on my nerves.

A few seats away from me, a lady wrapped in a red shawl, with a chic haircut and thin spectacles resting on an aristocratic nose, was throwing her head back in staccato, silvery cackles. Further to the front, an unshaven man with long, greasy hair kept up a running series of knowing chuckles. I glared about the room, at the faces of the clever and the beautiful, the well-read and the well-heeled; and the gaping grins that were scattered throughout. Then Giri Joseph said something further; the woman in the red shawl began tittering again, and I hurled a furious look at the back of her head, before swivelling towards Janhavi.

'Why are *they* laughing?' I said.

She looked at me strangely.

'He is mocking *them*! The joke is on people like *them*! Don't they get that?'

I had raised my voice. Somebody shushed me from the row behind, while Janhavi turned pointedly away, her face expressing an almost panicked incredulity. I was surprised myself at my outburst, it was completely untypical, yet I felt pleased and triumphant too, for my thoughts were surely true. Joseph was condemning these very people, 'people like us', hypocrites who claimed to be champions of a just and equal society, but were really quite happy to prop up its inequity. That woman in the red shawl, I was sure, did nothing at home; her maid did everything, and she paid her nothing, and would not dream of letting her sit on her drawing room furniture, those same sofas from where she and her friends must speak so feelingly about the emancipation of the underprivileged!

Outside in the grounds, I was still enthused with my epiphany, though I tried to be funny and charming for Janhavi's sake. She was having none of it. I suggested we drink *nimboo paani* and talk for a while, but already she was casting yearning looks at the adjacent studio, where people milled at the entrance. Suddenly I was annoyed and said so. She retorted that I seemed interested only in food and drink and didn't know how to behave myself during literary sessions. I began to laugh; the charge was so absurd, for I had actually listened and reacted to what the writer said, not come to gawk at the Booker Prize runner-up like so many others—Janhavi herself, for that matter. Very quickly, I was staring at her retreating back, her hair flouncing over jaunty shoulders.

Wrestling with my pride, I had just about decided to follow her, when I heard my name called out. Turning, I beheld Mihir. He was standing by the lane that led to the front gardens. In the same glance, I took in the lank figure of Giri Joseph, walking away quickly, flanked by two young volunteers with badges. Mihir was beckoning to me. I hurried towards him.

'Did you catch our session?' he called out.

'I loved it! He is so good! I mean, I haven't read his book, but—'

'Who, Giri? Yes he's quite sweet,' grinned Mihir. 'Come, I'll introduce you. What's the matter? Don't be shy, Dhruv, you're a superstar yourself!'

With my thoughts in a whirl, I fell in stride with him. Soon we were dodging the crowds, ducking towards a private region of the compound, where there appeared a courtyard—sheltered by trees—a second, smaller garden and a closed door. A young male face with bloodshot eyes swam into my vision.

'This is the author's corner,' it began to say, but already

Mihir was quieting the interruption. Entering steadily, he put out a hand to hold the door open for me.

The author's corner resembled a cut-price airport lounge. There were counters loaded with sundry food and drink, and a discreet distance away, tables and chairs clothed in white, about which a collection of well-dressed men and women sat, marinating. The first thing I saw was Karim Azad, in a dazzling orange kurta and silky red shawl, moving from the coffee machine towards the seating. He nodded absently at Mihir and myself, but his gaze was unfocused, and he seemed to be smiling all to himself. Then Mihir began to wave furiously. I noticed, waving back, a man and a woman installed at a table at the back of the room. Giri Joseph was sitting beside them. My heart began to race, but I tried to keep pace with Mihir as he bounded towards the group.

That morning, I was introduced to Dipankar and Ira Joshi, though I was too nervous to register their names. Yet they seemed to me a most kindly couple. I felt, in their presence, something warm and maternal, a memory of the atmosphere of my childhood in Delhi. Ira told me that Mihir had already spoken of me. Dipankar asked if I knew Giri, before introducing us, like equals. Their faces were fat and jolly, their moods seemed to rest on deep and generous reserves of comfort. The table was piled with food. I was pressed upon to have cake and coffee.

I found that I was happy merely to observe the faces around me, and listen to the sound of their conversing. But even in this dulled state of mind, certain things caught my attention. Giri Joseph, whom I had just that day begun to revere, was appearing oddly touchy, even as Mihir (who had removed his coat, and already finished a cup of coffee) was talking nineteen to the dozen.

'Yes, I think it was a reasonable success,' he said, 'especially considering I had no time whatsoever to even read the book. My apologies for that, Giri.'

'Well—,' began the writer, his lip curling.

'Oh I know you don't mind,' continued Mihir. 'You are a professional, you know how these things are. Also, you see, nobody in the audience had read it either. So it's probably good that we began from common ground.'

'It was a fairly capable discussion,' Joseph spoke calmly, 'if not on the book itself, then at least on subjects pertaining to the book.'

'By the way, I hope I didn't take you too deep into things,' said Mihir anxiously. 'I'm a journalist, so I sometimes get carried away, you understand!'

At this point, Ira said that she was surprised that Giri and Mihir had not met before (they had so many people in common), but that having known them both for years, she had felt sure they would put on a great session together, and therefore, had recommended their pairing to the festival organizers.

'I wouldn't call it *great*,' said Giri. 'Besides, what are these... displays really worth, if, when all is said and done, *nobody* is reading.' He raised his eyebrows meaningfully at Mihir, but was soon frowning as the latter's hand thumped his shoulder.

'Giri is being modest,' cried Mihir delightedly, 'and honest! He was the same in there—brutally honest, even about his own work. The crowd loved that. You know, we Indians are so used to fetishizing the Booker Prize—it's become a kind of national panacea. It was extraordinary to hear a Booker Prize winner—well, not a winner, I know, I know, but the shortlist is the big achievement, isn't it? Where was I? Yes, a Booker Prize shortlisted author admitting himself, that in practical terms, his novel is quite useless.'

'I'm sure I didn't use the word useless,' said Giri. He was clearly growing agitated, though perhaps he was too startled to be really expressive. Mihir had played such a deferential second fiddle on stage.

'You used many words where one would have done,' retorted Mihir, 'Ha! I'm joking, of course! Though it's true as well.'

I was baffled myself. Surely this was rank impertinence, towards such a celebrated writer! What was he trying to achieve? But Mihir's eyes were shining with pure pleasure. He seemed to be performing as naturally as he breathed. I watched in a kind of awe, as he suddenly turned serious and thoughtful.

'By the way, how have the reviews been so far? Or has it all been fluff coverage? I saw that piece in *India Today*, about your favourite colour or something like that. Amazingly nonsensical!'

'I suppose that's Indian literary criticism for you,' Giri shrugged, though uncomfortably.

'Awful! A book about India ought to be reviewed well in India! I'm sure you'd value that much more than anything you get anywhere else. Wouldn't you?... Yes...it's a shame! The truth is, you would probably have got more serious coverage here, if you hadn't been linked with the Booker!' Mihir grinned at the Joshis, and then (I smiled back, but he was looking away already) at me.

'There have been a couple of good reviews though,' began Giri. 'Meenakshi Roy in the *Express* for example, she was rather good.'

Mihir waved a dismissive hand.

'You deserve better than the likes of Roy! You know what, let me try to help with this. I'll speak to a few people. Let me see...I'll talk to Vinod.'

'Vinod...?'

Mihir stared back blankly. 'Vinod Paranjpe, of course.'

Giri Joseph hastened to reply. 'Of course! Well, that would be very nice indeed, if *he* were to review it.'

To my amazement, he was leaning in towards Mihir now, who sat back in his white-backed chair, neutral and pondering.

'I'll see what I can do.'

'Excellent,' cried Dipankar Joshi, who was watching closely. 'These days, we are surrounded by bright young people, Giri. Which reminds me, I believe you met Vishnu's sister? I am forgetting her name. Maithili...'

Later, I untangled the connections that had led to this encounter. Giri was known to the Joshis via their daughter Sukanya, whom he had taught years ago, as a young lecturer in Delhi University, shortly before he left India for good. Through Sukanya (they had remained close friends), he had come to meet her fiancée. Then some months ago, Vishnu had connected him with his sister, for at the time Maithili had been in the UK, working (so I gathered) on a novel.

Over the preceding half-hour, the expression on Giri Joseph's face had gone from satisfied to annoyed to anxious, which lessened the surprise of his gaze now turning dark with recrimination. It crossed my mind, however, that the atmosphere about our table had grown startlingly frank. But the Joshis appeared sanguine, as Giri began to speak, with palpable distaste.

'Maithili, yes. I met her all right. Tried very hard to help her out with her writing...such as it was...but it seems to me that she's one of those people who can't be helped.'

'Hmm,' grunted Ira Joshi, with interest.

'A talented girl,' Dipankar smiled faintly, 'beautiful and talented.'

'I saw precious little evidence of her talent, Dipankar,' said Giri coldly. There was a pause, before his mouth quivered and he spat out the story.

'What happened was, she wrote to me after Suki connected us on email. Said she was in Sussex, at some hostel, writing a novel and that she needed a "mentor". That's the word she used. I said I'd be happy to meet. So she came down to London. I took her to lunch in Liverpool Street. I found her very shy at first, she didn't want to talk about her book at all. I said all right, don't talk about it, write me about it on email, and send me the manuscript, I'll be happy to read. But even that prospect got her jittery. So I gave her a lot of my time. I took her out a few times, it wasn't just that afternoon. Really tried to make her feel comfortable, and also give her a sense of how the writing business works, because I could see at once that she was a dreadful amateur. For instance, she had this idea that she could get published "by the end of the year". I told her it took my first novel five years from the day I finished—to find an *agent*—and two more years to be published. And she hadn't even finished a draft. Well, so eventually she sent me something, a chapter, which, well, was frankly unreadable. If you had told me that an educated girl of twenty-six could spell and punctuate like *that*, I wouldn't have believed it. I really wouldn't have!'

He was sneering, of course, but I thought I detected in his voice a kind of wonderment as well. As he continued to the climax of this bitter memory, his mood seemed actually to improve, as though he were softening in the telling.

'If it had been anybody else, I would have ceased my efforts posthaste. But I thought I might have to answer to the two of you! [Dipankar and Ira smiled wanly back.] So I said to myself, well, after all, she has a presence, she has some flair, certainly personally she can be rather striking. Even if I don't quite see it, maybe there is a spark here that somebody else can do something with. So I called her home one evening. I was having a little dinner party, to which I'd also invited Peter Townsend—my agent, as you know. Maithili arrived, punctually enough. And she was fine, to be honest. A bit on the quiet side, but very well-spoken. I had already told Pete about her, so he was on his best behaviour too—thankfully! He was very gentle with her. Asked her some subtly leading questions about what she was writing, the genre, the themes, and so on. And at the end of the night, he invited her to send him the MS. So a very happy ending for all concerned—I would have thought!'

Giri paused, with his mouth working soundlessly. I was listening intently, until I noticed Mihir, with a bored expression, gazing about the room. Suddenly, he was grinning and nodding. Turning, I saw Karim Azad smiling back at him, and winking with extraordinary familiarity.

'About a week later,' continued Giri, 'I get a mail from Pete with some news about my American edition, and a postscript: 'Your young friend hasn't written to me.' I wrote *back*, saying Pete, she's shy, could you send her a reminder please? Now I should not have asked him to do that, I can't think why I did. But he did it—as a favour to me! Imagine my embarrassment and chagrin, therefore, when three days later, I get another mail from him. Just a blank mail, with a forwarded message attached. I'll...wait, let me quote verbatim.'

He pulled out his phone. Through the corner of my eye, I could see Mihir, still scanning the room.

'This is what she wrote him,' said Giri softly, '"I apologize that I will not be sending you my manuscript. It has become clear to me that the writing establishment in power does not include esoterically awakened souls. My words must remain secret. Perhaps some day. M'"

Giri looked up at us silently. 'Ha!' said Mihir. 'Excuse me,' he added, getting up quickly and striding over to where Karim was now standing, in a corner of the room.

'Wonderful talk this morning, Sir-ji!' I heard Mihir saying, 'Really fantastic!'

I saw Giri frowning. 'Didn't he only get in at eleven?' he muttered. But soon he was staring back into his phone.

'I'm trying to find that chapter she sent me,' he said, 'Strange, I must have deleted it. Though I don't remember doing that...'

Ira Joshi turned to me and said I must visit at their Greater Kailash home when I was next in Delhi.

'We keep an open house. It's full of young people all day long. Sometimes they put up performances in our ground floor space. We have music, we have theatre, it's very lovely, you must come. What is it, Dipankar?'

'Nalini is here,' said her husband, nodding towards the door.

Nalini Frances had entered the room. She had burst in with beauty and energy, in a crackling green sari, her eyes smouldering, her face flushed with colour. Everybody saw at once that she was in a high state of agitation.

'Karim!' she cried, rushing forward.

IX

'A Condemnable Incident'

In a few moments, Mihir came running back to our table. We all waited for him to speak but he moved wordlessly to gather up his blazer.

'What happened?' said Dipankar Joshi.

'Ahishor is hurt. No, it should be all right, he's at home, he's not in hospital. But I must rush. I'll call you up later.'

He bent to embrace, in a symbolic way, first Ira, and then Dipankar, before shaking hands swiftly with Giri Joseph, who was frowning as though he suspected some trick (a stupid expression, as I recall). But I was on my feet.

'I'll go with you!' I exclaimed.

'As you like,' said Mihir, turning towards the door from where Nalini and Karim had passed already. The Joshis bade me hurry on quickly. A silence had fallen over the room at large.

Outside, Mihir continued to stride three or four paces ahead of me. Suddenly he put on a burst of speed, as I spied, in the compound's main road, a black sedan, with Karim lowering himself into it. Then equally suddenly Mihir came to a halt. He turned his head, and I glimpsed an expression of annoyance, even as I realized that my presence made one too many for the car. The vehicle moved off (Mihir would have caught up to it had he kept going); I ran up alongside him.

'There'll be autos just outside,' I put in anxiously.

'Get one,' he snapped.

In the swirling traffic beyond the gates, it took me a minute or two to accomplish this. In the meantime, Mihir made no effort to assist. He stood by the gates sullenly, glaring at the road. His cropped hair had lost its combed-down appearance and the collar of his shirt was not straight.

When we climbed into the auto, I realized he was still upset about missing the sedan.

'I could have asked the organizers for another car,' he muttered, 'but they would have dawdled. Well, I suppose this is all right.'

Thereafter, he sat, plunged in silence. To my query regarding what precisely had happened with Ahishor, he opened his mouth, and then, appearing to change his mind, closed it with an exasperated grunt. After flinging several dirty looks at the adjoining traffic, he covered his nose and mouth with his hands, and lowered his head. His eyes fastened oddly on the floor of the vehicle. I wondered if he was asthmatic. But soon I was preoccupied with my own thoughts, because Janhavi had messaged asking where I was, and I had decided not to reply. We passed the journey in silence.

In Versova, my attention snagged for some reason on banal sights. I stared at the shop-signs glinting in the sun, at a garbage heap that never seemed to be cleared, at the dogs lazing on the pavements, the apartment guards on their plastic chairs, the predictable sequence of coffee shops. A little later, arrived the new gym beside the supermarket, and then the road turned full of shade, while trees sprung up amidst high buildings. Mihir began to direct the driver; I realized we were headed, not to Ahishor's, but to his mother's house.

When we had almost arrived, I saw the black sedan, minus Nalini and Karim, easing past us in the other direction. But a flaming red BMW was more conspicuous still. It was backing into a tight parking spot. There was no one inside but the driver.

Forcing our auto to halt at once, though it was still on the other side of the road, Mihir leaped out and ran to the apartment gates. I paid the fare quickly. The driver, however, was struggling to find the change. In the meantime, Mihir had finished scribbling in the visitor's register, and was lingering with obvious impatience. I abandoned the money, though it was not nothing to me, and hurried to join him. We ignored the lift and ran up the stairs; it was only two flights up. The door of the flat was open.

I recall a living room full of people, with everybody on their feet. Perhaps they had risen only moments before, for a man and a woman had entered just before us. But the nervous energy was palpable. I passed over the faces, both familiar and new; my gaze travelled quickly to find Ahishor.

He was the lone seated figure, situated on a sofa, more or less in the centre of the room. His head was propped back on a cushion, his body reclined in his favourite grey T-shirt and jeans. I associated these with his impish grin, and casual, brilliant speeches, but now Ahishor's face was pale and tired and he was breathing with concentration. Beneath the salt-and-pepper locks, a thick bandage was soaking up blood.

When he saw me staring, he began to smile.

'It's nothing, Dhruv,' he said, 'looks worse than it is.'

'It's not *nothing*!' A female voice cried aloud. She was even more loudly shushed by the man at her side, who then strode directly into the room. Standing over the sofa, he began glaring from Ahishor towards everybody else, and back again, evidently unable to contain his emotions. But no words emerged, until, with his gaze resting on the bath tub turned coffee table, he said quietly:

'Will someone explain what happened?'

I recognized him, of course. Ritesh Azad was a man of many talents, though he deployed them essentially as hobbies. He was an occasional actor, as well as the lead singer and guitarist in a rock band he had founded himself. But even if he had worked solely as an out-of-sight producer, I would have known him that afternoon. Karim was standing not a few feet away. They were both similarly big-built, and though the young man wore a pencil moustache on a puffy face, still the identical curly hair, and the stamp of the eyes and mouth, revealed the blood relation.

I assumed the woman Ritesh had quietened was his wife. (I had heard he had recently married.) She was wearing a rather sloppy sweatshirt and jeans, while her looks were paradoxically suggestive of high culture and breeding. She was a short woman, with long hair, high cheekbones, narrow eyes, and a grim mouth.

Quickly, I took in the other figures: Nalini had sunk into a chair; Karim was standing apart, staring, as usual, into space, with his arms folded across his chest. Strangely, I could not spot Mihir, though he had been right beside me only a moment before. Then I noticed Bharat Mishra. He was sitting on the carpet, cross-legged, his back hunched forward tensely. He was frowning hard—at me.

'Some fellows came to the office, looking for a fight,' Ahishor said, in tired tones. 'It wasn't really physical. We were arguing. Then one of them pushed me. I swore at him...He threw a punch at my head. I ducked, but he caught me from the side.'

His voice was frighteningly matter-of-fact. 'He got me from the side…and then I guess I slipped. I hit my head on the table. Everything went woozy after that. I guess when they saw me bleeding, they ran away.'

'They were that God-man's supporters,' Nalini interjected anxiously. 'They were chanting his name. They are upset about the movie!'

'Ma, please,' said Ahishor, with irritation, 'they are not upset about the movie. They are not upset about anything, they are just mindless pawns.'

'Wait, wait,' cried Ritesh, 'how did they come to know about it? Our film, I mean.'

'I shot an interview with their Baba-ji.'

'You've started shooting? You didn't tell me—*chalo*, never mind! Never mind! So you interviewed him? So what?'

Ahishor sighed and closed his eyes. At once, Nalini sprung to her feet. She rushed to check his bandage, even as he grumbled at her ministrations. In the meantime, from his position on the carpet, Bharat began recounting the story of our shoot in a dull and toneless voice.

'What a crook!' cried Ritesh's wife, when she heard about the God-man's 'magic' stone that Ahishor had bought in Istanbul. (I noticed, in passing, that Bharat did not go into what had prompted this purchase or why Ahishor had discarded the stone. In fact, he said it had gotten lost.)

'What a fucking crook! I'm so glad you exposed him in front of everyone! I'm *so* glad!

'All right Samira, enough,' grumbled Ritesh.

'What do you mean enough?' she retorted, her eyes flashing. 'What a bunch of hooligans! Did they have weapons? Gosh, I'm so glad it wasn't even worse! It could have been—!' She fell to shaking her head in silence.

'There were no weapons,' said Ahishor quietly. 'As I said, when they saw me bleeding they ran away. I was knocked out after that. Next thing I know, my phone was ringing... Good timing, man.'

He glanced at Bharat, who remained unsmiling. His eyes, in his thin face, were darting venomously about the carpet.

'Bharat was the one who took him to the clinic,' Karim informed us. 'He called us from there.'

We all looked at Bharat again. As he straightened his back and took a deep breath, perhaps preparing to speak, there came a pounding noise from the interior of the house. A moment later, Mihir was running into the room, waving his cell phone, his hair combed down again, and his eyes shining.

'I've made some calls!' he announced.

'Did you call the cops?' demanded Samira.

'Do we really need to do that?' cried Nalini. She was sitting beside her son now, her face pinched with worry.

'Well ya!' returned the other woman, 'It's criminal assault!'

'I know...but...'

In the pause that followed, Mihir regarded the two women with amusement.

'I haven't called the police,' he explained, 'I've spoken to my friends in the media. This is a condemnable incident, and they are best placed to take things forward.'

Karim and Ritesh both began to nod.

'*Accha kiya,*' (Well done) said Karim. 'That is the best way.'

'Yeah, and the cops won't take any action anyway unless some journos are pushing them,' muttered Ritesh. 'I'm just wondering...'

Screwing up his face, he began scratching his head, but said nothing further.

'Thank you!' said Samira, addressing Mihir, as though he had performed her a special favour. Mihir, however, was taking no notice of her. He had made his way towards where Ahishor sat. What he did next surprised me, for it was an odd gesture—and unexpectedly touching. Bowing down, he clasped Ahishor's right hand in both of his own, and stared earnestly, all in silence, into the other's face. His gaze was strained with meaning.

Ahishor managed to smile.

'Don't look so worried, all of you. This kind of thing was only to be expected. Anyway, that God-man is not exactly Sai Baba. He's small fry, he has, like, a thousand followers in all. He's done his worst—and I'm fine.'

He was full of assurance, yet I felt no lessening of the tension in the room. Indeed, as he finished speaking, a note of defensiveness, a rising inflection, seemed to have crept into Ahishor's voice. Perhaps our fears were infecting him too.

But will anyone blame us? The reader will hardly need reminding of the environment prevailing at the time, not only in the country, but all over the world. It seemed that religious fanatics were on the prowl, in the streets and public places of cities everywhere. Not long ago, an armed lunatic had taken people hostage in a Sydney cafe. Gunmen from the Taliban had murdered school-children in Peshawar. The Charlie Hebdo killings had occurred. Those men had shouted the name of Allah, but there were other fanatics with other names to rely upon, and we in India knew that. It was all very well to be told that the Navy Baba's goons had not been armed. One still remembered what had been, what might have been, what could be, the next time.

I have a clear memory of Ritesh Azad (at some point in that afternoon), staring up at the painting of Christ on the cross, that hung among Nalini's landscapes. He was breathing hard; a look of anger and indignation was spreading over his face.

'Why do you have such stuff?' he demanded of his father, who smiled wryly.

'*Hum na jaane,*' (I wouldn't know) replied Karim. 'Nalini has some fondness for such things. You'll have to take it up with her.'

She, at the time, was in an inside room with Ahishor (and Mihir), changing Ahishor's bandages. Ritesh sat down heavily, next to his wife. He threw an arm around her. She leaned her head on his shoulder.

'Does anyone want tea?' she asked suddenly. 'I would love some. Some masala chai right now would make me feel a whole lot better.'

'I'll make it,' said Bharat, climbing softly to his feet.

'Are you sure? I can help.'

'No need, I'll manage. I'll make for everyone. All right sir?'

Karim grimaced and nodded. But as Bharat went by me, he glowered at me again. There was accusation in his eyes. I was unnerved. Shortly afterwards, when I could not shake the feeling, I followed him into the kitchen.

* * *

Bharat was opening and closing the kitchen cabinets, hunting for the tea things. The stove was already flaming in readiness. I lingered behind him, but he ignored me pointedly, and I waited till his hands were free. Then I mustered my own indignation.

'Hey, why were you looking at me like that?'

He turned and stared. 'You don't know? I thought you are very intelligent.'

'Be straightforward, Bharat.'

'You don't like me *na*,' he smiled humourlessly, 'you think I am not straightforward.'

He was hovering, with a sieve in his hand, thin and lank, with a narrow, cunning gaze.

'No, I don't think that,' I said in irritation.

'Haha! You're lying! But whatever I am, at least I am not such a selfish person so as to risk somebody else's life for the sake of my career.'

'What are you talking about?' I exclaimed. Bharat remained quiet, simply peering at me knowingly, and it was I who spoke on.

'This documentary? Are you talking about this documentary? Firstly it wasn't my idea. It was Mihir's idea.'

'I know. And you were very happy to join in.'

'Of course I was happy! Why wouldn't I be?'

He stopped smiling entirely. 'Even now, you are asking that? Didn't you see what has happened to Ahishor? But you don't care about that. Doesn't make any difference to you.'

'For God's sake,' I cried, reflexively, 'Ahishor himself is taking it in his stride. He is being brave. I would rather support *that*. As for these kinds of goons, they exist, we know that. What does that mean, we should stop making movies? This sort of incident is the whole reason we're making this movie! And there has to be freedom of expression!'

'Shut up,' snarled Bharat. 'You are becoming like that *motu*, all words words words. You are not the one who got hurt, are you? I told Ahishor the moment I heard about it. This whole documentary idea is bad. These people should not be unnecessarily interfered with. They can do anything.'

'We are not defenceless either! Didn't you hear what Mihir said, he has already spoken to journalists.'

'Don't take that *motu's* name!' He broke off suddenly to

adjust the gas. Then he stayed with his back to me, stirring the brewing tea.

'You will laugh, I know. Until it happens to you personally. The truth is, babas and fakirs do have powers. They can do a lot of things...they can do black magic. I have seen it personally in my village. There was a man—then a fakir put a spell on him and he thought he was a horse. He used to sleep standing up. You will laugh, I know. But even you should realize. The media and police cannot do anything if these people get into your mind.'

He turned his head, scowling, as though prepared to see me smirking. But I was too surprised to make any response.

'My point is—I don't understand why we are unnecessarily messing with such people,' Bharat continued. 'They can destroy a person from the inside.'

Now I did begin to smile. For the first time since I had entered the house, I felt myself relaxing.

'This business of destroying people from the inside?' I reminded him, 'I remember earlier you were worried about Maithili doing it to Ahishor. Remember? Now you're worried about the Navy Baba.'

But his eyes only widened with greater certainty.

'Yes, exactly!' said Bharat, 'Maithili is like one of these people herself! I bet you she has such kind of powers herself!'

'If you say so,' I laughed, though I suddenly felt uncomfortable talking about Maithili. 'Anyway, never mind about her,' I continued quickly. 'But listen—you saw that Navy Baba... He's a total fraud!'

'Just because he does some frauds doesn't mean he cannot have powers *also*! And this is not the only baba out there. What about the next one you offend? *Motu* Mihir is loving all this, because it is getting him publicity! It's making him important! That's all he cares about. But Dhruv, I thought at least you are Ahishor's friend!'

I felt, momentarily, a tug of sympathy towards Bharat, because his anxiety was naked and sincere. But it was having on me exactly the opposite effect to the one he intended. My memory of that rundown 1 BHK, and the paunchy man in the red tweed cap fishing out Maithili's present, carried no overtones whatsoever of occult powers. Quite the opposite. How could I not smile?

'We'll talk later,' was the best I could say. With a furious look, Bharat spun away. The tea had begun to boil over.

X

Friends of Freedom

It happened almost imperceptibly, like the transitions in a dream. In no time, the news spread. As Ahishor lay convalescing at his mother's house, reports and reactions began spinning out all about him, quickly encasing in their web all of Versova. It was the same subject on everyone's lips, at every posh cafe and pub, in every struggler's cramped quarters. But the reverberations did not stop at our little community. Ahishor Frances's name was known beyond. It was not long before social media was resounding with outrage. Soon, too, there would be op-eds in national dailies and online magazines (besides two debates on major news channels), each decrying the perennial vulnerability of our artists, the increasing threats to free speech, and the vulnerability of religious minorities (though this last item did not gain impetus, Ahishor never having self-identified as Christian). These outpourings in turn would be shared and echoed on Facebook and Twitter, and so on and on.

What kept the emotions running high, apart from anything else, was Ahishor's continued ill-health. Though his wound was not severe, he had developed a fever in its wake, and was recovering his energy only slowly. We all paid him visits, while

Bharat practically lived in the house and Mihir was in and out constantly. One day, the Joshis arrived with Mihir, bringing with them angry wishes for the demise of the extremist right wing. I recall a hectic conversation in Nalini's living room, during the course of which we all ate and drank a great deal (except for the teetotaller Mihir), growing happily intoxicated (including, to all appearances, Mihir), even as we fulminated and despaired.

Late the next morning, I awoke to a phone call from Jatin.

'What are you doing today afternoon?'

I told him I didn't know; I had just woken. There was a muttering at the other end of the line.

'Are you following the Ahishor Francis incident or not?'

'Of course I am,' I was surprised, 'I was at his house just yesterday—his mother's house, I mean.'

'Good, good. Then you will be interested in this. If you are not doing anything—and you aren't, since you just got up—please come to the office today at 3. It's quite important.'

'What's the matter?'

'Just come please, Dhruv, I don't have time right now. At 3 p.m., okay?'

Jatin's office was high in a residential building, directly off the Lokhandwala Circle. It was only a short distance from my apartment, so I did not mind going there on a blind summon. As I exited the lift on the tenth floor, I found the door to the office open already. He was waiting, chewing gum vigorously, nodding his greetings in a knowing way, while his glasses twitched on his nose and his eyes gleamed continually.

'Not here,' he said, when I sat down as usual on the couch. 'Come inside. Everybody else has already reached. You're late, Dhruv. Though less late than usual, so I'm not saying anything. Come come come!'

Swivelling, he strode further in, past the kitchen counter where I had oftentimes made tea, and towards his private office, whose door was closed. As I followed, the door to the adjacent bathroom suddenly swung open. Ruhi Khanna walked out. Jatin stopped in his tracks. He began to introduce us.

'I know Dhruv,' interrupted Ruhi. 'We've met at workshops.'

'Hi, it's nice to see you!' I exclaimed. 'How do you...' A thought, perhaps silly, suddenly occurred to me. 'Are you both related?'

'Oh God!' Jatin declaimed, 'Everybody in India named Khanna is not related, Dhruv!'

However, he was smiling and I felt the idea had pleased him. Ruhi too was looking well. She was wearing a frilly, orange dress, and her face was glowing. It passed my mind that when she was not in a foul mood, she was extremely pretty.

'We met through a common friend,' she said gaily. 'Oh and then I discovered we have lots of things in common! Jatin is a Gemini, the same as me. And did you know—I suppose you must know—in his first novel he wrote about a character named Ruhi.'

'I didn't know that,' I said, in slight bewilderment, 'I haven't read it actually.'

'You should! I'm reading it now.'

She was washing her hands at the sink outside the bathroom. I glanced at Jatin, who coloured suddenly.

'Well, good,' he said, 'let's get the rest of the introductions out of the way.' So saying, he pushed open his office door. Then he held it open, waiting for Ruhi, while I passed through in front. 'Actually you know everyone already—except Tara. Tara, this is Dhruv, who used to work with me. Tara is—well—Tara is the mother of Maithili, whom I think you know. You do, right? Then say so, Dhruv, don't look blank! I mean, not that motherhood defines your identity, Tara! [He beamed at her] I'm just pointing out a connection.'

Tara Krishna sat by herself, on a sofa at the back of the room, smiling tensely. On either side of her, on chairs which I knew habitually belonged to the front room, Arvind and Sasha were seated quietly. An empty plastic chair furthered a rough circle. There was a plate of biscuits on Jatin's computer table and cups of tea in everybody's hands.

'Do we have enough chairs?' Jatin looked about busily. 'Yes, we do. What about tea? Dhruv? Have it, it's made already. Arvind, get him a cup please.'

I gave my successor a comradely grin as he went by me. Ruhi and I then seated ourselves, she beside Tara, I on the plastic chair, while Jatin took the big, plush one at the computer. (He had a horror of anyone else so much as touching that.) The room was cramped with our bodies, and rather warm. I wondered why we were not all sitting in the big front hall with the air conditioning. However, it was not uncomfortable.

'Are you Maithili's friend?' Tara Krishna was staring at me.

'We have common friends,' I explained, 'but I don't know her personally.'

'Oh.' An odd hope seemed to die from her eyes. 'I thought perhaps you've had some news of her... Maithili has been out of touch for—quite a long time.' As she saw me shaking my head, she forced a smile. 'Well, she does this sometimes!'

In the silence that fell, I felt a vague wonderment at the gathering. There was Tara, in a proper sari, beside Ruhi in her youthful dress. Sasha, I had seen only recently at Nalini's, albeit briefly, for he was one of the many visitors Ahishor had had in the past weeks. He was sharply turned out as usual, but his face was pale, and he looked unwell to me. He was fiddling with his watch-strap, in between darting strange looks at Tara, as though struggling to convince himself that she was really present, in flesh and blood.

'Hmm,' grunted Jatin. 'Well. Can we begin? Where is Arvind? Accha, your tea... Here he comes!...Come come...Don't spill it, please, both of you, be careful. Sit down, sit down... Wait, Dhruv, will you shut the door please? The door is open... Thanks, thanks... All right... Biscuits anybody? They are very good. I'm keeping them here. All right... Good.'

Cradling our teacups, we all looked up at him. On his high-backed chair he cut an imposing, if awkward, figure.

'Thank you all,' said Jatin, 'for being here today. Some of you arrived on short notice. Some came all the way from town—not only for this, I know, but still. I think most of you already know what this meeting is about, but anyway, let me start from scratch. Last Sunday, Ahishor Frances was physically attacked. In his office. By hoodlums working for a God-man, whom he had exposed on a movie shoot... Maybe I shouldn't have been surprised, given the intellectual climate we are living in. But this shocked me. Ahishor Frances is not just any film-maker. People may have personal issues with him [he glanced here at Sasha, who looked taken aback], but nobody can deny that he is a truly unique voice in these parts. He is someone who actually takes time to think about issues. Big picture, social, even philosophical issues. In this town, that's a miracle! Now, if matters have come to such a pass, that somebody as young and promising as Ahishor is being intimidated in this way, in our backyard...then what I would say is—A) anybody who is involved in film-making or the arts, or B) considers himself or herself a liberal—basically anyone who cares about where this country is headed!—needs to stand up and *do* something. I called you all specifically, not because you fit any grand objective criteria, but just because I know you all personally…and I feel that we share a certain sensibility. I may be wrong! [Here he glared at Arvind.] But I hope I'm right. So I want to start by getting your views. How do you all feel about this? You reckon this is worth doing something about?'

Ruhi, who had been nodding continually throughout Jatin's speech, began to talk at once.

'Oh, I'm with you. Everybody is. Everybody is talking about this. It's been trending on Twitter for days now. The most followed people on my timeline have been saying exactly what you're saying.'

'Politicians?' I inquired hopefully.

Her gaze flickered with annoyance. 'I am referring to my timeline, where I don't follow politicians. I'm talking about cultural icons. Youth icons.'

She rattled off a list of names; I recognized an RJ's, a singer's, and a series of stand-up comedians' and satirical columnists'. Jatin's enthusiasm, as he listened, was soaring.

'Varun is a great friend,' he cried, referring to one of the comedy writers, 'In fact, he was going to come today. He wanted to be here. Only he had something else he couldn't get out of.'

'We should do something for sure,' said Arvind decisively. 'I'm all for it.'

'Glad to hear you say that, Arvind!' Jatin cried with pleasure. 'It gives me hope in you!'

'I'm for it too,' I shrugged. 'Obviously.'

'What do you have in mind though?' Sasha was frowning.

'That's a secondary question,' snapped Jatin. 'The first thing is we should all feel this is important enough.'

'No, but that's what it boils down to!' Tara was suddenly animated. She looked far younger to me, than she had at the Film Festival. And I could see also, in the slant of her eyes and the firmness of her jaw, the face of her daughter. 'Everybody always wants to do something, right? Nobody wants such incidents to keep happening. But what exactly can we do? What's your idea?'

'Patience, patience!' Jatin grinned. He was in a good mood; the turnout had pleased him. 'Well, of course, I'm not saying we take up arms and storm the streets... Though, maybe, it will come to that... [For a moment a shadow passed over his face.] What I propose is that we make a set of videos...conveying the things we want to convey... We'll put them out on a YouTube channel. I reckon what Ruhi says is extremely true, there's a lot of support online for liberal ideas. We should tap that.'

'Lots of right-wing trolls too,' I said.

'You think I don't know that, Dhruv? In this country, there are many times more idiots than people with common sense. I'm not doing this to be popular. But the fight has to be fought. I don't plan to just sit on the sidelines and watch. In fact, the very first video we put out should say exactly this—it should ask people who care to get involved.'

Ruhi, endearingly, had her hand up, and a wise smile on her face.

'It will be popular,' she insisted. 'Liberals are not keeping silent any longer. In fact, they are waiting to be spurred into action. I can sense the mood. Even the police are with us on this,' she went on. 'I read online that they're arresting the Navy Baba. They've had other complaints about him in the past.'

Arvind, who was staring at Ruhi with great interest, began to nod.

'Fucking A,' he said softly.

There was indeed something in the air. A frisson of fear and excitement rushed through me, followed by a welcome feeling of enveloping security. I understood suddenly why we were huddled together in the back of the office. This work was conspiratorial, political; it needed the closeness of a womb. I looked at Jatin, looming anxiously over us, and felt myself filling with admiration. It was not for nothing that, all those months ago, I had chosen to link my lot with him, of all people in this industry. Neither his explosive temper nor his chronic insecurity, nor his commercial failures, had destroyed his capacity to embark on things that truly mattered.

Tara was sitting on the edge of her seat. I felt she was fighting her own excitement.

'But what kind of videos? We need to be very clear on this. YouTube is full of noise, there's no point if we're just going to add to that.'

'Absolutely!' Jatin nodded emphatically, 'What I'm thinking is simple, one-and-a-half to two-minute text-based videos, white letters on black, with background music, just setting out certain ideas, and expressing them smartly. We need to write them very smartly.'

'Won't that be boring?' Ruhi crinkled her nose. 'A video with only text?'

'That's exactly how we will avoid adding to the noise, and get people to think. Nor do we have the resources for anything fancy.'

'You mean,' said Arvind, 'you mean like a Facebook status update...with music?'

Jatin turned to him with fury.

'No Arvind! It is not a Facebook status update! But if you

can't understand that I can't explain it to you. Oh let me just say this! Nobody needs to be a part of this who doesn't want to be. This isn't my project anyway, you don't have to be involved just because you work with me or know me. This is something we should do only if we believe in it. There is literally no other reason.'

'I like the concept,' said Tara quietly. 'It's nice.'

'I like it too,' said Sasha. He seemed to have broken out of his brooding. 'We should write artistically. Maybe in aphorisms, or even poetry!'

'Well, I don't know about poetry,' said Jatin, good-humouredly, 'but let's see. What I was thinking was, let's start with nine videos. Each of us—that's you, Tara and me—will write three each. Dhruv will help me edit the videos, and Arvind, you will promote the heck out of them. Ruhi—you're welcome to write too—or just give inputs—as you like. That is, if you're still interested. Are you?'

The plate of biscuits was being passed to her, via Arvind and myself.

'Oh yes,' she said, biting into one. 'I think text videos will be kind of dull, but I'm curious to see what you come up with.'

'If you have a different idea,' said Jatin, 'do tell us. Please.'

I was surprised to note the real deference in his tone. In general, Jatin had little regard for the brains of actors. But Ruhi had been an economist abroad, before she came to Mumbai.

'No, it's fine.' She was chewing self-absorbedly. 'I'm in.'

The last thing we discussed was what to call ourselves.

'I reckon we should do it anonymously,' said Jatin. 'Not to protect our identities, but because our names are not important.'

'Yes, we must be self-effacing,' Sasha spoke thoughtfully. 'It's the principles that matter—the things we'll be putting forward. We could be anybody saying them, because they are universal principles. That's the whole point.'

'I have an idea,' Arvind grinned. 'We'll name the channel "Ahishor's Angels".'

Everyone fell about laughing. Tara's laugh was a delicious shock, high, girlish and piercing.

'Friends of Ahishor,' I suggested.

'This isn't really about Ahishor,' said Sasha earnestly. 'The attack on Ahishor was basically an act of revenge, because he exposed a fake. But there's a larger atmosphere of unfreedom and hierarchy and people one can and cannot question, that legitimizes it. How about "Friends of Freedom"?'

'I like it!' cried Jatin. 'I like "Friends of Freedom"! How about that?'

'I like it too,' said Ruhi instantly, 'Friends of Freedom.'

'Works for everyone?' Jatin was brimming with excitement; his huge chest rising and falling, his spectacles off-kilter. 'Works? Great! I'll set up the channel. And I'll send out a mail to all of us. I should be done writing my three videos by the weekend. Tara and Sasha will also try to finish by then. All right? We'll share them with each other. Ultimately, the videos should seem like they are written by one person—the sensibility has to match. That's very important.'

'One other thing,' his voice dropped, and filled with gravity. 'I've spoken to Ahishor too. Obviously what we're doing is not just about him. But he thinks it's a great idea as well. He is backing this project. Just wanted you all to know that... Oh, for those of you who don't know, Dhruv here works with Ahishor. He was there at the God-man's place.'

I faced with pride the admiring looks that were bestowed upon me. Ruhi was gazing especially curiously.

Suddenly, what I can only describe as an explosion of

lightness went bursting through me. I felt almost physically detached from my body; free and therefore invincible. It was a delightful feeling, and when it wore off, I wanted more.

XI

Tara Krishna

The driver had disappeared with the car. It had taken her several minutes and multiple calls to even get through to him on the phone. Tara stood outside the building gates, casting weary looks in both directions. The meeting in Jatin's office had left her strangely exhausted. She felt chilly as well. A sharp breeze was blowing, while clouds had enveloped the late afternoon sun. She stared down the empty road.

'Ma'am,' came a voice at her back. Turning, she smiled automatically. It was the young man from the office, with the wavy hair, the very thin, trousered legs and the slight hunchback, more prominent now that he stepped towards her.

'I wanted to say hello,' he said, 'I'm also a friend of Maithili.'

'I see.'

The young man sounded anxious, and uncertain of how to proceed.

'You said—you mentioned in the office—that she has not been in touch? I hope she is all right.'

'Oh yes, yes, she does that,' said Tara. 'Ever since she was a child, she's had a habit of disappearing'

Tara was smiling again, to her own surprise. But it was

difficult not to smile at the plainly lovesick young man.

'When she was little, she used to spend entire afternoons hidden away in the branches of some tree. She loves to be incognito.'

'The last email I got from her was about a month and a half ago,' continued Sasha. 'She said she was in Concord, near Boston. Studying raja yoga.'

'There's an institute there,' Tara nodded. Simultaneously, her worry woke and fluttered within her. It was simply a group of people Maithili had met over Facebook. She had crossed continents to 'train' with them (as she had put it), out in the ghostly towns and dark woods of New England. But Maithili had long ceased explaining her decisions to her mother.

'She is an exceptional person,' burst out the young man suddenly. His mouth was twisted with emotion. 'You must be proud of her.'

It seemed he was going to go on and perhaps embarrass himself with a declaration. However, though he blushed profusely, Sasha stayed silent—yet this too was eloquent. Instinctively, Tara began to probe the situation.

'It's Sasha, am I right? Yes, how is it you know Maithili? I haven't heard her mention your name.'

At once she regretted saying so, but (oddly) the young man showed no hurt. Instead, a glow of happiness was spreading across his face.

'I met her only this April,' he spoke feelingly, 'I was an extra—I was doing the job of an extra—in a short film that she was acting in.'

'I see,' said Tara. 'And do you act full-time, Sasha?'

'Oh no. I'm not an actor at all. I am doing some writing... I am actually studying—by myself—philosophy...theology, to be precise. It's difficult to study theology anywhere in India—in any institution I mean. I'm not making any money at the moment, of course, but I have some funds—from my father. I'm taking advantage of that!'

She nodded, smiling. The young man was rambling in all earnest. Of course, there was no need to tell her so much, but she felt a sweetness about his manner. As he spoke, his eyes were fixed on her in a kind of awe, which (like flattery) was a pleasant discomfiture. She was smiling still, as the car finally came up. She forgot to scold the driver.

'Can I drop you somewhere?'

'Oh no—thanks,' said Sasha. 'There's no need.'

'Are you sure? Well, all right… Goodbye then.' His gaze was still on her. Suddenly, she was filled with reassuring thoughts. 'Don't worry about Maithili,' said Tara, 'Maithili will be fine.'

'It was wonderful to meet you,' returned Sasha.

* * *

That evening, Tara sat by herself in the study room of the apartment in Malabar Hills. Through the closed door, the strains of Ustad Amjad Ali Khan's sarod faintly penetrated the air. Such was her husband's evening ritual.

She stared discontentedly at her laptop screen. The writing was hard going. She could see that she was producing little more than platitudes, which would be stupefyingly dull to read on YouTube. (These words of self-criticism came to her vividly, but not the ones she needed.) In fact, what she wanted to say was not banal. She wanted to say, how those who stamped down on critical inquiry stifled their own growth with their self-satisfaction. But to communicate this neatly, poetically—it was harder than she had expected—and she had read and written so much poetry when she was young! Perhaps a stricter form would help. She thought of developing a haiku. Then, as she bent her wrists to the keyboard, Tara winced. A burning sensation was shooting across her palms and, simultaneously, the soles of her feet. Her toes curled from the pain.

Rising, she hobbled her way to the door and into the living room. It so happened that Suraj too was on his feet, having just then risen from the sofa (in a loose white shirt and pyjama), refreshed and relaxed after his music session. He bestowed a vague smile in her direction, which turned into a look of alarm, as she sank, crying out, onto the carpet. Her back arched against the sofa he had just vacated.

'It doesn't go away,' she sighed.

'What is it?... The burning again?'

There was exasperation and even disbelief in his voice, but when Tara did not reply, instead only closing her eyes, Suraj felt a spurt of emotion. He moved to kneel beside her, and pressed her hands in his. She squeezed back desperately, yet their touch quickly turned clinical, and neither had much faith in the remedy. After a few moments, she pulled away.

'It's all right,' said Tara quietly, 'I'll manage.'

The trouble had come upon suddenly. (So, at any rate, it seemed.) About three weeks after Purushottam Krishna's funeral, Tara had woken in the middle of the night with an itching in her hands and feet. By the morning, this had intensified to a burning pain. The doctor prescribed certain changes of diet and exercise, but made clear that there was absolutely nothing wrong with her physically. He identified the return to India and old Purushottam's death as causes of damaging stress. Tara (though she knew the causes numbered more than two), had no compunctions in accepting that her condition was psychosomatic. In fact, it was she who used this term, while the others talked only of stress. Nor, after that night, did the burning ever fully disappear. She felt it always, to a greater or lesser degree.

Suraj Krishna now stepped back, frowning.

'Did something just happen? Or it started on its own?... What were you doing in—what were you working on in there?'

'I was trying to write—and failing.'

'You mean writing those videos,' muttered Suraj. 'I don't really get it. Everybody is condemning this anyway. I don't see the point of going overboard.'

'Who said we are going overboard?'

'You said it was Jatin's idea!' He threw up his hands, in a sardonic gesture. 'Jatin is not exactly the most measured person, you know that.'

Tara watched through narrowed eyes. She said nothing, but Suraj went on, struggling stubbornly to justify himself.

'What happened with Ahishor Frances was wrong, nobody denies that. The police are about to arrest that fellow already. My only point is, there's no need to be gloomy about the whole affair. It's under control. But Jatin likes the doom and gloom! He is very sincere, I grant him that, but he's one of those people who doesn't know how to let well enough lie. He doesn't know how to be content. You've said so yourself many times. That's why—just see—it's affecting you already. You haven't had this burning for the last week and now you go see Jatin and he drags you into his tirade, and bingo, it's back!... Well, isn't that correct? Why aren't you saying anything?'

She continued to look at him. She was aware of being in broad agreement with everything he was saying, but this awareness gave her no pleasure. One thing, felt Tara, was apparent. Suraj was dreadfully jealous. It was not her well-being on his mind, but his rights...

'It's one thing to be friends with the guy [he was going on speaking]. Okay, you've known him for ages. Although even that—but why would you get involved with his work? Nothing he does succeeds. Also, I haven't said this before, but I find it extremely odd that a full-grown middle-aged man spends such a lot of time with young men half his age. He only seems to hire twenty-year-olds. Have you noticed? He's childish—Jatin. If he wants to say something in support of Ahishor, why doesn't he write an op-ed? Why go to YouTube? The whole thing feels childish... Are you listening, Tara?'

A smile sprang to her lips, and her eyes flashed wickedly. 'Under control?' she found herself saying. 'Maybe that's an illusion. Maybe they're spiralling out of control. Maybe everything is on the absolute edge—and Jatin sees that!'

While Suraj's face contorted in irritation and he shook his head rapidly, speaking more knowing and superior words that she barely heard, Tara's laughter vanished, with the suddenness of a mask crumbling. She stared with desperation.

'You don't worry about anything, Suraj! What is happening with Maithili? Do you ever think about that?'

He came around slowly to the changed subject.

'You're worried about Maithili... I should have told you. She has been making withdrawals from the joint account. The last one was on Friday. So she's okay, wherever she is.'

'Oh.' Intense relief flooded over Tara. She got up from the carpet and sat down on the sofa. With his mouth twitching, full of a sense of achievement and (what, for him, often accompanied it) a sense of injury, Suraj lowered himself onto the chair alongside. He threw his head back and stared ruminatively into space. He began to speak softly.

'If you had only asked me before, I would have told you. You're worrying all the time about unnecessary things. Then what can you expect... Instead of doing these YouTube videos ['YouTube' here received a pejorative emphasis], why don't you draw up your guest list for the wedding? You've not done yours yet.'

Tara nodded. In a few months, their son Vishnu was to be married. It was such a glad happening, for at one time she had been worried for Vishnu, all alone on the West Coast, working himself to the bone. (She knew, also, how hard he had taken his first break-up—though he wouldn't show it.) Now she thought of old friends and acquaintances, warmly remembered but far-flung, who would come bearing good wishes, and that wide circle of relatives whom she would be proud to invite, as one who had helped grow this fresh branch of the family. Yes, she must write down the guest list. And yet something in her shrank from actually taking hold of the pleasure.

'If not before, at least we'll see Maithili at the wedding,' Suraj continued. 'Whatever she's up to, she'll come back for Vishnu, there's no doubt about that.'

'Yes, yes, of course,' said Tara. She had missed her grandfather's funeral, but she would never miss her brother's wedding. It was true that recently there had been some rancour between them, after Maithili had managed to offend Giri Joseph in London. Perhaps Vishnu had spoken harshly to her and that was why she had not called him up in America. But such quarrels were common between siblings.

'Everyone will be here,' said Tara.

Then her gaze went about the living room, to the old, beautiful furniture, the staircase to the children's rooms, the balcony, the blue sea beyond. Everything seemed massive, forgotten and empty. Suddenly tears pricked at her eyes. All her anxiety about Maithili rose up again in her heart. Was her daughter reduced to a wedding guest? Was it not important to know what she was doing, what her future would be?

She heard Suraj clicking his tongue. He was looking at her closely.

'What happened? What happened now?'

Tara said nothing. 'Any time you are not worrying, you worry that you ought to be worrying!' That was what Maithili had once told her. The accusation had made her smile and giggle, much to Maithili's exasperation. Now, however, she felt ashamed of the way her emotions turned. She glanced up at her husband. He was strong, sane, intelligent, such a fine figure of a man! Her shame deepened and she wished fervently that he would drop the subject, for she could not bear to think about it, to be questioned over it. But he was pressing her to explain her tears. Drying her eyes, she stared back.

'You haven't made your list either, why are you badgering me? You're talking as though all these domestic affairs are my responsibility alone. Just because I'm not working these days.'

'Tara, you are the one who said you wanted a rest! I have always encouraged you to work again. There are consultancies available, you know that. I got this Water Ministry one just like that, through Dipankar. You can work in the education sector any time you like! Shall I speak to somebody?'

His eyes were big in his head and his whole expression was one of concern. Tara felt a spasm of irritation, followed by guilt and helplessness, for what wrong had he done? He had merely taken her at face value. It was the very quality she prized in him—and oh, what a burden it was! Her expression turned droll. She smiled ironically.

'I don't want any consultancies right now.'

Grandly, she rose to her feet and began smoothing down the pleats of her sari.

'Are you going back to write?' inquired Suraj.

Her steps were taking her back to the study.

'Why don't you write later, after dinner?'

'I'm not writing right now,' Tara replied, 'I'm going to lie down for a while.'

After dinner, however, they sat close to each other on the same sofa, unable to take their eyes off the television. A panel debate was underway, though the word 'debate' does not begin to describe the spectacle. I trust my reader will know the sort of thing I am referring to. The cacophony; the shrillness; the raised voices; the borderline abuse; the refusal to listen to any point of view but one's own; the continual talking over one another, that had already become the staple format of our news programmes, was in full swing. Notionally, the subject of this outrage, was an allegation that a sitting cabinet minister had murdered his ex-wife (thought previously to have died of illness), which, in the nakedly prejudiced view of the channel, was being covered up by police, hand-in-glove with the government.

The shouting and screaming had quieted the Krishnas. It had entered, like a marauding army, over the tasteful apartment, the softly shifting sea. Suraj clicked his tongue several times over the course of many minutes, but he was too disturbed to voice what he felt. Such open disrespect for the processes of law and order, as he understood them, was shocking him. He felt personally aggrieved too. For Suraj too was now working for the government. In fact, he was specially proud of this new consultancy; it was going to be his most direct contribution to building his own country. But the faces on screen were impatient with authority, scoffing at the established norms, seeming to delight in destruction. He wondered what Dipankar would make of them—though Dipankar was probably used to them.

As for Tara, she had been wanting for a long time to simply switch the television off. What prevented her from doing so was the odd certainty, that if she were to admit how badly the noise was affecting her—the sheer absence of ordinary manners!—it would crush her in some fundamental way. She held out, with a half-smile moving her lips of its own accord. The tingling was returning to her hands and her feet.

'What a joke!' Suraj Krishna cried out at last. 'It's absurd!'

'Oh, absolutely,' said Tara gladly.

'How can they allow such things? It's a blatant media trial!'

'Relax, relax, Suraj.' She squeezed his thigh and rubbed his back, consciously rubbing out the pain in her hands. 'We are the silly ones to even be watching this.'

Reaching out, Tara pressed the button on the remote, and then turned, smiling radiantly, towards her husband.

To all appearances, and in their own reckoning as well, they were a loving couple again. The afternoon's quarrels and misunderstandings seemed forgotten. My reader, however, must have realized already that the fault lines in the Krishna household had not disappeared. On the contrary, they were to widen dramatically in the time to come, until, at last, only calamity could do the work of repair.

XII

Sasha's Red Letter Day

The office, on that day, was on edge. I wasn't present myself, but I can imagine from experience the exact atmosphere. Before Sasha arrived, Jatin and Arvind were huddled together in the front room, staring at a computer screen. Also looking on, with a guitar balanced across his gangly legs, was Sushant.

His presence there had come about thus. After a long period when we were not in touch, Sushant had called me one day, to complain about his myriad woes. His great work, *The Last Anarchist*, was still stuck, and he was cursing Samyak now, the producer he had (thought) he had found. In a bid to change the subject, I wound up telling him what I was doing with Jatin. His reaction surprised me. Apparently, the attack on Ahishor had offended him greatly, for he admired Ahishor personally, loved the philosophy in *Schrödinger's Cat*, and detested the religious right wing. On his insistence, I connected him with Jatin, knowing that it was one of Jatin's rare qualities that he was always truly curious about encountering new talent. As it turned out, in Sushant's guitar-playing (redolent to me of morbid, wasteful evenings post rehearsals in his flat), Jatin saw something he liked. Very quickly it was settled that Sushant would be strumming the notes of certain old classics for our videos. (For the music in them, like everything else, was going to be minimalist.)

'Twenty-two views,' muttered Jatin. 'How long has it been?'

'Two and a half hours,' Arvind reported.

'Is it that bad? Are people just not interested?'

'Friends of Freedom' had uploaded its first missive to the world. The good news had been shared on Jatin's and Arvind's Facebook, where it had received a combined total of twenty-eight likes, so far.

'There are more likes on Facebook than views on YouTube,' analysed Jatin. 'That means some people are just liking it for the heck of it. Who are these people?'

'There's no actual way to find out,' said Arvind.

'I know that, Arvind. My point is, is the video that bad? Sushant, you're seeing the whole thing for the first time. Tell us objectively. Be completely frank.'

'Oh, I like it,' drawled Sushant. 'I really like it. Only thing is—'

'Yes?'

'How about putting in some pictures?'

Jatin's face crumpled violently, as though something foul had been thrust under his nose. 'You just don't get it. That's not even up for discussion.'

Sushant shrugged and grinned shyly. He told me later that he had been enjoying the energy in the room. ('He was acting crazy, like way over the top, but it seemed cool, you know?')

'Why haven't the others shared it yet?' said Jatin suddenly. 'Okay, Dhruv has a cold, so what? He can still log onto Facebook, can't he? Remind him, Arvind, send him a message. Ruhi hasn't tweeted it yet either...I messaged her...no reply... Sasha—it's okay—Sasha is coming here. Where is he though? It's 1.30 already. *Khaana* (food) is ready, *na?*'

The homely smells of roti and sabzi were already filling the office. These dabbas of lunch that arrived every afternoon were one of my best memories of working with Jatin. I was thankful for his love of food, and for his insistence that we all eat together. Sometimes the need to eat seemed the only commonality between a crass, bumbling youth like me, and my masterful mentor.

'*Khaana* is ready. Although what's the point, I'm losing my appetite just looking at these views! Hang on, somebody's commented!'

He pounced towards the table, crouching over the laptop. The first YouTube comment had indeed arrived. I saw it myself the same day.

'*Powerful cautionary words in these times of intolerance and bigotry! Good on you, Friends of Freedom! One can only hope there are enough of you out there... Or I fear the worst!*'—*Anonymous*

Jatin read these words carefully, and, from the looks of it, many times over, moving his lips, and nodding especially at the last dramatic sentence. Then he pulled himself upright. Happiness had swelled his chest, and sent myriad, mysterious thrills running through his frame. He was a big-sized man, and it was most noticeable at such moments of excitement.

'I don't know about you guys, but I can't wait for lunch any longer! Let's eat. Let's forget about the damn views, they will come when they come. Aha! [The doorbell had rung.] Sasha's here too. Perfect timing! Perfect timing! Perfect timing, Sir!'

Throwing open the door, he bellowed at his visitor. Sasha slipped inside the office easily, as one who belonged. Yet in that fraught atmosphere, pulverized as it was by Jatin's emotions, an incongruity hovered about the new entrant. Previously (when I had seen him) he had seemed off-colour. Now his face was filled with a feverish brightness. His gaze was kindly, though also unnatural and abstracted, and the faintest of smiles lay permanently on his lips.

'Are you drunk?' inquired Jatin, not long after he had come in. 'Have you been drinking in the afternoon?'

'Of course not,' Sasha laughed.

He was not, however, strictly sober. He felt terribly happy that afternoon, for after many weeks he had received a message from Maithili. Not that it was a warm message. She had questioned his need to be interested in the goings-on of her life, and dismissed his queries as 'small talk', which she hated. It was apparent (she wrote) that he did not understand her at all. He had called her 'shy' and therefore distant, but she had not been shy since she was fourteen, and she was not distant with everyone, only with him, perhaps because he provoked her thus. In any case, she was on the esoteric path now, focusing on her own evolution. She was entering into a universal love, learning how to inhabit the oneness in all things and people. His constant, petty entreaties left her in no mood to respond. Was he not himself ashamed of his neediness?

The words were harsh, but even as he read them in pain, Sasha's heart raced with happiness. Why and wherefrom he could not say, but all his old hope rose up inside him, only more fervently than ever. With other people, in the weeks gone by, he had sometimes spoken as though his attachment to Maithili was past. Now he was almost afraid of having betrayed her! Reading her cold message, he felt desperately needed. He wrote back with confidence and urgency. Small talk mattered, it helped a person breathe, she must not strangle herself with the weight of great ideas, however noble-sounding. It was not only he who worried about her, her mother did too. He had spoken to her mother, so he knew. As for his feelings for her—they were not petty! It was no shame to him to need her—he felt proud! But how would it avail her to be a master of the occult if she could not see the person in front of her eyes?

Ever after he sent his reply, Sasha felt strangely certain that the miraculous was going to occur. They had talked so frankly, and about deep things. It was a rare interaction. Maithili would soften to him. This was the thought that filled him with happiness—more precisely, with relief, for he was not even nervously anticipating the future. The worst was over, he felt this in his bones. Their closeness was not merely to begin, but had already begun. She was close to him already, warm in his heart in Jatin's office, that afternoon.

'What do you reckon?' Jatin inquired, after Sasha had duly watched the uploaded video.

'It's good. It's turned out well.'

'You mean that?'

'Yes, yes.'

'But we aren't getting enough views! Kindly share it on your Facebook first thing after lunch.'

'The only thing,' said Sasha, a few minutes later, sinking onto a chair with a plate of roti-sabzi, 'is the music. It sounds too mournful, don't you think?'

'Mournful?'

'Lonely guitar string plucking away. I mean it's very well rendered, but it sounds melancholy, like we have already given up hope or something!'

He took a bite of his food, while Jatin stared. They were sitting on adjacent chairs in the middle of the room. Arvind and

Sushant were watching from the back, where the computers were.

'Spare me, Sasha,' said Jatin. 'If you have something constructive to say, then say it. Otherwise—'

'I mean this constructively. The music sounds a little defeatist.'

'Did you not notice that the tempo rises at the end? The whole idea is that we start slow and then gather momentum as the video proceeds!'

'That rising tempo seemed forced...like a desperate lunge. What I'm saying is, there's a kind of "quiet despair" in the music throughout.'

'You're talking rubbish! In any case, quiet despair is the absolutely correct mood for these times and this issue!'

'I don't agree with that,' said Sasha. 'Even if these are desperate times for freedom, we have to be confident. We still have to write as though we are on the winning side—because in a deeper sense, we are.'

'You're still talking rubbish! Why do you do this?'

'But maybe I'm reading too much into the music. I don't know much about music anyway.'

'You certainly don't! I have to tell you, it's irritating the way you go on about a subject you've no clue about. Don't laugh, I'm being serious!'

'Just because I told you once, I don't like Bob Dylan,' Sasha smiled.

'Which was a highly uneducated thing to say! Coming from someone who listens to trance and lounge music!'

'That has happened recently,' said Sasha thoughtfully. 'For me it creates a...a spiritual atmosphere.'

'Let's change the subject,' said Jatin, with distaste. 'I have to talk to you about the two videos you wrote. There are some problems there.'

'What problems?'

'I'm telling you,' said Jatin, menacingly. 'Be patient. You lack patience.'

A little smile rested on Sasha's face; he could not help it. It did not spring from mockery, but his peculiar lightness of heart. It was confounding, however, to Jatin. While Sushant was grinning with enjoyment at their to and fro, Arvind, I am sure, knew the danger, as I would have, in his place.

'The first thing is, your punctuation and the way you structure your sentences, is completely different from mine. That's not okay. These videos have to look like they have come from one common source.'

'I've tried to be poetic,' said Sasha.

'It's not working. That's what I'm telling you. Your style of writing has to match mine. Otherwise we are being chaotic and simply adding to the cacophony out there.'

'So long as the spirit of what we are saying is the same, I don't see a problem with differences in expression. Such differences are only good and natural surely.' But the more thoughtfully Sasha spoke, the higher the colour mounted in Jatin's face.

'I don't have the energy to argue about this.' His voice was raised noticeably, 'Also your content is extremely clichéd! This one you have written about speaking being a way of thinking, and—what was it?'

'Freedom of speech being vital for a society to think aloud,' explained Sasha. 'Often in order to understand your own views, or even to correct them, you first need to air them. So if you don't have an atmosphere of free speech, it's difficult even to think properly.'

'It's not fresh or interesting. One hears this sort of thing all the time. Also, your writing is preachy.'

Sasha paused, his eyes widening, and then, most maddeningly in Jatin's eyes, he laughed. 'All our videos are preachy, Jatin! The ones you've written are too! I'm surprised you think this is clichéd though. You could say that it's not exactly a defence of free speech, it's more an explanation of what it entails. After all, I'm not saying that all thoughts *should* be entertained. There are lines of thought it is sinful to go down, and shameful to go down publicly. I'm not denying that. Sometimes the law is right to intervene too. It would be clichéd if I simply said: free speech forever.'

'Hang on,' said Jatin slowly. 'Now you don't believe in free speech?'

'Oh, I do! But not simply as a slogan, obviously! Anyway, why don't we get a third opinion on this? What do Arvind and Sushant think? I mean, about using different writing styles and also whether my writing is clichéd.'

Here, he nodded towards the two onlookers. But Jatin was staring fixedly through his spectacles (which, at such times, always looked comically small for his face).

'It doesn't matter what anybody else thinks. Even if they agree with you, I cannot put out something that damages what we are doing. I cannot compromise on something so basic.'

'All right, then I won't write,' said Sasha, 'I can't write anyway, if you're going to control the wording of every sentence. I didn't know you wanted total control of this.'

'These videos were my idea, Sasha, everybody knows that. And this is not about wording, this is the basic sensibility. Let's not argue any further, I beg of you.'

Sasha was still smiling mildly, when Jatin's face darkened and contorted. His spells of remorse always appeared as a painful, chronic sickness.

'I'm not saying this to put you down, okay? It's for the good of the project. I still want you involved with it. You have a lot to contribute. You already have contributed a lot too.'

'Of course. It's fine, if you want to do it like this... And if I have more ideas to write about, I will tell you.'

'Good! Wonderful! Also, I want your feedback on everything I write, okay? I value it. Truly. What's the score now Arvind?'

'Is there a match today?'

'Views dammit, how many views?!'

Getting up himself, with his plate in his hand, he walked over to peer at the laptop. But though he clicked more than once, to refresh the screen, the news remained poor.

'There's another comment,' pointed out Arvind.

'I can see that. I'm not bothered by idiotic lunatic right-wing comments. But at least the liberals should be watching.'

'Low attention spans,' began Arvind.

'Don't be a fucking moron Arvind! It's a one-minute video! They're not even clicking on it! Where are all the people on Ruhi's Twitter? If there was a celebrity in this thumbnail, or some half-naked girl or a picture of a cat, people would be queuing up to watch! Are we such hypocrites? Are we so flaky? Do we only pretend to be interested in what's happening around us?'

Objectively, Jatin's impatience was extraordinary, yet in hindsight I realize he was onto something. The online buzz around the Ahishor episode, which we all thought was soaring, was in actuality, just then beginning to taper off—indeed, to fall off a cliff. In the news of the Navy Baba's impending arrest, those who had previously vented their outrage, had perhaps got their cue to celebrate, and be 'done with it'. Their tastes had turned, victoriously, to more titillating gossip, lighter-hearted affairs. I believe the trending topics on Twitter in that period included jokes about the IQ of a certain Bollywood actress, a cricketer's rumoured romance, the cabinet minister alleged to have murdered his wife, as well as a raging, worldwide debate about the true colour of somebody's dress. It was either blue and black, or white and gold.

After his outburst, Jatin fell back onto his chair, in an atmosphere that had grown carefully hushed. Then Sasha sat up, his eyes glistening like troubled waters.

'It's true, people are distracted. And afraid and insecure. It's a dangerous time. Listen, did you read the second piece I wrote? I think it's important. We should put it out there.'

'Your second piece?' said Jatin dully.

'Yes. About—about God.'

'It was moronic. I actually didn't want to talk about it, because it was shameful that you wrote it. I thought you had more intelligence than that.'

A moment's pause elapsed before Sasha spoke again.

'What was wrong with it?'

'I don't want to argue now, Sasha, please. How many times must I say that!'

'No, but tell me what was wrong. I'll read it out again.'

With his plate balanced on his lap, Sasha took out his phone and, a few seconds later, read aloud the following lines:

'Not Greater than God'

All things that grow on this earth
Whether tall, straight and beautiful
Or ugly and misshapen
Are overseen by the flawless sky.
Thus, however great or small a talent
For art, or beauty, or the occult,

None is greater than God.
Be a 'God-man' ever so gifted,
He is bound by God,
In the ordinary cord of right and wrong.

'Firstly,' began Jatin, 'it's far too arty, without actually being poetic either. It doesn't have impact. But worse than that, it's completely beside the point! Why are you talking about God?'

'The idea is to show that all people are subject to criticism, including God-men.'

'Then say they are subject to criticism, why are you saying "God"? And why are you calling God-men gifted? You sound like a right-wing loony yourself. Is that what you actually are? Are you a right-wing loony?'

'We can beat around the bush,' said Sasha, with sudden passion, 'or we can speak directly. All men are subject to criticism, that's easy to say. But what is the standard of criticism, and why should it be the same for everyone? This conundrum is solved only when we realize there is a God! People are equal only before God, and not in any other sense. There is no escaping this! As for God-men, why should we not admit their gifts? Are all mystics frauds? Are we going to ignore all the people who claim to have witnessed their powers?'

When Jatin did not reply, but, with his face screwed up in distaste, attacked his food, the warning signs were clear. Sasha continued:

'Think of an athlete. An athlete develops physical powers which appear literally other-worldly for ordinary people. Then why cannot someone who trains in the mind and spirit develop corresponding powers in those realms? Even if such babas commit frauds habitually—so do various athletes take drugs—it doesn't mean their prowess is all made up. We cannot say the followers of God-men are all sheep, all utterly misled! No, they are attracted by something real. It's the promise of unseen powers, the pull towards the supernatural. That's a very human thing! But they get waylaid by God-men who dominate them with their talents. If we take on God-men, we should do it in the name of God—I mean, that mystical...everything!—which is greater than any mystical talent. Then we'll be building up from the feelings of followers. That's better than tearing those feelings down in the name of rationality.

'As for the liberals,' he went on, earnestly, 'the rationalists and the atheists, yes this talk of God will offend them. But look, you said yourself just now, they are flaky and scattered. They don't really believe in anything! They need this message most of all. We shouldn't fret about alienating them, they are alienated already, they need uniting.'

'Shut up!' roared Jatin. A piece of roti flew from his mouth, landing in the vicinity of the wall TV. 'You are a moron! You are a bigger moron than the Hindutva bhaktas! No—all rationalists are not flaky! There are people who stand for their principles with courage and conviction! I am interested in reaching out to those people! I am not interested in alienating everybody with mystical mumbo jumbo!'

'Calm down,' said Sasha.

'I told you a hundred times I didn't want to argue! You insisted on talking! But you know what, I'm glad you did, because now I realize I was wrong about you. I thought you had brains—but you haven't got a clue! The idea with these videos is to make a practical difference! We have to get people to watch and we have to convince people. You have no notion how to do that! You're simply spouting your own theories to please yourself! And this is a real problem with you, I'm telling you for your own sake. You live in your own world, you are not capable of doing any actual work! Keep believing in unseen powers, see where that gets you!'

'If you were really telling me for my own sake, you wouldn't be shouting at me,' Sasha replied. 'You're simply being destructive. That's what happens when you refuse to let go of things and want to control them throughout—you become destructive.'

'Stop being sanctimonious! Even now! This is yet another unbearable habit of yours! You're making an utter ass of yourself!'

Suddenly a spasm passed over Sasha's face. With jerky movements he placed his unfinished plate on the table.

'I didn't come here to be insulted,' he said, getting up.

Jatin's eyes were popping madly. He stared from the abandoned lunch-plate to the figure opening the door, and then back. I suspect it was the sight of the wasted food which pushed him over the edge.

'Don't just stand there with the door open! Go, you asshole! *Ja, ja, chutiye!*'

All this while, Arvind and Sushant were watching wordlessly. Arvind had begun to smile in a knowing way, but Sushant could scarcely believe what was happening. He saw Sasha, who was on the verge of stepping out, halt and turn when the profanities began.

'Do you hear yourself?' cried Sasha. 'Is this how you talk to a friend?

Jatin jumped up, and charged, on pounding feet, the short distance to the door. Sasha flinched in shock, but stayed his ground until the other's manic face was filling his vision.

'Either get inside! Or leave, fucker, leave!'

Sushant records that when Sasha hurried out, Jatin, having slammed the door, turned with a strange look, akin to surprise. He seemed to have expected something else to happen.

'Arrogant bastard!' he yelled, after a moment. 'Let him go if he wants to!'

* * *

He had drawn blood, somewhere amongst his wild attacks, for such was Jatin's perspicacity. On his bed by the sea, Sasha lay in stillness. There was a hammering in his head, the aftershocks of the verbal assault. Yet he hardly paid it heed. What he felt most of all was a rampaging worry that he could not control; a doubt that was breaking through him like a sickness.

Sure, he believed in the things that he felt in his bones. Everyone did, at a certain age; he had simply continued to. He knew that, most often, if not always, these certainties ran counter to other people's advice. But he believed in them still. It was faith. And yet—what did that mean? What was it, after all, that he had faith in? *Pray now*, he told himself, and instead, a weary shame stole over him.

Was he, in truth, merely stubborn and self-harming? Perhaps it was not worldly wisdom he had avoided, but maturity? Perhaps, while others had grown, he had remained a child, away from life's glorious racetracks, where an eager crowd watched and cheered, where the prizes were coveted and the people flesh and blood? What if he was running his own imaginary course, observed only by the ghosts of his fancies, and excluding himself (because of his ignorance and childish snobbishness) from the great goings-on in that packed stadium? Oh, that was a pathetic figure!

The doubts were terrible in their persistence, and plaintively, he wondered why. Jatin had said nothing he had not heard before. True, it was the way he had said it, and true, also, that Sasha himself admired Jatin's insights into people, and liked him very much as a friend. It had been a grievous attack, from an unexpected quarter, difficult to recover from.

Outside his window, the daylight was dwindling, the sea was changing colour. Sasha tried to grow rapt in everything outside of himself. There was the twinkling horizon, where a small ship sailed gracefully, there were palm leaves waving, birdsong, and traffic, a child calling to another child, high-pitched squeals in the neighbouring building, there was the steady whoosh of the ceiling fan. He closed his eyes, trying, next, to lose consciousness altogether.

After an indeterminate period of time, he woke. Night had fallen. An electric glow hung over the apartment's boundary walls. The sea was invisible, melted in blackness. As though moved by premonition, he went to his table. He turned on his laptop, with his heart pounding. Moments later, he was light-headed with delight. Yes, she had written! His excitement twisted coquettishly inside him. Lunging to gain hold of it, his eye rushed eagerly to the end of her message. It was not a long message. There, Maithili's words, startling, final, bleak, knocked the breath from Sasha's body.

But I need not quote from her mail. The words were unexceptional. It was, indeed, their very plainness that made them so injurious, for they served to place Sasha's enduring passion at (nearly) the same rate as the briefest and most casual advance. 'I never had any feelings for you at any point' was the gist of what she wrote. 'Therefore, for your own sake, cease wasting your time and your energies.' She was angry, also, that he had spoken to her mother, and repeated her opinion that he was humiliating himself, unhealthily. 'I will not write to you again, and I hope you will do the same.'

Sasha leaned back on his chair, and stared out of the window. Nothingness lay before him, to the pounding beat of the ocean tides, as, within him, the edifice of his hopes, that had withstood so much, crumbled finally and unstoppably, into a silent abyss. He sat like that for a long time, blinking sporadically, disbelieving what had happened, but unable to look away. One thought continually revolved in his head—he returned to it again and again—that he should receive this message on the very same day that Jatin had damned him as being capable of nothing and warned him 'for his own sake' to change. It seemed an inescapable sign. And yet—was it really all so! His heart blanched, and filled with helplessness...

But here I must directly address those of my readers, who are perhaps growing impatient. Surely, it might be exclaimed, surely it was obvious all along that Sasha had no chance with Maithili? Can this really have been such a terrible blow to him? The final exposure of a wild and stubborn fancy may merit the victim a little sympathy, but for clinging so long to a delusion—bothering not just himself, but Maithili—he was more to be censured than pitied. And a delusion it certainly was, for he could not truly have believed what he said. Having met her twice, he had said he wanted to marry her!

Personally, I cannot quarrel with this point of view. Among the various people who had, in the preceding months, advised Sasha to 'move on' from Maithili, I myself was one. I had had no doubt that his love was never going to bear fruit.

Regarding its quality, however, I was always confused. Even at the time, I was never quite able to scoff at his dreams, or, when she didn't write, to mock his distress. Perhaps the sight of his constancy had chastened me, so fickle—without, of course, ever persuading me to alter my own ways. But looking back, I am glad I felt at least that much for what he felt, and did not entirely turn my back on what I did not comprehend.

XIII

A Family Gathering

This was in the early part of December, no season for rain. But it had poured mightily all day. Only well past nightfall did the deluge cease to batter the windows.

Ahishor threw them open, in every room of his apartment. Earlier that day, he had moved back home from his mother's. His injury had long healed, and now, with the fever gone and certain other complications cleared, he felt new-made. There was a great deal of work pending; he could not wait to return to it. Many things had struck him in the course of his convalescence. He looked more laid-back than ever, his hair and beard grown luxuriously unkempt, rubber chappals slapping his heels as he walked, and a sleepy expression on his face, but inside, he was teeming with ideas, his nerves tingling with fresh resolve.

'Ahishor, the candles will go out!'

Nalini's voice, high and musical, sailed out from the living room, as gusts of storm-swept air blew freely through the house.

She had cleared a space among the masses of things, and pulled three chairs around the central table. Four flickering candles were clustered atop it. From the kitchen alongside, came delicious cooking smells. A pot of pasta was boiling slowly, and cut vegetables frying alongside. Ahishor strolled over to stir and garnish them. With his back to his mother, he said:

'I feel much better in the fresh air.'

'Yes, all right, it is nice,' she agreed, 'and my candles are surviving too. Need any help?'

'No. Just ask them to hurry up, the food's almost ready.'

'Ritesh just messaged. They are near the D-Mart.'

Ahishor extended his left arm and made a thumbs-up sign, while under his steady gaze, the vegetables hissed and crackled confidently. Suddenly, a tremendous sigh rose up within Nalini and went juddering through her. She sat down at the table, her eyes welling up uncontrollably. Ahishor's grey cat leaped onto the table. She caught hold of it and pulled it down to her lap, stroking its back furiously as it mewed, first in protest, then purred.

'So naughty you have become, my bundle of naughtiness! Have you been missing your master? Are you happy he's well again? Yes, you are happy, aren't you?'

'Terrence is happy just as long as she is fed.'

'Nooo, that's not true! Terrence also worries about Ahi. Doesn't she? Doesn't she? Does Terrence also think Ahi should take some more days to rest?'

There was the sound of a spoon clattering. At the kitchen-top, Ahishor turned, glowering.

'Why are you still harping on that? I'm perfectly well now.'

'I'm talking to Terrence. Do you mind?'

She stared back stubbornly, her eyes drying quickly. Ahishor began to smile.

'Everything that happens, happens for the best.' It was one of his mother's own oft-repeated sayings.

'What does that have to do with not exerting yourself straight after a bad illness?'

'I'm fine, Ma. I'm fully recovered. And everything *has* happened for the best. That's what I'm trying to tell you!'

He laughed. 'Why are you being like this anyway?' She, now wearing a sulk, continued to stroke the cat. Ahishor came over to the table, beaming and brimming with bold new prospects, just as the sound of voices was heard from outside the door.

His mother dropped by often, but it was only the second or third time that Karim was visiting his Versova apartment, and Ritesh had never been before. It seemed to Ahishor that much fuss was being made over the end of his illness. Yet he was touched, very much. Karim, his gaze narrowed in good humour, chuckling and murmuring in a beautiful baritone, walked straight over to embrace him.

'I picked up some pizza and beers.' Ritesh lifted into sight a full plastic bag.

'Oh, Ahishor has cooked,' said Nalini. 'He's made pasta for us all.'

'Awesome! No, just that since I suggested dinner, I thought I'd bring some food along too. I somehow didn't expect you'd be cooking on your first day back.'

'I like to cook,' smiled Ahishor. 'It's all right, we can eat everything. The beers are very welcome. Let's get them in the fridge. This way... What's that?'

'Churros from Bandra,' grinned Ritesh, 'for later.'

Ahishor's other cat, large and black with white markings, padded into the room. He was a shy tomcat, usually found curled up on a crate in the corner, or on top of the cupboard.

'Look who's made an appearance,' said Nalini. 'Solar, what a pleasant surprise! Karim, it's you he likes.'

Karim Azad was fishing out a lighter, while Solar, the cat,

finished nuzzling against his legs, before proceeding to the mattress beyond the table and collapsing among the cushions. Terrence watched balefully from Nalini's lap.

'It's company they like. They like to be among a family,' said Karim. 'Now who will share a joint with me? Ahishor? Come on, come on, we'll eat right afterwards.'

'I'm trying to stop smoking,' Ahishor protested.

'Don't touch cigarettes, but this is good stuff. Once in a while. Ask your mother.'

'You do it more than once in a while, Karim,' said Nalini, but her slender arm was reaching out to take the proferred joint. Making a face of concession, Ahishor went indoors to put on music, The Moody Blues, ['That's the one!' called out Karim approvingly], and then joined them at the table. Ritesh, in the meanwhile, had laid down on the mattress, frightening the cat with his long limbs and big hair.

The songs came in on the breeze. At some point the candles went out, but nobody minded. The joint travelled around. Karim continued to talk about cats, while they watched with amusement a little fracas breaking out between Terrence and Solar. Another flash of lightning lit the sky, and a clap of thunder sounded, though the rain, thankfully, was past. Nalini remarked on the weather, and everybody agreed it was extraordinary, but rather lovely. When the joint was finished, Karim produced another.

Ahishor gazed at the others, through the haze of smoke. A glow of warmth, directed at everyone in the room, was descending upon him. It was a special feeling, even as regards his mother, whom, in general, he loved almost too closely to be aware of it. But she was always, always there for him. And Karim too, this great man, feared and respected at large, who, though not a father to him, was certainly a friend. He felt grateful even to Ritesh, currently belying his age and size by hugging Ahishor's cushions like a little boy. Ritesh was rather a fool, of course, but loveable, for his heart was in the right place, and after all, he was doing well with his production house, making good money. (Apparently, he had quite a fan-following among women too.) With a flash of pride, Ahishor thought how a support group of such quality would be the envy of anybody.

It did not occur to him that Ritesh was fidgeting and Karim smoking abstractedly and the conversation so desultory, because they were all tense.

'I wanted to say something,' he spoke out shortly afterwards, when dinner was on the table, 'I know we never do thanksgiving rituals, but I almost feel like we should today. But not to the guy in the sky,' Ahishor grinned. 'It's you all I want to thank. For—well, you know what! Anyway, I'm feeling better than ever now. To be honest—I was telling Ma—that punch I took actually knocked some good ideas into my head! Man, this film of ours...'

He turned to Ritesh (who was sitting up on the mattress, with his plate in his lap), and beamed meaningfully, before pausing to gather his thoughts. Karim looked up. A little smile reached his bloodshot eyes.

'*Khan pakaan ka maza leejiye, janaab* (Enjoy the feast, mister). There'll be time to talk shop.'

Ahishor laughed and ate with relish, though a little while later, he could not restrain himself.

'*Schrödinger's Cat* just won the Jury Award at Venice. I know, it's wonderful, right? But nobody ever punched me in the head for *Schrödinger's Cat*...I've come to realize how much I value that blow. It's worth more than any award. That these people felt so caught out...that they had the audacity... It proves our film is on exactly the right track. And we have to think big now. We can't be childish any longer. Mihir was wrong—we were all wrong—this is not a time to simply "raise questions" and "start a dialogue" and play safe. The country is hanging on a precipice, voices of reason are finally speaking up against the sort of people who punched me. Which side wins—hope and reason for the first time ever, or blinkered violence as in all of Indian history!—it all depends on the decisions that people like us make, right now. It's the Shakespearean moment, Ma, and we must take it at the flood.'

Through the course of his speech, his excitement hardened into determination, and his eyes, sunken in his bearded face, filled with that strange light of prophecy which is both beacon and reflection. He was looking back, not only to that afternoon in the office, but much before. Meanwhile, around the table, the silence was deepening.

'What do you suggest should be done?' asked Karim drily.

'The institution of the God-man is no accident of Indian society. It is a fundamental skeletal feature of Hinduism. God-men provide the organizational structure that Hinduism otherwise lacks. We must uncover the heart of the problem, which is the desire to escape the world—climbing up on the Guru's shoulders to get away—this inhuman obsession with hierarchy and "spiritual growth"—whatever that even means—and the neglect of material duties towards one's fellow man, and oneself for that matter. Which by the way also leads to the dirt and the degradation and the all-round shittiness of India. But what I'm saying is, as long as we do not attack the core doctrines of Hinduism, we cannot rid ourselves of the God-man menace. The two are completely related.'

'Very good,' said Karim, 'and what does this have to do

with your film?'

'That's the other thing I've thought a lot about. Cinema must step up now, it must become an agent for social change. Cinema, as a medium, is made for making change. Perhaps that's really the only thing it's made for.'

'Well!' said Karim, putting down his fork, 'So it's all decided then! Your documentary is going to attack Hinduism, dismantle the baba menace, and usher in the enlightenment!'

A flush passed over Nalini's cheek, and she drew in her breath with a fearful look at her son—but said nothing. Ahishor looked dully at Karim, without understanding. Then suddenly Ritesh, who had appeared childishly absorbed in his food, with cushions sprawled about him, straightened angrily.

'What if I told you that we've received death-threats in our office?' His voice grew high and wavering; it always did when he was losing his cool. 'Because of this documentary!'

'Have you?' Ahishor asked, astonished.

'We didn't tell you, because you were sick.'

'Thanks, though you ought to have told me. I hope you told the police.'

'They didn't take it seriously.'

'Well, they are probably correct there,' said Ahishor. 'You run a big movie company, you ought to be used to threats. I don't know why you're so perturbed.'

'You're talking as though nothing has happened to you.'

'Nothing has,' Ahishor shrugged and put on a bewildered look. 'Relative to what other people have faced, nothing at all has happened.'

A nasty smile spread across Ritesh's face—like something sinister breaking hitherto placid waters.

'So you're saying I shouldn't care... Let my investors and

employees be threatened with violence. All right... What about when your mother is?'

'What about when my mother is—threatened?' Ahishor repeated slowly, 'Who has threatened my mother?'

'I haven't been threatened,' frowned Nalini. 'When have I been threatened?'

'Arre bhai!' exclaimed Karim. 'You know perfectly well!'

'Are you talking about that Twitter thing?'

'You know what he's talking about.'

'What happened on Twitter?' said Ahishor.

'I hardly even check it,' said Nalini. 'Just that last week I logged on. Somebody—two people actually—had sent messages.'

'What messages?'

'There was a suggestion!' said Karim, raising his voice harshly—he was growing irritable, 'that the act that led to your birth was engaged in purely professionally. And so on and so forth. Then came threats of retribution. Use your imagination, Ahishor.'

'I deleted them,' said Nalini, 'and didn't give them a second thought.' But her pained expression said otherwise.

Ritesh glared at Ahishor, who, however, was looking merely thoughtful.

'The Internet is overrun with the extremist right-wing fringe. Women are targeted especially. Actresses all the more—even former actresses. I hope you know how to block people on Twitter, Ma. Because that's all one can do. These people are just jokes really, they're what's called Keyboard Nazis... Keyboard Nazis...'

The strains of the Moody Blues were still leavening the night. As Ahishor began to smile to himself, Ritesh put his plate aside and stood up on the mattress, in among the cushions. He was unsteady on the soft cotton, but apparently too incensed to care.

'Wake up, bro! Wake up and grow up! Since you refuse to take this seriously, let me tell you straight out. In the present climate, given all that is happening, I cannot produce this film. I have responsibilities, not just financially, but also in terms of safety. I cannot put people at risk. I actually thought we would discuss this tonight, and hopefully find a solution, because I didn't want to pull the plug. I absolutely didn't. I was still hopeful we'd find a solution. But the way you're talking—! It's kind of delusional! I really don't see a way forward!'

'Ritesh, sit down,' said his father quietly.

'Yes, do sit Ritesh,' said Ahishor witheringly. 'I don't know what to say really. I'm a little amazed. Karim, I hope you remember. You were pushing for this project even when others were sceptical. I'm sure you can understand, that now more than ever, this work must be done. The fact is—their attack on me was a huge mistake on their part, it has rallied all the liberal forces together. Hasn't it? What's the matter?'

Leaning back on his chair, shaking his head, Karim was staring into the middle distance.

'Too soon,' he said, with grim satisfaction. 'The shit has hit the fan too soon. You see, it's one thing when a film is already made and the right-wingers start protesting. I expected that to happen. But what has happened is different. The trouble has started already, and you have barely begun shooting.'

'What difference does that make? It had to happen sometime.'

'It makes a huge difference. You can pull together a lot of support once you have a product to offer. Because people don't want to be denied the pleasure of consuming it. But you cannot get the same support in the process of making it. Especially not this early in the process. In fact, in such a case, the opposite happens. You get looked at as incompetent, someone who could not even make his movie. *Main nahi keh raha hoon.* (I am not saying this.) I don't think like this. But people do.'

'You're wrong, Karim! Haven't you seen how much support we are getting?'

'It's illusory,' drawled Karim Azad, 'it's ephemeral. What was the expression you used just now? A little while ago? Keyboard Nazis? *Bilkul* (Absolutely), Keyboard Nazis. So the same logic that you apply to your haters, please apply it also to your supporters. Wait, I've not finished. The same logic applies—with one important difference! The difference is, that those who come to destroy don't need to have staying power—destruction takes no time, they can simply destroy and move on—but those who are needed to defend and support, they need to be committed. They can't be fly-by-night fellows. You see the point?'

As his query hung in the air, a thin smile appeared on Karim's lips. He resumed his dinner, in the manner of one who had earned it. But Ahishor was grinning incredulously.

'Then let's not *us* be fly-by-night, Karim! Karim—are you listening? At least let us show some courage. Maybe it will lead the way for other people too. And what courage is even required here? This was one aborted attack! Nothing more—except silly threats which I can't believe are bothering you all so much. Even the police are with us—the Navy Baba is being arrested.'

'He hasn't been arrested,' put in Nalini tersely.

'Yes, he has.'

'But he is out on bail,' she continued portentously.

'Well, that's the legal process. Anyway, don't change the subject, Ma! The question is, are you or are you not going to show support?'

'Of course I am!' cried Nalini. 'Of course we all are! The question is only—only what is the best way to move forward. Now listen to me please! Will someone switch the music off? Ritesh, will you please? Thank you!'

She waited, holding fast an anguished expression, until silence broke over the living room, and Ritesh reappeared. He was carrying a three-legged stool, which he now straddled, a little distance from the table. It was cool and quiet in the house, though somewhere windows were rattling in the breeze.

'Thank you,' resumed Nalini, 'Ahi, what I don't like is the way you are talking about "us" and "them". You mustn't get provoked by what has happened into losing your objectivity, and your balance. These are your sweetest—your finest qualities. Criticize God-men, by all means, but in the spirit of inquiry.'

'You mean the spirit of cowardice.'

'Why are you talking like this? It's completely unlike you! No! I do not mean the spirit of cowardice. Don't you understand, that if you become aggressive you only polarize people? We all want this movie to make a change, but to do that, we have to be respectful, mature and very, very specific in the targets we choose. Suddenly you're talking about attacking Hinduism! There are a thousand good things in Hinduism, so many rich traditions of debate, you have always said that yourself! You will damage your own case by being wild! There was an article in *The Telegraph*—today—I'm going to send it to you.'

'By whom? Saying what?'

'I will send it to you. Uff, I don't remember. Some Krishna, from the World Bank. Suraj Krishna, that was the name. It's a good piece, it's written in solidarity with you, but it's cautioning against exactly this kind of "us and them" polarization. Apparently that's going on a lot online, these days.'

Ahishor heard her, as though from a distance. He knew who Maithili's father was. A surge of unexpected emotions besieged him, released as though from some cage in his mind. Adrenaline was coursing through him, and his resolve growing supple and strong. A smile sprang to his lips. Nalini had finished speaking. She was staring at him, with anger and apprehension in her beautiful eyes.

'So am I to understand,' said Ahishor, 'that if I make this film in the detached, scientific way, as discussed before, not stepping on anybody's toes, not talking about Hinduism directly at all—if I do that, then Ritesh has no problem producing it?'

Under their combined gaze, Ritesh opened his mouth, closed it, smirked, shrugged, and looked at Karim.

'I really don't know. What Abba said is true. There are going to be problems throughout now. This thing has gotten too big already. One thing I'm clear on, safety is paramount. I have a responsibility to my investors—and my employees.'

Ahishor turned, with triumph, to his mother.

'He won't produce it. It doesn't matter how toned down it is.'

'Arre, why should you tone it down?' interrupted Karim, *'Tum bilkul theek kah rahe ho* (You're absolutely right...), it is not just God-men, the entire religion that props them up is bunkum! Let me tell you, I have no sentimental feelings about ancient teachings and traditions. All religions are superstitions! The older they are, the more entrenched their fakeries, nothing more. I'll give you an idea. Make this film as powerful as you like. But do it with the strength of numbers, because in the present context, you need that. Us three or four people, one production house somewhere—that's not enough. Involve the general public. Use crowdfunding.'

'That's a wonderful idea!' cried Nalini. 'Crowdfunding is

very much in vogue now. Do you know, they even raised money for the Film Festival that way? What? You're not audible, Ahi.'

'I am not interested in crowdfunding,' said Ahishor distinctly. 'An artist's job is to lead the public, not beg from it. I do not need thousands of gawkers who, out of mere curiosity, will toss a few rupees my way. I need a few brave people to take risks, not a mob that doesn't risk anything at all, individually.'

Suddenly, he fell back in his chair, sighing. 'Oh God, my God.'

'How ironic,' chuckled Ritesh, 'that you say that.'

Ahishor turned an unnaturally blank face to his half-brother, but did not reply. Nalini, dishevelled and flustered, with her mouth parted, leaned forward as though to speak again, but Karim reached out a restraining hand to her arm. His own face was pinched; his patience was at an end. A savage glance, like a sword thrust, went Ahishor's way, but fell upon the same impassive regard.

'This is why they win,' said Ahishor. 'No wonder they win. While we articulate our clever excuses to avoid entering the fray, they simply come out—with their fists.'

Taking hold of the arms of his chair, he lifted it up and let it fall with a clatter. Standing, he looked around at his family, letting his gaze rest upon each one.

Then rubbing his hands together, sticking them in his pockets, he walked unhurriedly to the front door, in a silence broken only by the distant traffic sounds.

XIV

Desires and Delusions

These and other developments came to me from an unexpected quarter. I was lying in bed at seven in the evening, feeling feverish in the unruly weather, when the doorbell rang. It rang twice before I pulled myself upright. Sushant was at the door, hair cropped and shaven, ears and eyes protruding, and his long, lithe body posed womanlike against the bannister.

'You've come for the edits?' I wondered, 'I thought you were going to come in the morning.'

'I got late bhai. What happened, were you sleeping?'

'Not sleeping. Just not been feeling well. Well I've finished the edits—except for the last one—'

'It's chill, chill,' he smiled gently. 'Just that right now the whole situation is changing. Jatin is going mad, bhai. He's going into overdrive.'

He slipped softly indoors and made place to sit on the ledge beneath my living room window, shifting aside a bundle of clothes without either fuss or permission. I stayed standing, watching his movements, which had a queer grace. I switched on the tube-light and the room was bathed in white.

'Is Jatin cursing me,' I said, 'for not having finished yet?

'Yes and no, bhai. He is so excited right now he wants to upload all the videos immediately. But the views have to be maximized *na*? So each one needs time for its own buzz.'

'Why is he so excited?' I said idly. 'Well—he always is, I guess.'

'Ohhh,' Sushant threw back his head, crooning astonishment. 'Don't you know?!'

'Know what?'

'You don't know! Ahishor *ki* movie is not happening! Ritesh stabbed him in the back. Producer fucker has ditched. He kicked his own brother in the balls.'

'*What?*'

'He told Jatin personally. Ahishor, I mean, Ahishor told Jatin. They have been in touch throughout *na*, since the videos began.'

'But what happened?' I was still on my feet, not far from the door. 'And when did it happen? I've not heard anything!'

'Sit down, I'll tell you... Okay, don't sit, haha! Basically, Ritesh Azad is chickenshit. Some guys had called at his office threatening to beat the crap out of him if he made this movie. He got scared, so he pulled the plug. Made excuses about safety first, responsibility to employees yadda yadda yadda. That's how these corporate guys are—talking fancy and pissing farce. See, Ahishor has balls. I really love that guy, bhai! He didn't step back, even though he is the one who has actually taken a punch... But Ritesh... But I'll make sure he gets beaten up anyway. Don't worry about it, bhai. Haha! He won't get away. Oh no, he—'

'Is this official?' I interrupted his reverie. 'Ritesh isn't producing?'

'Yeah yeah, it's official bhai, the documentary is officially fucked. Arre, he has posted on Facebook also!'

'Who has? On Facebook?'

I rushed to my room. Pulling open my laptop, I waited, impatient and at the same time apprehensive, my heart thudding uneasily, until the page opened. There, indeed, headlining my homepage with unrivalled 'buzz', was Ahishor's scarcely believable post. It was dated that afternoon. I felt myself filling with bafflement and a despair, which was not unmixed with anger (for surely this long-winded and dramatic public declaration could have been avoided), as well as worry, for myself, for the repercussions of this news. But perhaps I speak slyly. Perhaps that selfish anxiety was all I really felt. Yet why should I rush to name my sins, when all will emerge presently?

> Last week [ran Ahishor's post] I shared the news that *Schrödinger's Cat* had won the Jury Award for Best Film at the Venice Film Festival, beating out a world-class field. Today, I have something less happy to say. *Schrödinger's Cat* will be my last film (in a recognizable, 'artistic' form). The bigots have conquered. Rather, I should say, the bigots had already conquered. They have encroached very deep into 'our' territory, and recently I have become aware of just how deep. I want to thank you all for your sympathy and support over the last several weeks. I know there are those among you I can still rely on, the brave and the true and visionary ones. In you, I shall place my hopes and expectations.

Clutching my laptop (I was unable to let go of it), I went back to the other room. Sushant had not moved from the window. He was smiling sadly in the wash of the tube-light.

'Amazing *na*?' he mused. 'Here is a guy who has won I don't know how many awards. He has made a really really awesome film. Even he gets fucked. But what a guy, what a guy.'

'But I don't get it,' I cried. 'Even if Ritesh isn't producing it, surely Ahishor can find someone else? Why has he decided to drop the whole project? Does Mihir know? Does Bharat know?'

'They do if they're on Facebook! But *haan*, I'm surprised you didn't know already. Ahishor came to our office yesterday and told all of us openly. Jatin went mad. I have seen him mad before, but this was even crazier. If Ritesh had been there, he would have strangled him. That's for sure... Now the aim is to destroy Ritesh in our videos. Accha bhai, the CD? Give me whichever videos you've finished editing. Never mind the others.'

'You look like you need a drink,' he added, when I came out again from my bedroom, in a daze.

'I guess I'm quite shocked,' I managed to say.

'Let's have a drink! Come, let's go to Woodcon.'

'Don't you have to give the CD to Jatin?' I asked, in surprise.

'Not tonight. It can wait till tomorrow. I'm not going back to the office tonight. Come, come, let's have a drink, Dhruv! You'll get over the shock. Haha!'

'No, anyway, I can't drink,' I said, 'I still have fever. I don't know why. It's the weather, all these rains.'

'Yeah yeah...' He seemed to have lost interest.

'Nice place you have,' Sushant began to stare about the flat, without, however, making any move to get up and explore it. 'In this city, having a nice flat is like having a girl. You know what I mean?'

'I'm not sure.'

'I am losing my flat next month, bhai. Landlord is kicking me out.'

'Why?' I asked, coolly, after his own fashion. 'Too many parties?'

He chuckled to himself, his head hanging down. His right

hand crept over his thigh. Sushant looked used and shabby, like the clothes beside him. Yet I was riveted, just as I would have been, had those old bundles become animated, here and there, with languorous movements.

'Not parties, bhai. Hash... Too much hash... And too many women.' His laughter wheezed out again.

'Where are you going to live now?' I asked uncomfortably, and without knowing why, for I didn't care and didn't want to know. I was still standing, ill at ease in my own house. Suddenly, he looked up with bulging eyes.

'With Ahishor.'

'With Ahishor?'

He nodded. 'He offered that I can move in with him. I know, it's kind of surprising *na*.' A smile, awestruck and therefore endearing, brought dimples to Sushant's cheeks. 'A guy like him and a guy like me...'

His expression altered, for the worse. 'Heh! But we are all in the same boat, bhai. He can't make his film and I can't make my *Last Anarchist*. Bottom line is, we've both been fucked. By the fucking corporates.'

'So you'll be here in Versova?' I said blankly. I felt again my grasp on things slipping. Ahishor shutting shop, announcing it on Facebook, Ahishor choosing Sushant, of all people, to live with—it was all askew and amiss, and happening so suddenly.

'He liked Maithili *hunh*?' Sushant was leering from the ledge, his head cocked like a dog's.

'What?'

'Maithili Krishna. She was quite a bitch. But she was damn hot.'

'Did you know her?' Once again, I didn't know why I asked.

'*Na, na*...' He looked away, grinning with a faraway light

in his eyes that I suddenly could not bear.

'I have to go out,' I said, 'to the market. I'll walk you down to the auto. I guess you need an auto?'

'Let's go drinking,' he smiled.

'I can't! I told you, I can't, Sushant!'

'All right, all right bhai. Come, at least walk with me. I'll pick up some rum.'

It was cool outside, but humid, after successive rainy days. The traffic was peaking at that hour. Very soon, I was sweating, and fatigued. Sushant showed no interest in the waiting autos; instead I followed him up the road towards the wine shop—a long walk.

We did not speak as we went. He was mumbling something at intervals, but I paid him no heed. My gaze, though I tried to unburden it, snagged continually. I stared at a short man with ripped muscles taking a selfie on the pavement. A beautiful girl in a 'little black dress' was crossing the road. In front of a paan shop, two young men with beards leaned against a car, talking, with their arms folded, while alongside, a woman in a white dress fed biscuits to a dog. There was a continual play of colour, headlights, street lights, lighted shop-windows, and the noise of traffic, while in the distance, an old madman, well-known as such, screamed curses to the heavens.

They were like figures in a play, costumed and full of life, but the sheer vivacity of the scenes was weighing me down with melancholy. It was all too much life—and all to what end?

Suddenly, I stopped near a familiar cafe—or what had been one.

'What happened to Slake? Slake has shut down too?'

The once-brightly coloured interior was now a brutal wreckage of bare walls and plaster. But a board outside proclaimed the imminent arrival of 'Cafe Atavista'.

'How many cafes keep shutting down!' I exclaimed. 'It's incredible!'

For it was a recurring phenomenon, all down the road. In the past month I had counted fully three restaurants that had closed, and three new ones that had sprung up, disturbingly undeterred by the mounting toll.

Sushant was laughing. 'Woodcon doesn't shut down,' he said. The dark bar was filling already with the lonely and the merry. 'Bhai, come and have a drink,' he peered at me. 'Come, come.'

I felt myself weakening. What better things did I have to do anyway? Then suddenly, we were both distracted.

On the far side of the road, his hair standing high on his head, his head bowed, Sasha was pacing the pavement. He was wearing (I was surprised to see) nothing more decorative than an old T-shirt, and shorts, from which his thin legs stuck out like long sticks. He moved in one direction, then paused, threw up a look at the sky and turned, before seeming to change his mind once again and going back the same way.

As we watched, he walked towards where a pack of dogs lay resting, and stood there, gazing upon them. The flow of pedestrians parted around him.

'I know that guy,' said Sushant. 'He's a really cool guy.'

'I know him too,' I said, though I was surprised at Sushant's verdict. 'It's quite funny, he's always out on the road at this time. I see him often like this. He has a great flat, by the way. A beautiful sea-view. You ought to see it.'

'It must be amazing to drink there.'

'Oh, yes. [I waved wildly.] He's seen us now, he's coming over.'

'You know each other, right!' I continued talking loudly, as

Sasha emerged from behind a roaring bus. 'You met at Jatin's office. No, even before—in Bandra, right?'

In passing, I noticed the gleam in Sasha's eyes—a reckless gleam, like the unnaturally eager smile he was wearing. As Sushant and he began to talk, I said I had just remembered that I had someone to meet. As a matter of fact, I did seek out Bharat Mishra later that night. Then, however, I was simply anxious to slip away, and Sushant, having snared suitable company, showed no more interest in stopping me.

After I left, they went together to the wine shop, and then with clinking bags to the building where Sasha lived. He had made no protest; he had fallen in easily with Sushant's plans.

In the courtyard, they passed a girl in tight clothes, walking out from the parking.

'Who is *that*?' whispered Sushant.

'I don't know,' he replied, 'I think she lives here.'

'You should know her, bro. She is hot!'

'Maybe I should,' said Sasha. He threw back a glance at the woman's figure.

He felt glad to meet Sushant, for he wanted to talk about Jatin and what had transpired in the office after their fracas. That was one reason. And then there was the emptiness, knocking about inside him ever since Maithili's email, that cared neither for Jatin, nor himself, nor anything else—but was only knocking, ever louder.

Indoors, Sushant uttered a low whistle, before stepping over to the sliding windows of Sasha's apartment. He dragged them open. There came the crash of the tides, the twinkling lights of ships on the water, the wide open horizon, the breeze.

'Bhai, you are lucky!' he said excitedly. 'What a place! I had a beautiful house in Bandra, but I've lost it, I'm thrown out. Ha!'

From the kitchen, Sasha brought out glasses, and Coca-Cola for the rum.

'You were very calm that day,' continued Sushant, 'when Jatin was shouting. I really admired that. I think you are a person with a lot of strength inside you.'

He was speaking softly, almost earnestly. It was an attitude I had sometimes seen in him when he brooded, in his garbled way, on Nietzsche and Heidegger. Drawing back from the window, he dropped onto a mattress, and from there looked up at Sasha, with slow, respectful scrutiny.

'Has Jatin spoken about me,' asked Sasha, from a chair above, 'after that day?'

'Not really bhai. He has too much going on now. Ahishor's film has crashed, Ritesh Azad pulled out the funding. So Jatin wants to really hurt these guys now. So do I. I mean, if they can do this to Ahishor, what chance does anyone have?'

'I see,' said Sasha. He felt nothing, hearing the news. Even the names seemed removed—Ahishor Frances, Maithili Krishna—they were like characters in a book. Seaside characters, he thought, and smiled to himself at that quaint phrase. A tremendous detachment was filling him with calm. He tasted the rum; its warmth pounded through him. The sound of the sea was surging in his ears.

'You are a writer, *hai na* bhai?'

'No,' said Sasha, 'I am a philosopher, who lives off his father.'

He was about to smile and say that in truth, he did not know how to answer the question. But Sushant's eyes were shining. He was nodding furiously, in a knowing way.

'Ohhh... Then we are the same! Philosophy is my favourite thing in the world. Even more than theatre...even more than fucking. Ha! I want to tell you something, you will understand—

every night I read two poems of Rumi before I go to sleep... But you are lucky to be living like this. My father is mad at me. He thinks I am wasting his money. He wants me to go back to Patna and run a petrol pump... The thing is, he is right. I am not good enough. I tried to do a play, it failed because of the bitch producer and actress. I am not able to make my movie either. Now even the flat is gone. Bhai, you would know, so I'm asking you, what do you think of Nietzsche?'

'Well... I have only read *Thus Spake Zarathustra*.'

'It's great, isn't it? Nietzsche speaks the truth, he lays his subject bare! I find Bombay a very Nietzschiean place. It's like—if you have the will, you can make it here, you can make it your whore, do what you like to it. But if you are weak, it will chuck you out. I guess I am weak. But I have been fucked over by too many people also. They have not had faith in me.'

Sasha stared over the head of his guest, to the mirror at the back of the room. He saw himself, seated casually on the chair, one leg over the other, with a drink in his hand, and a smile on his face. But the smile was forced. Before him, on the floor, the gangly young man was sprawled humbly, staring emptily into his glass. Yet Sasha was conscious, even as he felt sorry for Sushant, of a warning tension in his limbs. He made himself stop smiling.

'Nietzsche talks too much about the will,' Sasha said. 'It's an empty philosophy, it's sound and fury, that's all. How are we to know what to will? Will needs an object—how do we find our object?'

'Yes bhai, you're right, you're right! But! The will makes all the difference. I know, because it's my weakness. I get distracted. I—'

'Maybe you get distracted because you are not doing the work you should be doing. You *can't* will to do the wrong work.

It's not possible. That way, you trip yourself up from the very beginning. You can only really will towards the good.'

'I don't understand that, bhai,' said Sushant. He grew immediately absorbed in a long gulp of rum.

'What I'm saying is—don't worry about your will. Worry about your conscience. Your willpower will take care of itself.'

'I don't have a conscience, bhai. Haha!'

'Yes, you do,' said Sasha. 'Everybody does.' But his voice was tired and strangely flat.

By contrast, Sushant was grinning with delight. His cheeks were slick. Sweat gleamed also, on his chest, where the buttons were open. He rearranged his spidery limbs on the mattress, and placed his glass of rum carefully in front of him, like a candle on an altar.

'I'm really glad to talk to you! Most people in this town can't talk about such things. I really liked how you stood up to Jatin... No, really, I appreciated it... Bhai... you don't mind if I call you that, *na*?'

'No.'

''Coz I feel we have a connection. And where I'm from, this is how we show respect. *Nai* you're smiling, but I'm serious. Bhai, you are right, I don't know what to do. That's the big problem. I really want to make something good, a really great play, a really great TV show. I know I can do much better than the shit that goes on here. But then, I also need to make money.'

Suddenly, his lips curved slyly.

'All I really want to do is live in a caravan, like a gypsy. Fuck women all over the world... Bhai, I'll tell you something. After I dropped out of college, I was travelling in Pushkar. There I met a Naga sadhu. We were smoking hash together. Yeah yeah! He told me I would always have this power with women. It's true...I don't leave any woman bhai...'

'But they all leave you,' said Sasha, still deadpan and toneless.

'Haha! Yeah! True! But I don't give a damn. By then, I know what they really are. For example, that actress who fucked up my play. She refused to do a kissing scene. That's not how she fucked up the show, but I'm just telling you. This same girl wanted to be slapped around in bed...she wanted it rough! And on stage you are a goody two shoes! Ha!'

Sushant's eyes roved eagerly about the flat.

'This is a great place to get women over. You must be having a lot of fun here, Sasha. Or do you have, like, a steady girlfriend? No? Somebody you like then? There must be somebody.'

'There's no one,' said Sasha.

'Nah, there is someone! Tell me, bhai!'

Sasha felt the hairs rising on the back of his neck. His infatuation with Maithili was known to enough people; it was quite likely Sushant had heard too. Besides, Sushant had been present that night in Bandra, when (though overshadowed by Ahishor) Sasha had made no attempt to hide his devotion. But for some reason, the thought of her name on those lips turned his stomach leaden.

'There's no one,' he said firmly.

'There should be,' said Sushant thoughtfully. 'You are missing out. Women are the one thing that make a guy feel alive...Though to tell the truth, even that gets boring. It's the same thing every time, you take off her panties, missionary position, you're going going going, you can't even see anything!' He grimaced, showing rows of small teeth, and drained his glass. Then, climbing to his feet, he darted towards a pair of cupboard doors.

'Is this the bathroom?' he asked, when he was almost halfway inside.

'No, that's a cupboard! The bathroom is that door. Yes, that one... The light switch is inside.'

When he was gone, Sasha felt steeped in tiredness. His thoughts were disordered. Again, he caught sight of his face in the mirror. It was blanched and grave. His muscles were hurting from smiling; it seemed the greatest lie in the world to be smiling. Yet his heart was beating hard and he felt, also, an undeniable thrill in letting his mood be, leaving it to twist and flap in a cunning breeze. As the bathroom door opened again, it was with a kind of desperation that he seized on Sushant.

'Why don't you start small, Sushant? Do something small.'

'What's that, bhai?'

'You're thinking in too grandiose a way. Why must you do your own productions? You're just pampering yourself by insisting on that. Why don't you start by assisting somebody on something, get an income, get a foundation first before you start on your own projects? Never mind what Nietzsche would say about it!'

'Hahaha! Yes bro, you're right. You're saying the right things... But who am I supposed to assist? The kind of person who would stab his own brother in the back, because of money? This guy, Ritesh Azad, he once tried to beat me on the roadside. Do you know what happened? It was over his chick, Samira. She was buying cigarettes in Pali Naka. I was there too, I was lonely bhai. I went up to her and started chatting with her. Haha! Ritesh came out of his BMW, throwing attitude. I recognized him of course. I told him, bro, I don't care who your father is, your dick ain't bigger than mine. His driver and his servant came out too, otherwise I would have beaten the crap out of him right there in front of his girl. Later, one of the junior people at Elevate even read my script and liked it. But I said no way am I giving my *Last Anarchist* to this guy. Even if it never gets made, I won't give it to him. And I was right! What he's done to Ahishor makes my blood boil! I really respect Ahishor—he's the only person in this town I look up to, as a film-maker. Now it's time for *badla* (revenge), bhai. I know, I know, it's a primitive concept—but I am who I am. I'm my father's son!'

He brought his face forward, leering madly. 'I'm going to punch his face. I swear!'

Sasha got up, sighing slightly, and then bent over the table to refill his drink. His hands were trembling.

'These are all clichés, Sushant. Revenge and so on are clichés. There's no life in them, they are dead, mechanical actions. We are expected to answer an insult with an insult—so we simply succumb to the expectation. It's like your behaviour with women. You do it only because you feel it's the done thing. It's not a genuine impulse in you—not all the way, I mean.'

'Oh yes, it is!'

'No, no, it isn't! You have heard stories of directors and producers who sleep with their actresses. And they do do it, I know. Just recently I heard—well, there's a story about Pankaj Pande.'

'Ahh! Ruhi Khanna!'

'You know?' asked Sasha, in surprise.

'She told me herself,' Sushant laughed. 'Ruhi was supposed to be helping us with the videos *na*? *Waise* she's only come to the office two times. Jatin's damn pissed with her. Ha! Not as much as with you, but bhai, that was not your fault. I told you, I really appreciated the way you stood your ground... As far as Ruhi is concerned, I know this type very well, they only want attention, they won't do work. We went drinking one day. She told me everything. She told me about you also.'

'What about me?'

'Don't look so innocent bhai! You like her, I get it.'

'I don't like her! I've tried to help her with some things... she's very troubled.'

Sushant's eyes, dancing with insinuations the moment before, suddenly narrowed.

'Fuck that! Pankaj Pande didn't force her. Like, I don't have any big respect for Pankaj. But she wanted the role so she slept with him. She is the kind of girl who will sleep with anybody. Ask me—I know! Such women take advantage of nice guys. They need to be controlled! For their own sake.'

'What did she say about me?'

'She said you're a good friend,' said Sushant, with a droll look. 'Take my advice, bro. Put her in her place. I'm saying it delicately, 'coz that's the way you talk! But you get my meaning. That's what she really wants! Mind if I smoke? I'll go to the window.'

'Wait—I'll give you an ashtray.'

Just then, however, Sushant's phone rang. He looked at it with a pleased expression.

'Hey brother!'

While Sushant listened eagerly, Sasha walked over to the window. The night sky had grown thick with clouds. From over the buildings by the sea, he heard thunderous rumblings.

'Bro, I have to rush—I have to go meet Ahishor!' announced Sushant, 'I am moving into his flat. Did I tell you?'

'No,' said Sasha.

'It's mad weather, no!' cried Sushant happily. 'I really enjoyed our conversation. Thanks Sasha—you take care!'

They clasped hands.

XV

First Blood

In front of my eyes, my fears were coming alive. It was all the more painful because throughout that period, I had no direct contact with Ahishor. Not that he shunned my calls; I lacked the heart to make them.

The first signs of things going awry appeared on his Facebook. His post about quitting film-making got too many likes, and it seemed clear that not all were offered in solidarity. Too many were ironic or even gleeful. Among the exclamations of shock and concern in the comments section, were various flippant remarks.

I saw veiled references to his 'drama' on other people's walls. One bitter soul who lived in Versova and had been knocking about producers' offices for nine years without anything to show for it, wrote a lengthy self-glorifying account of his 'struggles', the number of times financiers had betrayed him, the innumerable films he had almost made, and his 'won't give up' attitude throughout. It occurred to me, when I read that, and saw it being shared around, that Ahishor had never been a popular person. Too many people were jealous of his brilliant, early success. Hadn't he realized they would all come crawling out of the woodwork, to feast on his failure?

There were, of course, signs of support too. Liberal voices bemoaned the silencing of a great talent at the hands of the right wing. There were cries of 'shame!' directed at those who had let Ahishor down. Yet, although it quickly became known that Ritesh Azad was the one who had backed out of the project, hardly anybody came out openly to criticize Ritesh by name. For Ritesh was a 'complete package', a general favourite. He was talented, successful, modern and liberal and a person of influence to boot. He was also his father's son.

I had been sure that the news would be picked up for full-blown television debates. Surely it was 'breaking news' that an award-winning film-maker was abandoning his vocation because of pressure from bigots! But amazingly (or perhaps not, given the Azad clout), Ahishor's decision appeared mostly as an item of gossip on the entertainment programmes. Here I was shocked to encounter a rumour that the documentary had been canned because of Ahishor's own deficiencies in the form. 'He made an enjoyable fiction film—but he wasn't serious enough to take on a serious subject. He hadn't read enough,' ran this slanderous line. Ahishor's Facebook post about quitting cinema, it was further suggested, had been merely a tantrum; proof of his immaturity, and best passed over in discreet silence.

Among the few radical voices who were full-fledged in their backing of Ahishor and thunderous in their condemnation of the right wing and Ritesh Azad alike, the loudest belonged to us—'Friends of Freedom'. Jatin was in a state of continual fulmination. He was writing and uploading three videos a day. (I edited some—but he did most of that too.) The views we were receiving had shot up, naturally, yet the momentum was not building. There seemed a clear reluctance, on Facebook and

Twitter, to convert this into a 'campaign'.

Very simply, people were tired. As I have mentioned before, our liberal voices had already finished outraging for Ahishor's sake, at the time he was roughed up. This further hardship, while surprising, interesting and complex, was for the same reasons unwelcome. They were mobilizing only reluctantly, ripe to be swayed by a single countermanding command that would remove their responsibilities without burdening their consciences. This came from Pankaj Pande.

The venerable, white-haired director seldom used social media. At the time, he had not tweeted for six months. He broke his silence, days before the New Year, with this comment:

'Freedom is not enhanced by throwing toys out of a pram. A real director is not a quitter.'

In no time, he was retweeted a thousand times. A much-read indie cinema blog took the cue to publish an anonymous article contrasting Pankaj Pande's durability in the industry (had he not faced threats for the Hindu-Muslim love story in his third film, had he not gone through hell to fund his fourth, made with unknown actors?), against Ahishor's childish fragility. Another post followed, accusing the Versova community of habitually neglecting stalwarts of indie cinema like Pankaj Pande, for flavours of the month like Ahishor. Meanwhile, the 'toys and pram' tweet continued to spread across the web, and I stopped checking my Twitter account; it was too depressing.

Bharat gave me no opportunity to meet, but when we spoke on the phone, I found him strange and unsettling.

'Where is Mihir?' he kept saying.

'I don't know where Mihir is,' I said. 'Have you spoken to Ahishor? Why is he doing this with the film? There's no reason to overreact. Tell him to calm down please.'

'He is calm. I am talking with him.' Bharat's voice was strained and excited. Then he broke into unexpected exultations.

'Mihir has run away, *na*? Like a rat from a sinking ship. But you love Mihir, *hai na* Dhruv? He is your special friend. You should know where he is!'

'I want to know about Ahishor!'

'Don't pretend to be worried about Ahishor! All you are worried about is your career. Take career advice from *motu* Malhotra then!'

A few days later, the New Year broke, and the tide of bright-eyed sentiment and calendar-fuelled hope that flooded the Internet, washed away, as tedious and self-important, the complaints of one film-maker. As for me, I stayed at home and conducted lengthy, faux-emotional WhatsApp conversations with Jahnavi—my Lit Festival date—and one other girl. I messaged Mihir New Year greetings too, and inquired alongside whether he had spoken to Ahishor. But I got no reply.

* * *

At 9 a.m. on the second of January, Sasha woke to a phone call from Ruhi Khanna.

'Happy new year,' she said sombrely.

'Happy new year to you too!'

There was a silence, during which was audible her strained breathing. Then her voice came, in a rush, suffused with caught sobs.

'I want this year to be everything—last year was not. I'm fed up with giving and giving and giving and not getting— anything! It's shutting my body down! I cried all night—and I had a fever!'

'Is the fever still there?'

'It's gone now. Nobody is professional and courteous in this city! They are brats! I'm surrounded by people who take me for granted! I am far, far, far too good for them! And—!'

He pressed the phone to his ear to listen; but she was sobbing unrestrainedly.

'What happened, Ruhi? Did something specific happen?'

'Oh, I can't tell you like this! I have to tell you properly. Can you come over?'

He felt wide awake. A prickle of excitement was crawling over him. He found his voice emerging oddly—full of jerky, eager notes that he did not recognize.

'Of course, of course... In the evening?'

He got lost that night, though he ought not to have been. Abandoning the auto, he walked the last five hundred metres to her apartment. This gritty lane was spread with shadows. A bright moon sailed the sky, shining over misshapen buildings and the low lights of meagre shops; an electronics store, half-shuttered, a dairy, after hours. Presently, there came the distinct stench of a butcher's, where a lithe, sweaty figure was violently washing the floor. The bloody water spilled onto the street.

It was with a certain detachment that Sasha noted the wreckage of the road, the abounding pettiness, which was not mitigated, but compounded, by the glittering tower ahead, whose windows, like vacant eyes, stared and did not mind. Tonight, he felt he understood. He did not mind either. He looked at the buildings alongside, with their elaborate railings and balustrades. They had once been beautiful and beloved, and were now decayed and decrepit—and that too was all right. It was wisdom that had thought not to preserve them, wisdom to know that all things went towards night and blackness and destruction, that others would come by, that time was no arrow, but an infinitely turning circle, that a thing of beauty was to be grasped in the moment, not fetishized or fought over. Five thousand years of civilization had taught this: to be detached.

Stopping in the street, he mimicked taking hold of Ruhi, as she cried her bitter tears, and kissing her hard on the mouth. He felt the thrill of the act steeping inside him.

Somebody called out coarsely. Sasha turned, alarmed and affronted. Two workmen in tattered garments were mock-fighting near a garbage heap. He threw them hateful looks. His step quickened in a kind of panic.

At her door, pressing her bell, he felt his concentration returning. Then suddenly, while he waited, his body tingled with a sharp urge to turn and flee.

Ruhi appeared at the doorway. She was exactly as he had imagined. Her eyes were red from crying. She was pouting glumly; she was barefoot, in a pink dress of some thick material that rustled loudly as she waved him inwards. He entered to the familiar, stuffy living room, with the sofas mounted with cushions.

Bharat Mishra sat amongst them, holding a tortilla chip in front of his eyes.

'Bharat, Sasha. Sasha, Bharat,' said Ruhi in bored tones. 'You have a common friend: Ahishor.'

'We have met!' said Bharat enthusiastically, without moving from his seat. 'But I don't know if he remembers me. Haha, no he doesn't remember me. We met in Costa Coffee, Seven Bungalows... He still doesn't remember, haha! It was the day you went for Malik's film.'

'Ah yes, I remember now!' said Sasha.

'How are you? What are you doing these days?'

'Fine. I was, well—I've been helping—this is about Ahishor

in fact, helping to make videos supporting him in all this trouble he's had.'

'Friends of Freedom?' asked Bharat eagerly. 'Are you also part of Friends of Freedom?'

'Yes,' Sasha hesitated, 'at least I was.'

But Bharat was chuckling freely, while his eyes, in his long face, never stopped studying Sasha.

'And what else are you doing?'

'Can you talk later please?' said Ruhi coldly. 'Can you leave now please?'

The smile was swept from Bharat's face. For an instant he glared at Ruhi, but then got up smartly, clicking his feet together.

'Yes Ma'am! I will just take one more chip—if you don't mind. You don't mind right? Thank you... Well, it was nice talking to you... I hope I was of help... The whole idea was to help you, in your situation.'

A visible wave of emotion crashed over Ruhi, cracking, in an instant, her stern facade. Bharat stared curiously at her mouth, which was quivering wildly, and then extended a hand to Sasha.

'Bye! Hope to see you soon! Have fun, boss...,' he added softly, winking as he said it.

When they were alone, she grew very quiet and stepped over unsteadily to the far sofa, where she sat, wincing, as though every cushioned touch yet hurt her. Sasha wondered whether to sit next to her.

'The Universe is sending me strange signs,' said Ruhi, in a dazed way. 'First of all my horoscope was wrong. My personal life disappointments were supposed to end this week... I honestly feel I have nothing to live for.'

'You don't mean that,' said Sasha, sitting on the other sofa, where Bharat had been.

'Well, of course, I'm not going to kill myself! It's everybody else who needs to...just...'

'You can't say it,' said Sasha gently. 'You're a soft-hearted person, Ruhi.'

'What good has it done me? I finally found the man I love! And he loves me too! But he doesn't have the guts to stand up to his family!'

'Who is this?'

'You know his name. Everybody knows his name. He's famous. And everybody thinks he's happily married! But he's not! He can't stand his wife. His father is a bully. I'm perfect for him, I'm the one he's made for! He knows it! But he doesn't have the courage to have me!'

'Who is he?' repeated Sasha. He felt confused and troubled in his heart.

'Wait, wait! I'm telling you properly. We knew each other already from Twitter—though he didn't know my real name, because my Twitter handle isn't my real name. It wasn't just that I was following him. He was also following me! So—I often tweet things about relationships, emotions, just the way I'm feeling at that particular time. One night, past two o'clock, I had tweeted something and he sent me a private message saying: 'You speak my mind.' And I told him I felt the same about his posts. So we had an immediate connect. But we didn't meet for a long time. Then last month he posted about a gig in Blue Frog. He was performing. He plays the guitar. I messaged him saying I would try to make it, and he said, "You must say hi". So I did. It was amazing. It was like electricity. I saw him there, being congratulated by people after the gig, and I immediately knew that that was my life, waiting for me. I wanted to hug him and kiss him. He was mine!'

'This happened at first sight?' said Sasha quietly.

Ruhi nodded, the tears shaking out of her eyes. 'Yes! After that night he wrote me an email and then we shared everything on email. He confessed to me all his insecurities—the things he said he can't tell anyone. Including his wife. Especially his wife, because she's the subject of a lot of them. I would tell you about them, but I can't, you understand?'

'You still haven't told me his name.'

Ruhi glanced quickly from left to right, where her balcony opened out to distant lights over a sea of grimy darkness. 'It's Ritesh Azad,' she spoke quickly. 'I trust you to keep this a secret!'

'Yes, of course, I will... Ritesh Azad has been in the news. He's Ahishor's half-brother, who was producing his—'

'I know! That's why I'm saying the Universe is sending me strange signals. It's not letting me get over him! First of all—even before I met Ritesh, I did the workshop with Karim. You remember, I told you about that? So that was an omen! Then you connect me to Jatin and I get pulled into the whole Friends of Freedom thing. I was doing it for Ahishor but I was also doing it for Ritesh. I told him that! Any normal person would appreciate it! And now, when I want to forget all about him... because he froze me out. Oh, he treated me terribly!'

'What has he done?'

'The moment he realized he loves me—he panicked. He shut down. He unfollowed me on Twitter. He stopped taking my calls and replying to my messages. But then—when I said "I'm through with you, you don't deserve me", *then* he replied saying "Can't we still be friends? I really enjoy talking to you." You understand? He won't act on the attraction between us, because he's too cowardly, because he can't argue with his father, and get a divorce from his wife. But he won't let me go either.

He's destroying me! He's a monster to me!'

It would be a simple matter to step over and touch her shoulder, which was bare beside the strap of her dress, and her hair, where it fell, dishevelled, over her eyes, staring with indignation, and her trembling lips. She was endlessly troubled, forever wounded, she was self-centred and nakedly greedy for recognition and attention. Here, for instance, was this self-serving web of fancy she had woven around Ritesh Azad, with strands composed of Twitter posts, a few drunken emails perhaps, and probably only the one encounter—what did she rightly deserve for it? But though his gaze wandered her body and his mind thrilled to move towards her, he felt thwarted and paralysed. Almost against his will, he did not move, though he could see quite clearly that it would only take the slightest effort to snap the threads that bound him. Nor did Sasha stop listening.

'What have I done to deserve this pain?' she demanded, 'I've forgotten what it's like to be without pain! And every time I try to forget him... Now Ahishor himself contacts me, and of course I think of Ritesh all over again!'

'Ahishor contacted you?'

'Listen, don't interrupt, I'm telling you! Not personally. He contacted me through his friend. That was his friend who was here. You know that, surely.'

'I know Bharat knows Ahishor, but I didn't know—'

Her face rippled with irritation.

'Bharat Mishra was my friend on Facebook. I never check Facebook, but I happened to log in and see this. His message said he wanted to meet me about something important. I said if he wants to meet me, he has to come here, because I have no energy to go anywhere. I didn't even care that he may think I'm rude—and he works with Ahishor, you understand, so it's a valuable relationship for me. But I was past caring.'

'What did he want to talk to you about? A role?'

She breathed heavily, in silence. As Sasha looked at her, the thought crossed his mind that he was losing his chance, that another night was passing, shamefully, in mere talk. He jerked his head to his right, dismissing the thought.

'No,' said Ruhi thoughtfully, 'not exactly. I didn't exactly understand what he was saying. He doesn't speak clearly, he speaks with hints and winks. It was irritating me. I understood what he wants me to do though. And I understood that Ahishor wants to fix the culture of—of...the way some people behave! Which I fully support. Somebody needs to do it! There are no manners, there's no decency!'

'What does he want you to do?'

'Not suffer in silence anymore!' she said passionately. 'Not keep taking this shit—from everybody! Maybe if people knew what I've been through, maybe they'd think twice before stabbing me again!'

A sliver of apprehension went through him.

'Ruhi, I wanted to ask you—are you sure you are well? Your depression may well have a physical basis. To be honest, it sounds like that. Have you tried consulting a doctor?'

'Why are you talking about this now? If you think I should see a doctor, why haven't you taken me to one?'

'I can! We can go—tomorrow if you like!'

She smiled strangely, looking him over with fluttering eyelids. He spoke on hurriedly.

'Also—don't spend so much time alone, in this big house. You spend too much on Twitter. It's not good for you. And don't think so much about yourself, don't think about what the Universe has planned for you. Whatever the Universe has planned for us, it's beyond our understanding. So why fret about it?'

'I don't *fret*,' she frowned.

'All right, but can I take you to the doctor?'

'No, thanks, I'm fine, I don't need that. I just need to start standing up for myself. Ahishor wants me to go public about what Pankaj Pande did to me.'

For the second time that day, a crawling sensation grew all over Sasha, but now it was intense and unpleasant.

'You mean, he wants you to go to the police?'

'No!' Her eyes flashed angrily. 'I said, go *public*. I'm going to tweet about it. Then Ahishor and all his people will support me. We'll make sure Pankaj never does this to any girl ever again!'

'Ruhi, wait,' said Sasha, 'I've told you before—I don't think you should do that—you should go to the police instead. Even if you go public like this, you'll anyway have to go to the police later. Or you should confront Pankaj Pande directly—that may be best of all. But on Twitter this can snowball out of control. It'll be very difficult for you.'

'I didn't ask you to question and criticize me! I've already done it! I tweeted it when Bharat was here! It's being retweeted all over already. Even Ritesh must have seen it! He follows Ahishor, and Ahishor has retweeted it already! So he must have seen it or if he hasn't seen it, he will soon! Then he'll realize how much I've been through!'

Sasha was sitting on the edge of his seat, his brow crumpled. 'Bharat made you do it,' he said unhappily.

'Are you going to support me or not? I don't know why you're here, if you're not going to support me!'

Fear and aggression stared blackly from her eyes. Then, when he failed to reply at once, she was enraged.

'Leave then! Don't stay here if you're going to question and criticize! I didn't call you for that!'

'Why did you call me?' he asked, with a flash of bitterness. But it passed immediately. 'I'll leave now,' said Sasha, getting up. 'I'm glad you called me. I do support you. Only this will be a difficult time for you. Do call me again, anytime—okay?... Okay?'

Ruhi seemed not to hear. Her gaze was fixed and unblinking at the wall behind his head. She stayed unblinking for unnaturally long moments, then, closing her eyes slowly and opening them again, she rose and walked rapidly away. There came the firm click of her bedroom door closing.

* * *

As Sasha walked past the guttering lights of the lane to the main road, a voice called out to him from one of the dingy holes. Alone in the 'Lucky Dragon' restaurant, Bharat Mishra was finishing a dinner of chowmein and coke. He was eating unhurriedly, though it was noisy all around him—the owner at his table was upset over something in the accounts, and the staff was out in force, waiting to leave.

Sasha went in, but did not sit.

'You sure you won't have anything?' Bharat sounded astonished. 'How are you? How do you know Ruhi? She's a close friend of yours?'

'She's a friend.'

'You came out very quickly! *Aaya Ram Gaya Ram*! What happened?'

'Nothing.' Sasha looked away, back down the road. Bharat grinned.

'I would like to talk to you sometime. If you're not in a hurry right now...sit and have a chai at least.'

'I need to get back,' said Sasha. 'Talk about what?'

'Just generally,' said Bharat, licking his lips with satisfaction. 'Some things may be happening... You are a friend of Ahishor, so... I would like to get to know you better.'

'Sure. We can meet properly later.' Then suddenly, swivelling, Sasha looked him full in the face.

'It was wrong, what you did to Ruhi.'

'What?'

'You persuaded her to tweet about Pankaj Pande. You don't know how fragile she is, what impact this can have on her!'

'Hello, hello, hello!' Bharat laughed unpleasantly. 'I didn't make her do anything. She has done it of her own free will. And we are there to fight this matter! Pankaj Pande *ko rulaana baaki hai*! (We are yet to make Pankaj Pande cry.) Why? Don't you think he deserves it? Hey! What happened?'

'Nothing. I told you I have to go. We can talk later.'

'Ok ta-ta, bye bye!' Bharat raised a hand. 'Listen! If you won't be a friend, it's all right, but don't be an enemy! All right? I'm telling you as a friend!'

He forked mouthfuls of chowmein, but his eyes, dancing with unguessable meaning, stayed on the retreating figure of Sasha.

XVI

Maithili's Messenger

Of the spark that had been struck that night, of the fire that was smouldering and would soon erupt with such destructive and tragic consequences for us all, the reader will learn in due course. First, however, I must tell of significant goings-on that were taking place elsewhere, in a quiet, leafy corner of Greater Kailash-I, New Delhi—far from teeming Versova—in the lavish but tasteful two-storeyed apartment of Dipankar and Ira Joshi.

Their house, that Sunday, was full of new faces, shot through with heightened excitement and rapidly shifting moods. Anamika had arrived from Greece three days ago to tearful embraces, a passionate reunion with Delta, her collie dog, her favourite foods specially prepared, gulab jamun and ice cream after dinner, hysterical Bollywood-watching sessions in front of the TV, and stories of college told to her mother late into the night. But on the third day, she was irritable, with the maid, who worked noisily and spoke in a rough voice, with the freezing Delhi winter, with the upholstery that her mother had chosen for the sofas, and, when pressed for deeper reasons, she made a bitter face and went out for a long walk, returning later to go straight to her room.

Nor did she come down when the Krishnas arrived. As part of the consultancy on the waste management project that Dipankar had helped deliver him, Suraj Krishna was meeting with Water Ministry officials in the capital. Tara was travelling with him, for it was an opportunity to meet and greet old friends in the city, and together deliver the wedding cards for their son. Their energy and cheerfulness, those days in Delhi, was therefore natural, right and proper. But a shadow hung over husband and wife; there was a worry in their bosoms that waxed and waned frantically. Every night, Tara had been sobbing herself to sleep in the IIC guest house. No wonder that it should all come out that evening; they had no one closer to unburden themselves to, than the Joshis.

'How is Maithili?' They had answered the question with vague politeness at the beginning of the evening, forestalling further queries. But later, when the wedding card had been admired at length, and congratulations given and received over cups of tea, when the consultancy too had been discussed, and they were all quite warm and comfortable in the living room—then came breaking out in Tara the terrible canker that devoured her happiness.

'Won't Anamika meet us?' she cried suddenly.

'Well, I told her you're both here,' said Ira, with slowly building surprise, for the desperate lilt in Tara's voice was audible to them all. 'She's been a bit up-and-down since she returned. I thought I ought to give her some space. But let me try again.'

'Don't bother!' said Suraj. He threw an anguished look at Tara.

'Oh, but this is important!' she cried again. 'I am worried about Maithili. Perhaps you're not!'

'Of course, I am,' he muttered.

'We don't know where she is or how she is!' Tara turned to the Joshis, who were watching with widening eyes. 'We've not had word for months. She's done this before, of course, but it feels different this time, I don't know why... And then, just before we came here!...I was wondering if Anamika knew something.'

'Anamika has had only a handful of phone calls from her since she went to America. She's been quite upset about it, though of course she understands how Maithili is. But I will certainly call her now. Anamika!... Anamika!... Anamika, come down please! Oh, here you are!'

Halfway down the stairs already, Anamika was glowering at her mother. She was still broad and big-shouldered, but she had lost weight since she was last in India. Her hair was growing back fast, and her skin was tanned and gleaming beneath a low-cut, black top. Black fitted her well, like the kajal she wore at all times.

Saying nothing, she smiled curiously at the Krishnas and made her way to an empty armchair in a corner of the room.

'I was just telling Tara Aunty,' her mother explained, 'that you haven't heard from Maithili either.'

'Not since Concord,' said Anamika eagerly, in her high, clear tones. 'Is there news?'

Worry flashed in her eyes, which was held and reflected in Tara's.

'Yes,' Tara hesitated, 'I mean, I think so. But we don't know what to make of it. Just a little while before we left Bombay—we got a letter.'

'From Maithili?'

'No! Not from her. We don't know who it was from! The

maid was cleaning and she found the envelope on the side of the carpet, almost under the carpet. I don't know if it was shoved under the front door, because it was quite a long way from the door! But how else could it have come?'

Dipankar Joshi grunted with interest, and sat up straight in his seat.

'It was a plain white envelope,' said Tara. 'It said on top: "To The Progenitors". "To the Progenitors", yes. That's what it said.'

Suddenly distraught, she looked at her husband, who, a moment later, continued the telling.

'Well, it seems like a prank to me. Although who would do it... Tara, you have the letter, show them. Yes, yes, show them, God, it will be a weight off to discuss this thing! The two of us have been going nuts all by ourselves. No word from Maithili herself, you see. Her last bank withdrawal was a big sum, about a month and a half ago. Since then no activity in the account either... Here it is... Shall I read it out? Or here, take it Ira, please!'

Crossing the carpet fitfully, he delivered her the white envelope with a sigh, as though setting down a heavy load. Ira Joshi was already putting on her reading glasses. Dipankar moved up closer on the sofa, and Anamika ran up behind it, to peer over their shoulders. This is what they read:

We do not belong to the past nights, but to the dawnings of tomorrow!

Greetings to the Progenitors!

Man is a creature that must evolve! It is blessed to evolve! We rise up from our animal and insect nature into exalted and ever more exalted states! Unto the swirling clouds of Moksha!

Oh, how blessed is the spiritual path! But how miserable and anguished to inhabit the lower state! I am Shonar by name, the one made of gold, yet I am still searching for my true metal. I am yet tin. But Thalia! Thalia shines already!

'Who's Thalia?' Anamika spoke aloud, but didn't stop reading.

Shines she, yet ignorant is she. Lost is she, far from her Master. Believe it or do not believe, I met her on the T, here at Haymarket. We were both going to Brigham. My prison was her destination. My walls were her doorways. How I laughed and cried! He who has never allowed me to approach Him (Wise is He!), He who knows I am unworthy (Just is He!), He craves her. And she has found her way— to me!

O Progenitors of Thalia! I cannot once speak of Him without singing of Him! India was once an elevated land! Today it lies degraded, filled with greed, tension and violence! Our age cries in pain and confusion. It cries out for its Saviour! His mission is our rejuvenation in the modern day. His mission is to fill the streets of our cities, just as much as the fields and the mountains, with fully realized beings! Oh, I loved Him the moment I laid eyes on Him. Out He came from the palace between the palm trees, with the full moon rising above the casuarina groves. His shoulders rippled like the temple walls. When He spoke, it was like the waves striking the holy rock, the way they have for centuries upon centuries! Even longer than the seven temples has His nobleness and self-sacrifice endured! For He has planned His mission for aeons—through all His past lives!

'Good gosh,' murmured Ira, turning the letter face-down. Anamika clicked her tongue and tugged it back upright. They read on.

> *At last I understand His plan for me! Miraculous plan (though He hates that word)! At last I understand, why I was forced to stay on in this land, this land far from knowledge, this land where people pretend but do not dare! It was all so I could meet Thalia! And now we return, she and I, to Him. The tin of Shonar has gained a gleam from this act! He sees what I have discovered, and is pleased. For if He were not pleased, would He undertake the delivery of this letter Himself? I say again He has contempt for the workers of miracles! Yet I know you shall receive this, though I shall leave it here, on my wooden desk, underneath my Christmas paperweight, with the big birch tree at the window.*
>
> *As to the contents of this message, they come to you at Thalia's behest. Thalia wishes you to know, that she shall not return to you, for she belongs now to all humanity and the Universe. You may wish her well for her mission, though it will not change her destiny. She sends her love and asks for your understanding. In your understanding, O Progenitors, lies the hope of your own evolution!*
>
> *Peace and Joy to You All!*
> *Shonar!*

When they had finished reading, they were all silent, in their different ways. Ira looked up from the letter, holding Tara's gaze with a sincere performance of tenderness. Dipankar appeared to be rereading the sentences, a frown creasing his bald head. Anamika was looking away at a spot on the carpet, evidently thinking hard. It was she who broke the silence, turning suddenly towards the Krishnas.

'And this just appeared? Didn't, like, the guards say if anyone had come to your door?'

'The guards said nobody had come,' Suraj Krishna replied gruffly. 'They are not reliable anyway, they are sleeping half the time.' He shrugged. 'Well, I don't even know if this is about Maithili. It says Thalia. The whole thing may be some silly prank.'

'You know that's not true,' cried Tara. 'It's about her! What I can't believe is—there is no mention of Vishnu! It says the message is at her behest…surely she would have wanted to say something to Vishnu! At first, I thought he might have got a letter separately, but no, he says he's not heard anything! How could she ignore him? It makes me think this is happening by force! This isn't my Maithili. She's been kidnapped. Or drugged! Oh, I don't know!'

'And you haven't showed this to anyone else?' Dipankar was looking thoughtful. 'Hmm... Well... Ahem!'

He was preening suddenly, nodding significantly. They all looked at him.

'I think I know who this fellow is,' he continued proudly. 'You see, when you look at this letter closely…you see…this talk of the waves striking the rocks?… and the seven temples…. Right? Now, my guess is this a reference to Mahabalipuram. Mahabalipuram, in Tamil Nadu, it was called the city of the Seven Pagodas—as you know. As a matter of fact, there's only one temple there, but they say the other six are underwater. Of course, that's just our typical legend-making…everything was marvellous 3000 years ago!'

'They found them!' said Tara animatedly. 'During the 2004 tsunami, they did find some ruins in Mahabalipuram that were underwater before!'

'Did they? Well...are you sure? Well anyway, very close to Mahabalipuram, off that same road—it's called the East Coast Road—there's an ashram belonging one of these new-age gurus. You might have heard of him. He calls himself Sadhguru Narayanan.'

'I've heard of him!' It was Anamika who had spoken, while the Krishnas looked on curiously. 'My friend Sachin follows him on Facebook.'

'Sadhguru Narayanan, yes of course,' Ira Joshi was nodding too, 'I've heard him speak once—in Kovalam, in fact. He was at the Kovalam Literature Festival two years ago. I found him quite a compelling speaker. Very calm and reasonable. Unlike most of his tribe...reasonable-*sounding*, I should say.'

'Narayanan is doing very well for himself,' Dipankar informed them. 'I believe his foundation does a lot of charity work in rural Tamil Nadu and Karnataka. And then he's also got this modern touch. There are others like that too, of course—they're all doing well. Anyway, he speaks excellent English. Which translates to lots of rich, influential clients.'

He shrugged. 'He doesn't impress me. Self-styled Mahatma, like the rest. But a successful chappie.'

Tara was staring at her husband, her mouth parting strangely, in both horror and relief.

'Then Maithili is being taken to his Ashram! By Shonar! What does that mean?'

'People go there and disappear,' said Dipankar grimly. 'Husbands leaving wives, mothers leaving children—all headed for salvation—I mean, that's the party line. The ashrams are like little kingdoms of their own, you see, where only the Guru's writ runs.'

Mr Krishna was thinking furiously, patting down his hair continually.

'Well, thank you so much,' he muttered. 'I'm so glad we came here—that you made this connection! So it's Mahabalipuram then! Narayan, Narayanan? We'll go there and get her back then!'

'Assuming I'm reading this letter correctly and if it's not a bunch of rubbish to begin with,' cautioned Dipankar.

There came a gasp from Tara, a stricken noise. Then she began to talk, in an odd, set tone that caught everyone's attention.

'Maithili is not a child... We can't forget that... If she wants to be there, there's nothing we can do... Not one thing... Ira, you did say he is not like the other God-men. Is he real? Do you think he could be a real God-man?'

'Real?' Suraj exclaimed with disbelief. 'None of them is real! You said yourself just now that this...this [he gestured with contempt at the letter, still in Ira's grasp], this isn't Maithili. She's not acting of her own free will. "Thalia", these affectations! This absurd friend she's made! It's all farcical!'

'Don't shout, please...'

The next sound, after a moment's sudden silence, was of Tara sobbing. Ira uttered an exclamation and stared at Suraj, who hung his head with a sigh. Dipankar Joshi took up the letter again. Anamika looked in turn at each of the other three, her own eyes wet and angry, and then (even as, at the front door, a knocking and scuffling was heard) moaned 'Oh Muttl-e-e-ey!' to the ceiling.

Moments later, a beaming Mihir Malhotra, warm and rounded in a knitted pullover, padded into the room. He had just begun to appear confused by the fraught scene (Mr Krishna alone was trying to force a smile), when Anamika caught him by the shoulder and pulled him back to the foyer.

'Come upstairs!' she hissed.

* * *

The heater was on. The bedroom was warm and humming, done up in pastel colours. The bed, with a floral patterned cover, was arrayed with fluffy and lifelike soft toys of animals. Paintings hung on the walls, many of them Anamika's own. An easel stood beside her desk-cum-bookshelf, which was crowded and messy, while above it, stuck on a corkboard, many rows of photographs showed happy scenes from her travels, dinners with her family, cherished memories with beloved people. These included (many times) Mihir's own laughing face. They did not, however, wander in the direction of the photographs. She sat at once on the bed and sat him down beside her.

'What's going on?' he asked cheerfully.

She stared at him. 'I'm hungry,' Mihir declared. 'I just came from Jorbagh, Alisha's office. It's a nice office but she offered me no food.'

'Oh... Didn't you demand it?'

'Of course I did. She acted like I hadn't spoken. I can't stand her, but she's doing very well. She's already the go-to lawyer in all these harassment cases. The high profile ones, I mean. She's got a finger in every pie. Oops! No pun intended! [He laughed merrily.] Now she's gotten onto this Khanna Commission too. She is doing very well, no doubt about it.'

'You sound like Dad,' said Anamika suddenly.

'Really?' Mihir continued to smile. Then, perceiving the steady, brooding regard of his old friend, his expression faded slowly.

'Maithili has gone off,' said Anamika. 'That's why everyone's upset downstairs.'

'Oh, Maithili...'

'She's gone off to join a God-man in South India.'

'Well, I pity him.'

'It's not funny, Mihir.'

'Look,' he said, turning to her seriously. 'She's been a bad friend to you. You ought to just cut her off—mentally, I mean. She doesn't deserve your concern. After all you've done for her, hosted her for so long in Greece, if she can't even have the basic gratitude to stay in touch, then screw her! I had a similar experience with Ahishor Frances. There must be something wrong with the water in Bombay. They're all crazy.'

'Have you cut off Ahishor?'

'What else can I do? He insisted on converting our documentary into some extremist anti God-man propaganda. Which is exactly what we had discussed not doing! He's alienated everyone in his family, including the producer guy. Now he's surrounding himself with a coterie of thugs and failures...which Versova is crawling with, by the way. They prop up his ego. I can't tell you how disappointed I am in him!'

'Anti God-man propaganda is a good thing,' said Anamika, glancing at the floor.

'Oh, it's very good! If you're looking to make two headlines and then disappear! I think Ahishor imagines himself a kind of cultural messiah. Going to usher in a cultural revolution, overthrow the big bad right wing with wonderful liberalism, et cetera, et cetera. It's so childish. Imagine if I was associated with something like that! People will laugh! Did I tell you what he said to me? He said, "We need to sweep everything aside, Mihir. It's all rotten! We need tabula rasa!" I told him we aren't in a video game. I don't think he liked that... What?'

She had reached out a hand and shoved the side of his head, with disdain. Now Anamika stared into space, her eyes welling up again, her mouth grim.

'You and Ahishor are not the same as me and Maithili.' She was controlling, with an effort, her shaking voice. 'I loved Maithili. I loved her! I still do. I miss her...'

'I know, I understand...,' said Mihir, trembling suddenly himself. At the sight of her emotion, carrying her far from him, his flippancy had vanished entirely. So it had always been, ever since they had played together as children, and he had wanted only to impress Anamika, bigger than him, older than him, the girl whose emphatic hugs made him feel safe to such a degree, that fear too was mixed in his affections. Indeed, he now resembled very much an anxious and afraid child, startled again, as she chastened him.

'You don't understand! You don't understand...You think she's full of drama. I think she's a genius. Yes, she is. Maithili is wonderful. She's something clean and shining. She's like the sun! A new sun rising up, bringing a new light... There is nobody like her! It's my fault if I lost her.'

'You were always,' said Mihir, 'a good friend to her.'

'But I wasn't good enough! She used to talk of how petty our modern civilization is. It's just things. It's just being comfortable. Just a bunch of living rooms. And I always agreed with her! But really, she was talking about me! No—don't try to argue with me—I've thought about this. I'm petty too! Those things fill up my world! At least they used to. But Maithili was right. And now I feel it too! Because we really are not good enough! Look at us! What do we offer someone like her? A colony... surrounded by slums! Dirt and spit on the streets! Rape on the news and a police that does nothing! My friend from Greece, Yulia, she's backpacking right now through South India. I was on the phone with her last night, and she was telling me how her necklace was stolen from her, while she was walking out on the street. And then the way the cops behaved! I was so ashamed to hear it! They're still as awful and primitive as ever! God, everything and everybody is so cramped here! I switch on the TV and what do I see? Just idiotic, sensationalist quarrels about everything under the sun!'

'It's interesting that Maithili's back in India,' said Mihir. Signs of concentration were appearing over his face; he was thinking once more. 'She might have stayed abroad where things are better. Freer.'

'I know! But she didn't. And that's what I would have done! I'd have stayed in Greece forever if I could! That's why I'm not her!'

Mihir slid his arm about her shoulders, and began to stroke her back.

'Let me tell you something,' he said quietly. 'It's not "things" you're fond of. It's people. You and I are the same that way. We like people and we like people to be happy. We want to give them things only to make them happy. That's the way we are.'

Anamika nodded. 'You're right. But I couldn't make Maithili happy. And I don't feel happy myself.'

He squeezed her shoulder, even as the frown deepened on his brow. Then he smiled briefly, unnaturally, as though someone had tugged on his lips, and then let go.

'Well, now what? Do you want to join the God-man too?'

'God, no!' She tried to laugh. 'I could never become, like, a devotee and stop thinking for myself. I know Maithili couldn't either. She loves her freedom! But at the same time, she's very vulnerable. She's a child really. She needs a secure surrounding, in which to blossom. If only she had found that here—maybe she wouldn't have gone away.'

Inclining her head towards Mihir, Anamika looked gravely into his eyes.

'I want things to really transform, Mihir.'

'You are the second person today who's said that to me,' he answered slowly. 'Alisha also said the very same thing.'

Her eyes flashed. 'Oh really? I'm the second? What is Alisha doing about it then? Why don't you go talk to her about it then? Why are you here?'

'It's your saying it that matters for me.'

He let his hands fall to his lap penitently. Presently, she softened, and placing her palm on his cheek, turned his face back towards her own.

'I don't want you to become like an old person. Just because they like you, you don't become like them. You must set your own agendas.'

'Like you do,' murmured Mihir, 'but I usually don't know what I want. That's why I always need...'

His breath rose up within him, overwhelming his speech. Anamika smiled and stared.

'I don't want you to drop Ahishor. If he's taking more risks now, it's good, isn't it? If nobody takes risks, how will anything here transform? A cultural revolution is exactly what we need, Mihir! You said people will laugh at him... It's only the old people who will laugh! And for how long will they laugh—if you, and me, and people like us are with him?'

He stared back, wonderingly, taking stock of the intensity of her feeling. She nodded in silent confirmation.

It cannot only have been Anamika's influence. It was Mihir's own genius, that he really did see 'the big picture' differently in the space of seconds and then did not hesitate.

Suddenly, his eyes were shining, and a glow of happiness was burning his cheek.

'You're right, you're right,' he whispered, in soft, excited tones, 'I understand it now. I understand what has to happen.'

Getting up, he faced her tentatively and then leaned down to kiss her forehead.

'Thank you, my angel sister!'

'Again,' said Anamika, after a moment.

'Oh!' He bent again and this time, quite mashed his lips against her brow, till they were both giggling.

'When are you going to call Ahishor?' she demanded, pulling a warning face.

'This very night!' said Mihir ecstatically. He took a step to the door. 'Are you coming down? I'm going to speak to your Dad.'

Then he hesitated, nursing a new thought.

'Dipankar Uncle and Ira Aunty are not like the others... they're not just wishy-washy old people. They are dynamic.'

'If you say so,' said Anamika. 'Maybe you're right...I hope so. Go on! I'll come in a minute.'

He skipped and bowed after an old way of his that traditionally made her laugh. Then he was gone from sight. But his voice came again, a moment later, from the landing: 'This very night!'

Alone in her room, Anamika shuddered, in a long, wracked breath. When she had finished exhaling, she stood up and was still and unmoving for several seconds. Then she bent to the floor-rug and pulled it aside. From there she moved to the bed, dashing the cover from the sheets that shone blankly beneath. She threw aside the fluffy animals and the pillows that surrounded them, before crouching over her desk, peering into every corner, and tugging open each drawer, and rummaging through them all.

She looked and looked, but there was no letter from the ether, no miraculous message, from the girl with the pixie hair, and the mask-like face, who stared from the photographs on the wall.

Here ends Book 1 of *The Outraged*

In Book 2, *Times of Strife*, Ahishor propels forward his cultural movement, attacking the religious right wing while purging his liberal society of hypocrites. He is backed by both Versova's strugglers and Delhi's pundits. But can Ahishor really tell his enemies from his friends? And who is the mysterious investor who has now begun to fund him?

Maithili's journey takes her to the starry heights of occult power. She leaves broken hearts and a breaking family in her wake—and finds herself on a collision course with Ahishor's anti-Godman project.

And Sasha discovers his calling, as a peacemaker. Even as he struggles to shield the vulnerable from destruction, he will make enemies on every side, and his faith will be pushed to breaking point.